WAITING FOR
REDEMPTION

NASHVILLE NIGHTS 3

SARAH PIRTLE

Cover Design and Formatting by Kate | Kate Decided to Design

www.katedecidedtodesign.com

Edited and Proofread by Erica Rogers | Logophile Editing Services

To those who thought they had nothing left to live for, and kept living anyways.
And to the ones who are fighting like hell for the ones they love and refuse to give up.
This one's for you.

CONTENT WARNING

Please note, this book contains sensitive subject matter.
My hope is that I have handled all subjects delicately and
respectfully, in the process of bringing our characters their happily
ever after.
Please visit www.authorsarahpirtle.com for a full list of trigger
warnings.

PLAYLIST

BROTHER - KODALINE
SYMPATHY - TOO CLOSE TO TOUCH
PAIN KILLER - WARREN ZEIDERS
PRETTY LITTLE POISON - WARREN ZEIDERS
WORK SONG - HOZIER
IRIS - THE GOO GOO DOLLS
TENNESSEE WHISKEY - CHRIS STAPLETON
LAST NIGHT - MORGAN WALLEN
SATURDAY NIGHTS - KHALID
YOUR BONES - CHELSEA CUTLER
HOW DO YOU LOVE ME - NICOTINE DOLLS
HOME - MGK,X AMBASSADORS & BEBE REXHA
BROKEN PROMISES - JON DRETTO
SAY YOU WON'T LET GO - JAMES ARTHUR
LEAVE A LIGHT ON - PAPA ROACH
MIGHT LOVE MYSELF - BEARTOOTH
SIN SO SWEET - WARREN ZEIDERS
FALLING - TREVOR DANIEL
RAIN - SLEEP TOKEN
HEARTBROKEN - DIPLO, JESSIE MURPH & POLO G
HIGH - STEPHEN SANCHEZ
WHATEVER IT TAKES - STEPHEN STANLEY
IF YOU ONLY KNEW - ALEXANDER STEWART
MY BOY - ELVIE SHANE
PERFECT - ED SHEERAN
CHANGE YOUR MIND - ALEX WARREN
FALL INTO ME - FOREST BLAKK
USE ME (feat. 070 Shake) - PVRIS
BULLET - NF
HAPPY - NF
HALLELUJAH - CITIZEN SOLDIER

Prologue

TANK

6 MONTHS AGO...

"WHAT BRINGS you here today Mr. Landry?" my therapist asks me from her brown leather chair. She's wearing glasses propped up on the bridge of her nose, her hand is steady as she holds a pen against the notebook in her lap, and the stark blue eyes I can't seem to shake the attention of, are trained solely on me. It's making my skin crawl to see someone waiting so patiently for me to speak, so they can begin picking apart everything that went wrong in my brain to get me to where I am today. My leg shakes furiously against the leather couch I'm sitting on and my jaw is set tight, refusing to let any words escape from my lips as I let my gaze drift to her through my hooded eyes. She offers me a soft smile, likely trying to put me at ease. It doesn't work the way I'm sure she's hoping it will, however, I can appreciate her effort.

"That would be my brother, ma'am." I give her a humorless smirk, doing what I always do. Using humor to deflect confrontation

1

and the possibility that I may actually have to face the things I'd much rather keep hidden away. She returns my smirk with one of her own before setting her pen down in her lap.

"I see. And what reason would your brother have to think we needed to meet each other?" she asks rhetorically. I let out a deep sigh, realizing there's no use in fighting the inevitable. I'm far too aware that Tucker would come *into* the next session with me if he found out I wasn't actually trying to talk out my issues. With doctor/patient confidentiality I'm not sure how he would even know, but I wouldn't put it past him to have some sixth sense about it.

He's been on my ass for the last two weeks about when I would be coming in for this session after recommending this therapist. Apparently, she's experienced in dealing with Veterans and comes highly recommended by those who have seen her.

It's not like I don't *want* to get better—to get to the bottom of what's been going on with me and make sure I leave it in the past—I just needed some time to sit with my thoughts before I was ready to talk to someone else about them. My eyes are glued to my running shoes and my nose begins to sting at the emotions creeping through my body as I remember the day all too well. From writing Tucker a note while my hand wouldn't stop shaking, leaving my dog tags on the coffee table, hearing the click from my handgun, and the color draining from Tucker's face when I finally saw him standing in front of me—witnessing what I can only imagine to be a big brother's worst nightmare.

Some may take my hesitation as a sign that I don't *want* to work out my problems—the ones I don't even know I have but I'm sure will become evident soon enough—I just don't know where the fuck to begin.

So, I start by answering her question with the truth.

"I'm here because I tried to kill myself," I admit, swallowing past the lump in my throat. My eyes finally come up to meet hers, and there's not a trace of pity to be found. She just looks at me like she sees my hurt, and really wants to help me overcome it. She doesn't move, or pick her pen up and flip open her book. Her attention remains on me, and this time I appreciate the focus she seems to bear.

"What do you think it was that led you to that decision?" I let out a humorless laugh, unable to answer. "Remember, Mr. Landry, I need your complete honesty if I am going to be able to help you. That is why I'm here, after all. To help you," she says, giving me a soft smile and a gentle nod.

"That's a question that comes with many answers, Doc," I admit, finding it hard to look up from my wringing hands. She takes a quick breath, repositioning herself in the leather chair. When I steal a glance at her, the expression on her face changes.

"That's alright. I know it can be difficult to find a place to start. Why don't you tell me how you're feeling instead? After everything that's happened, how are you feeling?" For the first time in 14 days, I allow myself to open up and find an answer to that question. The one I've not dared ask myself, knowing what my dark truth will be. I swore I would keep these demons locked up until the day that I died, but that day may not be as near as I once thought it was. I take a shaky breath, as I hear my truth spoken out loud for the first time.

"Broken and weak."

And the journey that got me here was a fucking wild one.

"I am going to do whatever I can to help you see the strongest parts of yourself while you work on feeling whole again. I am so glad you are still here, Mr. Landry, and that you reached out for help."

Part One

2 YEARS AGO...

Chapter 1

TANK

IT'S BEEN a long time since I've seen my brother, Tucker. He and I have always been close—seeing as how he basically raised me after our dad died—but our careers have kept us from seeing each other regularly over the past few years. Our father, Mitchell Landry, was one of the most well-respected officers on the Nashville police force, and the best damn dad we could have ever asked for—losing him turned mine and Tuck's whole world upside down. After he passed away, our mom was so devastated and heartbroken that she started drinking and simply never stopped. With her living in a drunken denial all the time, Tucker was left to pick up the broken pieces of our family. No middle school-aged kid should have that much responsibility, but Tucker handled it in a way that made me feel like everything was going to be alright.

I did my best to stay out of trouble throughout my adolescence, but with a loss like that at such a young age, the grief would come in waves at the most inconvenient of times. Specifically any time Jimmy Halloway—the most obnoxious middle school bully—had the fucking audacity to make jokes about my family. I found myself in so many fights with him that the guidance counselor at our school finally suggested I join the wrestling team to keep from getting expelled and help me channel my *angry energy*. It didn't take long for me to see the difference wrestling made in my life, and I quickly became the school's top wrestling champ. The last time Jimmy ever messed with me was the day I tossed him in the dumpsters behind the school after he made a crass joke during PE about my mother. He finally left me the hell alone and things started looking up.

I wrestled all throughout high school, and even started taking MMA classes in my free time. I probably would have dropped wrestling altogether when I started MMA, but I knew I had a better chance of landing a wrestling scholarship, so I stuck with it. Sure enough, before I graduated high school I was offered a full ride to UCLA where I eventually joined their Taekwondo team. I knew to stay sharp on fight weeks, but that didn't keep me from getting into trouble any other time.

After four years of nonstop fights, parties, and getting in just enough trouble to appease my rebellious streak, I graduated with my bachelor's degree in business management. I spent the next few years traveling and ended up training at a handful of the best MMA gyms in the world. Getting to see some of the most beautiful places on earth, all while perfecting my skill, was a high I don't think I'll ever match.

Once I was back home from my travels, I realized I never stopped moving from one fight to the next long enough to settle down. Not in the *get married and repopulate the earth* kind of way, more in the *having a regular drinking buddy* kind of way. The only friends I'd ever made were ones I never let myself get too attached to since I had a bad reputation for causing trouble and leaving things broken in my wake. So I just kept moving—never in one place long enough to make any real connections.

Being back home felt good for a beat, but after a week of silence and not being able to contact Tucker while he was deployed, I had to get my ass out of the house before I died of boredom. I spent most of my time at the gym and soon realized how desperately I needed to find a job. Since I had the most experience in fighting, and couldn't fathom a job where I had to sit behind a desk all day, I started looking for openings as a martial arts instructor. When I finally saw an ad for a position needing to be filled at a gym down the street, I was over there in no time—but I never made it inside.

After stopping to talk with a Marine recruiter set up outside, I left there with my mind made up about what I would do next. At 26 years old I joined the Marine Corps, and at 31 I am on a plane headed home—permanently.

It fucking sucks when you find something in life you believe to be your calling, to have one thing you're doing that will actually make a difference, just to have it ripped away from you in one fell swoop. I've spent the last three months in a recovery center, forced to interact with an entire staff that looked at me with respectful pity every time they laid eyes on me. As if breaking my back and having to stop doing the one thing I love isn't bad enough, every sad, puppy-eyed expression that crossed their faces made me want to bash my head into the wall. So I'm downright giddy to be back home with my brother, and more than ready to see what's next for me.

When I finally step off the plane and see the big ass grin on Tucker's face, it causes one to creep across my own as well. This is probably the first time I have smiled, genuinely smiled, in months – it feels so foreign and of course, he's the first to point it out.

"What the fuck is this? I thought you broke your back, not your face." Tucker says, squeezing my cheeks to smush the smile I was attempting.

"Shut the fuck up dude, you wouldn't know how to smile either if you spent the last three months where I was." I swat his hand away, rubbing at my jaw.

"Sorry, I couldn't be there with you man. I would have been–" Tucker says with a pained expression.

"Ah, don't worry about it. I know." I cut him off before he starts feeling down on himself for not being there with me. Sure it would have been nice to have someone by my side that didn't walk on eggshells the whole time they were around me, but I knew Tucker had a business to run here and I had no intentions of letting him drop everything just for me. Not again. He gives me a small nod and looks down at the duffle I'm carrying.

"Here, let me throw this in the back and we can get going. You hungry?" He grabs the bag, tossing it in the back of his Bronco before we climb into the cab.

"Fucking starved." He gives me a grin before speeding off down the road.

Tucker and I have spent almost every second together that he's not working since I've been back, and to be honest—I'm fucking exhausted. Don't get me wrong, I love my brother to death, but he's acting like he's seconds away from getting me a life-alert bracelet, and that shit's annoying the hell out of me. After finding an apartment for me a couple of days ago, he took off work today so we could shop for furniture and get it set up, that way I'm not sleeping on the floor or his god-awful couch that might as well be made of stone. That's one thing he and I actually agreed on—I need a real fucking bed as soon as humanly possible.

"So, you got everything moved in already?" Max asks, sitting back in his chair. He props his ankle on top of his knee as he takes a drink of his beer.

"Yeah, thanks again for letting us use your truck man." Tucker's Bronco didn't have nearly enough space to load all the furniture we bought and since my truck was in the shop, Max was kind enough to let us borrow his.

"Anytime." Max nods in response.

"*Yeah.* What can I say? I'm a pro." Tucker sighs dramatically, propping his hands behind his head. Unfortunately, Tucker had to drop everything he had going on to help me since I'm not supposed to be doing any heavy lifting for a while. I'd rather eat glass than feel like an inconvenience to someone, and that's exactly how I've felt these last few days, no matter how many times they tell me not to worry about it. Luckily everything we bought came in boxes that he was able to either carry or drag on his own.

At least I can still use a fucking screwdriver.

It made me feel even shittier than I already did, not being able to do more, but I tried not to focus too hard on it and just accept the help.

When we finally got done putting everything together and Tucker asked if I was hungry, I thought we'd swing through a drive-through or order a pizza. I did *not* expect to show up to a bar-b-que for three at Max's house.

I'm not complaining though, this is the best meal I've had in... maybe ever, honestly. We're sitting in the backyard around the bonfire with a cooler full of beer while Riley, Max's service dog, finishes off her very own steak.

"I'm glad you're coming to work at the bar, man. We're starting to get a little outnumbered," Max grumbles. Tucker snickers and my eyes shift between the two of them. Tucker looks pleasantly amused, and Max looks annoyed as shit—the usual for these two.

"I feel like I've missed something, but yeah I'm happy to help." I offer before finishing off my drink. I feel the self-loathing trying to creep its way out of the dark hole I keep it in, but manage to shove it back down before it dares to show its face.

"Max is just suffering from a severe case of blue balls over the new girl." Tucker rolls his eyes, causing Max to turn a deep shade of red. I honestly don't know if he's mad or embarrassed, but seeing him this way is amusing nonetheless.

"I do not, so kindly, fuck off," Max threatens unconvincingly.

"Stay away from the new girl, got it." I raise my brows and try to hide my smirk, but when Tucker barks out a laugh I can't help but let it slip.

"*Ohhh,* little bro, are you trying to get some action already?" Tucker teases. "It may be a little too soon. You're supposed to break her back, not blow yours out again." He slaps my chest with the back of his hand as he obnoxiously laughs.

"Fuck you, dude." I close my eyes, shaking my head in disapproval.

"Well, this immediately stopped being fun, you two are free to leave," Max says, throwing an empty beer can at us.

"I actually do need to get going. When do you need me to start, *boss*?" I ask Max, as I stand to leave.

"Stop by sometime this week and Ruby will get you an application, go over the schedule with you, and start your training." He stands from his seat and claps my hand before bringing me in for a hug, then repeats the motion with Tucker.

"*Ruby*, got it." Tucker and I walk back to the Bronco in silence as I try to convince myself it won't be so bad to be a 31-year-old bartender with a fucked up back and having some chick show me how to serve drinks.

Fuck my life.

Thank God whiskey was one of the essential things I picked up for my new apartment. Because I need a damn drink.

Chapter 2

RUBY

"HENDRIX, love of my life, please, I am begging you. Tell me where you put my keys." I stare at him through narrowed eyes with quiet desperation, causing his smirk to grow into the biggest grin that melts my heart. The dimple on his left cheek, as well as his warm brown eyes, match my own, making it damn near impossible to ever stay mad at him. He shakes his head *no*, making his dark brown hair that falls just past his eyebrows flip around as a little giggle falls from his lips.

"I will let you take *two* packages of fruit snacks to Betty's if you tell me." I wiggle my brows as I look at him, encouraging him to give in to my offer. His eyes grow wide and he finally nods his head in agreement.

"Deal?" I ask, putting my hand out.

"Deal!" he shrieks, shaking my hand vigorously before running through the house. I follow quickly behind him, hoping to catch a glimpse of where they are. You never know when a list of your toddler's favorite hiding places will come in handy, especially since his new favorite game is *taking mommy's phone and keys hostage right before she leaves for work.*

I'm not sure how complex a three-year-old's brain is, but it's not lost on me that he seems to know when I have to leave, and does everything in his power to keep me home. I sometimes catch myself wondering what life would be like if I weren't a single mom. Would it be easier to go to work every day if I knew his dad would be around to fill in the gaps when I'm working late or taking on doubles to make ends meet. Though, if I were married, I may not even have to work doubles, stay late, or even work at all. What a dream that would have been to spend all of my time with Hendrix up until he started school. Never missing a single thing.

As always, I stop that train of thought before it picks up enough memento to crush me because none of those things are options for us—it's simply a fantasy that will remain shoved into the back of my mind. No matter how hard it is to accept, the guy who gave me Hendrix is not the man I would want to bring that fantasy to life with anyhow. He's the very one who shut down any hope I may have had to build a family like the one I had growing up—simple, happy, and full of love. It may just be me and Hendrix now, but it's better this way, that much I know for sure.

It still doesn't make it any less hard—leaving him every day to go to work, having to miss out on important milestones, and never feeling like I have enough time to truly be in the moment with him. Those things alone give me enough mom guilt to last a lifetime and a half. But there's *nothing* I wouldn't do for him, so if busting my ass to make ends meet is what I have to do, then that's what I'll do.

Betty has been my saving grace ever since I moved here almost four years ago, determined to start over no matter how impossible it may have seemed. I'm not sure what I ever did to deserve the world's greatest neighbor who also conveniently runs a daycare out of her home, but I count that blessing twice *daily*. She has gone above and beyond for Hendrix and me by watching him after her normal babysitting hours when I have to work the night shift, and being available when I'm needed to work on short notice. I always try to show my appreciation by bringing her a coffee when I drop Hendrix off after running errands and putting together little gratitude baskets during the holidays, but it never quite feels like enough.

"FOUND THEM!" Hendrix shouts, pulling my keys from beneath his mattress.

"You are one sneaky little dude," I tease, snatching him up off the ground and blowing raspberries into his neck until he's squealing that beautiful little laugh of his. "Alright, let's go. Mommy is still training someone this week and I can't be late." I plop him back down on his feet as he takes off towards the door.

"Don't forget the fruit snacks!" he calls back over his shoulder.

"I wouldn't dare." I giggle to myself as I tuck my keys into the back pocket of my jeans. I grab the snacks from the cabinet, swipe our bags from the bench by the front door, and give myself a once over in the mirror before following Hendrix to Betty's.

"How is Hendrix feeling? Any better?" Shane asks as she places two drinks on the bar for her customers.

"Yeah, much better. Thanks for asking. It must have been a virus or something, he was fine after about 24 hours." I shrug, mixing a martini in the cocktail shaker.

"Poor thing, I'm glad to hear he's doing better." She smiles, before whipping around to grab a couple of bar coasters.

Shane started here about a week ago and is catching on surprisingly quickly. She's easily the nicest human I've ever met, which makes Max's extra grumpy demeanor around her confusing as shit. Not that it's any of my business though. I know they had a bit of a disaster the night I had to leave to pick Hendrix up—the same night prompting her to ask how he's feeling now—but who doesn't have a bad night after starting a new job?

I sure as hell did when I first started here.

I was about seven months pregnant with Hendrix and the bar still hadn't quite made it on the map yet. I walked in and barely got out the words *are you hiring* before Max offered me a job bartending. I started the next day and have worked my ass off every single shift since then. I knew that, if done right, bartenders have the capability to make seriously good money, and I desperately needed all the cash I could get. Despite my hard work and efforts to do the job flawlessly, there was this one time I had a really *really* bad night.

I was working the Friday night rush alone and wound up leaving the beer tap on a tad too long. I had turned around to set a coaster down for the drink I was pouring and someone else caught my attention. They were asking where the bathroom was, and in the amount of time it took me to point down the hall, beer overflowed *everywhere*. Of course, that wouldn't have been a big deal to clean up and keep going, for someone who didn't have swollen ankles and a massive hormonal imbalance. But I had both of those things and I ended up bursting into tears right there behind the bar—causing my water to break.

Max had to shut down the bar and drive me to the hospital, which made me feel both humiliated and grateful. That was the night that sealed Max as a lifelong friend in my book. He didn't get mad, or freak out and overreact. He simply dismissed all of the bar patrons, called Jackie to have someone clean up behind the bar, and guided me to his truck before rushing to the hospital. When he asked if there was anyone I needed him to call, I did my best to hide the hurt in my answer. *"No, you're about the closest thing to family I have these days."* I laughed, then groaned immediately after, from a contraction. I had meant for my comment to land more sarcastically, but I saw the look on Max's face when I said it and knew he had picked up the truth I'd hidden in plain sight. From that day on he was like the big brother I'd never had.

He's been there for me and Hendrix without hesitation ever since that day and told me I never had to worry about losing my job at the bar. He said when I was ready to come back to work after maternity leave, my job would be waiting—if I still wanted it. How could I *not* still want to work here after that? He never fussed when I had to miss work because Hendrix was sick, or had a doctor's appointment, and even offered to let him stay in his office if I ever needed to bring him with me for some reason. I believe his exact words were *"I don't know much about babies, but I know they sleep sometimes, and I am fully capable of watching them do that and getting you when he cries."* I begin laughing as I think back to that day, and the absolute shock I was in from hearing him offer me such thoughtful accommodations.

"Rubes," Max calls, snapping me back to reality from my wandering thoughts.

"Yeah, boss?" I turn to face him as he walks over from his office.

"Tank is going to be starting as another bartender soon. You good to get his paperwork, scheduling, and training done?" I know his inquiry is just a formality since I've been taking care of those things ever since coming back from having Hendrix.

"Sure thing. Tank is… Tucker's brother, right?" I ask for clarification and Max nods. "Do you know when he's supposed to come by?" He looks up from his phone and nods towards the entrance.

"Now, apparently."

"In the middle of lunch rush, nice." I roll my eyes and give a sarcastic smile, as Max gives me a warning look.

As soon as I turn to face the new guy, all my hardass-wittiness disappears. I'm suddenly unable to peel my eyes away from the burly, tattooed statue in front of me. I haven't bothered giving a man the time of day in the past four years, because the *only* good thing that came from the last guy I was with, was Hendrix. That little man has been my sole focus and love of my life ever since he came into this world, and I have no intention of changing that any time soon. However, my mouth does involuntarily pop open when he flashes a toothy grin at Max.

Holy hotness.

When he finally glances my way I quickly school my features, giving him the good ole closed-mouth grin—you know, the one you give to the coworker you don't really like.

Off to a great start, Ruby.

"Ruby, this is Tank. Tank, Ruby." Max introduces us. My smile morphs into one a little more friendly, and a lot less... creepy. Though he softens his from the big grin he just gave to Max.

"Hey." He tips his chin up at me, shoving his hands into the front pockets of his blue jeans.

Big talker, this one.

"Hey, nice to meet you." He nods politely without another word and I start to wonder if he just needs time to warm up to people or if it's *me*.

"Man, this place hasn't changed a bit," he says to Max as they look around the bar.

"Why mess with perfection, ya know?"

"So you've been here before then?" I interrupt, wondering if we've met before but I somehow forgot.

"Just once," he answers simply.

"Tank came by when he was home on leave a few years back. You may have been out on maternity leave now that I think about it." Max gets quiet as he calculates the time to himself. I glance up at Tank, suddenly curious what he may be thinking. He stares down at me with an unreadable look before Max shakes his head, giving up his mental quest of finding out when exactly Tank was here last.

"Anyways. I'll leave you to it." He walks off, leaving us standing at the bar together. I try to repress the thoughts slowly creeping into my brain about how casually gorgeous this guy is.

There's not a single thing about this man that doesn't scream *rugged*. His towering height, the way his muscles press tightly against every seam of his shirt, and don't get me started on the veins in his huge, tattooed hand that have all but demanded my attention. His dark brown hair is longer on top but buzzed around the sides and looks as though he simply ran his fingers through it to style it. His five o'clock shadow makes his bright green eyes almost hypnotic, like emeralds with just enough darkness behind them to make me curious about what they've bared witness to. Throw in the tattoos emerging from his Marine T-shirt and my chance at any kind of focus is shot.

"Okay, so... here's your application, we just have to have it on file for legal purposes. Once you're done with that I'll show you around and if you have any questions feel free to ask." He lets his eyes glide slowly up my body before landing on my own and he smiles. Still, the soft closed-off smile he gave me before, but a smile nonetheless.

"Got it." He clicks the pen open and gets to work on his application, but I stand unmoving as I watch him. I see his jaw tick a few times as he looks over the sheet of paper, and I can see his eyes dart around as his hand hovers over the *previous job history* section of the application.

"You know, you've basically got the job, you don't have to worry about filling that part out. Unless of course, you've been working the mail room in a prison, then maybe add that." I tease, trying to ease some of the tension I can feel growing around him. He smirks at me and lets out a deep chuckle and moves down to the next section of the form.

"Thanks," he says, so quietly I almost miss it. I feel a small sense of pride in my ability to get a laugh out of him, no matter how small it may have been. I don't realize how entranced by him I am until Shane calls my name.

"Hey Ruby, Lenny's asking for you." Tank glances up at me through his eyelashes causing my cheeks to heat instantly, embarrassed I was just caught staring at him.

"Right, okay so just let me know when you're done. I'll be—over here." I hike a thumb over my shoulder awkwardly, as a smirk appears on his face.

"Don't worry. I'll find you." His gaze lingers on me another moment, stealing the breath in my lungs before he turns back to his paper, but his less-than-enthusiastic expression has me hanging back a little longer.

"Bartending, not exactly your dream job?" I scrunch my nose playfully, trying to tread lightly on the subject.

"You know, out of all the things I've done in my lifetime, I never imagined I would be working in a *bar*." He scoffs.

"Oh, it's not so bad. We do weekly wet T-shirt contests, beer pong tournaments, and some of the guys even play Russian roulette in the parking lot, though that's not one of the approved bar games but Drengr kind of does whatever they want." I wave a hand dismissively in their direction.

"Are you serious?" He looks at me in mortified disbelief.

"Have you met the owner of this bar? Of course, I'm not serious." I laugh as he lets out another small one of his own and his tongue peeks out to wet his bottom lip, momentarily altering my brain chemistry.

"Right." He agrees quietly.

"But hey, even if it's not a *forever* job, maybe it'll still be fun for a while." I smile, hopeful to shine some light on what seems to be a gloomy situation for him.

"Maybe." Right on cue, Lenny calls me again from the other end of the bar.

"Calm your tits, Lenny. I'll get to you when I get to you," I holler back at him, offering Tank one last smile before leaving him to his paperwork.

Chapter 3

TANK

EITHER MY NEW boss likes what she sees, or I actually look as shitty as I feel and she notices. After leaving Max's last night and thinking about just how fucked my life got so quickly, I got re-acquainted with my old friend Jack Daniels. Before I knew it, the bottle was empty and my alarm was going off—sounding like fucking war horns might I add. But I figured prolonging this process wouldn't do me any good, so here I am—hungover and trying my best to remember how to spell my own name for this application.

Working at Chattahoochies isn't my first career choice—not by a long shot—but while I'm still taking it easy to make sure I don't agitate my back, this is probably my safest bet. Max knows my situation and I don't have to tell the story repeatedly to possible employers until one finally considers me a suitable fit. On the bright side, the person who will be training me seems to have a tolerable personality, and is easy on the eyes—she's pretty fucking gorgeous, actually—which just feels like a reward for having to take this job in the first place.

"So that's pretty much everything. It's a simple job if you have common sense. Which is probably why Marco struggles around here." Ruby leads us through the door from the kitchen, where she just gave me a very detailed tour of the freezer—which seemed absolutely pointless. Her voice drops as she mumbles the end of her sentence but I still hear it.

I remember the last time I came here, Marco was still new to the staff and someone ordered a drink he wasn't familiar with. The poor kid looked like a deer in headlights and that look apparently never went away. I scoff at the thought, and Ruby's eyes grow wider when she realizes I heard her.

"Uh, any questions?" I take the opportunity to study the sleeve of tattoos covering her right arm, as she folds them over her chest. It's like a kaleidoscope of colors, unlike the black ink covering my own skin. I take notice of the bright blue water and purple mermaid tail leading up to a... "Okay, great! You start tomorrow at ten thirty sharp." Before I can make out the rest of the tattoo she begins to move, blocking my view. "What size are you?" she asks, as she bends down to reach into a box beneath the bar.

"Excuse me?" I ask in confusion, as she stands back up holding two T-shirts in her hands.

"What size T-shirt do you wear? You'll need a uniform." She shakes the fabric in her hand as she explains. I examine the two shirts in her hands but don't offer a response.

"Would you like me to just guess or something?" She presses impatiently.

"Extra large," I answer simply, earning a playful scoff from her.

"Right. That checks out." I raise a brow at her and her cheeks instantly flush. As though that thought wasn't supposed to be said aloud. "Here you go." I take the shirt from her hands, taking note of another purple tattoo along her wrist. She quickly pulls her hand away and offers me the same tight-lipped smile from earlier.

"Okay, so I'll see you tomorrow."

"See you tomorrow, boss."

I pull my bike into the parking lot behind the bar at exactly 10:29, cut the engine, and place my helmet on the handlebar. When I walk through the back door it's eerily quiet. I've never been here before opening, and the deafening silence makes my skin crawl. However, the silence is shattered almost immediately after I walk inside.

Startled by a crashing sound, my hand instantly reaches for my sidearm and my heart rate starts to pick up. Before I can unholster it, I scan the room and my eyes land on Ruby. She is sitting on the stainless steel table off to the side, eating Sour Patch Kids and rolling silverware with her headphones on. Well, she *was* rolling silverware, until it all fell to the ground. She pulls her headphones down around her neck and holds her hands up.

"Oh, hey. Relax. It's just me," she says quickly. I slide my gun back into the holster fully and glance around the rest of the kitchen instinctively.

"Sorry about that." I can feel the scowl on my face, but it's not towards her. I'm sure I probably just scared the shit out of her and that's not the kind of first impression you want to give someone you're about to be working with. "You alright? I didn't mean to scare you. I just didn't see you there. Then I heard the–"

"No, I'm okay. I get it." She cuts me off as she hops down from the table to start picking up the mess.

"Here, let me help with that." I bend down next to her gathering as many spoons as my hands can hold—which is pretty much all of them. I notice the way her eyes fixate on my hands for a second before she tears her eyes away.

"Thanks. I guess I'm done with that task until all of this is re-washed." She laughs, tossing some dirty forks back in the bin.

"I can wash these and finish rolling them. If you want." I don't look up when I offer, but I can feel her eyes on me.

"I actually have another job for you. Marco can do this when he gets in." She goes to pick up the bus tray but I grab it from her before she can.

"I've got it." I smile at her before taking it over to the sink. I wipe my hands on my jeans making my way over to where she's shoving her headphones into her bag. When she pulls the last sour candy from its package a small frown appears on her face before she tosses the trash in the bin.

"Alright, follow me." She smiles, making her way through the swinging door that leads to the bar. "You can start by getting all the chairs down from the tables, then sanitize the surfaces. When you're finished with that, come see me." She turns around just fast enough to cause her long black ponytail to whip around behind her.

"Will do." I unzip my jacket hanging it on the coat rack next to me, when I turn back around her eyes are fixed on me and there's a hint of a smirk on her face.

"What?" I ask, drawing my brows together.

"Um, nothing." She shakes her head, but I can tell she's lying.

"That smirk didn't seem like nothing," I press. She laughs, taking in the sight of me in the T-shirt she gave me last night, giving me a feeling of self-consciousness I'm not too fond of.

"You umm... you have it on backwards." She points to the T-shirt, drawing my attention to the large Chattahoochies emblem across my chest that should be on my back.

"Shit," I mumble. "That's the last time I get dressed in the dark." I pull the T-shirt off to turn it around properly, as Ruby's eyes grow slightly before she turns her gaze away from where I'm now standing shirtless behind the bar. Did I think about this being awkward for her? *Nope.* I guess that's what I get for being surrounded by nothing but men in barracks and locker rooms for— well, my whole fucking life.

"Well, well, well, *excuse* me. Didn't mean to interrupt," Marco says, strolling in with a defensive hand up and his headphones on.

"You're not interrupting anything, Marco. Tank here is just getting his uniform on." She looks at me with those soft brown eyes, giving the illusion that the warmth from them is washing over me just from one simple glance. Though the feeling ends as soon as it begins when she looks behind me, pinning Marco with an annoyed stare.

"There's silverware that needs to be washed in the kitchen." She gives him a sarcastic smile, as Marco grumbles.

"I hate dish duty."

"Heard that," Ruby calls after him.

"I said it pretty loud." Marco flips her the bird as he disappears into the kitchen again. I have the sudden urge to break his finger, but if she's not bothered then maybe I'm just overreacting.

"Sorry, I didn't mean to make things... weird. Or anything," I apologize, sliding the shirt over my head, where the small *What's your poison?* logo rests on my chest now.

"Oh, it's...fine. *You're* fine," she says, bringing a smirk to my face. "No, not like that. I didn't mean *you're* fine. I mean, you're not... *not* cause I mean... congratulations on all of that." She waves her hand up and down the length of my torso, as the shade of red on her face deepens while she rambles.

"Ruby..." I interrupt.

"Hmm?" She rolls her lips together, bringing her eyes up to mine.

"We're good." I give her a reassuring wink, and she nods her head.

"Fantastic, here's the sanitizer and a towel. I'll be right here when you're done." I throw the white bar towel over my shoulder and give her a nod before starting my tasks.

Well, one good thing came from my mindless wardrobe change and her rambling. That's the first time I've felt even a little bit good about myself in *months*. Though, I'm sure the feeling will flee in no time. It always does.

Chapter 4

RUBY

"You are a lifesaver, Betty. Thank you so much for keeping him late today."

"Oh please, how many times do I have to tell you, it's no problem at all. We have tons of fun, and he's such a big help when the little ones are here." Betty grins as she rustles Hendrix's hair. Working doubles at the bar all week has been absolute hell. Not because of the long hours though, *that* I'm actually used to. Having a six-foot-five, tattooed grizzly bear that also looks like he probably models for Marine holiday calendars and bench presses *trees* in his free time, *that* I'm *not* used to. Not to mention the fact that I can't seem to get on his good side to save my life. If there even *is* a good side to be on.

Every shift is full of one-word responses or head nods until he clocks out and it's starting to drive me crazy. Maybe I'm being paranoid, but I can't stand it when I feel like someone is mad at me. So if I have to coax an emotion out of the broodiest man I've ever met, then so be it.

"Mommy, can we watch Spider-Man tonight?" Hendrix pulls my attention back to him as he squeezes my leg with a death grip.

"Of course we can buddy. How does chicken casserole sound for dinner?" I gently scratch at his back as he fist pumps the air.

"Heck yeah!" Betty and I start giggling as Hendrix shakes his butt all the way out the door.

"Goodnight, Betty. We'll see you on Monday." I wave over my shoulder as we walk across her front yard to our own.

Our little two-bedroom house has been my safe haven ever since Hendrix and I moved in. I was lucky enough to find a landlord who was willing to work with me on rent when I didn't have enough money right away to be able to move in, and I will be eternally grateful for that. I saved every penny of my first few paychecks at Chattahoochies and added it to the money I had in savings from my previous job to be able to afford this house. It's nothing fancy but it's *ours*, and that makes it special to me.

Hendrix and I sit down at the table to eat our leftover chicken casserole—the only thing he will eat most days—and talk about anything and everything. We've done this every night for as long as I can remember, and it's always the highlight of my day.

"So, were you good for Ms. Betty today?" I ask, adding a little hot sauce to my bowl before forking a bite into my mouth.

"Yes ma'am. I helped with baby Boaz when he was crying. I sang and did my booty shakin' and he stopped crying." He beams with pride as he tells me about his accomplishment.

"Well, I'm not surprised. You're the best singer and booty shaker I know." I wink at him causing a cute little grin to spread across his face. His little dimple is so deep I just want to press it like a button.

"Ms. Betty says I'm the best helper. She says I'm like the big brother of daycare," he explains with a mouth full of food.

"Is that so? Well, those babies sure are lucky to have you."

He suddenly throws his arm around my neck and pulls my face down to his, planting a kiss on my cheek. "I love you, Mommy." He goes on eating his dinner, not knowing just how much little moments like this mean to me.

"I love you, too, Hen." I kiss the top of his head and we scarf down the rest of our food in silence. After giving him a bath and taking a shower myself, we snuggle up in my bed and play a couple of rounds of Go-Fish before turning on Spider-Man. We only watch about twenty minutes worth before he passes out and begins snoring beside me. Most nights I take him to his own room to sleep, because I think we *both* sleep better when we have room to spread out. But tonight I let him stay with me, I snuggle up to him and brush his dark brown hair to the side before drifting off as well.

"Park day. Heck yeah. Come on Mom!" Hendrix sings from the doorway with his monster truck in hand.

"I'm coming dude, chill out." I tickle his sides as I bend down to put my shoes on.

"This is going to be so much fun. I hope they didn't move the big dirt so my monster truck can go really high!" He swooshes his hand above his head, watching it in slow motion before it comes crashing down.

"Well, let's go find out. Grab your shoes." I pinch his cheeks, glancing down at his sock-covered feet.

"Oh, right." He slides his boots on with a stomp and smiles. "Ready!"

Thank God it's not crowded today.

Listen, I'm as polite as one can be to other moms when they're here, but sometimes I just want to watch my kid play in the dirt and not pretend like I'm going to set up a play date between Hendrix and a child who thinks it's funny to throw rocks at squirrels. There's one other dad here, but he's playing with his son on the other side of the field, so I'm enjoying the peace and quiet on my empty park bench.

I often wonder if Hendrix notices the lack of male presence in his home life, and if it bothers him. He's used to being around Max and Tucker, but there's a big difference between that and having a father who's present in your everyday life. It's been just me and him since day one and although I know it's for the best, I still hate feeling like he's missing out on something major. Not having a father figure, a role model that he can look up to and think *I wanna be like him one day*, has to be hard on a little boy, right?

Even if his biological dad *was* in the picture, I would pray daily that he would *never* want to end up like him. I close my eyes, trying to take a deep breath and let go of all the suffocating feelings I get when my mind takes me down this path. Just as I do, I hear a loud kick of a soccer ball across the park followed by,

"Heads up!" My eyes shoot open as the ball flies past my head, hitting the stone wall that lines the bike path behind me. The dad mouths *sorry* as the little boy runs in my direction to retrieve the ball. I take the opportunity to stand up and grab it for them before he makes it too far.

"Back at ya." I glance at the runner who's taking a break on the bench near mine, ensuring my yell doesn't alarm them before throwing the ball as hard as I can back to the little boy. I watch as they start their game back up, keeping my eyes on them as I start walking back to my park bench, but instead of the short trip to my seat, I make a more abrupt one to the ground as a runner comes crashing into me.

"*Shit*. I am so sorry. Are you okay?" I try to regain my bearings, as I take the hand being offered to me.

"Yeah, I think so." I stand up, brushing some loose gravel from my jeans as I check myself for scrapes—which I surprisingly don't have. I may have a new rip in my favorite black jeans, but that's about the only damage done.

"I should have been paying more attention." When I finally look up, I'm shocked by who I see.

"Tank?" I do nothing to hide the surprise in my tone, but it's less about him being here and more about the fact that I think this is the most I have ever heard him speak to me at once since his first day at the bar.

"*Yeah?*" he says, drawing his brows together as he looks at me more closely. "Are you sure you didn't hit your head?"

"No, I just... I'm surprised to see you here I guess." I cross my arms over my chest, feeling slightly embarrassed by how nervous I am around him.

"This *is* a public park, isn't it?" he teases. Or at least I *think* he's teasing, I'm not sure I've ever heard anything but a serious tone come from him.

"*Yes.*" I roll my eyes, giving him a playful attitude. Next thing I know a tiny blur comes running up and starts kicking Tank in the shins.

"Stay away from my mom, dirt ball," Hendrix yells, as I quickly pull him back towards me.

"Hendrix, stop, what are you doing?" I ask, unsure where this new aggression is coming from.

"That man pushed you down!" he yells again, flailing his arms and feet as I pick him up off the ground.

Oh, *that.*

"It was just an accident, Hendrix, look at me." He stops kicking and hesitantly looks back at me through his long brown hair, as I give him a reassuring smile to help calm him down. "Check me out, see—" I say, planting his feet back on the ground as I start moving my arms around to show him I'm not hurt. "I'm okay. Really. This is actually a friend of Mommy's." He holds my cheeks in his dirt-covered hands, looks over my face, and kisses my nose before cutting his gaze back over at Tank like he's mentally adding him to his shit list. Tank gives Hendrix a friendly nod but Hendrix ignores him and looks up at me.

"Can I go back to my dirt now?" Hendrix asks.

"Don't you think you owe Tank an apology?" Hendrix's face turns to stone as he looks up at Tank.

"No." My eyes grow to twice their normal size and my face immediately heats with embarrassment.

"Hendrix Ranes," I scold, and his shoulders slump.

"*Sorry,*" he mumbles, without an ounce of conviction in his tone. Tank simply smirks as Hendrix stomps back over to the dirt, while I stand with my mouth ajar a little mortified by everything that just happened. Hendrix is not an aggressive kid at *all*, so for him to come running over to kick a total stranger had me caught off guard enough—but refusing to apologize for his behavior has left me absolutely speechless.

"Good little man you got there." He smirks, raising a brow at me.

And the surprises just keep on coming.

"I am so sorry about that," I apologize, but Tank waves me off.

"Don't be. Little boys *should* look out for their moms. Especially when they've got a good one." His subtle compliment makes a warm feeling grow in my chest as he looks over at Hendrix and smiles. There's a sadness behind his striking green eyes I've never noticed before that has my gaze lingering on him.

I take a moment to study him while he's still looking away, trying to get a better read of him and what he might be feeling, but his nearly impenetrable exterior doesn't budge.

"You sure you're okay though?" he asks, checking on me again. I nod my head in reassurance.

"Alright, well. I'll see ya around," he says, nodding back before stepping around me to continue his run.

"Hey, Tank?" I stop him before he even has the chance to take off.

"Yeah?" He turns back around with a waiting expression, and it takes everything in me not to try and absorb every single one of his distinct, manly features.

From the way his T-shirt fits snugly around his chest and biceps, to the tattoos that go all the way down his right arm and up his neck that I'm dying to observe more closely, and the perfectly scruffy facial hair accentuating his strong jaw. I shake my head, blinking away the brain fog as I continue.

"I was just wondering... Uh, are we good?" I ask almost timidly. I'm typically more sure of myself and assertive in conversation, but something about Tank's aura makes me feel as though I need to *handle with care*, if you will.

"How do you mean?" He quirks his brow and I bite on the inside of my cheek, trying to think of what to say next to keep myself from sounding childish.

"Things have just felt kind of weird since your first day at the bar. You hardly speak to me, and some days you simply *don't*. I just —did I do something to piss you off that I'm unaware of?" I study his face as his lips turn down into a frown.

"No, not at all. Honestly, I've just never been great at making friends. I've been told I'm socially awkward—by my own brother mostly—but I can assure you, *you* haven't done anything," he says with a sort of embarrassed laugh.

"So... we're good?" I confirm.

"We're good." The wave of relief I feel at his words makes me realize just how much this has been bothering me.

"And you'll start talking to me at work?" I press further, giving him a playful grin. He takes a deep breath, taking in his surroundings before his gaze lands on me again.

"I'll do my very best." One corner of his mouth turns up in a smirk.

"Okay then." I smile, standing with my arms crossed, unsure where to go from here. Though he seems to share no such predicament.

"See you tomorrow, boss." He casually salutes before turning and jogging off. Well, that's progress I guess.

Chapter 5

TANK

I HAD a feeling going for a run was a bad idea. As it turns out, I was right, and for more reasons than one. I started feeling a twinge of pain in my back halfway through, but I was determined it would go away after getting warmed up.

Oh, how wrong I was.

Another pain hit and when it did it sent my mind right back to the day I broke it.

"Fuck! Landry, talk to me. You good?" Asher calls from above me, but all I can get out is a loud groan when I realize I can't move without severe pain shooting throughout my entire body.

I wasn't too fond of the unwelcome memory, and when I stood up from the bench ready to run the thoughts away, I almost took Ruby out right there on the bike path. As if I didn't already feel like enough of an asshole for that, she then pointed out that I never really talk to her at work. I'm kind of glad she noticed *that,* and not the fact that anytime I look up from what I'm doing my eyes seem to magnetically find their way to her. It's not intentional, the fact that I don't talk to her, my mind has just been elsewhere lately and it's really taking everything I've got to be there in the first place.

I feel like I'm going crazy, living my life on a loop. All I do is work, go home to pour myself a glass of whiskey, then fall asleep in front of the TV. It's like I'm 81 not 31, which is why I finally dragged my ass out of the house to go for a run this weekend. If I don't find some kind of hobby soon, I'm going to *actually* lose my mind—or drink myself into liver failure. Here's to a new day and trying to hold a simple conversation with Ruby so she doesn't start thinking I hate her or some shit.

"What's up, Steamroller?" Ruby smiles as she wipes down some glasses. I smirk and shake my head as I throw the bar towel over my shoulder while unloading more glasses behind the bar. Her giggle gets my mind lost in the fact that she's so unlike anyone else I've ever met. Because even though I haven't made the best first impression, she still seems optimistic about our friendship. I can't for the life of me figure out *why* though—she barely knows me and so far it seems like I'm doing a *bang-up job* matching her efforts. Not speaking to her and almost giving her a concussion don't exactly seem like qualities someone sees and goes *yeah, let me be friends with that guy.*

"Landry, snap out of it." Ruby's voice breaks me from my thoughts just as a lemon wedge hits me in the head.

"Did you just throw a lemon at me?" I accuse, making her force a clueless expression.

"I would never. That's highly unprofessional," she says, dropping more wedges into their canister. "But I do need you to count down the register."

"Uh huh. You know, blinding your coworker by getting lemon juice in their eye is also highly unprofessional." I grab the bar towel from my shoulder and try popping her with it, barely missing her as she hops backward.

"Whatever, you'd look fine with an eye patch." She cuts her eyes over to me, giving the brief feeling she might be flirting with me. But then again, she's probably just being nice.

The bar is super crowded today and I'm about at my wits end with the amount of blatant stupidity I've dealt with already—and it's only 4 PM. Much to my dismay, the obnoxiously loud drunk guy that's been at the pool table with his co-workers since about noon, decides to plant his ass on the barstool right in front of me.

Fan-fucking-tastic.

"What can I get you?" I ask, grabbing a coaster from behind the counter.

"Ah, shit. Wrong seat." His head falls back like a toddler that's delirious.

"By all means, go find a new one." I grab the coaster to drop it back behind the bar as his head turns from side to side.

"Where's that sexy tattooed babe that's always working back here? Let me grab a seat in front of her." He sways in his seat as he chuckles, but his comment stops me in my tracks.

"On second thought, why don't you stay *right* where you are." I tap the counter, grabbing his attention. His brows knit together in the most dumbfounded way, and then his face smooths like a real- ization has hit him.

"*Oh.* I get it. Don't worry buddy. I'll only look, no touching. Unless she asks nicely." He snickers to himself.

Yep. I've heard enough out of this guy.

I slam my fist on the bar and grab him by the collar, bringing his face just inches away from mine.

"Here's what you're going to do." I smirk at him humorlessly. "You're going to shut your fucking mouth, pay your tab, and get the hell out of this bar before I break your jaw." I release his collar with a little more force than I intended, sending him stumbling onto the floor.

"What the hell, man!" he yells.

"Hey, what's going on?" Ruby runs up beside me, looking at the guy on the floor and then up at me.

I see the predatory spark in the guy's eyes as he looks over at Ruby and my jaw immediately tightens, my hands balling into fists as he stands back up. One more fucking word out of this guy about her and I'm going to jail.

Before either of those things can happen, Ruby nods to Marco to handle things out front and pulls me into the kitchen.

"What's going on? What just happened?" She releases my hand looking up at me with those big brown eyes. My jaw seems to relax at her touch, and I'm surprised by the immediate effect she has on me.

"He was just talking shit. I told him to cut it out and when I let go of him, he fell over." I shrug, trying my best to spare her the details.

"*Okay.* Well, drunk bar patrons always talk shit, you can't threaten all of them or you'd never get anything else done." She narrows her gaze like she knows I'm leaving something out.

"I didn't say I threatened him. I said I told him to cut it out," I correct. She crosses her arms over her chest, raising a brow like she doesn't buy a single word out of my mouth.

"I don't threaten *all* of them. Only the ones talking shit about *you,*" I admit, holding her gaze as she processes what I said.

"Hmm." Her cheeks turn pink as the shock settles on her face. Next thing you know, Ruby storms back out front.

"What are you—" I follow her through the door, but she holds a hand up to me and my mouth snaps shut. My eyes widen and a spark of excitement shoots south at her boldness as she leans slightly on the bar top right in front of the guy—his face instantly morphing into a sick smirk.

"Hey there," Ruby's voice is sweet as sin as she speaks to him and it makes my blood boil instantly.

What the fuck is this?

"Did this gentleman over here threaten you?" she whispers, nodding over to me.

What. The. Fuck?

"Sure did. All I said was that I wanted a better view than he could give me. Promised I wouldn't touch—unless it was asked for," he says with a wink, making me want to slam his head into the bar repeatedly until he's left without any sight at all. I see Ruby's shoulders stiffen slightly as she leans a fraction closer.

"Well... If you ever come in here again insinuating you plan to touch *anyone*, asked for or not, I'll let him do whatever he threatened to do and more. Understand?" Her words come out so commanding, like a perfect breeze fanning the flame burning inside of me. I feel myself start to calm down as the guy's face turns ghostly white.

"Y'all are fucking crazy," he argues, standing from his barstool.

"Yeah? Well, the owner of this bar takes no bullshit, and neither do I. Get the fuck out and don't come back." She stands up taller, flipping him off before pulling me back to the kitchen again.

"It better have been a good threat." She points her index finger at me and I notice the way her hand is shaking before she pulls it back.

"It was decent. I think yours was better," I say, making her smirk. Just as I'm about to ask if she's okay, Shane comes rushing through the door to the kitchen.

"There you guys are. What the hell happened out there?" She asks, her eyes bouncing between me and Ruby. I raise a brow at her, giving her the opportunity to answer instead of me.

"Ugh, some drunk idiot talking shit, and Tank had to put him in his place. I was just following up. Nothing new." She rolls her eyes with a shrug, and Shane scoffs.

"Ew. Those are never fun. Well, Marco closed him out and sent him and his *lovely* friends on their way." She fusses with her ponytail as she hops up on the counter where some of the staff sit for their breaks.

"Tank, I'll have to point out the guy that comes in here and stares at me like he's trying to put a hex on me. Maybe you can put him in his place too. Or blacklist him from the bar. I'm cool with either." She shrugs as Ruby starts laughing.

"Oh my god, yes! Tank this guy is seriously so disturbing. We'll definitely have to point him out next time he comes in." They continue talking about the amount of people who have come in the bar and made them uncomfortable that I now have to apparently play bar bouncer with.

The thought of being needed is appealing, sure. But after seeing the way Ruby handled that guy I'd say they don't need *me* for shit. This is exactly why I didn't try to go out of my way to belong here—because I don't. I belong somewhere I won't want to threaten every piece of shit that looks at my coworkers the wrong way. Somewhere I won't count down the minutes until I get to leave and be by myself. Somewhere I don't have to connect with others to do my job well. Because I had that, and I lost it—and nothing will ever be like that again.

ME

Gym?

TUCKER

Holy fucking shit. The hermit is crawling out of his hole!

ME

Hermits live in shells, also known as their homes.

TUCKER

Yes, but they hide in holes.

ME

Oh my god. Are we going or not?

TUCKER

You're a cranky crab.

TUCKER

MR. KRABS GIF

TUCKER

I can meet you in half an hour.

ME

I think I changed my mind. I don't want to go with you anymore.

TUCKER

TUCKER

TUCKER

ME

Meet you at Hall's in half an hour. Leave the sass at home will ya?

TUCKER

"How's work been at the bar?" Tucker asks, taking a drink from his water bottle while I use my foam roller.

"It's fine." I would pay all the money I have right now to *not* talk about work.

"That's...good?" He gives me a look urging me to elaborate.

"It's not what I want to do, Tuck, but I'm not gonna complain." I sigh, standing up to grab my water.

"Look, I know it's not the best, but Max was being a good friend by offering you a position there until you can find something else," he says almost defensively.

"I know he was. I'm not discrediting the gesture." I take a deep breath, trying to choose my next words carefully. "It's just... I need *more*. I need to be doing something that makes me feel like I'm making a difference." He nods his head slowly at my response.

"Then start looking for more, brother. You won't find something if you're not actively looking." He claps my shoulder, sending a shock of pain down my side. I close my eyes as my jaw tightens in an effort to keep me from wincing.

"1...2...3... UP!" The pain shoots all the way down my legs as the guys lift me into the Medevac. "You're gonna be alright man. We'll get you back out here in no time." Dom nods reassuringly, though I have no hope of that happening with the way my spine currently feels.

"Just hang in there, Tank. You're gonna be fine."

"Tank?" Tucker snaps in front of my face, as my eyes fly back open. "You good man?" he asks, staring at me a little more closely.

"Yeah. I just..." I swallow hard, debating whether or not to bring up the flashbacks to Tucker. But he already concerns himself with me too much, I don't need to give him another reason to worry about anything.

"I'm good. You're right. I'll start looking." I agree as we grab our stuff to leave.

Maybe Tucker is right, maybe I just need to start looking for something that will make me feel... *useful*.

Because these days, I feel anything but. Especially with these flashbacks that do nothing but remind me of what I'm *not* doing.

Chapter 6

RUBY

I HATE MALLS. I truly, deeply, hate them. As if they aren't bad enough on a regular day, I am shopping in *November* when everyone seems to lose their minds, manners, and driving skills. If I could shop online for everything, all the time, I would. However, my darling child—the sun, moon, and stars of my life—wants a LEGO set for Christmas that is sold out online, and only *one* store near me showed it in stock. So here I am, full of anxiety and dread, looking for a parking space in an overcrowded lot. When I finally snag a spot about two football fields from the entrance, I throw my car in park and give myself a good pep talk before booking it inside.

I probably should have grabbed a jacket, but I came straight from work and never seem to need one there. So instead, I'm currently freezing to death in nothing but a Chattahoochies T-shirt and blue jeans. I keep my head down and my feet moving straight into the LEGO store, and lo and behold, the exact set he wants is sitting on the shelf just waiting for me. Snatching it up before anyone else has the chance to, I let out a sigh of relief that my shopping is officially *done*. As soon as I turn around to make my way to the register I'm frozen in place by a figure that looks eerily too familiar.

It couldn't be.

There's nothing telling about him that should make me think it could be the man who haunts my past, only this *feeling* accompanying his very average look. He has the same shade of brown hair, is the same height, and has on an expensive winter coat I'd imagine he would wear. All I can see is the back of him, but it's the feeling in my gut that brought me to a halt. And if there's one thing I've learned in my 26 years of life, it's to always trust your gut. I'm only broken from my trance when a pair of perfectly pink manicured nails grab onto the box.

"Oh, excuse me. I was *just* about to grab that one." I turn to see a woman devilishly smiling at me, her face made up with a shade of pink lip gloss that matches her nails and puffer jacket perfectly. Of course, I'm gonna have to fight *Barbie* over this damn toy.

"Yeah, but you didn't. It was *fully* in my possession before your hands touched it so... Good luck." I pull the box away from her, turning around once again before she latches onto my arm, spinning me around to face her.

I really fucking hate malls.

"Listen. That's the *only* toy my kid asked for this year. I can't let him go giftless, so why don't you give me that one, and you can take... *this* one." She pulls a different box down from the shelf that looks *nothing* like the one I am buying for Hendrix. I look at the box and then back up at her with a raised brow.

"Or...you can buy that one for *your kid* since you were too busy batting your eyelashes at the store manager to turn around and find it yourself, and I'll keep this one." I give her one final look, assuring her this conversation is officially over, then head to the register and secure the gift that will no doubt have Hendrix's booty shaking with excitement on Christmas morning. I do one subtle sweep of the store, looking for the man from earlier, but he's nowhere in sight, giving me the chance to finally exhale.

When I get home, I run straight to hide Hen's gift at the top of my closet before picking him up from Betty's. Once we are in for the night, we both hop into our pjs and turn on *It's the Great Pumpkin Charlie Brown* while I make my famous chicken casserole for dinner.

One of my favorite things about working at Chattahoochies is all of the regulars I have connected with throughout the years. Drengr—the biker gang that stays around here—is always in here, and their president Lenny is a fucking riot.

"Hey gorgeous, how about another round for the boys." He winks at me as he walks outside to smoke.

"You got it, Len." I get to work putting their drinks on a tray, but as soon as I finish, I look up to see a familiar face walking through the door. Along with two others, I don't recognize.

Mall Barbie.

"Why the fuck is she here?" I mumble to myself, looking around for Heather.

"Oh, Heather. Could you grab that table please?" I ask, nodding to the booth they just sat down in, hopeful I won't have to interact with this woman again.

"Sorry, Rubes, I just clocked out for my break. Want me to run those drinks first though?" she offers.

"No, it's fine. Have you seen Tank?" I ask, desperate to find a way out of having to go over there.

"I think he was taking the trash out." She scrunches her nose before walking through the door to the kitchen.

Shit.

"Okay. Thanks anyway," I mumble, taking a deep breath to try and maintain my composure and not let my anxiety start taking over.

I pick up the tray of drinks for Lenny's table, which is inconveniently right behind theirs, and make my way over. I try not to make eye contact with them until absolutely necessary, but before I reach Drengr's table, I trip over a strategically placed foot and the drinks spill all over me.

Giggles erupt from the table where said foot is attached to none other than *Barbie*. I grind my teeth so hard I'm sure the enamel on them is chipping as I place the tray of fallen drinks on an empty table nearby.

"Wow, the bitch is clumsy too, why am I not surprised?" I hear the woman from the mall say, making her friends scoff and cast judgemental glances in my direction.

I feel my face turning red as I decide how best to deal with this. Old Ruby is really trying to come out and slap the makeup right off of her face, but this is my place of work and I have to handle myself in a *professional* way. Before I get the chance to say anything, I feel the warmth of a hand grabbing me gently by the arm, turning me around.

"You okay?" I'm still slightly in shock as I look up and see Tank staring back at me with an intensity behind his green eyes I've never seen before. I glance down at my favorite purple work shirt, now covered in beer, and swallow hard before nodding. I see his jaw flex and his nostrils flaring—- like a bull seeing red. He cuts his eyes over to the women at the table, then stands up a bit taller. He pulls his baby blue Chattahoochies T-shirt over his head, now standing in front of the entire bar bare-chested, with his eyes solely on me. It's not the first time I've seen him shirtless, but it sure *feels* like it is. My eyes fall to the ink on his skin that reads *"No Quarter"* and I make a mental note to ask him about it later.

"Here. Take this and go change. I'll finish up here." I know I should be making eye contact with him. I should take the shirt, go change, and just walk away. I should not be looking at him like this, but *shit*—this man is beautiful. Before I can peel my eyes away, his fingers tip my chin up, forcing my eyes on his. "Go."

I blink away my wandering thoughts and take the shirt from his hands, heading straight to the bathroom to change. As I am walking off I hear one of the girls begin to flirt with Tank, which for some strange reason pisses me off more than being covered in beer, but what he says next surprises me.

"Go be immature brats somewhere else ladies. Maybe pick up some manners on your way. Whatever you do, don't ever come back to this bar." I hear his footsteps getting closer, meaning he's probably headed towards the bar, and though I'm itching to turn around and catch one more glimpse of him in nothing but his blue jeans and tattoos, I won't chance getting caught. With my eyes trained on the bathroom door, I hear an appalled scoff and several small footsteps stomping away. They exit the bar at the same time I enter the lady's bathroom.

I wonder if Tank has an extra bra lying around somewhere, cause mine is soaked.

As I'm rinsing my shirt in the sink, I hear the bathroom door open.

Guess I could have locked that before stripping down to my bra.

I don't bother freaking out nor do I apologize for being indecent, since anyone who just witnessed what happened would probably expect to see this. When I hear the door lock my head snaps up in a panic, but when I see *who* locked it, my heart starts racing for a completely different reason.

"Tank, what the hell are you doing in here?" I stare at him wide-eyed until he turns to face me. When I see his eyes drop and his jaw tighten I follow his gaze to my exposed body. I quickly drop my shirt in the sink with the water still running and cover my stomach with my arms. His eyes finally make their way up to mine and he takes a step closer.

"You don't have to do that, you know?" He nods towards my arms. "Hide from me."

"You didn't answer my question. What are you doing in here?" I repeat.

"I wanted to check on you." He shrugs so casually, like we're not both locked in the women's bathroom shirtless right now.

"I'm fine. I smell like I've been on a week-long binge, and wish someone would rearrange Barbie's face—or give her a bad haircut at the very least—but I'm fine." I huff, causing an amused smirk to come across his face.

"You say the word and I'll find some scissors." I want to think he's joking, but there's absolutely no hint of sarcasm in his voice. I finally let myself study him for a moment, no longer worried what he might think by my staring. One of his brows raises slightly, but he doesn't say a word or comment on my silent assessment of him. He simply lets me look at him.

He's so unreadable, always so quiet, never gets in anyone's business, and definitely doesn't let other people into his. So I can't figure out why he stepped in and put himself in mine today?

"Why did you do that?" I ask, letting my eyes bounce between his.

"What? Offer to cut her hair?" he asks, his brows knitting together.

"No, this," I say, holding up his shirt from the dry part of the counter. He takes in a deep breath, and another step closer to me.

"I don't like bullies. Never have. No one is going to treat you like that as long as I'm around," he answers, stealing the breath I've been holding captive in my throat since he walked through the door.

"And what about when you're not around?" Though I mean for my voice to sound strong and playful, it comes out as barely a whisper.

"Then you give me a call and I'll grab my scissors." He smirks, making me laugh.

"Tank?"

"Hmm?" The deep rumble of his simple response and the fact that his eyes fall briefly to my lips send goosebumps down my arms.

"Do *you* have another shirt to change into?" I ask, my eyes falling on his still-exposed chest.

"Umm. No. That's another reason why I came in here," he says, glancing down at himself. "How about I take *this*," he says, reaching behind me to grab his shirt, "and I go grab you a uniform from the box under the bar?" With his chest grazing my shoulder and the scent of sandalwood and musk surrounding me, I almost forget to respond. When he pulls away, leaving his intoxicating scent embedded in my memory, I nod my head in agreement.

"Tank…" I call before he opens the door. He turns his head to face me. "Thank you."

"No problem, Honey." The soft and genuine smile he gives me before walking out the door sends a twinge of heat to my cheeks as I wait for him to return.

Chapter 7

TANK

I'VE SPENT the last week and a half filling out more applications than I would ever care to admit to. I've applied to every Police and Fire department within a ten-mile radius, as well as assistant instructor positions at gyms around town. I've gotten rejections from some, silence from others, and am starting to lose any hope I may have had about hearing from the rest. It's the week of Thanksgiving so I'm sure some places may be waiting until after the holidays to go through applications or reach out to applicants, but the waiting is fucking torture.

In an effort to distract myself from the chaos of my own mind, I came to Mulligan's for a beer. Mulligan's is a small pub right down the road from my apartment and is *nothing* like Chattahoochies. It's very... plain. No Viking aesthetic, no war memorabilia, pictures of motorcycle clubs, or neon signs. It actually almost makes me *miss* being at work.

"Landry?" I hear a voice call from behind me. I spin on my barstool to see an old buddy from my days on the high school wrestling team walking in my direction.

"Rodgers. Holy shit man, how the hell are you?" I stand, shaking his hand.

"I'm good, man. Busy as hell. What about you? I ran into your brother the other day, said you got discharged from a back injury? That fucking sucks man, I'm so sorry."

It does fucking suck, so why the hell would you bring it up, asshole?

"Umm, yeah. I, uh, got back a little while ago. Been working at a buddy's bar but I'm looking for somewhere a little more permanent to land," I answer vaguely. "Actually, one of the places I'm waiting to hear back from is your department." I nod to the Nashville Fire Department logo on his T-shirt. "But I figured with the holidays and all it may be a minute." An uneasy look washes over him, and though he tries to cover it quickly I still notice.

"Yeah, maybe so." His tone and body language change immediately, a dead giveaway for when someone's lying.

"What?"

"What do you mean?" he asks, looking confused.

"There's something you're not telling me. What is it?" I press. He looks around, trying to avoid eye contact before rubbing his hand along the back of his neck.

The universal sign for bad news.

He lets out a sigh, giving me the same look of pity I seem to be getting from everyone these days. "Look man, you didn't hear it from me, but I saw your application come through, and *I* was excited about it, honestly. But... I heard the chief talking and he said he's worried about the back injury and the job being too strenuous so soon after your discharge. I think he just doesn't want to risk you getting hurt again. I'm sorry man. I really am."

"Yeah, I get it. Thanks for letting me know," I say, trying not to let the rage that's fighting to get out become too apparent through my expression.

"Rodgers," the waitress behind the bar calls out with a to-go bag in her hands.

"I better get going. It was good to see you, Tank. Something will work out soon, don't sweat it, man. Yeah?" He claps me on the shoulder, and all I want to do for a moment is break his arm.

I don't need his fucking pity or his empty words of encouragement because what the hell does he know about how things will work out for *my life*. I manage to nod and force the smallest hint of a smile to appear on my lips before he turns and walks out the door. In almost perfect unison, the bell above the door to the pub rings at the same time as the reminder on my phone.

Work. 15 minutes.

Fan-fucking-tastic.

I wasn't missing it that *much.*

Ever since my little encounter with Ruby in the bathroom the other day things have been quieter than usual between us, and now I'm worried I overstepped. She didn't seem upset by it, but she's almost as hard to read as I assume I am some days—the girl has a poker face you could take to the bank. As if my morning didn't start off bad enough after running into Rodgers, Marco is being especially annoying today. If he drops one more cup into the bus bin with the force he's been using since the beginning of his shift, I might just lock him in the walk-in freezer. Maybe if his hands are too frozen to use, I won't have to listen to him throwing shit around all afternoon.

"Hey man, I think that lady is undressing you with her eyes." Marco bumps my shoulder, nodding discreetly to the other end of the bar. I glance in that direction to see a woman—who looks like she needs a lot less gin martini and a whole lot of Jesus—looking at me in a way that leaves no room for interpretation.

"Maybe I'll hand you over instead and solve two of my problems at once," I threaten, giving him an unamused stare.

"Sheesh, who pissed in your Cheerios this morning?" he teases, pushing the door open to take the bus bin into the kitchen.

The fucking universe, that's who.

"I'd pay all the money in my wallet to see you pair those two up," Ruby's voice chimes in from her place at the sales terminal.

"I'd pay all the money in *my* wallet for you to send him home," I fire back.

"Just *today*, or indefinitely?" I glance over at her and see a smirk on her face that gives me a weird feeling in my chest. Like a calming effect on my otherwise rage-infested soul.

"Today, I don't have a preference," I scoff, a look of concern appearing on her once playful features.

Ding.

"Sorry. Forgot to turn that off," I say, hearing my phone go off inside my pocket.

When I grab it to silence it, I notice two new emails have come in, *both* with application rejections. My grip tightens so hard I think I may shatter my screen. I rip the towel from my shoulder, slamming it down on the counter so loud it grabs the attention of everyone seated at the bar. I turn to push open the kitchen door just as Marco is walking back through it, causing me to absentmindedly shove him out of my way.

"What the hell man?" Marco yells as he lands on his ass on the bar floor.

"Tank!" Ruby calls after me. "Marco, you good?" I hear her ask as her voice fades away.

I have to get out of here. I need some air, I need to be alone, and I need to feel something other than pure fucking anger. I push the back door open, causing it to slam against the brick wall.

"Fuck!" I yell as I throw my phone against the dumpster.

Is this it? Am I just destined to be a bartender for the rest of my life? I can't seem to get a job serving anywhere honorable because of my injury and so far I haven't heard back from any of the gyms I applied at where I could do something I actually *enjoy*—something I'm good at. I'll just feel like shit for the rest of my life while miserably serving drinks to people who think I'm their new therapist and keep every bit of self-loathing I feel over it bottled up. Because, why bother telling anyone how useless you feel when the only response they can muster up is *But you're so lucky to be alive.*

Fuck. That. Shit. Because some days I wish I wasn't.

Before I know it my fist goes flying into the brick wall.

Once. Twice.

I feel my demons being appeased by my pain, but it's not enough. I need to feel *more*. More than this fucking *emptiness* that leaves me as worthless as if I'd never come back from that mission at all. I rear back, ready to force my head against the wall, but a small, cold hand makes contact with my face before I get there.

SLAP.

The sound of skin on skin, and the slight tingle on my cheek snaps me out of my trance. I look down to see Ruby staring at me, her poker face perfectly in place.

"Rear back like you're going to hit your head on these bricks again and I'll kick you in the balls so hard you'll be able to taste your own ass." My demons crawl back into hiding and my dick jumps when I note the intensity behind her sweet brown eyes.

Apparently, I like it when Ruby threatens me.

"What the fuck is the matter with you? Do you have any idea what kind of permanent damage that would do to you?" she asks, continuing lighting into my ass.

"Maybe a permanent solution is what I'm going for," I answer back in an arrogant tone. She crosses her arms over her chest, narrowing her gaze at me.

"Promise me you won't do that again," she demands, earning a scoff from me.

"What makes you think I'll do that?" I ask, squaring my shoulders to accentuate our height difference.

"Because if you don't, I'll follow you everywhere you go to make *sure* you don't."

"Maybe I'd like that." I huff, giving her a sinister smile to see if there's *anything* that will get her to leave me and my problems the *hell* alone. "Or let's say I promise you. Who's to say I'll even keep the promise?" I pester, her brows scrunching in further before her features soften completely.

"No one. But I hope you'll prove to both of us that you're capable of not only the self-control but the loyalty that keeping that promise will require." Her tone is still calm and collected, pushing me deeper into my uncontrollable rage.

"You know, I've known you for a *very little* amount of time. What makes you think I owe you any kind of loyalty?" I respond in one last attempt to drive her away. Her eyes narrow and I'm suddenly held captive by the way it feels like she can see through me. Straight down to my torn and tattered soul.

"You know what. You're right. You don't owe me a *damn* thing. *I* must have made the mistake of thinking we were friends." Her hand moves from her chest, as she shoves a finger at me accusingly. "Seeing as how *you've* stepped in on multiple occasions for me, which is something I've only *ever* seen friends do for each other. My bad, please… *as you were.*" She scoffs, turning to go back inside.

Why the fuck does my heart sink when she turns to walk away? That's what I wanted, the only reason I said any of that shit to get in the first place was to get her to leave me alone. To make her not feel whatever need she has to protect me. So why am I about to undo it all? Maybe because, outside of my brother, she seems to be the only one who's ever cared about what happens to me.

Goddammit.

"Okay. Fine," I say through gritted teeth.

"Fine, what?" She turns around slowly, looking at me impatiently.

"I'll promise," I bite out.

"And *why* should that mean anything to me now? You just made it *very* clear you don't give a shit about being loyal to *me*," she says, leaving me with a sour feeling for being so harsh.

"Because I only make promises that I intend to keep." She shakes her head like she's listening but not believing a word I say. I let out a heavy sigh, running my hands along my face. "And because I didn't mean any of the other shit I said before. I was just *really* fucking pissed about something and was trying to get you to leave me alone."

"You know, *asking* to be left alone, also works. You don't have to resort to being an asshole right away," she says, showing that boldness of hers I'm beginning to grow fond of.

"I'll uh, have to make a mental note of that," I say sarcastically. Trying to melt some of the ice I created between us.

"You do that..." She studies me for a minute before speaking again. "Do you want to talk about it?" she offers in a softer tone.

"Not really," I clip.

"Well, do you need to go home?"

"That depends. Are you going to make me apologize to Marco?" I ask, making her grin.

"I'll let you decide if you need to or not." Her smile grows a little more, showing a hint of her perfect white teeth. The same calming effect settles over me like it did before and I realize—Ruby's smile is like a pain killer for my soul. It takes all the rage I have simmering inside of me, and lulls it to sleep until my mind is right again—and she has no fucking idea.

"Fine." I hold a hand out, prompting her to walk back inside. When she walks ahead of me I instinctively place my hand on the small of her back to lead her through the door. Suddenly my bloody knuckles aren't what's holding my attention. It's the itch I feel in my fingertips to know what it's like to touch every other part of her. I pull my hand away quickly, trying to erase the curiosity creeping in, because no matter how her smile can affect me, or how it feels to have any part of her body on mine, I won't go there with her. Everything I touch and everything I do only ever ends in disaster. And I refuse to be the fall of Ruby Ranes.

Chapter 8

RUBY

"OH MY GOD, I thought this day would never end." I lock the front door of the bar while Tank stacks chairs on top of the tables. He huffs out a laugh and my eyes fall to the gauze wrapped around his knuckles. My heart stopped earlier when I saw him outside about to assault the building with his forehead. I held my breath as soon as my hand made contact with his face, but at that moment I had no other ideas on how to stop him. His attempts to get me to leave him alone pissed me off, but even more than that, they hurt a little bit too. All I've done since Tank started working here is be nice to him —and *maybe* admire his genetics from afar, but honestly, who could blame me? I thought we were on the edge of friendship after he stuck up for me that day with the whole *here, take my clothes* gesture, but after today I'm not so sure that I didn't make it all up. I'd still like to get to know him a little better though, he seems lonely and a little sad. And if anyone can relate to that it's yours truly. So here I go… putting myself out there and doing something bold.

"You drink, Landry?" I ask, placing two beers on the bar top. He rears back slightly, showcasing the tattoo on the side of his neck.

"*Psh*, it's what I'm best at." He smirks, making me smile back at him.

"Let's drink then." I hold my beer up in the air and wait as he grabs his and does the same.

"As you wish." Our bottles *clink* and I pull myself up onto the counter as he turns to lean against it with his elbows.

"So... what else are you good at? Besides drinking?" I tease, making him scoff.

"What?"

"What other skills or talents do you have?" I press further.

"Why are you asking me this?" He lets out a bashful laugh.

"I wanna get to know you." I shrug.

"Why?" The look of genuine confusion on his face breaks my heart. Like he truly can't understand why someone would want to get to know him.

"Well... I think if you want to pursue a friendship with someone, it helps to know things about them. Things they're good at, things they like. Things they're *bad* at and *don't* like are good to know too." I continue, making him laugh again.

"So, you think you want to *pursue a friendship* with me?" he asks sarcastically, but I meet his sarcasm with sincerity.

"I do. If you're okay with that." His gaze narrows as he studies me.

"Alright, fine." He finally agrees. "Let's start with you though." He counters.

"What do you wanna know?" I encourage with an outstretched arm.

"I'm dying to know the story behind this tattoo," he says, pointing to the mermaid on my arm.

"*That's* what you're starting with?" I look at him in disbelief. He raises a brow at me but doesn't answer. I roll my eyes, taking another drink before setting the bottle on the counter.

"It's a mermaid." I roll my lips together to keep from laughing when his face drops.

"No shit, I wasn't born yesterday. Explain the rest of it." He demands with a smirk.

"She's a stripper mermaid and she's very talented," I say in a serious tone. Looking down at the mermaid holding a pole tattooed on the inside of my left bicep.

"That so?" He nods.

"Yes."

"I have... so many questions." He laughs. "Like first of all, what the fuck?" We both laugh this time and I pick my beer back up, turning to face the same direction as him.

"She's feeling judged now, and will be taking no further questions."

"My deepest apologies," he says, looking at my arm like he's speaking directly to the tattoo. I give a nod of approval at his apology.

"Okay, your turn."

"What? You wanna know about my tattoos?" He assumes, and though that's not what I intended to ask, I'll take any reason to stare at his arms a little longer.

"Well, the logo for the Marine Corps on your hand, tattered American flag, smoke background, *1776,* and cannon covering your left arm all seem pretty self-explanatory. Very patriotic." I give him a smirk, earning a raised brow in return before letting my eyes fall to his neck. "Though the little skeleton guy with a spear through his head on your neck *does* pique my interest, as well as the tattoo on your chest, the raven with a heart in its talons on your other hand, and whatever words are tattooed above it." He nods slowly, taking a sip of his beer before placing it on the bar. Then he points to the tattoo on his neck.

"It's like a mashup of the insignia from Blackbeard's flag."

"Blackbeard?" I raise a brow in question.

"The pirate."

"Right, of course," I say sarcastically, earning a playful glare from him.

"The tattoo on my chest basically means no pity, no mercy. And the raven, heart, and quotes are from two of my favorite pieces by Edgar Allen Poe."

"Curious." I narrow my gaze, but when he doesn't elaborate further I move on. "Okay then. Do I want to know about the haunted mansion with the dead tree and ghost on this arm?" I nod to the arm closest to me, making him turn it slightly to look at it.

"I like spooky shit." He shrugs, making me laugh. "Does that mean it's my turn now?"

"No. You totally hijacked my turn and picked the question. What I *really* want to know is what you were like as a kid."

"Why?" He rears back, clearly surprised by the inquiry.

"I don't know. Something tells me I would have wanted to know you when you were little." I shrug, answering with pure transparency.

"Nah. You definitely wouldn't have wanted to know me then. I'm not sure you really wanna know me now either," he says, hanging his head.

"Tell me anyways, please." He shakes his head and then lets out another sigh.

"Honestly? I was bad as shit." He laughs. "My dad passed away when I was seven, and my mom just kind of stopped living when he did."

"I'm so sorry, Tank. I'm sure that was really hard for you guys" I say, rubbing his hand with my pinky. He gives me a sad smile before he continues.

"Yeah... She was there but not really, ya know? Anyway, Tucker always tried keeping me on track but I was dealing with the grief in my own way and he couldn't always be there to put me in my place. When I got to middle school there was this one guy... he was the biggest bully I'd ever met. I was getting into so many fights with him that I was on the verge of being expelled. But there was this one guidance counselor who made the suggestion to join the wrestling team to keep me out of trouble."

"Did it work?"

"Yeah. It did, actually. He tried fighting me one more time, but I shut him down and that was the end of my fighting days. Off the mat at least." The thought brings a smile to my face and I just want to hear more.

"Were you any good? At wrestling?"

"The best our school ever had."

"He says with such humility," I add jokingly. He smiles, showing off his perfect, pointed canines. "What happened next? Did you keep wrestling?"

"I did. I started doing MMA in high school and fought all throughout college and some after." He nods, turning to face me.

"That's so interesting. I would have never guessed that about you." He smirks and I feel my cheeks heat at the distance that is lacking between us.

"Your turn," he says, nodding to me.

"Suddenly, I can't remember a single interesting thing about myself," I admit.

"It doesn't have to be interesting. It can be something simple."

"What, like my favorite color?" I say sarcastically.

"Something I don't already know." My brows knit together as I think back on if I've ever told him this.

"You don't know my favorite color." He raises a brow at me and leans in even closer, causing me to stop breathing momentarily.

"Plum. Not lavender, not true purple. The deep, almost black looking purple."

"How..." Is the only word I get out before he smirks, taking my hand in his as electricity shoots from my fingertips all the way to my core.

"Well... Your nails are almost always painted this color. Even when they chip and you get them redone, they're always the same color. The same color as," he flips my hand over, displaying the other purple tattoo on my wrist, "this tattoo. Which I am also curious about, but I don't know if you want to tell me about it yet."

He looks into my eyes, waiting for an answer but I simply shake my head.

"That's alright. A story for another time." He smiles softly, winking at me as he leans back to put distance between us. "It's also the same color as your favorite work shirt. The purple tie-dye shirt that only *you* have. I assume you had it specially made?"

Did I just fall in love?

"How'd I do?" He smirks, forcing me to clear my head of the *many* thoughts going through it right now that are causing my cheeks to burn.

"I would have accepted *purple*." I tuck my hair behind my ear, unsure of what to do next. "So what, you just know all about me then?"

"Hardly. But I do think I'd like to." He holds onto the same wrist with the tattoo he pointed out before and gives it a gentle squeeze. "If that's alright with you."

"Yeah. I'd like that." We sit in silence as we finish our drinks and then play a round of pool while I try to convince him why I need to see the pictures from when he was on the wrestling team. I've never heard Tank laugh so much or look so comfortable, and by the end of the night, I finally see the start of what I hope will be a really great friendship.

"You're not fucking leaving this house until this is settled. I'm going to have a say in this," he shouts, gripping me tighter as I will my tears away.

"Do you even hear yourself right now? After the other nasty things you've said to me about this you're delusional if you think you have a say in this," I fight back.

"Try and make this decision, the WRONG decision, without me, and it'll be the last thing you ever do." When he throws me to the ground, I don't

bother standing up. I have no fight left in me, and my arm is throbbing from the pain.

Keys.

Front door opens.

Front door...

SLAM!

My body lunges forward at the sound and my heart is already racing. I look around and don't see Hendrix in bed with me and immediately begin to panic. I throw the covers off and run straight to his room.

There he is.

Sound asleep on his bed with his arm hanging off by his dresser, and his storybook on the floor. I exhale with relief and place it back on his bookshelf. I stare down at him, watching his peaceful features as he sleeps before brushing back his dark locks of hair and kissing his cheek. I'm wide awake now, too shaken to possibly fall back asleep. I turn on *Supernatural*—which is ironically a comfort show for me—and try to get my mind off of the nightmare that woke me. As soon as I'm comfortable enough to fall asleep, my phone goes off.

DING.

Who is actually texting me in the middle of the night?

TANK

Guess what I'm eating right now?

ME

If this is a dirty game, I don't want to play.

TANK

photo of plums

ME

I'm concerned that that is your midnight snack.

TANK

Why? Plums are good. They're healthy. They're your favorite color... I see nothing wrong with them. What's your choice?

ME

Wine… and popcorn. Like a normal person.

TANK

Noted.

ME

Why noted? What's that supposed to mean?

TANK

Night Honey.

Well… I'm never going to sleep *now*.

I got quite honestly the worst night's sleep *ever* last night. Between the nightmare that shook me and the very vague and mysterious texts from Tank, my brain wouldn't shut off until almost sunrise. Today's shift has had me in full zombie mode, but seeing Hendrix run through the front door has all my troubles washing away immediately. I love it when Betty brings him by the bar to see me randomly. It doesn't happen very often since she rarely ever has *just* Hendrix, but it always had the power to turn my day around.

"Mommy!"

"Hey, Buddy!" I squeeze him into my arms before taking him behind the bar with me.

"We were on the way to the park and he wanted to stop by and see you. I told him if it didn't seem too crowded we would, I hope that's okay," Betty says with a grin on her face.

"Of course it's okay." I set Hendrix on the counter, taking in his sweet features.

"I'm gonna run to the ladies room before we head out," Betty says, making her way to the bathrooms.

"Hey, do you want me to get Jackie to make some of his special fries for you before you and Ms. Betty go to the park?"

"Heck yeah!" Hendrix yells, making me laugh.

"Okay, you hang out here for a minute. I'll go let him know he has a special order coming in." I wink at him and run my fingers through his hair before heading to the kitchen. "I'll be right back, do you mind keeping an eye on him for a second?" I ask Tank as he looks over at Hendrix, then he smirks and nods,

"Sure thing."

TANK

"Mommy!" I look up from wiping down the bar to see Hendrix running in Ruby's direction. Not far behind him is a woman holding a small blue jacket that I assume is his babysitter.

"Hey, buddy!" Ruby rounds the bar to sweep him up into her arms and I can't help but smile. Ruby in mom mode is when she's happiest and that's a sight that surprisingly makes my childhood wounds hurt *less*. I couldn't get her off my mind last night to the point that the fruit in my fridge made me start to *miss* her. Not sure how one night of drinking and talking about wrestling and the color purple could lead me to that, but I'm convinced that's when it started. Her smile, her laugh, the random ass mermaid stripper on her arm, the fucking color purple—it's engrained into my mind now and I can't seem to think about anything else.

Am I pathetic? Cause I feel a little pathetic.

"Hey, I'll be right back, do you mind keeping an eye on him for a second?"

"Uh, sure thing," I agree, walking a little closer to where Hendrix is sitting.

"Hey, little man." I smile at him but the angry look on his face makes me freeze in place. "You excited about going to the park?" His face softens slightly as he nods. "Whatcha gonna do there?" No response.

Making conversation with kids is harder than I thought.

"Hendrix. My man. Give me some," Max says walking through the bar towards his office. Hendrix's face immediately lights up and he gives Max a high five. "Yeah. Where's your mom?"

"She's getting me some Jackie fries," Hendrix says excitedly.

"Right on. I'll catch you later. Be good for Ms. Betty, you hear?" Max smiles, clapping me on the shoulder as he moves past me.

"Yes Uncle Max," he calls out, I watch as the door closes to Max's office before turning back to Hendrix who has already put his poker face back on.

God, he looks just like her.

So he's not a *shy* kid, he just doesn't like *me*. But why?

Then I remember the first time I met him. I literally clobbered his mom on the sidewalk right in front of him.

Shit, I wouldn't like me either.

So, I do the one thing I know to do. I ask him an honest question, knowing I'll get an honest answer. Cause if there's one thing I *do* know about kids, it's that they're brutally honest creatures.

"You don't like me that much, do you, Hendrix?" I ask, folding my arms over my chest. He shakes his head *no* while giving me an emotionless stare.

"Is it because you thought I hurt your mom that day at the park?" He nods *yes.* "I get it. I wouldn't like me either." His face twists in confusion and he finally speaks.

"You wouldn't?" he says quietly.

"Of course not. You thought I hurt someone important to you–"

"The *most* important to me," he corrects, making me stifle a laugh.

"Right. You thought I hurt the most important person in the world to you. I would have reacted the same way."

"You would?" his eyes grow wide as saucers and I nod.

"I would. And you know what, I would do it for your mom too." I watch as he absorbs the information, then he looks up at me.

"Is my mommy an important person to you too?" He finally concludes.

"Can I tell you a secret?" I ask, leaning my elbows on the counter.

"Mommy says we don't keep secrets."

"Right. No secrets." I take a moment to think. "Not a secret then. I'll tell you something true, how's that?" He nods, accepting my offer.

"I think your mommy is becoming one of my most important people too."

"So you won't hurt her. You'll protect her?" Hendrix asks, giving me a very serious look.

"I will," I admit, feeling a depth to the statement that I wasn't expecting.

"We cool?" I ask, holding my hands out, awaiting his answer.

"Yeah, we're cool." Hendrix slaps the hand I had no intention of getting a high five on and we go back to sitting in silence. He looks at me with squinted eyes and I look around to be sure he's not looking *past* me, before asking what's wrong.

"Is there something else on your mind, buddy?"

"Why do you look like The Hulk?" My mouth opens to answer just as Ruby walks back into the bar.

"Okay, special fries for my most special guy," she says, placing the basket of french fries on the counter. I laugh off the comment about me looking like The Hulk as Hendrix sticks his tongue out at me as if to say *haha I'm most special*. Ruby's brows knit together as she looks at me confused, but I simply shrug my shoulders and walk back to the other end of the bar.

"Okay, who's ready to go to the park?" Betty says, reappearing from the restrooms.

"Me!" Hendrix exclaims as he holds his arms out for someone to help him down from the bar.

"Bye buddy, have fun and be good for Betty," Ruby says, kissing his cheek before planting his feet back on the ground and handing Betty his basket of fries.

"Yes ma'am." He grabs Betty's hand and waves over his shoulder.

"Bye, Tank." I rear my head back, a little surprised that I made it off his shit list and onto his *worthy of a goodbye* list that quickly.

"See ya, buddy." I salute him with two fingers and he mimics my motion, making me grin. When the door closes behind them I look back over at Ruby who seems to be in a state of shock.

"Umm... No offense but, I kinda thought he hated you after your last encounter. What was that about?" she says, hiking a thumb over her shoulder.

"Ouch," I say, placing my hand over my heart causing her to roll her eyes playfully.

"I'm serious. What happened while I was getting those french fries?" She laughs, throwing a fry at me.

"We talked. I told him I understood why he didn't like me. Which shocked him. That if someone hurt somebody I loved, or I *thought* someone did, I wouldn't like them either. Then I told him that I would never hurt you on purpose and I think we came to an understanding after that." Her features soften as she twists the bar towel in her hands.

"Okay then," she finally says.

"Okay then."

Maybe it was a little soon to qualify Ruby as one of my *most important people*, but I don't think it is. As someone who's never had long-term friends, I have a feeling this is one that has the potential to last. Man, I hope I'm right. Because these days God knows I could really use a friend.

Chapter 9

RUBY

1 YEAR LATER...

ME

Are we sure we trust my kid with these rings? I love him to death but he likes to hide shiny things.

TAYLOR

Of course we do!

TAYLOR

Especially since he won't get them until we send him running down the aisle.

ME

Smart choice.

LEAH

I still can't believe one of us is getting MARRIED 😭

LAUREN

I can. I'm just glad it's with someone we won't have to stand in objection to. 😈

TAYLOR

Agreed.

SHANE

HEY!

ME

They're not wrong. I met the guy for five minutes and wanted to throat punch him.

SHANE

That's fair. I definitely upgraded. 😅

TAYLOR

Now that that's settled. Let's get this girl MARRIED!! 😵

SHANE AND MAX'S wedding is one that *dreams* are made of. You'd never guess by how immaculately it came together that it was planned in one week. We all helped in every way possible, and the lovestruck look in both the bride and groom's eyes when they swore forever to each other, made every seemingly impossible task worth it.

I look away from where they're swaying in each other's arms when I feel a tug on my dress.

"Mommy, can we dance too?" How could I ever say no to my favorite guy in the world?

"Of course we can!" I look around at the other couples on the dance floor, and the tiniest hint of what feels like jealousy hits me when I see Taylor and Tank together. I quickly turn my attention away from them, unsure where this feeling is coming from. Instead, I focus on the one little guy who looks at me like I hung the moon. I sweep him up in my arms as we start dancing to the slow song playing. He giggles and smiles as I twirl him around, making me unable to hold back laughter of my own. As we come to a stop I see Shane rushing out of the room holding the back of her dress.

"I think we're having a little fashion emergency. All bridesmaids have been requested to help," Leah says, waving me over.

"Shall we continue this dance later?" I smile at Hendrix and he nods excitedly.

"Yes, ma'am."

"Oh, my. What a gentleman." I wink at him and kiss his cheek before sending him over to Max. We rush over to where Taylor and Tank are still dancing and that stupid little feeling comes back.

"Hiii, we have a bridal emergency and we need you," Lauren says, taking Taylor by the hand. When neither of them moves I decide to put a rush on the situation.

"Stat." I smirk, I can feel Tank's eyes on me as he chuckles, but I don't bother looking in his direction. Whatever is festering in my chest needs to go away before I give him any of my attention.

"Okay, let's go," Taylor agrees as we rush out of the room.

"Umm, okay so were you just dancing with *Tank?*" Lauren asks, still walking swiftly through the hotel. I want to kiss her for being the one to bring it up because I'm sure it would have sounded a lot different coming from me.

"Yes, he said Tucker was getting *territorial* over me with Zander, and that he was causing a distraction before things got out of hand. How crazy is that?" She laughs in disbelief. We all come to a halt in the middle of the hallway as Leah and Lauren glance at each other and then back at Taylor.

"It's not crazy at all. What's crazy is pretending you don't notice the way he looks at you," Leah says, as if pointing out the obvious.

"Who? Zander?" Taylor asks, confused.

"Oh, my god. You can't be serious." Lauren shakes her head in disbelief.

"TUCKER!" We all shout in unison.

"Honestly, you'd have to be blind not to see it," Leah says accusingly. Taylor rolls her eyes and begins walking towards the bridal suite.

"You guys are crazy. Tucker and I are just friends, and he's always been flirty like that. It doesn't mean anything." She places her hand on the doorknob but Lauren stops her from going in.

"I say this because I love you. Everything you need to know about how a man feels can be found in the way he looks at you, you just have to be paying attention—and I don't think you have been." Taylor's face twists momentarily, but she doesn't say anything else.

After fixing the buttons that popped off of Shane's dress, the reception is back in action as if nothing ever happened. Shane and Max are back on the dance floor, getting lost in each other's eyes. Hendrix is passed out *on* one of the reception tables, and I can't help but notice the way Tucker is storming the dance floor to get to Taylor as she and Zander are dancing.

Damn, Leah and Lauren weren't kidding, with the way he's looking at her right now, there's not a single person who would question the way he feels about her—except maybe Taylor.

"You look absolutely stunning tonight." The deep swagger of Tank's voice sends shivers down my spine, and I quickly straighten my posture to try and hide any indication.

"Thanks, you don't look so bad yourself." I look him up and down and damn if his tux isn't doing the Lord's work. Every bulging muscle this man has is poured into perfectly tailored polyester.

"May I have this dance?" He extends his hand and much to my surprise, a petty part of me I hardly recognize comes out to play.

"Are you sure you don't want to steal Taylor away for another dance?" I raise a brow and his gaze slightly narrows.

"No." His tone is sure as his eyes narrow on me. "*That* was just a necessary precaution. My brother is hopelessly in love with that girl and I knew if someone didn't step in during whatever was happening earlier, the guy she invited as her date would have been leaving a little more broken than the way he arrived," he explains.

I'm slightly embarrassed by the relief I feel hearing he isn't interested in Taylor.

"However, dancing with *you* is something I've been wanting to do all evening." The corner of his lips turns up in a grin, and I can't help but smile back.

"Is that so?" I take his hand and we begin swaying on the dance floor.

"Come on, Honey. Don't pretend you don't know you're my favorite person to be around. Makes me feel like I don't do a good enough job showing ya." Tank winks at me and without warning, I feel a flutter in my stomach.

Tank has easily become one of my best friends since he showed up a little over a year ago, but an established friendship doesn't mean I never wonder if those winks or comments like *you're my favorite person* mean something more.

While Shane and Max have been on their extended honeymoon, things have been a little more chaotic than normal at the bar. Them both being gone meant having one and a half employees *less* than we're used to and making schedules to accommodate everyone has almost killed me. Tank and I are closing together tonight, and things have *finally* begun to slow down.

"*Woooo hoooo. Bar crawl, bitches!*" I turn around from mixing a drink to see a large bachelorette party walk through the door.

Damn, spoke too soon.

I immediately glance over at Tank who already looks annoyed. I don't even have to wonder what he's thinking because every time a group like this one it's the same thing. *Why do they come here? This is not their kind of bar.* We get more bachelorette parties through here than anyone would ever believe.

"Why do they always come here? There are plenty of flashy bars that have karaoke and shit that they could torment instead," he grumbles under his breath, making me smile at how accurate I was.

"I have no idea. But they can't stay forever, it's almost time for the last call anyway. It'll be fine," I assure him before I go over to the table to take their order. When I reach the group I am shocked to see who the bride is.

"Bethany?" I question, getting her attention. She stops her assessment of the bar and looks in my direction before her mouth pops open.

"*Ruby?* Shut up!" she screams, standing up to hug me. "What are you *doing* here?" she asks, her eyes comically wide.

"I work here," I say, pointing at my shirt.

"Get out of town! I would have never pictured you in a place like *this*," she says, not hiding the judgment in her tone in the slightest.

"And yet, here I am," I answer with a forced smile.

"You know I thought you were studying something super brainy when we were in college?" she asks, popping her hip out as she takes a slow evaluation of me.

"I was a psychology major. I actually *graduated* with that degree," I remind her.

"Right. I guess the *dancing* got you a little derailed, huh?" she says with a sinister grin.

"You know what ladies, I was actually just coming to tell you it's past the last call so you're gonna have to leave," I say forcing a dramatic pout.

"Come on Bethany, someone just posted they saw Blake Shelton on Broadway!" One of the girls exclaims while dragging her out the front door.

"Congratulations." I wave with a smile as fake as my disappointment that they're leaving plastered across my face. "Poor bastard," I mumble as they exit.

"Last call! Pay your tabs and get the hell out of here you heathens!" I yell to the rest of the bar patrons with a genuine smile on my face. I can feel the anxiety I was actively shoving down begin to crawl up my chest as I walk back behind the bar.

"Wanna tell me why you made the last call an hour early," Tank says, raising a brow at me.

"Nope. Wanna close the bar and do some shots?" I ask, pulling a bottle from the shelf.

"You don't have to twist my arm." He tosses the towel that lives on his shoulder most shifts onto the bar and starts closing out tabs. We waste no time getting people out the door and saying bye to the kitchen staff before locking up.

"Shall we?" He wags his eyebrows, grabbing the bottle of whiskey and two shot glasses before walking over to the pool table. I follow him over and sit down on the edge of the table as he pours us each a shot.

"Alright." He clears his throat. "What do we toast to?"

"Heavy baggage we left behind." I raise my glass and he nods mirroring my motion.

"Fucking cheers to that," he says, tilting his head in agreement as we both down our shots. He's completely unphased by the liquor as he fills our glasses to the brim again, and I take a moment to appreciate the friendship that's developed between us.

Tank was the friend I never saw coming, and the one I couldn't imagine not having around these days. Even though he can still be really closed off most of the time, and he struggles letting anyone get to know him on a deeper level, I still consider him one of my closest friends. He always works hard and has a way of showing up for me that I find respectable. There have been little moments over the last year or so that I thought he might be flirting with me—the way he invades my space to whisper something funny in my ear instead of letting everyone else hear, the heated stares or subtle winks he gives me here and there—but the man is so unreadable there's a good chance it was all just in my head. I'd be lying if I said I wasn't exhilarated by the idea of him wanting me in that way though.

Do I date? No.

Do I steer clear of trouble at all costs to protect myself and Hendrix? Yes.

Do I think Tank Landry would be the most delicious kind of trouble? Absolutely I do.

But is it worth the risk? Letting someone in only to end up getting hurt again? No. It never will be. Because taking a chance like that wouldn't only affect me, it would affect Hendrix too.

It's still a nice fantasy though, to think he could see me that way. It's been a *very* dry five years for me. I would probably come apart just from sweet nothings being whispered in my ear at this point. Which is probably why after only three shots, I find myself staring at Tank like he could be my last meal. Or I could be his.

Speaking of, I probably should have eaten something before we started drinking.

"So what did *sorority bride* say earlier that got to you so bad?" Tank asks, clearing my mind from any dirty thoughts I was on the verge of having about him.

"Was it that obvious?" I ask sarcastically.

"You shut the whole bar down after she walked in. What, did she sleep with your boyfriend or something?" He assumes as he pours more liquor into our glasses.

"Worse, she insulted my intelligence," I say in disgust, throwing my shot back. The warmth of the liquor slides down my throat no longer leaving a tingle in its wake.

"What a bitch. Want me to go cut her hair?" He slams his shot glass down on the green felt playfully, making me laugh, and I realize two things.

One, he remembers the comment I made over a *year* ago about the woman who came into the bar and tripped me.

Two, he has the most devastatingly handsome smile I've ever seen. This is the first time in forever I've ever seen Tank *really* smile —and it's a sight to behold. Unlike the little sarcastic or flirty smirks he typically gives, his straight, white teeth are on full display and it sends butterflies fluttering in my stomach.

Or maybe it's the liquor.

I should really find some pretzels or something.

"No, I think we can let bygones be bygones with her." I sigh.

"So," he waves a hand of encouragement, "tell me what happened there."

"Ugh. Can't we just do another shot?" I groan, sliding my glass towards him on the table.

"We can, but you're still gonna tell me about it," he says, filling our glasses again. I narrow my gaze trying to figure a way out of this conversation, but he looks back at me expectantly and once my eyes lock on his hypnotic green ones, I cave.

"Fine." I sigh, rubbing my hands along the blue jeans covering my thighs. "*Bethany* and I went to college together. We were actually friends at one point if you can believe it. We joined the same sorority our freshman year and clicked instantly. I received an academic scholarship right out of high school and was a *model* student. I never missed class, kept a GPA that would make any grandma proud, a real *teacher's pet* according to everyone else. I didn't mind it so much at first, hearing the whispered remarks about what a *goody-goody* I was, but when we would go to parties and I would leave early to make sure I had time to study or be up on time for my classes, people started to make fun of me for it. *A lot.*" I huff out a sad laugh thinking about how immature it was.

"Anyways, the beginning of our junior year there was this one guy that I had liked from a distance for a while–"

"Oh, so you were stalking him a little," Tank interrupts playfully.

"Do you want the story to be over?" I threaten, rolling my eyes at him.

"*No...* Proceed." He waves his hand for me to continue.

"*SO...* he showed up at one of the parties our sorority house was throwing one night, I introduced myself and one thing led to another and we started dating shortly after. He was… amazing, honestly. But, before too long I let myself get completely consumed by him. I was staying out later, which made me late to class almost every day. I wouldn't study as much because I was so wrapped up in spending time with him and my grades started to drop severely. By the end of the school year, my GPA dropped so low I lost my scholarship. My parents did *not* hold back on telling me how disappointed they were in me and how irresponsible I had been to let that happen. I couldn't even blame them because they were right. I come from a lower class family and there was *no* way we could pay for my college tuition outright so… I had to come up with a way to pay for it myself."

We've officially taken a break from doing shots, and I'm nervously playing with a loose string hanging from the rips in my jeans as I gather the courage to finish the story.

"One day while I was hunkered down job searching and brain-storming with some of my roommates and boyfriend, he made the very *loud* suggestion that I start *dancing*." I air quote the word. Glancing up through my eyelashes I see Tank looking at me so intensely, his jaw ticking as he swallows hard, listening closely to every word.

"He told you to start stripping?" he asks flatly. I nod my head, scrunching my nose remembering how the conversation went.

"Basically… It was so weird, you know? He told me about this place he and his friends liked to frequent—a comment I did my best to ignore at the time—and he said I would be great at it. We all laughed because we thought he was joking, but later when it was just the two of us he gave me the address and told me I should check it out. I couldn't believe that he was so okay with it, ya know? How was he so casual about letting his friends see me like that, let alone anyone else. He had never acted so… *douchey* before. I told him that he was crazy and that I would find another way, but once that seed of information was planted and I found out how much I could be making, the idea was hard to get rid of. A few months of looking for another solution and a *lot* of confidence-building later, I actually went for it. Next thing I knew I was dancing at *Bad Bunnies,* this *very* prestigious strip club in Las Vegas. It wasn't the club he had told me about though, and I never actually told him I started stripping. I didn't tell anyone. I wasn't very fond of the idea that he and his friends might show up, so I just kept it to myself." I can't help but smile when I notice Tank smirking his quiet approval.

"However, I later found out that *Bethany* had walked past the door the day he mentioned it the first time and ended up telling anyone who would listen at one of our parties that I was stripping. She didn't even know that it was true but needless to say when my boyfriend—my very drunk at the time boyfriend—heard about it he was *not* happy. I tried to tell him he was being unreasonable because he's the one who told me to do it in the first place, but he wouldn't hear it. He grabbed me by the wrists and pinned me against a wall while yelling at me, telling me what a whore I was, and ended up leaving a bruise on me for days after from where he was holding onto me. I was so heartbroken, I never in a million years would have thought he would treat me that way. Of course, that night was the end for us. I broke up with him and told him not to contact me again and lucky for me he listened—because I never heard from him after that." I sniffle, wiping away a stray tear from my cheek. I feel so silly still crying over something that's nothing more than a distant memory most days. But talking about it for the first time out loud must have hit new depths of my emotions.

"You know, he's *really* fucking lucky you haven't said his name yet," Tank grumbles, grabbing his shot glass and filling it up.

"Why? You gonna grab your scissors?" I choke out through my sniffles, as he shoots me an unamused glare.

"It wouldn't be for his hair, I can assure you of that," he bites out before tossing his shot back. "So the mermaid stripper on your arm? There's more to it than what you told me before," he says softly, reminding me of the conversation that really opened the door to this friendship.

"Yeah." I smile, "Even though how I started wasn't *ideal.* I really did love it once I started. I would feel so strong and confident when I danced. It was a way for me to be in control and there was something so empowering in that. I always felt like I was…"

"A mermaid in water? You felt like you were where you belonged," he finishes for me. I look up at him and see the understanding in his eyes. There's no hint of judgment or disapproval for my choices. I feel a lump forming in my throat because no one has *ever* gotten that before, but *of course*, Tank does.

"So, what happened next?" he asks, bringing out conversation back around.

"I might need a refill for this one," I say, shaking my glass in front of him. He fills it up and I tip it back, immediately feeling the confidence to bare my soul to him.

I guess we're doing this.

Chapter 10

TANK

I CAN BARELY SEE straight after hearing how this guy treated her. If she slips up with his name, the missing persons board at the local market is about to have another flier added to it. Thinking about him putting his hands on her is an anger all of its own, but him calling her a whore because she started doing something *he* told her to do in the first place, makes me want to bury him with my own two hands.

"I stopped going to parties, only danced on weekends, and graduated at the top of my class with an almost perfect GPA. I left that school and never spoke to any of the people I had once been so close to, again. Until tonight..." She rolls the shot glass between her fingers and I take it upon myself to fill it halfway. It's been a heavy night, and I'm sure she could use it.

"What did you major in anyways?" I ask, realizing she never mentioned that either.

"Psychology." She grins to herself before lifting her gaze to meet mine, as a memory resurfaces from the day this friendship *really* began.

"Do you have any idea what kind of permanent damage that will do to you?"

I may not have known the extent of it, but she sure as hell did and was adamant about not letting it happen to me. That was the day I knew I needed her around. She wasn't gonna put up with my shit and was gonna give me hell if I tried.

"Do you remember the day you followed me out back? I was having a bad moment and punching the wall and you came out and slapped me?" She tilts her head and her eyes go wide.

"Vividly," she scoffs, setting her shot glass down.

"I never apologized for the way I spoke to you that day," I say with a pained expression.

"Oh, *pfft*. It's fine. Our friendship, if you would have even called it that back then, was fairly new. I probably had no business inserting myself in the first place." Her voice drops along with her head.

"It's *not* fine. I would kill anyone else for speaking to you the way I did, and if I'm being honest, I hate myself for everything I said to you that day. I hope you know how truly sorry I am." I curse myself inwardly as I remember every hurtful word that left my mouth that day. If I could go back in time I'd tell her to slap me harder because I definitely deserved it.

"Well... thanks for the apology, but you've made up for it ten-fold by now. No hard feelings." She smiles at me and I find myself wondering how I wound up lucky enough to call this woman my friend.

"So... psychology, huh? Did you ever practice anywhere?" I ask, bringing our conversation back around as she readjusts her position on the table. A deflective response to my question.

"I planned to..." She looks past me straight at the wall, her eyes glistening and almost doe-like.

"But?" I move my head slightly, trying to get her attention back on me. Her honey-brown eyes refocus on mine and she takes a sharp breath in.

"I got pregnant shortly after I graduated, had to leave Nevada, and all my plans changed." Her answer is vague, and I don't love how she said she *had* to leave, but I can tell she isn't ready to divulge the circumstances behind that statement so I don't press the matter. I take a deep breath, standing from the table to grab two beers from behind the bar before rejoining her.

"I can relate to plans changing, whether you want them to or not." I pop the caps off and lean against the wall opposite of Ruby.

"What happened to your plans?" she asks, bringing the bottle up to her full, pink lips.

God, I bet she tastes fucking amazing.

"I got injured and was left with no choice but to leave," I say, taking a sip from my own beer.

"That's vague," she says timidly.

"It is what it is." She tilts her head, brows knitting together to display her confusion. I know she wants to know more, and after everything she just shared it only seems fair I give a little more detail. I let out a sigh, gathering the courage to talk about the incident that I hadn't spoken about since the day it happened.

"How much do you know about what I did in the Marines?" I walk over, sitting right next to her on the pool table.

"The fact that you were a Marine is about the extent of my knowledge," she explains, causing me to let out a small laugh. I take one more quiet moment to gather my thoughts, then I tell her my story.

"I was part of the Marine Raiders special operations group. On my last mission, my team was sent to clear a building. We got word that it had been marked as the target of an impending attack, so we had to make sure all civilians made it out safely. We were headed to clear the last floor and since I was leading I went up first. Slowly rounding the corner of the stairwell, I made sure there weren't any undetected threats. I was almost to the last step when this guy came out of nowhere and started charging at me. He was unarmed, and we had very strict rules of engagement, which meant we held back fire unless fired upon.

"Me and my guys started stumbling back on impact from this grown ass man just fucking *lunging* towards me. So I'm face to face with this guy, trying to subdue him *without* taking him out completely, but... he was panicked and absolutely incoherent. He ended up shoving me so hard that I went over the railing before I could even comprehend what was happening. As *my* luck would have it, I didn't just fall down one floor, I fell down two whole stories before landing on the concrete stairs below. I broke my back on impact and... that was it for me." I grind my teeth so hard I'm almost certain I hear one of my molars crack. "Turns out, the guy was just a civilian—freaking the fuck out simply because of my team's presence." Reliving the story is still just as infuriating—even a year and a half later.

"Holy shit. I had no idea, Tank." Ruby rests her hand on my forearm and I can suddenly feel the buzz from my anger and alcohol begin to mix, causing a hyper-awareness of her touch. It feels as though her fingertips are lighting my skin on fire as they graze along my tattoos.

"I mean, if I had just seen him a second sooner or grabbed the rail when he put his hands on me—I wouldn't have let my team down, and I might still be over there doing something that makes me feel worth a damn," I spit out angrily, standing up as the rage begins pulsing through me. I grab my beer bottle and white knuckle it before throwing it against the back wall. She hops to her feet and stands in front of me, for a split second I think she might be star-tled, standing to walk away from me for acting so impulsively. But she doesn't walk away, she stays. She sways briefly, most likely from the alcohol rushing through her from the quick movement, then takes my face in her hands.

"Listen to me. What happened to you was cruel and unfair. I know if you could go back and change what happened, you would. But you can't, and yes, that sucks *so much*—but you can't go through life thinking that you're worthless just because you can't serve anymore either. There's so much more to you than that." My eyes shift, burning with what I assume are tears, but I blink them away angrily.

"What is it?" she asks, rearing back a little bit. I shake my head, letting out a humorless laugh.

"Tank... Talk to me." Her thumb caresses my cheek, such a small yet intimate gesture, and that's all it takes for me to give in to her.

"You're the only person who's ever told me there's more to me than a fight." My voice is barely a whisper, as I admit that out loud for the first time.

"What?" Her brows knit together, her big brown eyes fixed on mine.

"You know, I spent my whole life getting into fights, whether it was in the locker room, on the mat, or behind the school. But when I was over there, with my team, my fight made a difference. I don't know how to do anything else. I don't know who I am without that part of me."

"Could you ever go back? If you love it so much, and you're so unhappy *not* being over there, wouldn't it be worth it to at least *try?*" she asks, the genuine curiosity and *care* in her voice doing something unexplainable to my heart.

"There's plenty of times I catch myself wondering if I could. If I could somehow pass the physical and make it back to my team but... When it comes down to it, I couldn't live with myself if I made a selfish decision and something happened to them."

"Are you living with yourself *now* though? Because to me, it looks an awful lot like you're in survival mode most days." Her face is clouded with sadness as she runs her hand along my jawline, causing my eyes to fall shut at her touch. When her thumb caresses my cheekbone again, my eyes find their way to hers, and the same calming effect I've felt every time I've been around her for the last year washes over me like rain. I take a step back, trying to gain some composure before I give in to the temptation to touch her. To pull her into me and finally see what it feels like to have her body pressed against mine. But before I get too far, before I allow myself the clarity, she pulls me back into her, wrapping her arms around my waist as her head rests on my chest. It takes me a minute to fully understand what's happening because the last thing I expected was for Ruby to embrace *me* like this. Like she's trying to patch me up from the inside out.

"I'm finding moments where it feels more like I'm living," I say, wrapping my arms around her shoulders. Running my fingers through her long black hair, my head and my heart are at odds about everything I'm feeling right now.

"Care to share what moments those might be?" she asks, still wrapped safely in my arms.

"You really want to know?" I sigh, hoping my answer isn't too much for her. I can feel my chest tighten when she squeezes me a little tighter.

"Yes," she breathes out. I loosen my grip, taking a small step back as she looks up at me.

"Any moment I spend with you, Honey. *You* make me feel like I'm living." I swallow hard, afraid of how she'll react to what I've just said.

I can't take it back now even if I wanted to. But *I don't* want to take it back, because it's the truth. Having Ruby in my life has given me glimmers of hope that life might not always have to be such a goddamn shit show. But any fear of her rejecting me dissolves when her eyes start to glisten and she smiles up at me. I hold her face in my hands, and even though all I want to do right now is take her lips in mine and thank her for all the ways she's been there for me, I kiss her forehead and thank her outright instead.

"There's so much more to you than a fight, Tank Landry. And I can't wait to watch you find out what it is."

"Thank you, for your friendship. I really don't know where I would be without it." Her eyes flutter open, and she smiles.

"Anytime."

"Honey?"

"Yeah?" She looks at me questioningly.

"Will you dance with me?" Her smile grows wider.

"Anytime."

I walk over to the jukebox in the corner and select *Tennessee Whiskey*, when it begins pouring through the speakers I pull her back into my arms and we dance.

No one else in the bar but us.

No one to cut in.

Just me and the woman I'm convinced is changing my entire world.

But before the song comes to an end, her phone starts ringing.

"Sorry," she apologizes as she swipes it out of her pocket and slides to answer when she sees Betty's name flash across the screen.

"Hello," she answers, clearing her throat after a slight voice crack. "Oh no. Poor thing. Okay, tell him I'll be home soon. Thanks, Betty."

"Everything okay?" I ask, walking to grab our shot glasses and whiskey from the pool table.

"Yeah, apparently Hendrix has a stomach ache and was asking when I would be home." She runs her fingers through her hair as she blows out a breath and looks around the room. I know that look —it's the face she makes when she's trying to prioritize what needs to be done in order to close the bar the fastest.

"You go ahead, I'll close up tonight." I nod her towards the door but she immediately starts shaking her head at me.

"No. I'm not leaving you to do all of this by yourself," she argues, trying to move past me. I grab her shoulders gently, guiding her back to where she previously stood.

"Yes, you are. Your boy needs you and if I had to guess—after tonight—you need him too. Go." She lets out a sigh, finally surrendering as she grabs her bag from behind the counter.

"Thank you, Tank." She walks over and stands on her tiptoes to plant a kiss on my cheek. "I really needed this."

"Yeah, me too." I smirk at her, getting a smile in return before she heads towards the door.

"Hey, Ruby."

"Yeah?" She turns around quickly, making her long black waves swoosh around her.

"Text me when you get home. So I know you made it there okay."

"Sure thing."

Once she's gone I get to work cleaning up the broken beer bottle and then start closing down the rest of the bar. The entire time my mind can't seem to think of anything other than Ruby. The way she opened up to me tonight—and got me to open up to her—it felt like our friendship reached an entirely new level. Though tonight was one of the many times I've wished I could be so much more to her than just a friend. The war waging inside of me over not kissing her tonight, *really* kissing her is downright painful. I told myself I wouldn't be the one to ruin Ruby, but the more time that passes, the more I want to do just that. And I'd have a damn good time ruining every last inch of her.

RUBY
Hey, made it home safe!

ME
Glad to hear it. How's little man doing?

RUBY
Not great. 🤢 I think he's actually got a stomach bug and I have no food to support his current dietary needs. Mom of the year, go me. 😣

ME
What does he need?

RUBY

Oh, no. You don't have to do that. I'll just Instacart
something.

ME

That service is such a rip off. I'm leaving the bar
now. Send me a list.

RUBY

I really owe you one for this. Thank you.

ME

Nonsense Honey. I'm happy to help.

RUBY

If you say so.

Chicken noodle soup. (he likes the ones with the
alphabet but I'll take anything they have)

Gatorade. (lemon lime is his favorite)

Crackers.

And Ben & Jerry's ice cream. Half baked or
brownie.

ME

Okay, I know I'm no expert, but he may not need
ice cream right now.

RUBY

LOL. That part is for me. It's my comfort food while
I stay up all night making sure he's okay.

ME

Got it. I'll be there in half an hour.

RUBY

I still owe you for this.

ME

Hush, woman.

Chapter 11

RUBY

I just knew he was going to kiss me. After a night like that, it seemed like the only thing left undone. But right when I thought I knew where things were going, he pressed those beautiful lips to my forehead and thanked me for being his *friend*. The hope I had been holding onto shrank immensely when those words left his mouth, but the logical part of me knows it's probably better this way. After all, it's not just *me* I'm thinking about, but Hendrix too.

I've always known bringing a man into my life, into *our lives*, would potentially complicate everything I have worked so hard to build for us.

Safety, security, and no broken hearts—for either of us.

The last thing I want is for Hendrix to end up attached to someone who will just up and leave one day—or worse, someone we have to run from. Not that I think of Tank as becoming someone I would ever have to run from, but I've been burned before so I don't count anything out. It still doesn't change the feelings I find myself having towards him though. I want to know what it feels like to have his lips on mine, to be wrapped in his arms in a passionate and needy way, not just in a comforting, friendly embrace. But if I want to keep him in my life, I have to push those feelings down and accept that the only way he's willing to offer himself to me, is as a friend. And a damn good one at that.

When he dropped groceries off after insisting I not use Instacart, he added in little treats of his own for both me and Hendrix. A bottle of my favorite red wine, Sour Patch Kids, and a soccer ball. I remember telling him the other day how Hendrix has been talking nonstop about how he wants to play soccer and the poor kid has absolutely *no* idea how. But I didn't expect *him* to remember that. When I texted to thank him for everything, I asked if he would send me some beginner videos so I could be prepared before taking Hendrix to the park. I stared at my phone for an entire minute buffering when he told me to just call him before we go and he'd come show us how to get started. There was an immediate swarm of butterflies in my stomach at his offer, and I promptly opened my bottle of wine to try and get my mind off of the amazing *friend* I have who's offering to teach my kid how to play soccer.

Why does he have to be so kind and *so damn hot though?*

"You know I probably could have figured this out on my own. You really didn't have to come out here and do all of this," I say, watching Tank set up the little cones for them to kick the ball through.

"Don't you go trying to take all of my fun, Ranes." He smirks at me, and I instinctively roll my eyes. "Besides, if you sprained your ankle or something out here and I had to pick up your slack at the bar, I'd never let you hear the end of it."

"Okay, fair. But you still have to teach me too," I insist. "Hendrix is going to need someone to play *with* and I can't just call you every time he wants to get the soccer ball out." I laugh.

"Sure you could." He smiles, throwing the rest of the soccer gear to the side.

There's not nearly enough time for me to overthink that right now. Is there?

"Alright, get over here." He waves me over and we spend the next two hours learning so many soccer terms that I'm not sure my brain has room for anything else at this point. Hendrix caught on pretty quickly and shocked both of us at how well he was doing. By the time we finished my stomach was growling and Hendrix looked like he was about to fall out right in the middle of the park.

"Mommy, I'm hungry. Can we go eat now?" he asks, splayed out across the park bench.

"Of course buddy, you wanna see if Tank wants to go with us?" I ask, nodding over to where Tank is gathering all the soccer gear.

"Yeah!" He perks up instantly and runs over to him. When I hear him yell *"Heck yeah!"* I assume Tank said yes. No way am I letting him spend this much time helping Hendrix *and myself* learn how to play soccer and not offering to feed him.

"I hear we're getting food," he says, throwing the mesh bag over his shoulder. My eyes instinctively land on his biceps and the way his shirt looks like it's holding onto its seams for dear life. My stomach flips when I remember what it felt like to be wrapped in his arms the other night, and how I've wondered more than once how effortlessly he'd be able to hold my body flush against his as he–

"Yeah, I'm *starving*," Hendrix groans loudly, making me clear my throat as I refocus. He relaxes his shoulders into a dramatic slump like he's moments away from being completely famished.

"That's the plan. What do we want? We could go to Spurs," I offer, knowing how much Hendrix loves their strawberry milkshakes. I keep my eyes on Hendrix, though I can feel Tank's gaze burning into my skin.

"Can we go home and have chicken casserole?" Hendrix asks, pulling on my leg. I glance up at Tank whose gaze is still settled on me as he shrugs, then I look back at Hendrix.

"Buddy, that's just leftovers, and Tank may not like it. Why don't we go out somewhere instead?"

"*Nooo,* I want some casserole and Spidey. My legs are sleepy," he pouts. I feel a sense of pride that he's actually picking *my* food over a milkshake, but I'm nervous to offer Tank leftover casserole in place of a fresh cheeseburger—or fresh *anything* for that matter.

"Casserole sounds good to me. As long as you have enough. I'm fu–" Tank stops himself, letting his gaze fall to Hendrix who's already eyeing him judgmentally. "*Freaking* starving." Tank's eyes grow wide when he looks my way, making me laugh.

"Oh, we have enough to feed an army. Are you sure?" I ask, wanting to be sure, as Hendrix bounces up and down while holding my hand.

"Hell yeah. Let's go." Hendrix stops bouncing and holds his index finger up at Tank.

"I mean, *heck* yeah." Tank corrects himself. Hendrix adds his thumb making a finger gun motion and tries to wink as he clicks his tongue. We both laugh as we walk to the car and head back to our house for casserole.

With Tank.

Why does this feel both super normal and extremely weird?

"That was the best casserole I've ever had in my entire life. You have to give me the recipe. I'd eat this sh– *stuff* weekly," Tank says, sitting back in his chair.

"No chance, I can't have you sharing my super secret recipe," I tease, winking at Hendrix. He winks back at me before forking a massive bite into his mouth.

"Fine. Maybe you can just show me then. I have a terrible

memory and with no written recipe to remind me, I think we'll be safe." Tank winks and it sends involuntary flutters to my stomach.

Shit, stop it, Ruby.

"Hmm. I'll take it under consideration." I narrow my gaze at him and he holds his fist up to Hendrix earning a fist bump from him.

"Finished! Can I go watch Spider-Man?" Hendrix asks, holding his bowl up to show me that it's empty.

"Just one episode." I nod, and he takes off to the living room. I smile and shake my head, thinking just how lucky I am to be his mom.

He's the sweetest kid and has such a big heart. I find myself praying often that the world will treat him well. Being a mom is so hard because you literally have a piece of your heart walking around in the world. You know you would do anything and everything to protect it but don't always know when you need to. I'm pulled from my thoughts when I hear dishes clinking and look up to see Tank grabbing his and Hendrix's bowls from the table.

"Oh, I can grab that in a minute. You don't have to–" I start, but Tank cuts me off.

"Hush woman, eat your dinner. I got this." He gets busy cleaning their dishes and places them back into the cabinets while I sit at the table watching his every move. I'm pretty sure I'm in a state of shock because I am so used to everyone I know using a dishwasher or the *let it soak* method.

"Ruby?"

"Hmm?" My eyes refocus and I see Tank looking at me with an amused concern.

"You okay?"

"What? Yeah." I shake my head and finally take a bite of my food. "Why?"

"No, nothing. You just kind of had this look on your face like I was drowning your cat or something," he says so nonchalantly.

Oh, he is, but not the kind he's thinking.

The thought makes me snort and when I look up his eyes grow wide. I slap my hand over my mouth, embarrassed by the noise.

"Oh, that was fucking adorable."

And now my face is red for a completely different reason.

"Whatever," I say, rolling my eyes at him. "Don't be mean to me, I'll start crying."

"I'm serious. Pigs have always been my favorite farm animal." He laughs, making my mouth drop open in disbelief.

"How *dare* you?" I say dramatically as Hendrix runs back into the room and straight over to Tank.

"Tank, can you come back to play soccer with us next time?" I feel my breath catch in my throat as I wait to hear Tank's response. I have a bad habit of answering for other people before they have a chance to let Hendrix down, but tonight, for some reason, I don't step in. Because part of me is confident he won't let him down.

"I'm there, little man. Just tell your mom to call me and I'll bring the gear." He smiles at Hendrix as they fist bump and the realization hits me—I have to do anything I can to protect my friendship with Tank. Because no matter how I *think* I feel about him, I can tell that Hendrix looks up to him already and considers him a friend as well. And there's no way I'll do anything to jeopardize that now.

Chapter 12

TANK

EVERYONE except for Tucker is currently at the airport getting ready to fly out for Shane's art exhibit in San Francisco. Max is the only one who's seen the pieces being displayed tonight and the only thing the rest of us know is that it's military-themed. I'm kind of looking forward to getting out of town for a little while, even if it *is* just for the weekend. Don't get me wrong, I enjoy my routine of going to work, the gym, and soccer practice with Hendrix and Ruby —but I think it'll be nice to have a change of scenery.

Apparently, this event has been advertised widely enough that there's supposed to be a massive turnout, with members from multiple military branches expected to attend. The amount of anxiety I had to fight off when I first found that out was intense, but the more I thought about it the more I convinced myself there's a very slim chance I'll run into anyone I worked with directly. I miss those guys like hell, but I just don't think I'm quite ready to talk about what happened or re-live the *good ole days* just yet.

"What seat are you in?" Ruby slaps my arm with her boarding pass and nods to the one in my hand.

"Uhh. 15B." I flip the paper over to show her my seat number.

"Oh, hell yeah. 15A." She sinks her teeth into her bottom lip, and it immediately does something to my brain chemistry—something I'm becoming more and more accustomed to. "I'm gonna annoy the shit out of you the entire flight. I hope you know that." She points at me as she backs away, heading towards some of the other girls standing by the charging station.

"*Greaaat*," I drag out sarcastically. "You better at least have snacks," I call out, granting me a *come on son* look as she pulls a bag of candy from her backpack. I let out a chuckle because, of course, she has snacks. Then Taylor's voice catches me by surprise.

"Hey, where's Tucker, he said he'd be here?"

"Ah, don't worry. He'll show." I adjust my duffle bag on my shoulder. As if on cue, my phone silently buzzes in my hand with a text from Tucker.

> TUCKER
> Just got here. Have a safe flight.

> ME
> I mean, I'm not the one flying the plane but I'll eat my snacks safely.

> TUCKER
> You're an idiot.

> ME
> Don't be jealous of my quick wit.

> TUCKER
> Jealous? Who do you think you picked that up from?

> ME
> Max. Definitely.

> TUCKER
> 🦢 Good one.

> ME
> See you in a few hours.

"Flight 429 to San Francisco, now boarding."

I'm not sure what plans she had to *annoy the shit out of me* for the entirety of the flight, but making me share an earbud while she played the first five songs of the *Clueless* soundtrack didn't bother me at all. I think she may have actually glitched when I started to sing along to one of the songs. After realizing how unbothered I was, she rolled her eyes and turned on a podcast called *Dark History* that I found rather interesting, though it *did* lull both of us to sleep after about 20 minutes.

The feeling of the plane preparing to land wakes me, but Ruby is still out like a light with her head propped up on my shoulder. She's hands down the most beautiful woman I've ever met—captivating in a way that could bring any man to his knees. Not only does her long black hair make me want to run my hands through it, her lips make me want to taste every sweet smile she gives and her body makes me ache to touch her in a way I've never experienced before. She also makes me laugh, stands her ground when bar patrons get a little too rowdy, and doesn't let anyone push her around. To top it off, she's the best damn mom to Hendrix, which makes me feel things for her I don't dare try to unpack right now.

I know Ruby and I can never be more than just friends, so I am content with the way things are. There's less of a chance I'll fuck everything up this way.

"Psst. Ruby." I nudge her head with my shoulder gently, doing my best to wake her without startling her. "Hey, Honey. We're about to land." Her eyes begin to flutter open as she yawns and looks around the plane. She pulls her charging case out for her earbuds and drops hers in, looking around for a moment before I pull the other one out of my ear, wiping it off before I hand it to her.

"Oh, yeah." She laughs. "Wait, you listened to it without me?" She pouts, making it damn near impossible not to fixate on her fucking lips.

"Nah, I slept for a while too. We can finish it later." She looks at me with an unreadable expression before placing her case and the rest of the Sour Patch Kids we were sharing into her backpack.

When she steps into the main aisle, I notice a small red candy stuck to the back of her black leggings. I look around us and then make the quick decision to remove it in hopes of saving her from any potential embarrassment. When I go to pull it off I accidentally pinch her skin and she lets out a little gasp that makes my dick jump before turning on her heels to face me with wide eyes. I hear another small gasp from beside me and turn to see Lauren in her seat with her mouth hanging open.

"Did you just pinch her ass?" Lauren whispers.

"Umm, yeah kind of." I look between the two of them and the blush that coats Ruby's cheeks makes my dick stir even more at the thought that she *liked* that I pinched her ass, but I quickly redirect my train of thought. "There was a Sour Patch Kid stuck to your leggings." I hold up the red candy and Ruby nods in realization.

"Oh," she says, turning to exit the plane.

"Whew, I really thought I was gonna have to kick your ass right here on this plane, Landry." Lauren tosses her brown hair over her shoulder as she readjusts the strap on her fanny pack.

"Lauren, you're the same size as this Sour Patch Kid, I'd like to see you try." I tease, making her narrow her gaze at me before she exits her row in front of me. She links her arm with Ruby's as they make their way through the airport.

"Come on, gorgeous, we're rooming together. I can't wait to see you in that dress again. We did *good*." It's Lauren's voice I hear, but I can't seem to peel my eyes off Ruby as she struts through the crowded building.

"You're going to run into a wall if you don't look up soon."

Max's voice catches me by surprise as he throws his arm around my shoulder.

"What?" I ask, only partially aware of how long he's been walking beside me.

"How's that X-ray vision working out for ya man?" He raises his brow at me, making me scoff.

"Maybe I *did* get my wittiness from you," I mumble under my breath.

"Huh?" Max rears back in confusion.

"Nothing. I'm stopping for a coffee, I'll catch up with you guys later." I have no intention of having this conversation with Max right now—or ever, for that matter.

I've got to get my shit in check before I see Ruby in whatever dress Lauren was talking about tonight. There's no doubt it'll be something that will steal what little breath I have left when I'm around her. I'll probably end up jerking off in the shower to thoughts of her perfect ass and the way she smells like cherry candy all the goddamn time like the desperate-for-her man I am.

Chapter 13

RUBY

LAUREN and I are sharing a hotel room and I don't think I ever realized just how long it takes her to get ready. She's always been the one who knows everything there is to know about clothes, hair, and makeup but oh my *god* I could not do this every day. I think the worst part is that she doesn't even need it. Her skincare routine is just as high quality as her makeup routine. The woman's skin looks like untouched butter, her brows are perfectly shaped and don't even get me started on the length and fullness of her eyelashes. If I didn't love her so damn much, I'd probably hate her out of pure jealousy.

"Which shoes go better with this dress?" she asks, holding up a pair of black platform heels and a pair of beige strappy heels.

"You're asking *me?*" I look at her in disbelief. Lauren, the fashion guru of our group, asks the one who wears the same t-shirt and jeans at least twice a week for wardrobe advice.

"Okay, I hear your point. I know which ones *I* would choose, but I want a second opinion." She fusses, so I take a moment to look at the options again. The wine-colored dress she has on could really go with either pair. The dress is knee length and has short ruffle sleeves, her brown hair is set in loose waves, pulled up halfway in some cute ass hair twist, and she's wearing a simple charm bracelet that wouldn't clash with anything.

"The black ones are a little more edgy, the beige ones are more classy. Go with the beige," I say confidently. She drops the heels at her side and holds one hand to her chest.

"Is this what being a proud mother feels like?" she teases. I give her a playful eye roll as I finish curling my hair.

Lauren helped me pick out a black satin dress for this event at a boutique in town last week, and it might be my favorite thing I've ever worn. It's similar in style to our bridesmaid's dresses for Shane's wedding, but this dress is mid-length and has a slit going up my thigh. It hugs my mid-section a little tighter than I'm usually comfortable with, but the cinching in the bodice makes any self-consciousness a thing of the past.

"Here. These shoes are screaming to be worn with that dress." She winks at me and holds out the black platform heels. I tilt my head at her and give an accusing stare, but she shrugs me off like it's no bother. Once my heels are on we take one final look in the mirror before heading to *The Gallery*.

I'm not sure what I was expecting when we showed up tonight, but this place has surpassed any expectation I could have fathomed. Shane's artwork is absolutely stunning, as I knew it would be, and every inch of *The Gallery* is covered in coordinating designs. From the olive green dress shirts the caterers are wearing, to the red, white, and blue floral arrangements, not a single detail has been missed. No wonder Shane hated to leave this place, I'm sure it's every artist's dream to work at a place like this.

Lauren and I met up with Taylor and Leah in the lobby and all rode together since Shane and Max came early to make sure everything was ready for the event tonight, but I haven't seen Tank yet—or Tucker now that I think about it. I try to casually glance around the room without making it obvious who I'm looking for, though I'm not sure why I'm so worried about it, we are friends after all. Just as I think I catch a glimpse of Tank, Hugh takes the stage to welcome everyone so I turn my attention to him. He's wearing a suit that's tailored perfectly to every line and muscle and I'm sure not a single female in this building is letting it go unnoticed.

With the exhibit officially open, the crowd only seems to keep growing. Everywhere you turn there are groups of people talking about the paintings, making the room about ten times louder than it was when we first arrived. With Leah, Lauren, and Taylor all mingling elsewhere, I take the opportunity to visit one of the paintings displayed in a more secluded area– my small attempt to find a place where I can hear myself think. I take a deep breath as the conversations begin to fade, causing one booming voice to catch my attention when I hear it.

Tank.

I don't bother turning around since I can tell he's in the middle of a conversation with someone else, but I can't help but notice the edge to his voice. I can't quite place it, but he doesn't sound like himself at all, and I can tell something is wrong. I hear him clear his throat right before he excuses himself from the conversation, and just as I turn to see if he's okay I catch a glimpse of him darting towards the back hallway– pulling aggressively at the tie around his neck.

Something is definitely wrong.

TANK

It took me longer than I care to admit to tie the tie I was instructed to wear, which caused me to arrive much later than the rest of our group. I've been tying ties since I was in middle school, but my nerves about possibly seeing old team members tonight had my hands shaking so damn bad I almost said screw it and tossed the damn thing in the trash.

I slid in the door just before the gallery owner took the stage, and stayed towards the back so I wouldn't cause a disruption. I was on my way to look for the rest of the crew when I got stopped by a few familiar faces. Faces that, no matter how much I tried to prepare myself, I wasn't quite ready to see just yet. Some of the guys I was closest to from my old team are here, and seeing them makes me feel like I've just hit those concrete stairs all over again.

"Landry, long time no see." Asher walks over, extending his hand with the other tucked into his front pocket. He's always walked around with an air of confidence about him—something I envy now that I have little to none.

"Back at ya brother, what the hell are you guys doing here?" I greet each of the guys with a handshake and quick hug, trying my best to play it cool.

Asher, Dominic, Mike, and Keller.

"Well you know, we heard about this thing through the grapevine. And by grapevine, I mean one *very* persistent and proud husband of the artist. I had no idea Max got married until he reached out to tell us about this though." The guys met Max and Tucker *maybe* twice when they came to Nashville with me on leave, but that's the thing about those two–they make a lasting impression. Regardless of how grumpy most people think Max is, the ones who understand his background can see the depth behind it.

"Oh yeah. That shit happened super fast." I laugh, remembering their engagement night like it was yesterday.

"Well, how have you been man? What are you up to these days?" Keller asks.

Here we go. The question I would like nothing more than to never have to answer.

"Ah, you know. I've been working at Max's bar for a while. I applied to a few other places but nothing's worked out just yet." I grit my teeth while doing my best to fake a smile, waiting for them to lay on the impending jokes or judgment about working as a bartender. It's different when you own the damn bar and build it from the ground up—*that's* a respectable career. But the jokes and judgment don't come, instead, it's something far worse.

"We really miss you out there man. We could have really used someone with your skill set leading our last mission. Hell, we could use it now, we head out again next week," Dom says, earning an elbow in the back from Keller, as the other guys shoot me sympathetic glances.

"Shit, man. I didn't mean it like that. I just meant there will never be another leader like you." The tone of his voice puts me on edge and immediately my chest begins to tighten. A faint ringing hums in my ears as short, yet vivid flashbacks of our last mission start running through my mind. The feelings I've been pushing down for over a damn *year* come bursting through to the surface.

Regret and disappointment.

Regret for things so far out of my control it makes me angry in a way I've never experienced before.

And disappointment that I let my team down when they needed me most—that I am *still* letting them down, even now.

I manage to clear my throat, hoping I don't choke on the words I'm forcing out of my mouth.

"Man, I miss being out there with you guys too. Sorry to cut this short, but if you gentlemen will excuse me." I nod behind me—*to where I have no fucking clue*—but they accept my excuse and I bolt.

"Yeah, man. Maybe we'll catch up with you later. It's good to see you doing so well," Dominic says with a smile on his face. That damn smile of his. He always stayed so positive—even during all the bad shit we saw.

If he only knew how unwell I truly am.

I make it back to an empty hallway, surrounded by nothing but doors with studio numbers on them and, as luck would have it, a small chaise against the back wall. I loosen my tie and unbutton the top few buttons of my dress shirt, taking in as deep of breaths as I can catch, but all it does is make me feel like I can't breathe at all.

I put my head between my hands with my elbows resting on my

knees, doing my best to find something to focus on. There are no spots on the pristinely white floor for me to count, there's ironically no art on the walls for me to try and focus on, and all I can think is *I need to find Ruby.* She's the one person I'm confident could distract me long enough for me to catch my breath. I squeeze my eyes shut in an effort to will her to me, but my mind derails in the worst possible way.

"How are we feeling today?" the doctor asks as he steps into my recovery room. It's been two months in this recovery center and I'm more than ready to get the hell out of here.

"Better than yesterday," I respond in hopes that they'll believe me and release me sooner.

"Well, that's good news." I can hear the distress in his voice and when Captain walks through the door I know I'm in for some shitty news. I swallow hard and try sitting up a little straighter, though all that does is agitate my back making me wince. A dead giveaway that I'm not better than yesterday at all.

"We need to talk," he says, bringing an ominousness to the atmosphere.

"So you're telling me that I could break it again over something as fucking stupid as tripping?" I ask in disbelief.

"With the extent of your injuries, yes, landing on it with any amount of force could cause you to end up right back here. Not to mention you sustained a severe concussion and we will want to keep an eye on the long-term effects that may have on you as well," the doctor answers.

"And it's unlikely you would pass the re-entry physical—not to mention the liability you would be to the rest of your team," Captain chimes in.

"I understand." There's a burning in my throat as I force the words out. My nose stings as I try to keep my emotions in check while the only thing I've ever loved in life gets ripped away from me. "I would never want to potentially put my team in danger." The amount of rage I feel burning in my chest makes me wish that the fall had taken me out completely. I shut off any part of my mind that harbors thoughts of "what ifs" until I can't feel anything but indifference to the situation.

Unfortunately, those same parts of my mind I closed on that day, have been forced back open. I sit back abruptly, slamming my head into the wall as I groan in frustration.

"Fuck. Not this shit again," I mumble to myself. I thought I was done being haunted by these fucking memories.

When my eyes snap open desperate to see anything besides the past that torments my mind, I hear the clicking of heels headed my way.

Please be her.

"Tank?"

There she is.

Her voice—smooth and sweet like honey—already has my heart rate slowing down. But when I catch a glimpse of her, it immediately picks back up.

Goddammit, she looks gorgeous.

"Hey, are you okay?" She rushes over and bends down in front of me. I think I might go into cardiac arrest between why I came back here in the first place, and the way the slit in her dress is dangerously high on her thigh as she's squatted down in front of me.

"Look at me," she demands, and my eyes drift up to hers. "Are you having a panic attack?" she asks, her demeanor seeming as cool and collected as always. Her eyes are the only giveaway that she may be a little panicked herself. I can't find words to answer her at the moment, so I nod my head in response.

"Okay. It's okay. I'm here. I'm not gonna leave until you want me to." She grabs my hand and I grip it back tightly, as the panic dissolves behind her gaze.

"I'm gonna do something to try and help calm you down a little, okay?" I nod in agreement. "Tell me what you see." She begins gently tracing lines in the palm of my hand while I look over her body.

"You."

"Okay." She giggles. "That's a good start. Can you be more specific?" Her voice is so mesmerizing, encouraging me to keep going.

"Your dress." I bite out, trying to keep my tone neutral. It should be a fucking crime for someone to look as good as she does right now.

"What can you smell?" Her finger continues swirling around my palm.

"Cherries." Her cheeks blush but she keeps going.

"Okay, good. What can you feel?"

"You," I answer again, knowing she's going to ask me for more.

"More specifically?" She pinches the inside of my hand. I focus my eyes on hers, saying every word as clearly as possible.

"*You*, Honey. I feel you everywhere. Not just in the palm of my hand." I see her teeth grab ahold of her bottom lip, as her fingers still dance around my hand. She gives me a soft smile, and I run my fingers through her hair. Gripping around her neck, I bring her forehead to mine.

"Thank you," I whisper, looking down into her honey-brown eyes.

"For what?" she whispers back breathlessly.

"For being exactly what I needed tonight." My jaw ticks as every nerve in my body tells me to kiss her. To say to hell with this friendship bullshit and just go for it. But before I make a mistake I can't come back from, I think better of it and reign those feelings back in. Because if tonight showed me one thing at all, it's that even if she's everything *I* need. I'm far from what *she* needs.

Unstable and unpredictable are the best ways I can to describe myself in this moment, and those are two things I would never burden her with.

So I press my lips to her forehead and say a silent prayer that one day I will be a man that's worthy of her.

"What are friends for, right?" She lets out a soft laugh, and while her voice and laughter will always be one of my favorite things, the words leaving her mouth set my soul on fire.

I burn for her in a way that is getting harder and harder to conceal, while she'll always remain just out of my reach.

Because even though I've placed myself in a friends-only position with her, I never let it cross my mind that maybe that's all she sees in me anyway. That the feelings I'm harboring for her may not be mutual.

"Hey, Tank?" She whispers, bringing my eyes back to hers.

"Yeah?"

"Who were the guys you were talking to? Before you came back here?" Of course, she was around to hear that. Because the magnetic pull I've felt with her since we first met seems to keep us in each other's orbit, and like a moth to a flame, she always knows where to find me.

"Asher, Dominic, Mike, and Keller. The team I had to leave behind after the fall." I can't get much more out without starting to spiral again, but with Ruby that's never an issue. She doesn't require *more*, she takes what I give her at face value and heals little broken pieces of me with her touch. Or at least that's how it feels when she wraps her arms around me in an embrace, without uttering another word.

The plan to go out to dinner after the event at *The Gallery* tonight sounded like a great idea at first. But running into my old team has thrown my mind completely off track. It just reminded me of the life I left behind and how much they need me out there, while I've been back home serving gimlets to old ladies, having panic attacks that drain me, and falling for a woman who may see me as nothing more than a drinking buddy or a soccer coach for her kid.

Lovely.

Here goes shot number five. Because if there's one thing I know about myself, it's that drinking to forget is my specialty.

Chapter 14

RUBY

TAYLOR

I think I'm going on a road trip with Tucker

ME

Interesting…

LAUREN

🍿👀

LEAH

Are you on something? Are you taking drastic measures to avoid Zander? What's happening?

SHANE

I'm very confused, but very invested in your answers. 👀

TAYLOR

I don't know. He just asked and I said yes. 🙈 It will be nice to not see Zander for… however long it takes to drive from San Fran to Nashville. Oh god, was this a mistake?

ME

No, not at all. Enjoy the time away. Clear your head. Just keep us posted so we know you're alive. BOTH of you.

SHANE

Ruby's right. You deserve a little road trip vacay.
Have fun. But not like, TOO MUCH fun. 😏

TAYLOR

As if. 😌

Those two are just trouble waiting to happen.

Returning home after traveling is always the weirdest transition. It takes me about three days to unpack, and just as long to readjust to my routines. I hated leaving Hendrix but I knew he would be in good hands with Betty. Not to mention he would have either been extremely bored or extremely destructive at *The Gallery*, and I didn't want to gamble on which of the two it would be. We've been attached at the hip every second I've not worked since I got home—eating, playing with Play-Doh, Go-Fish, watching TV, or doing puzzles—and I've soaked up every single second. He's currently passed out in my bed using my arm as a security blanket while Scooby-Doo plays on my small television. Just as I close my eyes to try and doze off with him, I feel my phone buzzing. I grab it with my free hand and see Tank's name lighting up my screen.

That's so weird, he never calls me.

"Hello?" I whisper, doing my best not to wake up Hendrix.

"*Heyyyy,* Honey." Oh fantastic, he's drunk off his ass.

"Tank, what's wrong? Where are you?" The sounds of boisterous laughter floods through the other end of the line, as well as glass breaking which has me sitting up a little straighter.

"Oh, I'm just hanging out with Drengr. Lenny is super cool. We've just been chatting about *stuff.*" Someone says something I can't quite make out that makes Tank snicker.

He snickers. Tank never snickers.

He's worse off than I thought.

"Could you maybe come pick me up? I rode my bike and I don't think I should drive it home." The slur to his words makes him sound almost childlike and I'm alarmed thinking about what could have caused him to drink this much.

On a damn Tuesday night for that matter.

"Umm. *No.* In case you forgot I have a five-year-old, and he's currently asleep on my arm." He clicks his tongue as if he's disappointed by my answer.

"Man, I don't want to be alone. I'm so sick of being alone," he says in a sad, cry-like whisper. My heart sinks a little at his words but I try to wave it off because he's *clearly* incoherent right now.

"You're not alone. You said you were with Drengr. I'm not gonna bother asking *why* right now. But you're not alone," I remind him.

"It's not the same. I wanted *you.*" My heart jumps into my throat as his words flood through my ears. I bite my lip, trying to tell myself not to get too worked up as I contemplate what I want to do next. In the next second, I'm slipping out of bed and into my bathroom, turning the light on and sitting on the floor next to my bathtub as I click the FaceTime button on the screen.

"What the fuck?" I hear Tank say in a confused tone, making me giggle. "I think I'm getting another phone call." Poor drunk thing. He finally catches on and clicks accept, bringing his face into view a moment later.

"There you are," he says, with a more content look on his face. His green eyes are shining from the street light above him and his teeth look even whiter next to his dark facial hair when he smiles.

God, even drunk he looks amazing.

"Here I am. See, I told you you're not alone." He slides down a brick wall, taking a seat on the ground outside of what I assume is Drengr's bar.

"What's going on Tank? You wanna talk about it?" I ask, curious about what drove him to get so drunk tonight.

"No. Can we… Can we just sit together for a little bit?" he requests, deflecting any potential conversation about what's happening right now.

"Of course." We sit in silence for a while—aside from me humming to the music playing through the bar speakers where Tank is—until he finally starts dozing off while we're on the phone.

"Okay, Tank. Why don't you call Max to come get you?" He groans in response.

"Nah. Maybe I'll just stay here. Or call a cap or something."

"Do you mean a ca*b*?" I say, enunciating the b.

"That's what I said." He blows a raspberry into the phone and I shake my head at him.

"Either you call Max, or *I* will."

"*Fine*," he finally grumbles in agreement.

"Tank, I swear to God, I'm not playing around. I will text him in five minutes to make sure he's coming to get you."

"Okay, Ruby. I got it." For the first time I realize, I don't like when Tank uses my real name. He's called me Honey for so long now that it feels…*strange* when he doesn't.

"Be safe, please."

"Will do, Honey." He salutes me lazily with two fingers then the line goes dead before I can say another word. I have a bad feeling in the pit of my stomach after we hang up—the same one I got when I saw Tank's head hit the wall while we were in San Francisco. He's been off ever since that night and it's starting to worry me.

I hate seeing him revert back to the quiet, to himself guy that he was when I first met him. He's still friendly, but there's a look in his eyes telling me that something's changed. It's like any good moments in his days are few and far between, and I just wish I could do something to help.

> **ME**
> Please tell me you're going to get Tank.

> **MAX**
> On my way now. How'd you know?

> **ME**
> He called me to come get him, but Hendrix is already asleep so I told him to call you.

> **MAX**
> Don't worry, I'll get him home safe.

> **ME**
> Okay, good. Thanks

I bite the inside of my cheek, still staring down at my phone while my mind swirls with so many thoughts about Tank. I feel a little better knowing Max is the one in charge of getting him home safely tonight, but it still doesn't change how uneasy I feel over the way he's been acting lately. Maybe he just needs a little bit of normalcy to get him out of this...*funk?* Whatever it is, I'll do my best to pull him out of it.

After crawling back into bed with Hendrix I toss and turn until I get a text that helps put my mind at ease.

> **TANK**
> Thanks for not letting me feel alone tonight.

> **ME**
> Anytime.

Almost immediately after, I nod off and dream of the night we danced together at the bar. I never knew your heart could physically ache from missing someone's touch during a dream that's supposed to make you happy. But somehow, it does.

"I am so excited. Okay, so we'll all meet here for pre-game shots and then head over around six o'clock." Shane claps her hands together excitedly while Leah and Lauren sit next to her at the bar. Max grumbles in disapproval as I stand back watching in amusement.

"And where are y'all going?" Tank asks, wiping down the other side of the counter.

"Oh no, you're coming too. I got you a ticket and I will drag your ass there if I have to." Max slams a ticket down on the counter, sliding it over to Tank.

"*Country Music Festival*...The fuck I am," Tank scoffs, sliding it back to Max.

"Come on man, I will buy your first three beers if you go," Max offers. It's the closest thing I've ever seen to him begging, and I have to say—it's entertaining. My eyes bounce between the two of them as Tank contemplates his decision.

"Are you going?" he asks, looking directly at me. I hate the fact that my cheeks instantly heat at his inquiry because I can feel all three girls staring at me intently.

"Yeah, I am," I answer, turning to organize *nothing* just to keep myself busy.

"Alright, fine." Tank swipes the ticket from the counter and glances over at me. For the first time in days, he actually looks like himself.

"You think our seats are next to each other again?" He laughs, looking over the ticket.

"Well, we're on the lawn so... you get to *stand* by whomever you'd like." He lets out a disapproving grunt then flicks the ticket and slides it in his pocket.

"Then I guess I'm standing by you." He winks at me and then

disappears through the kitchen door. I brace myself for their reactions, but nothing could properly prepare me for these three.

I glance at Shane, Leah, and Lauren and they're all staring at me with their mouths hanging open. Shane's finally snaps shut before she begins talking.

"Since Taylor isn't here, I'll say it. What the shit was that, *ma'am?*" she says, impersonating Taylor perfectly.

"*Nothing,*" I deflect, but none of them break.

"Try again," Lauren says, folding her arms over her chest.

"What? Can we not just be friends?" They all look at each other in disbelief.

"*Sure.* Only problem is, friends don't look at friends like *that,*" Shane says, pointing to the door Tank disappeared through. I zone out looking over at the pool table, remembering the dream I had, and the night we spent talking and dancing.

"Oh, my god!" Shane exclaims, jarring me from my thoughts.

"What?" I ask, matching her urgency.

"I know that look." She glances over at the pool tables. "You guys did it on the pool table too?" she whispers excitedly, leaning in closer to me.

"What? Oh my god no!" I rush out, making her sit back looking at me in confusion. "We just... we stayed late one night and did some shots and *talked.* I told you, we're just friends." The three of them study me for a moment and when they come to the conclusion I'm telling the truth, they hesitantly drop it.

"The pool table, Shane? Really?" Leah says, redirecting the conversation. Shane shrugs and her cheeks instantly turn red.

"Atta girl," Leah says, and we all burst out laughing.

I try not to dwell on what Shane said, "*Friends don't look at each other like that,*" but it's kind of hard not to when I spend so much of my time wondering if his looks, his winks, or his flirty remarks could mean something more. I keep telling myself I cherish our friendship too much to jeopardize it, but what if it wouldn't jeopardize anything. What if it could open a door to an opportunity for us to become something even better?

I never have been the country music type, but ever since moving to Nashville and gaining a girl group that lives and breathes it—it's starting to rub off on me. I still stay true to my own taste but I don't mind rocking a pair of black cowboy boots with cutoffs and my favorite Bon Jovi T-shirt.

Max and Tank both look less than thrilled to be here, but God knows they'd rather be miserable here than let us come alone. I respect that about them, and I know Tucker would be right by their side if he were in town. Having friends who will protect you no matter what is something my soul has desperately wanted for so long, and now that I have it I can't imagine ever having to live without it. While Shane, Leah, and Lauren all talk around me, and Max has his head on a swivel like a guard dog, I notice Tank staring at a group of guys not too far away, but he looks completely spaced out.

"Tank." I walk closer to him, but he doesn't seem to notice or hear me. I gently bump his arm with my shoulder, finally breaking him out of his trance. "Hey, you okay?" He grunts in response, rolling his neck as he begins scanning the area around us.

"Honestly? I'm not sure yet. There's so many goddamn people here. I hate it." His blunt response takes me by surprise since he usually just brushes things off as *fine*—but not tonight.

He squares his shoulders back, taking in an exasperated breath as the same group of guys start hooting and hollering. The concert hasn't even started yet so I'm sure Tank and I are thinking the same thing right about now—*this is only going to get worse as the night goes on.*

"How about this-" I grab his hand and his eyes finally focus on me. "Just stick with me tonight. Focus on me when you feel like it's getting to be too much, and if that still doesn't help, we can go somewhere quiet or we can just leave," I offer with a smile.

"You don't have to do that. I don't want to be the reason you have to leave, and I really don't want people asking *why* we're leaving." He cuts his gaze to the rest of our group, before looking back down at me.

"No one will ask why. Just pinch the inside of my hand if we need to take a minute, and if you decide you wanna go, just leave the explaining to me. No one's going to know anything is wrong unless you want them to." I squeeze his forearm, getting only a nod in response.

"Thanks, Honey, I owe you one." The corner of his lips turn up into a sad smile.

"I was hoping you'd say that." I wag my eyebrows, making his knit together in confusion. "I'll take a Jack and Coke, thanks." I smile brightly at him, making his smile grow into one that makes me think he actually feels it. I wrap my hand around his bicep and call back to the rest of the group.

"Going for drinks, we'll be right back." As I turn back around, I almost run into a group of people that are coming down the hill. Before I can even blink, Tank has his arm around my shoulder pulling me into his side. I was already taking every one of his veins to memory while touching his arm, but being tucked beneath his shoulder with the sandalwood and musk scent that's easily become my favorite sending my senses into overdrive, I may never leave his side.

"This may be the shortest concert you'll ever attend," he says, shooting me a warning look.

"Eh, I think I'd be fine with that." I shrug, settling into him.

We get through the first band's entire set list with no mishaps, and at one point I think I actually saw Tank mouthing the words to one of their songs. But as soon as the second band takes the stage, people around us start losing their ever-loving minds. The screaming is so loud I can't even hear my own voice while I am trying my hardest to ask Tank if he's okay. When they start playing their first song, the same guys Tank was watching earlier start stumbling around and bump into not only Tank, but me as well—sending him immediately over the edge.

I can see the exact moment he starts seeing red and I immediately grab his hand. He squeezes mine tight, moving his fingers to my palm to pinch it gently.

"Oh my god, are you guys okay?" Lauren asks, staring daggers into the guys that just trampled us.

"Yeah, Tank is just about to walk with me to the bathroom,"

"Want me to come with?" Lauren asks, still swaying to the music.

"No, I'm good." I smile, trying to end this conversation as quickly and politely as possible. I turn around to leave the lawn, pulling Tank close behind me. With everyone now in their seats the rest of the facility is pretty much empty at this point—making it easy to find a quiet place for us to talk. We stop along the brick wall lining the sidewalks, and I can see Tank's chest rising and falling more quickly now.

"What do you need?" I ask, unsure how exactly to help right now.

"To snap a few necks maybe. What the fuck is wrong with people?" he spits, slamming his fist into the concrete behind him.

My heart aches when I see it happen, but I keep trying to think of how to get him to calm down.

"Well, alcohol along with the fact that they probably have a few less brain cells than the rest of the population," I tease, trying to distract him. He huffs out an angry laugh as his eyes fixate on my arm. I follow his gaze and notice a small cut there, possibly from one of the guy's beer cans. I thought I felt something pinch me when they fell into us, but I don't know how I missed *this*.

"They fucking did that to you?"

Shit.

He pushes off the wall and begins stalking back towards the lawn but I quickly run in front of him, bringing his steps to a halt.

"Tank, stop. I'm fine. It's just a baby cut, I have probably done worse to myself working at the bar."

"That's different," he says through clenched teeth.

"Look, just... focus on something else."

Gee, what a great plan Ruby, I'm sure he hasn't thought of that yet.

"Unless you *give me* something else to focus on, someone's nose is about to get broken." I take his face in my hands, noticing the distant look in his eyes. Like he's looking at me, but he's not actually here. I try to get his eyes focused back on mine but when I can't seem to bring him back to reality, I am flooded with so many thoughts and emotions that I feel dizzy.

Panic and adrenaline course through my veins as I stand on my toes and pull his face closer to mine, and I do something absolutely insane.

I kiss Tank Landry.

His body stiffens slightly as my lips land on his, causing me to pull away immediately. The panic from before suddenly becomes the only thing I feel.

"I'm so sorry." I gasp. "I just–" He doesn't let me get another word out before he pulls me in harder. His hands wrap around my waist as he presses his body flush against mine, sending me a clear message of how well my distraction is working. His tongue swipes against my lips and I can't help the soft whimper that escapes from my throat. Nothing about this feels like a friendship being potentially ruined, it feels *right*.

Kissing Tank Landry feels better than I ever imagined it would.

Which, if I'm honest with myself, has been more often than not.

When we hear footsteps approaching, he pulls me away, brushing his nose against mine before standing back to his full height.

"I don't think there will ever be anything better to give my full attention to, than you."

"So, you're okay?" I ask, breathlessly.

"Better than okay." He smirks, kissing the top of my head.

Tank grabs my hand and leads the way as we re-join our group, but when we make it back up and Lauren turns to face our direction, I pull away from him on instinct. I look up to gauge his reaction, worried he might be upset about my sudden need to put distance between us, but he simply smirks at me and shakes his head. He places his arm around my shoulder and watches the band play like it's the most natural thing in the world. I do my best to enjoy the rest of the concert, but my mind keeps swarming with thoughts of what this might mean for us now.

Did I just kiss him to calm him down or did I do it because deep down I know I want this?

Did he only kiss me back to keep from breaking someone's nose?

Does he *want this to mean more than it did?*

Have I blinked in the last 15 minutes?

Looking up at Tank, he looks more carefree than I've ever seen him before. He's singing along to whatever song is playing right now and the smile on his face is the one that makes part of my brain unable to focus on anything but him. The butterflies I'm growing more and more used to, are fluttering around viciously in my stomach as he pulls me closer to him, planting another kiss on the top of my head.

Chapter 15

TANK

Out of all the things I've experienced in my life—from fist fights, to combat, traveling the world, to the best buzz I've ever had —nothing comes close to the feeling of kissing Ruby. I've dreamt of that moment almost every day since the night we danced at the bar. She tastes like cherries and I don't think I'll ever crave another flavor more.

No matter how good that moment felt though, I still can't pinpoint if it happened simply to keep me from breaking someone's nose, or if a part of her wanted that as much as I did. *I* know I was probably seconds from blacking out again, but *she* didn't know that. So I can't help but wonder where her motivation came from. She's mentioned before that she hasn't been with anyone since having Hendrix, and a part of me wonders if she's ready to take a chance with someone... with *me*.

I would fight every day to put my own darkness to rest if I thought I would ever have the chance to truly love Ruby—even if I know there will be a war within me as I try to prove to be a better man for her.

Because if there's one thing I've learned during the time I've gotten to spend with her, it's that my demons don't like how happy I am when she's around. They immediately start reminding me that

I'm not good enough, that I'm unworthy, and that even if she were ready to take that chance with me, that I would likely end up doing something to ruin it all. Which is why I tell myself, once again, that she was just being a good friend, and nothing more.

RUBY

I have a massive favor to ask you.

ME

Shoot.

RUBY

Hendrix needs to be picked up from school but we are slammed right now and I can't leave and none of the girls are available to go get him. Would you mind just picking him up and bringing him here?

ME

So I'm just a last resort? You know, you could have just called me first instead of checking with the rest of the spice girls.

RUBY

I don't even know how to respond to that except to ask, which one am I supposed to be?

ME

Hmm... This feels like a trap. Which one is Baby Spice?

RUBY

Wrong. Are you getting my kid or what?

ME

Yep. See you in a bit.

RUBY

Thank you so much. I'll let the school know you're
coming.

I'm halfway to Hendrix's school when I realize I don't own a car
seat. After making a pit stop at the nearest store to grab one,
ensuring it looks almost identical to the one I've seen in the back of
Ruby's car, I install it and book it to the school to pick him up.
While sitting in the pickup line I start overthinking things and get
nervous that Hendrix won't want to ride with me. I'm not even sure
what the circumstances are to explain why I'm here instead of Betty,
but when he sees my truck and a smile spreads across his face, all
my worries fade away.

"Tank!" he yells, as he runs up to the door. His teacher helps him
in and gives me a curt smile that rubs me in all the wrong ways.

"Hey little man, how was school?" I ask, watching him throw his
stuff into the floorboard.

"It was good. I got to help pass out snacks today," he says,
pulling his seatbelt on and clicking it into place.

"Heck yeah. That's like one step down from being a teacher." I
give him a playful smile over my shoulder, making his face
completely light up.

"Why are you picking me up? Are we going to play soccer?" I
laugh at the way he connects our interactions, but it also gives me
an idea.

"You know what, that sounds like a great idea. Let me call your
mom and see if that's cool with her." Hendrix nods his head, excited
by the idea.

I pull into a parking space and pick up my phone to dial the bar.

"Chattahoochies, what's your poison?"

That's always been my favorite line when she answers the phone.

"Hey, it's me."

"Tank? What's wrong? Is Hendrix okay?" she asks in a panic. I can hear just how loud the bar is in the background and she wasn't lying, they're fucking slammed.

"Yeah, yeah. Everything is fine. Listen, I know you're insanely busy there so I was just gonna see if I could take him to the park for a while instead of bringing him there?"

"Well…" she trails off, contemplating my offer.

"Look, I'll do whatever you want. I just know he'd probably be bored in Max's office and I wouldn't want you worrying about him while you're working. Plus I still have the soccer stuff in my truck and he asked if we could play," I finish, watching as Hendrix waits patiently for an answer.

"Are you sure? I don't want to put you out on your day off."

"Are you kidding? This is much better than what I had planned." *Nothing.*

"Okay. if you're sure that would actually really help me out. Thanks, Tank." I can almost hear the appreciative smile on her face.

"No problem, Honey."

"Let's go play some soccer." The enthusiasm in my voice sends Hendrix into a fit of excitement.

"*Yessss!*" I laugh as we pull out of the parking lot.

"Tank? Why do you call mommy, Honey?" Hendrix asks, giving me a curious look through the mirror.

"Well, because *I* think your mom is as sweet as honey. Don't you?" He smiles at me so big his dimple is showing more than ever. He's a little young for me to divulge that it's because her eyes, when in the right lighting, are the perfect honey color, and her voice is just as soothing.

"Yeah! She's the sweetest. Like sugar. Hey, you could call her that too! Or chocolate. I love chocolate. Do you like chocolate, Tank?"

"Yeah, buddy. I like chocolate too." He keeps naming every candy and sweet thing his little mind can conjure up, making me belly laugh as we walk over to the soccer goals.

RUBY

How's it going? I'm so sorry. Betty had to cancel at
the last minute cause she's sick. You can still bring
him here if you want.

ME

Nah, it's going great. We played soccer for a while
and now we're at Spur's getting some food.

"Wanna send a picture to your mom?" I ask Hendrix who is dipping
his french fry in my chocolate shake.

"Yeah!" He hops over to my side of the booth and I pull up my
camera. I fully expect him to open his mouth or do some crazy face
that boys his age usually do. But instead, he throws his arms around
my neck and smiles ear to ear. A foreign feeling grows in my chest
and I lean in slightly, smiling big before snapping a photo of us.

"Okay, now a crazy one," he says, growling as he holds his hands
up like a dinosaur.

Ah, there it is.

I snap another few photos as he changes poses and send them to
Ruby.

RUBY

RUBY

If he starts getting tired you're more than welcome
to go to the house. I'll be off in an hour and there's
a spare key behind our street number sign above
the door.

ME

Yeah, I think he's about to pass out in the booth.
We can head that way now.

RUBY

Honestly Tank, I owe you one.

ME

Hush, woman. You owe me nothing.

"You ready to go home?" I ask Hendrix as he slurps the rest of his milkshake.

"Yes!" He shimmies his butt as he scoots out of the booth, making me shake my head with a laugh. I get Hendrix buckled in his seat as the excitement from the day seems to catch up with him. He lets out a big yawn as I shut his door, and just as we're pulling out of the lot I hear his little voice from the backseat.

"This was like the best day ever. Thanks, Tank." His eyes fall shut and open again only halfway before I turn my eyes back to the road.

"No problem, buddy. Anytime." I smile, swallowing past a lump in my throat.

This isn't the first time I've hung out with Hendrix, but it's the first time we've ever been together without Ruby—and it felt so... *normal*. For the first time in my life, I'm actually starting to picture what my future would look like with a wife and a kid—or *kids*. Being someone they can rely on, someone who can teach them new things, who they run to when they're sad, need help, or simply want to share something that made them happy. My heart squeezes at the thought as I look back at Hendrix passed out in the backseat of my truck.

They have no idea the impact they're making on my life.

Chapter 16

RUBY

WORK TODAY WAS ABSOLUTE MADNESS. For some reason every customer today was extra needy and Heather does not do well under pressure, so that left Max and I running the show the entire day. I've missed working behind the bar with Max, ever since Tank started, and with Shane still helping on nights her studio is closed, he and I hardly ever see each other anymore. Unfortunately, I barely got to enjoy our shift because we were going nonstop all day.

When I finally pull into my driveway I try my best to take a deep breath to release the stress from my day and get into mom mode before seeing Hendrix. I'm sure he'll be bursting at the seams to tell me all about his day with Tank, and I need to be ready to receive it and match his excitement. Even *if* all I can think about is a bubble bath and rubbing my feet until I can't feel my thumbs.

I cut off the engine and grab my bag from the passenger seat, but when I shut my car door something in the back seat of Tank's truck catches my attention.

A booster seat.

I stop in my tracks, then look back at my car to see an identical seat *still* sitting in the backseat of my car and two thoughts cross my mind.

1. *How did I forget to mention Hendrix would need a booster seat?*
2. *I can't believe* he *remembered and…* bought *him one?*

I smile at the thought and am overwhelmed with gratitude at the way Tank showed up for me…for *us* today. This may have been the first time I haven't had to actively stop myself from thinking about the kiss we shared at the concert the other night, but as I walk in the house and see Tank standing at the stove while Hendrix sits on the counter next to him, he's suddenly *all* I can think about.

"Mommy!" Hendrix yells as he grabs Tank's arm for support while climbing down from the counter.

"Hey bud! How was your day today?" I ask, bending down and bracing myself for the impact of his running hug.

"It. Was. The. BEST!" he squeals, his dimple on full display as he smiles at me.

"I am so glad you had a great day. I'm really sorry I couldn't pick you up today," I apologize, feeling that twinge of mom guilt seep in. No matter who shows up for him on days like today, I always hate when it can't be me.

"It's okay, Mommy. Tank took me to the park and we played soccer, then we went to Spurs and I got to have *two* milkshakes…" I cut my eyes over to Tank as he turns the burner off and moves the pan he's using to the back burner.

"Whoa, hold on. Don't go getting me in trouble now," he says, lifting his hands in surrender. "You got *one* milkshake, I just let you dip a few fries in mine," he explains, glancing back over at me. "They're not the same dipped in strawberry."

"That sounds like a *very* fun day." I smile at Hendrix who lets out a huge yawn. "You getting sleepy?" I ask, brushing his dark hair away from his eyes.

"Yeah. Will you scratch my back on the couch?" He pulls my arm in an effort to drag me to the living room.

"Sure, buddy. Why don't you go get your comfy clothes so I can talk to Tank for a minute?"

"Okay!" he shouts, taking off down the hallway towards his room. I stand back up and it's only then that I realize, Tank didn't just cook, he cleaned too. My house is absolutely spotless. Not a spare toy or sock lying around anywhere. He even has a candle burning in the living room making the scent of cherry blossom mix with whatever that delicious smell is coming from the kitchen.

"Hey," he says, sliding his hands into the front pockets of his blue jeans in an almost bashful way. And dammit if it isn't working for him. He's wearing a simple white T-shirt and blue jeans with a gray ball cap and running shoes and I could literally stare at him for the rest of my life and never get bored.

"Hey," I say, sounding as exhausted as I'm *sure* I look right now. When I realize he seems a little more awkward than usual I realize we haven't really talked since the concert. "Did you not get full at Spur's?" I tease, nodding to the stove.

"Um, no. I couldn't eat another bite if someone paid me to. That's for you."

"You made me dinner?" I ask, with a shocked expression.

"Yeah."

"And you cleaned my house?"

"I did."

"After you had to buy a booster seat and pick my kid up from school, took him to play soccer for a few *hours,* and then fed him his favorite food, you came here and cleaned my house and cooked me dinner?"

"That is correct. Excellent recount." He smirks.

"But... why?" I ask, genuinely confused.

"Why not?" He shrugs.

"Because it's not your responsibility," I say, dropping my bag on the counter. "You could have said no, or told me you didn't have a seat. You could have taken him to the bar after picking him up, or you could have brought him here and sat on the couch watching cartoons until I got home and then bailed. But..."

"But?" he presses.

"But you did all of *this*." I laugh, waving my hands around my house. "You went and *bought* him a car seat. You took him to do his favorite things, you cleaned my house. You even lit my favorite candle and I am *very* curious to know what's on the stove." At this point, I'm rambling and repeating myself so much I can't believe he's still here listening. But alas, here he stands. Arms crossed over his chest, looking like a mountain I'd love to climb, listening to me go on and on about all the things I'm sure he's well aware he did.

"Look… If I overstepped," he says, his features mirroring the sincerity in his voice. "I'm sorry. I just wanted to help. It seemed like you had a long day and I just didn't want you to come home and feel like there was more work to be done."

Speechless. I'm rendered speechless.

I stand here blinking at him like an idiot because I actually have no words. He didn't overstep—at least not in my opinion. He helped me more today than anyone else ever has, besides maybe Betty, but he did all of this without me even asking. He went above and beyond because he *wanted to.*

"I'll go." He nods. "Umm. That's stir-fry on the stove. If you don't like it you can just toss it." He goes to step around me but my hand wraps around his forearm, stopping him before he gets too far.

"You didn't overstep," I assure him, as my eyes begin to water. "I'm not used to people showing up for me the way you did today. I think I'm just having a hard time processing it all," I admit, rolling my eyes in annoyance as a rogue tear streams down my cheek. He turns to face me completely and wipes the tear away with the pad of his thumb.

"You're worth showing up for, Honey. As long as you're calling, I'm gonna answer." I swallow hard as another tear breaks free.

He studies me as he cups my face in his hands and my heart begins hammering behind my chest. There's still so many unanswered questions I have about *us*, but all I can think about right now is how much I wish he would kiss me again. Our eyes are locked on one another, and just as he leans in and I think he might, Hendrix's footsteps echo through the hallway and he presses his lips to my forehead. The warmth of his embrace and the way his lips gently caress my skin makes me melt into him. I wrap my arms around his middle and squeeze him tight because whether we're friends, or bordering on something more, I am *so* grateful for him. We both pull away just as Hendrix shows up in the kitchen in his Spider-Man pajamas.

"Mommy," he calls, making scratching motions with his hands. I choke out a laugh, blinking away the rest of my unshed tears.

"I'll be right there buddy." I smile at him.

"Can Tank stay?" he pleads. Tank and I glance at one another and he simply shrugs, leaving the decision up to me.

"Only if he wants to," I answer Hendrix, but my eyes never leave Tanks.

"I'd love to stay." The tension between us is so heavy I can hardly breathe, but Hendrix can't tell a thing. He simply whispers *"Yes!"* and runs to the couch.

"Okay." I smile, feeling the heat rising to my cheeks.

"Go have a seat, Mama. I'll make your plate." Tank kisses the top of my head before walking over to the stove, leaving me feeling like I'm in a dream. I join Hendrix on the couch, watching as Tank prepares my plate before pouring me a glass of wine. The amount of thoughts I'm having about this man right now is leaving very little space in my mind for anything else.

After I finish my food, Tank takes my dishes into the kitchen, cleaning them completely before returning to the couch with Hendrix and me. He doesn't rush out the door, or look for reasons to, he just *stays*. Once Hendrix has passed out, I turn on *Unsolved Mysteries* as Tank pulls my feet into his lap to begin massaging them.

"What are you doing?" I whisper to him.

"I'm rubbing your feet," he says in an obvious way. I try pulling them away, but he doesn't allow me to.

"No! That's gross." I say, scrunching my nose.

"Ruby, you've been mindlessly rubbing at your feet for five minutes. They're obviously hurting."

"Okay, well they're *my* feet. I'm allowed to touch them when they're dirty."

"Woman, will you hush and let me do it?" He begins rubbing the arch of my foot with the kind of pressure that makes me want to moan. And mortifyingly so, I do. I look over and see Tank smirk with a little spark behind his eyes I've never seen before.

"Atta girl. Let it happen." He laughs, tugging my foot until I slide a little closer to him. Once I've let go of the fact that I just *audibly moaned* while he was rubbing my feet, I look over at him again.

"Hey, Tank... Can I ask you something?" I ask hesitantly.

"Always." He smiles at me, making me nervous to voice my concern.

"The other night at the concert, right before... Before I kissed you," I whisper, glancing down at Hendrix who's still sound asleep. "You had this distant, almost vacant look in your eyes. Like—like you weren't really there." His jaw ticks as his gaze stays locked on my feet in his lap. After a moment, he finally looks up at me.

"Yeah... I've recently had these *occurrences* where I kind of mentally space out and it's almost as if my subconscious takes over. Sometimes they're triggered by things, sometimes they're completely random. *Then* there's times I'll end up somewhere and have no idea how I got there." My eyes grow wide at his confession, stirring a major concern for him in the back of my mind.

"What do you mean you just show up places?" I press further. He lets out a deep sigh, as he begins rubbing my opposite foot.

"Remember the night I called you? When I was at the bar with Lenny?"

"Yeah?"

"I was headed home from work that night, I stopped at a red light, and the next thing I knew I was parked right outside of their bar. Lenny came out right about the time I realized where I was and asked to buy me a drink, a few hours later I was on the phone with you."

"Is there a way to stop that from happening?" He smirks and glances in my direction.

"I've only found one method to pull me out of it so far." he teases. I give him a concerned smile but he brushes it off before the conversation goes any further.

"Don't worry about me, Honey. Just sit back and enjoy your foot rub, yeah?"

I roll my eyes at him playfully as I lay my head down on the throw pillow next to me—before I know it, I'm out like a light. I'm woken up by the feeling of Tank's lips on my forehead, I try to tell him bye and thank him again for everything he did today, but the words never come. I hear the door shut and lock behind him then I let myself fall back into a deep sleep. When I wake up the next morning the kitchen is completely clean, my phone background is changed to the picture of Tank and Hendrix from Spur's and I have a new outlook on my relationship with Tank.

I only hope that when I decide to tell him how I feel, he'll feel the same way.

Chapter 17

TANK

YESTERDAY WAS a real eye-opener for me. Spending time with Hendrix, and seeing the impact it made on Ruby to have someone help her with some of the simplest everyday things made me realize how regular I want to make that. I don't want to just show up for her though, I want to be there before she ever has to call. She's the most amazing woman I've ever met. She's the best mom, a loyal friend, and has a way about her that makes me feel like she sees *me*. She sees through the bullshit, she doesn't pity me or try to tell me she understands what I've gone through, she just helps me see that I can make it through the hard things. Ruby isn't a ray of sunshine, she's a raincloud, helping to bring the dead parts of me back to life. So when I show up to open the bar with her this morning, I have actual butterflies about talking to her. Didn't know until today that guys got butterflies but they're definitely fucking there.

I've walked around the entire bar already and haven't been able to find her, which is strange because normally she's bouncing back and forth from the bar to the kitchen to make sure everything is done from the closers. Just as I'm giving up on finding her, I hear the door to Max's office shut.

There she is.

Looking as fucking beautiful as always with her long black hair down in loose waves, her favorite purple tie-dyed uniform on with a pair of black jeans that make me want to wrap her perfect thighs around me and demand she never let go.

"Hey, there you are," I say, unable to fight the smile demanding to be present on my face as I look at her. She smiles, making her way next to me at the bar.

"Back at ya."

"What were you doing in the office?" I ask, nodding towards the door.

"There was a schedule change and Max asked me to put a post-it on his computer so he won't forget to change it before they're sent out tomorrow." She waves her hand like it's no big deal. Then her demeanor changes to one a little more playful. "You been looking for me Landry?" She smirks, sending my pulse into an irregular rhythm.

"Always." I smirk, looking down at my feet trying to gain the courage to do what I've been thinking about all morning. "Hey, come here." I tilt my head, guiding her closer to me. She gives me a curious look but does as she's asked. When she stops in front of me I extend my hand to her and she places her small fingers in the palm of my hand.

God, I bet her hands would look perfect around my cock, and mine would look right at home around her throat.

"Tank?" her voice cuts through the volume of my own thoughts. My eyes shoot up to hers and I stand from my barstool, pulling her closer to me. A small gasp escapes her lips, bringing a smile to my face. I quickly spin her and grab around her waist to set her on top of the bar, as she lets out a little squeal. We're nose to nose now and damn if I don't love how it feels to be this close to her. I run the tip of my nose along the bridge of hers and my hands up her thighs, letting my thumb slip through the rip in her jeans, as I listen to the way her breathing pattern picks up. The goosebumps that run down her arms and the quick breath she sucks in as my finger digs into the skin under her jeans has me weak in the knees.

"Tank, what are you doing?" she asks, almost breathlessly.

"Shit, Honey. I wish I knew." I press my forehead to hers, clenching my jaw as I wish away all the negative thoughts telling me I am about to ruin the only friendship I've ever truly had. But dammit, I can't *not* try to have something more with her—the woman who makes me feel like there's more than just the bad and the terrible things I've faced in life.

"Tell me—when you kissed away my anger that night at the concert, did you only do it for me?" I lean back a fraction, trying to read her answer through her honey-brown eyes. "Or did a small part of you want it too?" Her eyes fall to her lap as a redness settles across her face.

"I… I don't know." I grip her chin with my index finger and thumb, encouraging her eyes to come back to mine.

"I think you do. Had you imagined it before? What it would feel like to have those perfect lips of yours on mine?" I run my thumb across her bottom lip. "Did you think about the way the taste of you would potentially ruin me for anyone else? Because I can tell you right now, that's exactly what you've done." My jaw ticks, as I run my fingers through the base of her hair. "Ever since that night–" I nod to where the pool table sits, "when I had to fight every instinct in my body telling me to kiss you because I knew I didn't deserve you—I've wanted to." Her eyes are glued on to mine as she hangs onto every word.

"Did you want it too, Honey? Because I'm coming apart inside right now trying not to kiss you right here, right now." I take a small step closer to her, standing between her legs while she's still perched on the bar top.

"I wanted it. More than I thought I would," she whispers, her eyes flicking up to meet mine.

"Thank God." I don't waste another second tightening my grip on her hair and letting our lips collide.

I grip her ass, squeezing her as I pull her body flush with mine. This bar could be full of people right now and I wouldn't give a single fuck. Because at this moment, it feels like every doubt I had about not being good enough for her was just a figment of my imagination. Right now, Ruby Ranes feels like *mine*, and that's enough to bring my dead soul back to life. When we hear the back door alarm go off, our kiss comes to an abrupt end, the noise sending me into a spiral.

"What happened?" I hear a voice ask urgently. The pain has gotten so bad I can't bring myself to keep my eyes open, but I know by the numerous beeping machines, overhead speakers, and a code blue being called that we've arrived at the hospital.

"A distressed civilian pushed him over a stair railing. He fell two stories and landed on his back. Hasn't been able to move on his own yet." I hear Keller explaining, trying his best to mask his concern, but I can make it out clear as day.

Fuck. It was a civilian?

Wait, two stories? Fuck. Fuck. Fuck. How the hell am I coming back from this?

"Any feeling in his legs?" I hear the doctor asking.

"I don't... I don't know."

"Yeah. They fucking hurt," I'm finally able to grumble a response.

"We've got him from here."

"So..." Ruby's voice brings me back to the present. When I look up she's walking back over to me, and I can tell by the obnoxious singing coming from the kitchen that it must have been Marco that set off the alarm.

She gently brushes my pinky with hers, standing close enough to me that it would raise suspicion if someone were to walk in right now, and when I meet her gaze, she looks *happy*. Really fucking happy, and that's enough to make me put my worries about the flashbacks that have started up again to the back of my mind—for now at least. Though it's hard to rid the concern completely when I've never had one while being *with* Ruby. They've always happened before she shows up or when she isn't around at all.

"Do you want to come over tomorrow and learn how to make that casserole? Maybe we can talk about... whatever is happening here." She grins, linking her pinky finger with mine.

"I'd love that." I smirk, glancing toward the kitchen door before planting a quick kiss on her forehead. I give her a wink as I back away and start getting the tables ready while she starts counting the register down. Everything about our shift together is as normal as any other day, except now, every time I catch a glimpse of her, I imagine what it would be like to bend her over any one of these tables and make her mine in every sense of the word.

I don't think I've ever been this nervous in my entire life. I was less anxious before going on missions where there were active threats on my life, but that was something I was trained for. Having an honest conversation about what I want with the woman I'm falling in love with? *Nothing* has prepared me for this moment.

Knock knock knock.

"I got it!" I hear Hendrix yell through the front door, easing some of my nerves. The door swings open and he immediately runs out and hugs my legs.

"Tank! *Finally*, I'm starving and mom won't let me have a snack." He pouts, pulling me into the house behind him.

"Well, yeah little man, can't be spoiling your appetite before dinner." I shut the door behind us before walking into the kitchen to see Ruby setting ingredients on the counter.

"That's exactly what I told him." Ruby gives him a warning look making him slump his shoulders.

"*Okay...* Can I watch TV while you make dinner?" he asks, not looking up from the floor.

"No, buddy, no TV right now. Why don't I get your crayons and some paper so you can color and hang out here with me and Tank. Then you can watch TV *after* dinner," she counters, winning a smile from him.

"Okay! I can get my crayons, I know where they are!" Everything this kid says sounds like the most exciting thing in the world. He runs to a closet in the hallway and I take the opportunity to pull Ruby to the side for a quick kiss. She relaxes into me immediately and I love how natural this already feels. She pulls away and smiles just before Hendrix re-enters the room.

"I brought you some wine." I clear my throat, setting the bottle of her favorite red wine on the counter.

"Thank you so much because *I...* am out," she says, finishing the glass she already had poured. "Okay," she claps her hands together. "You ready to bake a casserole?"

"Let's do it." I nod in agreement. Ruby pulls out her recipe, and we get to work assembling the casserole.

- *Combine chicken, cream of chicken soup, sour cream, and rice.*
- *Place in a greased 13x9 baking dish.*
- *Combine crushed crackers and butter—sprinkle over mixture.*
- *Bake uncovered at 350° for 30 minutes.*

"*So...* what's the secret to the recipe?" I ask, unable to pinpoint which basic ingredient we used is supposed to be the *magic touch*. I wipe the rest of the counter down as Ruby pulls herself up on the already clean end, holding her drink.

"I use rotisserie chicken or cajun seasoning to give it more flavor." She giggles as she takes a sip of her wine.

"Wait, that's it?" I tease.

"Hey, it makes a *big* difference, thank you very much. Just wait until we add the hot sauce." She wags her eyebrows at me, making me shake my head.

"How much longer?" Hendrix grumbles, laying his head on the table dramatically.

"Just ten more minutes buddy," she says sweetly.

"*Okayyy,*" he drags out, making us both snicker.

I'm always amazed at how easily the conversation flows when I'm talking to Ruby. No matter the subject, it's never boring. I often find myself daydreaming about late-night conversations with her about what our future might be like, but up until tonight that was just some distant fantasy I thought never had a chance to see the light of day. But now? Who knows, maybe it had the potential to become our reality.

I walk over to where she's seated on the counter and run my hand along her thigh. Her eyes—much like mine—watch in anticipation for what might happen next. I rest my fingers along her hip and wait for her eyes to meet mine. When they finally do, I catch a glimpse of the same desire I can feel burning in mine. The microwave timer goes off—woefully cutting through the growing tension—as Ruby takes a quick breath in and looks over at Hendrix who has suddenly perked up at the sound.

"Okay buddy, get the table cleaned up. Dinner is ready!" I take a step back, giving her room to get the casserole from the oven, never taking my eyes off of her.

"Tank, do you want to see what I drew?" he asks, sorting through the papers on the table.

"Yeah buddy, but why don't we eat first, huh? Since you're *so* starving." I remind him.

"Oh, yeah. Good plan. I'll just put this one over here to show after." He slides a piece of construction paper to the side as he gathers the rest of his supplies to return to the closet.

"Hey, do you mind grabbing Hendrix's cup while I take the casserole to the table?" Ruby asks while sifting through her spice cabinet.

"Here, I can take it for you," I offer, reaching for the casserole dish.

"Oh, okay thanks," she says, turning back to face me once she grabs the hot sauce. I grab the casserole from the stove top and start towards the table but as soon as I do, Ruby is yelling, "Tank, wait!"

As soon as I hear it, the sensation makes it from my brain to my hands and I can feel them burning.

I am barehanded holding a piping hot casserole dish.

"Fuck!" I yell.

Before I can reach the opposite counter, I drop the casserole dish on the floor.

Glass shatters, sending a ringing to my ears almost immediately.

When Ruby yells I find myself flashing back to a memory I'd all but forgotten.

Suddenly this kitchen is a battlefield, and things go from bad to worse.

I'm unable to catch my breath, feeling exposed and helpless with no idea how to ground myself, as reality and a flashback fight for my attention.

"Mommy, I need help!" Hendrix yells, making the flashback hit me full force—becoming the only thing I see.

"The child was last seen on the second floor. Snipers saw movement up there but proceed with caution, our view is obstructed and it's unclear if the movement detected was from the child or something else." I nod, waving Dom and Asher to follow my lead. After clearing the first floor we make it to the top of the landing where a ragged tapestry with burn holes is hung. I catch a glimpse through one of the holes of a small figure huddled in the corner next to some beat-up old furniture and give the guys silent instructions on what to do next. We walk through the threshold one after the other and clear every angle of the room before I make my way over to the child. He has his ears covered, rocking back and forth on the floor and my heart aches for him thinking of how scared he must be right

now. Before I reach him to let him know we're here to help, an arm pops out of a credenza and grabs my shoulder. I turn around, pulling the person out of the furniture, and pin him against the wall with my forearm. As Dom comes to my aide, Asher goes to retrieve the child who is now frantically screaming.

"Mommy! Mommy!" When I hear him scream again, chills shoot down my spine.

"MOMMY! TANK, STOP! YOU'RE HURTING HER!"

All at once the flashback fades and I'm brought back to an even more devastating reality. I have Ruby pinned against the pantry door —in the same way I'd pinned the terrorist to the wall all those years ago—and when I can finally focus back on her eyes, they're full of fear and heartbreak. I pull away as fast as I can, completely in shock over what just happened.

What the fuck have I done?

"Mommy!" Hendrix cries, running into Ruby's arms.

As the adrenaline and shock wears off, I'm left with nothing but panicked breaths and self-loathing.

"Ruby… I am—I am so *so* sorry…" My voice cracks as the magnitude of the situation hits me. Tears begin streaming down her face as she holds Hendrix close to her, silent sobs racking her body. She pulls in one deep breath to steady herself.

"I think you should go." Her voice quivers as she stares back at me.

"Please, please let me explain," I beg, taking a slow step forward. I see her features harden as she stands a little taller.

"Tank, please hear me. I don't need an explanation right now. I just need some time…*we* need some time. *Alone.*" She looks down and Hendrix, who still has his face buried in the crook of his elbow while his arms are wrapped tightly around her waist. When she looks back up at me, her brows knit together with a pained expression that doesn't require words for me to understand.

No explanation I give is going to change what her son just had to witness because of me.

My heart begins to break—slowly and painfully—as I see everything I was beginning to love slip away from me with each passing second.

"I think we all need some space, and you need to figure things out." She looks up at the ceiling fighting back more tears that dare to fall down her cheeks anyways. "Because this can't happen again." Her eyes well with tears that are so thick her eyes look golden.

He saw you. She mouths.

"Ruby, please–"

"I can't, Tank. I... I can't. You have to understand that. Please." She sobs, shaking her head as she grips Hendrix tighter. Just when I think I have no heart left to break, it's ripped from my chest completely.

"It's not just me I'm thinking about here, it's Hendrix's too. This isn't the first incident you've had like this, but you're starting to lose more and more control over the situation. I think you need to talk to someone about this, someone who can help you be *you* again."

"Honey, please..." I choke out, unable to see clearly through the tears blurring my vision.

"Please don't make this harder than it already is. Can't you see how this is killing me?" she whispers, choking back her sobs. I nod, silently and resistantly agreeing to go. I take one last look at her before walking out the door, not knowing what will happen the next time I see her. Or *when* I'll see her next. My whole body feels numb, my mind is unable to stop the night from playing on repeat.

I don't remember how I got home from Ruby's house—but here I sit. In the darkness of my empty apartment. Contemplating what the fuck I'm supposed to do now.

"Someone who can help you be you *again..."*

The fucked up part about it is, this *is* who I am. Outside of the good Ruby has always been able to bring out in me, *this* is me.

I knew I would ruin this.

Fuck it, maybe I will finally try to go back to the Marines. They don't know how fucked in the head I am so maybe I could mask it and go back. I can just disappear from Ruby's life without hurting her any worse, and make myself useful in the only way I know how.

I knew trying to be part of her life would only end badly, but I selfishly went there anyways, and in one *fucking* night, I've ruined everything. I scared her, I scared Hendrix, I *hurt her* and I lost them both.

I hate myself for hurting her.

Just as I am about to pick up my phone to reach out about my going back, the voice of the news reporter on the TV breaks through even my loudest thoughts.

"Marine special forces underwent an enemy ambush while trying to eliminate a terrorist threat. As of now, there has been one death recorded while multiple other team members were wounded during the mission, as we have been informed by the state's officials."

I can feel the blood drain from my face completely as the voice echoes in my mind.

It can't be them.

Please don't let it be them.

Chapter 18

RUBY

I WAS SO sure by the way things were looking that Tank and I would be officially *something* before he left the house tonight. The way he so comfortably fell into place here, the chemistry, the way his touch feels as though it's lighting my entire body on fire. I've wanted him for longer than I care to admit, but like every other time in my life when I thought things were going one way, they go rogue and I'm left hurt and confused. When I noticed Tank grabbing the pan with *bare hands* I couldn't form a sentence fast enough to warn him or remind him to grab the pot holders. He grabs the 350-degree casserole dish from the stovetop before the words ever leave my lips. He notices a moment later and yells out in pain.

"Fuck!"

The dish falls to the floor and shatters everywhere, a piece of glass flying past my leg and leaving a small cut in its wake.

"Shit!" I yell, shocked by the pain. As soon as I'm able to check my cut and see that it's not very deep, I rest my hand on Tank's shoulder to see if he's okay, but his eyes are glazed over and it's like he's looking right through me.

"Hey, are you–" In one swift movement, he has me pinned to the wall with his forearm resting on my throat.

"Tank... Tank, stop. What are you doing?" I struggle to get the

144

words out as the pressure of his arm keeps my voice at a whisper. I push against his arm, but it's no use. He's three times my size and my strength is no match for him.

When I look into his eyes, I can see that Tank isn't really here. Wherever his mind is right now, is someplace dangerous. I know he's been going through some things—spacing out, not knowing where he is, angry outbursts, but *this* is a level I never knew he was capable of reaching. I squeeze my eyes shut and for a brief moment, I'm no longer here either.

"You fucking bitch. You never listen, do you? I thought I told you to take care of this! I'm going to be generous and give you one more chance to make this right. If you won't, you leave me no choice but to do something about it myself." His hand releases my throat and I gasp for air between my sobs.

"You don't mean that. You can't mean that." I'm grasping at straws trying to make sense of what he's saying.

"I'll give you one last chance to take care of this, or I'll do it myself."

My eyes snap back open as I can feel the air getting thinner as the pressure from his weight increases, but no matter how much my heart was aching before, it completely shatters when I see Hendrix out of my peripheral vision.

"Mommy! Mommy!" he screams, making me wish I could somehow break free—that I could turn him around so he doesn't have to see this, and tell him we're going to be okay. But, I have no air left to even whisper those words when crocodile tears start pouring down his cheeks. He yells out once more, "Tank, STOP! YOU'RE HURTING HER!" And like that day in the park, he comes running up and kicks Tank in the shin. By some miracle, that pulls Tank back from whatever memory he was facing and he pulls his arm away, taking a few steps back as he does.

I take in a deep breath, coughing once before I try taking in another. Hendrix turns to me, wrapping his arms around my waist as I squeeze him close, rubbing my hand along his back to let him know I'm okay.

He tries to apologize. He tries to come to me. But my defenses are up so high, he couldn't possibly get over them. I can feel my heart breaking more with every word out of his mouth. Every desperate plea for me to hear him out, every apology for hurting me crushed my spirit a little more, but my son is watching. He's seeing what is acceptable and forgivable behavior, and right now, my mind can't make up what is and what isn't.

"Ruby, please—"

"I can't, Tank. I... I can't. You have to understand that, please." My sobs are completely consuming me while it feels like my heart is being crushed under the weight of the world.

"Honey, please..."

God, I can't fucking take this.

No matter what's happened, I still can't look at him and see how much he's hurting without wanting to kiss away the pain. But I can't do that—I *have* to be stronger than that.

"Please don't make this harder than it already is. Can't you see how this is killing me?" I whisper, breaking my own heart as I send him away. He stares at me a little longer, blinking rapidly as tears keep falling down his face. Once he finally leaves and the door shuts behind him, I take a deep breath and drop down to Hendrix's level.

"Hey, are you okay?" He shakes his head up and down, being the brave little soldier that he is. "You can tell me if you're not okay. I know that was a little scary." I remind him, giving him a safe space to share how he's feeling.

"I'm sad, Mommy. Why did he do that?" he asks, hanging his head.

"I don't really know, baby." I swallow past the lump in my throat, doing my best to keep my composure.

"He said he would never hurt you... but he did. He said he would protect you because you're one of his important people. Was it an accident?" he asks, showing me yet again what an old soul he truly has.

"I don't really know. Maybe it was." He stares back at me with his big brown eyes and they're so full of *concern*. Not the fear I would expect from a kid after such an event. He wraps his little arms around my neck, squeezing me ever so gently as he whispers in my ear.

"We're okay, Mommy. We're safe." The same words I always whisper to him when he's hurt or sad. I always let him know he's safe with me, and at this moment I'm so proud of the little man I'm raising. I fight back more tears, as I pull back to look at his sweet face.

"I tell you what, why don't you go ahead and turn on Spider-Man in Mommy's room and I'll order us a pizza." His face lights up as I smile back at him.

"Yes!" He runs down the hallway and as soon as I hear the TV turn on I slide down to the floor with my hand over my mouth, trying to hold back the sobs threatening to escape.

We were so close.

I know Tank—at least I *thought* I knew Tank—he's been one of my best friends for almost two years, and whatever happened here tonight wasn't him at all. It's taking everything in me not to call him to see if he's okay. To tell him we'll be okay and that once he works through whatever is haunting his mind, I'll be here. But the truth is, I can't do any of those things. Because I don't know if we'll be okay. I don't know if he'll actually find someone to talk to and work through this. And I don't know if we'll ever come back to a place to give *us* another shot.

Because tonight I saw the man I thought I could potentially love turn into someone I could fear, and I'm worried that all I'll see when I look at him is the guy with vacant eyes and his arm against my throat.

But he's so much more to me than that.

My heart is shattered into more pieces than there is glass on my kitchen floor, and I can barely muster up the energy to stop crying long enough to clean it and order a pizza. But being a mom is weird in that way. No matter how severely broken you are, you find the will to pick up the pieces and be there for your kid. It's me and him against the world. Always has been, and always will be.

As soon as I set my phone down from ordering our dinner, and my tears have finally dried, I glance over to see the picture Hendrix drew while we were making dinner. I walk over to the table and pick it up, and my eyes immediately begin to burn with more tears.

I didn't think I had any left in me.

Before I have the chance to fall apart all over again, Hendrix pulls out the seat next to me.

"Aw, man. I forgot to give Tank his picture," he says simply. As I place my fingertips on the edge, pulling it closer to me.

"That's okay, Buddy. I'm sure we'll get it to him soon." I assure him, forcing a smile as I look back down at the picture of Tank, Hendrix and me playing soccer together.

So. So. Close.

I toss and turn all night, unable to get Tank out of my head. The night replays over and over and the tears just don't stop coming. Between what happened with us, and the memory that forced its way out of my past, I was staring at the ceiling until sunrise.

I thought we had a real shot at something. I feel so stupid for letting myself want something—*someone*—so badly. This is exactly why I've stayed single all these years. Because as soon as my heart gets involved, everything starts falling apart.

I knew things with Tank would be anything but simple, but he was the one person I was willing to take the risk on. Until I realized just how big of a risk that truly was.

The craziest part about everything that's happened, is none of it made me scared of *Tank*. Believe it or not, no matter what demons he's facing I'm not afraid of them. Because I *know* the real Tank—the one that gave me the shirt off his back and danced with me in the bar. The one that looks at me like I'm his saving grace and kisses me like it's the only thing keeping him alive. The one who loves my kid, cleans my house, and rubs my feet. He isn't someone I fear at all, but the darkness he's getting lost in is. He may feel like he's broken or damaged by the things that take over his mind and send him into survival mode, but against all odds, I still love him.

But my love for Tank will never outweigh my love for Hendrix, or my need to protect him. So I'll hope and I'll pray that he finds someone to help him find the light again. And maybe then we can see what's next for us.

TAYLOR

Moving day bitchesssss. 🐦 🏠

SHANE

🐑🐑🐑

ME

Can't wait babe! Also, Hendrix is very excited to be helping today. He has a hard hat and everything. 🐣

LEAH

I fucking love that kid.

LAUREN

We'll have you packed up and shacked up in no time. 😌

TAYLOR

I'm not loving the use of "shacked up" like I'm crashing on his couch until I get my life together but... sure, let's shack me up. 🐣

LEAH

🏠

ME

LAUREN

TAYLOR

I hate you all.

SHANE

You know you love us.

Chapter 19

TANK

THE SUN SHINES through the window in my living room, illuminating the almost empty bottle of whiskey sitting on my coffee table. My leg shakes vigorously as I scroll through every news outlet looking for information on the attack made in Iraq. I've texted every contact I have that could tell me anything about what happened and not a single response from any of them. Suddenly I feel bile threatening to escape my throat when I refresh the website for the Nashville Times Local News and see the headline for the story posted five minutes ago.

Dominic Slater, 35, Marine Raider, killed in Iraq on Thursday during the Raider's attempts to stop terrorist attacks.

Fuck. Fuck. FUCK!

"No. No, no no," I whisper, tears fill my eyes instantly as I run to the sink and heave into it, emptying my stomach of all the whiskey I've put away over the last *however* many hours have passed. I can feel my chest caving in, almost as if it could touch my spine.

I can't catch my breath, and my mind won't wrap around the fact that Dom is gone.

"We could really use someone with your skill set man."

"We ship out next week."

"GODDAMMIT!" I slam my fist down on the counter. "FUCK." I swipe my arm across the surface, clearing it of every single glass and appliance.

What kind of sick torture is this?

I thought my not being there as a potential setback would keep them safe. That they would be better off without me. But now Dom is gone and God only knows what's happened to the rest of them; I'm wondering if I should have fought the decision made for me *not* to return to my team.

I can't go back now.

I wouldn't dare show my face after leaving them like that.

I thought I could start over by coming back to Nashville—make something of myself here and leave the tragic past in the past. I thought I had a chance at a future with the only woman who's ever made me see past the moment we're living in, and the little boy who made me believe I could be a man worth looking up to. And I lost both of them too.

There's nothing left for me here.

I could move and start over somewhere else, but all of my mistakes wouldn't just suddenly disappear. My past would still haunt me and I would end up leaving more damage in my wake as I crash through life like the fucking wrecking ball I am.

I'm done. I can't keep fucking doing this.

I'm done acting like I have a shot at something better. There is no *better* for me. Just what I've already destroyed and what I'll ruin next.

Suddenly an eerie sense of tranquility rushes through my blood like ice, and I know how to make it stop. Just like any other mission.

Eliminate the threat, and protect the innocent.

I take a deep breath, pick up a notepad and pen, and begin writing. I fold the paper and write Tucker's name on it, take my dog tags off and place them on the table next to it, and grab my SIG from the safe. I stare at it a few moments before doing something I told myself I wouldn't.

I pick up my phone, click into my texts with Ruby and the photos of Hendrix and I illuminate on my screen. My heart feels like it's being smothered under the weight of all my regret. With shaking hands, I send one last text to the person I will miss the most, and I place my phone face down on the coffee table. I sit on the couch, a numbness taking over my entire body as I think back on my life.

I think about Tucker, and how he was so young when our dad died and he had to start taking care of things, of *me*, when he was still just a kid himself. The way he has always dropped everything to come bail me out of trouble or sent someone to look after me when he couldn't. I wonder what his life will look like without a brother he feels the need to parent more than befriend.

I think about the guys on my team, tears burning across my face when I think about how they all must feel right now. We served well together, but in the end, I let them down. Another wrong choice under my belt, and now Dominic is gone.

I think about the group of friends I've acquired over the last couple of years, simply from being in Tucker's life and the way they immediately considered me part of their family.

But ultimately, I think about Ruby. From the moment I stepped foot in Chattahoochies, she was like this magnet trying to pull me out of my darkness. Her kindness and confidence, the way she's taken *none* of my bullshit and has always been a safe place for me when I've been at my most vulnerable. I give myself a minute to remember how it felt to have hope. That I might actually make her mine, that the feeling of kissing her wouldn't be a memory I had to replay but a habit I would create. That taking Hendrix to the park, and cooking together would become a regular part of my life, and not something they would have to remember me by.

They'll all be better off without me in that way.

I'm doing this for them.

Closing my eyes, I take in one final breath.

No one tells you what to expect in these last moments. It's not fear or panic I feel, but peace and quiet serenity. Knowing I'm finally making a choice that won't ultimately ruin someone else's life is a sort of freeing feeling. So as the cool rim of the gun's barrel makes contact with my temple, I don't fear the end of my seemingly doomed life, I welcome it.

Click.

Almost immediately my front door flies open, while I sit with my gun still pressed to my skin. My eyes are locked on nothing, but through blurred vision, I can see a figure that looks almost like Tucker moving in slow motion through my peripheral. He's saying something but I can't hear him over the ringing in my ears from the adrenaline. I slowly bring the gun down to my lap and finally hear his voice break through.

"Tank!" He gently grabs my firearm, removing the magazine before setting it on the coffee table beside him, then takes my face in his hands.

"It...It didn't fire," I whisper, stating the obvious as I'm still sitting here with him.

"You–" he starts, but can't quite seem to get the words out.

"It misfired." All at once the anger starts rushing in, taking over any other emotion I may have had leading up to this moment. I stand up, pacing the room while my eyes involuntarily bounce from one wall to another.

"It didn't work. *Why* didn't it work? I can't even do *this* right. Why the fuck can't I just be put out of my misery already?!" I yell, pulling hard at the hair on my head.

"Tank, look at me. *TANK!*" My eyes hesitantly meet his, and I know he can *finally* see the depth of my struggles. "Sit down, let me get you some water." He tries to guide me to sit down, but that's the last thing I want to do. Sit and talk about what went wrong, *yet again.* I shake my head and try shoving him away.

"I don't want any fucking water. I don't want to sit down. I want *out!*" I yell.

"No, you don't. You hear me? You're not leaving me like this, Tank. I won't let you." He grabs me by the shoulders and shakes me, in an effort to pull me out of my panic.

"Look at me," he demands. "You are *not* giving up. You are a motherfucking Marine. You are *my* brother, and so help me, you will *not* leave this world without a fight. You're gonna fight, Tank, and if I have to fight for you until you're ready to do it yourself, then that's what I'll fucking do." His voice shakes as he struggles to get the words out and his hands are wrapped around my neck to keep my focus on him.

"Why bother? What's the point? I don't have a purpose here, not anymore," I manage to choke out.

"You think that just because you left the Marines you don't have a purpose? Try again. I left, Max left–" he begins, trying to calm me down, but fuck all this talk about *choices*.

"Yeah, Tucker. You *chose* to leave. I wasn't given a fucking choice! One stupid fall and I was done. I *was* fighting my fight. I was making a difference over there, and just like that—it was taken away from me. I didn't get a fucking choice! THIS WAS MY FUCKING CHOICE!" I yell, straining my voice as I point to the spot he found me in. "And it was just taken away too."

"And I will be thankful every single *fucking* day that fate knew you weren't done here." Tears begin spilling from his eyes. "Because you have so much to live for, brother. You just have to find something that you love, find a reason, and fucking *live* for it. And you won't find it at the bottom of a bottle or a barrel." Little does he know, I found my reason—she just probably wants nothing to do with me anymore.

With that thought my breaths are short and quick, chest heaving as I struggle to get air into my lungs. With so much anger and adrenaline pumping through me, it winds up morphing into a severe panic attack. In this moment, the one person I need is–

"Tank!"

It can't be.

"Ruby? What are you doing here?" Tucker asks in a confused tone. She shoves her phone at him and takes my face in her hands. My eyes are still zoned out on nothing, though I can tell perfectly what's going on around me.

"Tank, look at me."

There she is.

That calm and steady voice, and those warm brown eyes looking up into mine.

Why did she come here? I thought she hated me.

"Take a deep breath in through your nose." Her fingers caress my jawline and I can feel my heart squeeze in my chest at her touch. I do as she asks, breathing in a deep, shaky breath.

"Another one. Deeper." I draw in a longer, more steady breath and I can feel her relax through her grip on me.

"Good. Now, can you tell me what you smell?" she asks, as I take another breath in. Breathing *her* in.

"You," I whisper, slightly worried how she may feel about my answer. Ruby cuts her eyes in Tucker's direction, then turns them back to me.

"More specifically."

"Cherries," I answer, with a sad smile.

"Now tell me what you can see."

I smirk, knowing how to get a rise out of her. "You."

She lifts a brow in disapproval and I know I have to clarify my answer.

"Your brown eyes. Like melted chocolate and caramel."

Or honey, but I'll keep that between us.

"Good." She lets go of my face and I immediately miss her touch.

"Don't you *ever* scare me like that again." The anger in her voice is accompanied by tears welling in her eyes and all I want to do is kiss her forehead and tell her how sorry I am—for everything.

"You're a lot of things, Tank Landry, but a quitter is not one of them. You better figure your shit out and realize that there are people who are counting on you being around." Unable to fight the need to have her in my arms, I pull her to me, looking at Tucker with reassurance when I answer.

"I will."

Ruby swipes a fallen tear away angrily, her voice shifting into humored annoyance.

"I hate closing the bar with Marco, he still doesn't know how to make a gimlet and it's literally the easiest drink in the world to learn." We both choke out a laugh as we stand there for another moment.

"Why don't we sit down for a minute?" Tucker encourages, leading us all to the kitchen table.

He walks ahead of us and as Ruby pulls away, I can see so much emotion on her face. So many things she wants to say—or yell—and I intend to listen to every single one of them.

"Would you guys mind not telling anyone else about this?" I see Ruby and Tucker give each other a concerned glance.

"Listen, brother. I understand this is a lot to process, but you can't just keep all of this bottled up and act like it never happened," Tucker says first.

"Yeah, I'm with Tucker. You need to talk to someone who really knows how to help you," Ruby adds.

"Just, not yet. Okay? I know I have a lot of shit to figure out, but I'm not ready to talk about it with other people. I can't handle having this conversation with all of our friends. You guys knowing is enough for right now. Okay?" I ask, hoping they'll respect my request.

"Well, I won't tell anyone else. You have my word. But Max knows *something* is up," Tucker says simply.

"Shit. How?" I ask, running a hand through my hair.

"We kind of figured it out together when you didn't show up to work today," he says, making me scoff because of course they did.

"Anybody else?" I ask, looking between the two of them.

"No. Nobody else." Ruby shakes her head. "I told the girls I was going to run out for coffee as soon as your text came through. I didn't want to worry anyone in case... in case I was wrong," she says sadly, looking down at her lap. My fingers twitch to reach out and squeeze her hand, to try and comfort the pain *I* caused.

"Thanks. I appreciate you both keeping this to yourself. And..." I swallow hard past the lump in my throat. "And for showing up for me." My voice betrays me, breaking as I let myself be vulnerable to the fact that someone actually cares about what happens to me. More than one someone, apparently.

"I'll always show up for you, Tank. Just please don't make me show up like *this* again, okay?" Ruby says, squeezing my forearm. Tucker watches as it happens, and lifts a brow at me in return.

"I won't. I promise." And that's a promise I intend to keep. No matter what I have to do to make it happen.

"Okay, well, I better get going. I have coffee to pick up now." She laughs, squeezing my arms one more time before standing from the table.

"Yeah, I can walk you out," I offer, standing from the table. When we reach the door, I open it, and Ruby steps outside, quickly turning around to face me.

"Tank, you didn't... I mean, last night I–" She looks up at me with her eyes full of tears, swallowing hard as she squares her shoulders back. "My life will always be so much better with you in it, Tank. I just wanted you to know that. No matter what." She reaches up and kisses my cheek before rushing off to her car. I close the door and return to the table where Tucker is typing on his phone. I hear the *swoosh* of a sent text message and he locks his phone before looking up at me.

"So," he says expectantly.

"*So...*" I clear my throat, sitting back as I run my hands over my face.

"A lot has happened here today. We're getting a safety crisis plan set up for you immediately and *so much* other shit that you're probably going to despise me for, but it's for your own good. But putting all of that aside, *for now,* can we just go ahead and talk about what the fuck is going on between you and Ruby?"

"Really Tuck? *That's* the first course of action you want to take? Figuring out what's happening in my love life?"

"*Love life?* So there *is* something going on there?" he asks in his annoying, overly amused tone.

"You are unbelievable." I shake my head at him.

"And I'm so glad that you're still here for me to aggravate about it," he teases before his features morph into something much more serious.

"Seriously, Tank. I don't know how I missed so many signs of what you were going through when I went through them myself not that long ago. But I'm so fucking grateful to be sitting here with you right now. I love you, brother. I see you and we're going to get you some help." Tucker's eyes fill with tears, much like my own and I shake my head in agreement.

"Yeah, I uh… I love you, too, Tuck." We stand from the table and he wraps me in an embrace that feels like he's trying to protect me from any harm that may try to come my way—self-made or otherwise.

"Okay." He takes a deep breath, grabbing my shoulders as he backs away. "Grab your shit. Let's go."

"What? Where are we going?" I ask, drawing my brows together in confusion.

"Well, I'm planning to propose to Taylor, and since I'm not letting you out of my sight for the rest of the day, you're coming with me to get a soft pretzel and pick up the ring."

"You're getting *married*? What the hell happened on that road trip?" I laugh, crossing my arms over my chest.

"Grab your shoes and I'll tell you." He wags his eyebrows, making me instantly regret my question.

"You know what, I actually don't want to know. But congratulations."

"Oh, it's too late for that. I'm gonna tell you and next thing you know you'll be asking Ruby to drive to Canada with you." He keeps on while I lace up my boots and we head out the door.

Maybe the darkness that's been taking over my life isn't just my fate after all. Maybe it's something much more complex that I need to face. Something that I need to remove to see that there are actually people in my life who care about me, and *want* me around.

Having Tucker and Ruby both show up for me today made me grateful that by some miracle I've been given a second chance—to dig deeper into what's going on inside my head, and start living a life where I learn to love myself, instead of hating and hurting myself.

After all, if those two think I'm worth saving, then... maybe I am.

Chapter 20

RUBY

SHANE

The game starts at 10 right?

ME

Yes ma'am. You guys coming?

SHANE

Of course! We wouldn't miss it for the world.

TAYLOR

Tucker and I will be there too!

LEAH

If Lauren doesn't forget to come get me I'll be there!

LAUREN

How could I ever forget you, beautiful? You've texted me 15 times to remind me this morning.

LEAH

😊 😊

LAUREN

Leah and I will be there.

ME

 He will be so excited.

SHANE

They're gonna win today. I can feel it.

"COME ON, buddy, we're going to be late!" I call for Hendrix as I finish loading the car.

"I can't find my other shoe!" I barely hear him yell back. I let out a little groan as I unzip his duffle bag and begin sifting through it. After taking out his extra clothes, snacks, and practice ball—I come up empty and shove it all back in before running back into the house.

"You find it yet?" I call out from the doorway.

"No!" He frantically screams from the back of the house. I quickly look through the shoe basket by the door first, then all around the kitchen before finally seeing little black laces sticking out from beneath the couch.

"Found it! Let's roll." Hendrix comes barreling through the living room and snatches it from my hand.

"Thank *you*," he says, plopping down on the couch as he pulls his shoe on.

"See, this is why we are supposed to put our shoes in the basket, and not kick them off like a heathen because you're in a hurry to watch TV." I remind him as I tie his shoe.

"Yes ma'am." He stands up straight and salutes me like a nervous little soldier.

"Okay, we're officially late. Let's run."

"AHHHHH," he yells, as he runs out the front door. Never a dull moment with this endlessly energized child of mine.

"Go Hendrix! You got it, buddy. Take your shot!" I know I must look like a maniac, yelling so hard for a recreational team of six-year-olds, but I don't care. This is the last game of the season and Hendrix is playing his heart out today. His little legs move as fast as they can running down the field and as soon as he's close enough, he takes his shot.

GOAL.

Our little group immediately loses all control as we scream and shout in celebration.

My heart swells with pride seeing him make his very last goal of the season, but it also sinks with a hint of sadness when I see him looking up and down the sidelines for someone who isn't here.

Shane is sitting in her foldout chair with her hand propped up on her belly. Taylor, Leah, and Lauren are all on their feet right beside me—since my anxiety is keeping me from staying still long enough to sit in one of the many chairs we have lining the field. Tucker and Max are standing right behind Shane, talking about all things *sports* and shouting *"Atta boy"* and *"Way to stay on it"* like the proud uncles they are. But the person I know would be the most proud of him, besides me probably, isn't here. He hasn't been here all season, and even though I knew he wouldn't be, a naïve part of me thought he might come today. Tucker makes it a point to drop hints that he asks how we're doing and checks in on us, but it's not the same.

Tank quit his job at the bar shortly after trying to take his own life, started going to therapy, and has been working really hard on getting better. At least that's what I was *told*. About a week after I saw Tank last—the day he quit—Tucker handed me an envelope with my name on it.

"He asked me to give this to you since he doesn't know when he'll see you again. Said the letter should explain everything."

As if my heart hadn't already broken enough at the hands of Tank, that day my heart turned to ice. After everything we'd been through, we were over just like that, and he couldn't even tell me himself. I never bothered opening the letter he gave me because I knew it didn't matter what was inside. If the decision not to see me needed to happen as part of his healing process—if it would help him get better and keep him from wanting to take his own life again —then I was going to accept it, regardless of how much it hurt. So I didn't read it, because I didn't want to hurt anymore. Though, I'm not convinced that method actually worked.

When Hendrix stopped asking where Tank was every time I took him to play soccer at the park, and the spark left his eyes on park days, it felt like someone had shoved a dagger into my heart. The ice protecting it had cracked and the pain was back, because we both missed Tank, and there was nothing I could do to fix it.

Eventually, the time came to enroll him for fall ball. I suffered the worst case of anxiety I think I've ever had because I was worried he would ask if Tank would be there—and as many times as I racked my brain to come up with an answer that wouldn't disappoint him, I came up empty. Much to my surprise, he never asked about him. He simply told me he still wanted to play and never asked who would be at his practices or games. But in this moment—after making the winning goal for his team—I can see that he's looking for *him.*

I've been grateful that some, if not all of the rest of our group has shown up for every single one of his games so long as their work schedules didn't interfere. He's always so excited to see them and I think it helps take the sting of who *isn't* here away.

"Hey Rubes, I think we're gonna head out," Shane says, waddling over with a pained expression she's doing her best to hide.

"Of course, I'm so glad you guys made it." I smile, leaning in to give her a hug. "You okay? You look a little… uncomfortable." Shane is almost 40 weeks pregnant and has been complaining about little pains here and there that remind me of the days leading up to having Hendrix.

"Yeah, I think I just need to lie down and drink some water. He did so well this season, we are so proud of him," she says, waving off my concern as she gazes at Hendrix.

"You did good with him. He was by far the best one on that field," Max agrees, earning a swift elbow to the ribs from Shane. She quickly looks around and grins apologetically at the other parents who just heard Max indirectly insult their kids' skills.

"Yeah, I don't care. It's true." He shrugs, making me laugh as they walk towards the parking lot. I wish I could take credit for how well he's done, but most of what he learned was from Tank, I just kept doing what he'd taught us. Plus he had a decent coach this season.

"We're gonna head out too. I have a few late showings today," Lauren says as she and Leah take turns giving me a hug.

"Thanks for showing up, you guys. I know it means a lot to him."

"He's our guy, of course, we're gonna show up for him." I smile through the pain of her words as they wave goodbye.

"Mommy! Taylor and Tucker want to buy me an ice cream for scoring the winning goal, can I have one?" he pleads, giving me those *please don't say no* eyes.

"Of course, you can, superstar." I bend down and squeeze him tight, giving him a quick kiss on the cheek. "I am so proud of you, Hendrix. You played so hard this season. I hope you're proud of yourself too." I smile at him, quickly taking to memory the joy on his face before he takes off towards Taylor and Tucker. I mouth *"Thank you"* to Taylor who gives me a big smile in return before scooping Hendrix up as they make their way to the concession stands.

I stand there watching a little longer as Tucker lifts Hendrix onto his shoulders and even though they're about a football field away, I can hear Hendrix laughing as Tucker leans from side to side like he's going to drop him—which I know he won't. I giggle to myself and just as I'm about to start packing our things, all of my attention gravitates to a familiar sound. A voice I feel like I haven't heard in ages carries across the field like it's riding on the current October breeze.

Tank.

I don't have to look long before finding him, and a wave of mixed emotions floods through me. I can't quite see *who* he's talking to but I could care less when I hear what he says next.

"Yep, number five. Never been more proud in my life." His deep laugh booms through the air, stealing all of my breath and melting every bit of ice that's lived around my heart these last six months.

Number five. Hendrix's number. He showed up for him.

I feel tears forming in my eyes just as a crowd of people walks in front of me, obstructing my view of him. I swallow past the lump in my throat and politely excuse myself, backing up a few steps to let them through. I'm seconds away from leaving all our belongings behind to head in his direction, but when the crowd finally clears he's nowhere to be found. I look up and down the entire field, and over by the concession stands to see if he was headed to see Tucker, but he isn't there either. It's as if he's just vanished—no matter where I turn there's no trace of him at all.

I feel my heart sink again as I turn back to finish packing our things.

Did I imagine that?

Have I gotten delusional?

Do I actually miss him so much that I'm hallucinating him?

I try to shake it off so I can meet up with Taylor and Tucker, but as I'm putting our chairs back into their bags, I get this sinking feeling in my stomach that I can't quite place. It's not just sadness from thinking about Tank though. It's similar to that anxious/frightened feeling you get when you leave your baby for the first time after having them and your mind is going through all of the horrible thoughts of what might happen while you're not around. Or when it feels like something is about to go horribly wrong, you just don't know what it is yet. But the last time I had this feeling was last year at the mall when I thought I saw–

"So. It seems as though you *didn't* take care of our little problem, did you Ru?" My stomach immediately drops, not stopping until it feels six feet underground. I turn around slowly, coming face to face with the same man who's haunted my dreams for the last six and a half years, and panic immediately sets in.

Mark.

Part Two

Chapter 21

TANK

PRESENT DAY

Full commitment to focusing on myself and the journey to heal my mind.

By far the worst—albeit necessary—thing I've ever committed to. Cutting ties with Ruby to become someone she can trust and feel safe around feels like the most contradictory thing I could possibly do, and I'm not even doing it well. I've resorted to asking Tucker about her and Hendrix and lurking around the soccer fields just to see for myself that they're okay. In the short amount of time I got to know Ruby she completely inhabited every part of my mind. Not a day went by where I wasn't thinking about her—her laugh, her eyes, her smile, those *lips*. There wasn't a thing in the world I wouldn't do for her, and in the process, I was losing pieces of myself I didn't realize were missing. After starting therapy I realized that I had to let her go, only for a while, if I ever wanted to become a version of myself that could get her back and *keep her*. Even though our time apart didn't start as a plan to focus on myself, I know now that it was needed. I did the right thing, I did what she *asked*. But that still doesn't guarantee everyone will be happy about it.

Shit, *I'm* not even happy about it, but the fact that my flashbacks have only been in occasional nightmares, the blackouts have stopped, and the anger I was harboring over things out of my control has been faced and forgiven makes it all seem worth it.

Giving myself distance to get my mind right was definitely necessary, but the day I've been waiting so impatiently for– the day I'm finally back in Ruby's orbit– may be here much sooner than I thought. Because the same guy that was just asking me who I was here to watch is putting a look of fear on Ruby's face I wish I'd never seen. Though I don't normally worry about Ruby being able to handle herself, she seems completely frozen right now and there's not a single one of our friends around to have her back if need be.

After assessing the situation and seeing how uncomfortable Ruby is, I immediately grab my phone to text Tucker.

ME

Keep Hendrix by the concession stands until I say otherwise.

TUCKER

Wait. You're here? This is getting really sad dude.

ME

Not now Tuck. I'm so serious.

TUCKER

Ok. He won't leave my sight.

Within 30 seconds I'm approaching Ruby's side and while my outward appearance is as stoic as ever, my heart is about to hammer out of my chest, worried how she may respond to my sudden reappearance.

Six months. It's been six months since I've seen her and I'm probably about to cross so many lines.

I don't even bother second-guessing myself though, because

when I see her up close she's ghost white and looks so scared that it makes me want to snap necks and ask questions later.

"Hi, Honey. Surprise." I wrap my arm around her shoulders protectively, planting a kiss on the top of her head.

"Tank." She breathes my name out like a confused prayer and every part of me wants to kiss my name right off her lips. To breathe her in and give myself the time to take in every last beautiful feature I've missed for six months. "What are you doing here?" she asks, looking up at me as a little bit of pink paints her cheeks.

"I know you thought I had to work today but I got off early. I wouldn't miss our little man's last game." I wink at her, seeing the confusion deepen in her eyes.

"*Our?*" the guy asks, his tone nothing short of repulsed. "Wait, are you... You're *married?*" His entire demeanor changes, as a look of shock washes over him. I knit my brows together as I look down at Ruby, seeing something change behind those sweet brown eyes when she barely hums out, "Mhm."

Mhm? As in, yes mhm?

I have no idea what's happening, but that's not about to keep me from playing along. I drop my hand to her waist and pull her in closer, making her look up at me.

"What is it, ten short days now until I get to watch you walk down the aisle?" She doesn't say anything in response. She simply looks up at me, eyes wide as can be as the blush in her cheeks darkens. I smirk at the fact I can still make her blush, and then she turns back to stare at *him*, allowing her features to immediately harden when she does.

Don't look at him. Look at me.

"I'm sorry, and you are?" I ask, looking back as if I forgot he was there at all.

"Someone you'll be seeing again, *very* soon," he scoffs, giving Ruby one final look of disapproval before walking away. I watch with my jaw set tight as he gets into a blue Tesla and drives away.

"Oh my god, what the hell did I just do?" she asks, pulling away from me slightly, the anguish on her face making me feel unsettled.

"Who was that?" I ask, though I'm not sure she hears me.

"*Why* would I do that? Why would I *say* that? *Mhm.*" The panic in her voice puts me more on edge than I was before.

"Ruby, who. Was. That?" I demand. I have my suspicions but I need to hear it from her. I need to know for sure.

"That was Hendrix's father," she answers, looking as though all the life is draining from her while she stares blankly into the parking lot. "The man who didn't want me to have him." Tears fill her eyes as she looks up at me. "The man who threatened my life if I didn't *get rid of him*," she says in a whisper, looking around self-consciously as she wipes a stray tear that's fallen.

Fuck. I'm going to kill him.

"I need to go find Hendrix." Her breaths are quickening and I can tell by the look in her eyes she's on the verge of a panic attack as she begins frantically walking away. I step in front of her and grab her by the shoulders gently.

"He's with my brother. He's safe—and so are you. I've got you." As if the dam of emotions within her breaks from those nine words, she lets herself fall apart in my arms. The frantic gasps for air mixed with sobs take turns stealing her breath.

"Okay, okay. Ruby. Hey." Keeping my voice as steady as possible, I bend to pull her focus back to me, holding her arms to steady her as I try my hand at one of the only things that's ever helped me in these situations.

"Tell me what you can see." Her eyes dart around for a moment before they lock with mine.

"Trees, your tattoos, your green eyes. They look like emeralds." I smirk, loving how it feels to know she's looking at *me*.

"What can you smell?" I ask, remembering vividly the order she's asked me these questions in.

"You. Sandalwood and musk and your peppermint gum." When

her eyes fall to my mouth, it takes everything in me to stay focused on the task at hand.

"Good. Now, what can you feel?" Her eyes begin to water as she squeezes my forearms. She doesn't answer but she's breathing more steadily now, so I pull her into my chest, holding her tight and running my hand through her hair as I plant kisses on the top of her head. I can't believe I went six whole months without holding her.

God, I fucking missed her.

"Are you actually here?" I hear her muffled voice ask, as she squeezes her arms around me.

"I'm here, Honey, and I'm not leaving you again," I assure her. Her fingertips dig into my back, like she's scared I'll disappear from her grasp. I close my eyes to savor the moment. though it doesn't last nearly long enough.

Parents begin cheering as the next game starts up, startling Ruby and causing her to step out of my embrace. When I see the tear stains on her cheeks I pull her over to an empty area near the parking lot so we can talk.

"Forgive the ignorant question, but are you okay?" I ask, watching as she spaces out again. She shakes her head no, not meeting my gaze.

"Did he say anything to you? Before I got over here." Her eyes shift, but she doesn't answer.

"Do you have any idea why he would show up here?" Her lip quivers and her eyes well with tears again as she shakes her head once more. I take her chin between my index finger and thumb, tilting her head back just enough to make those beautiful eyes of hers focus on mine.

"Why did you say yes when he asked if we were married?" I ask, not at all upset by the idea, simply curious given our distance these last few months. She scoffs, wiping her tears away angrily as she tries to shake her head no again—avoiding answering the question.

"*Ruby.*" She stills in my grip, eyes unwavering from mine as she visibly swallows.

"I got scared," she whispers. "It felt safer to make him think–" she trails off, mentally talking herself out of finishing that sentence.

"To make him think what?" My hand caresses her cheek before tucking a strand of hair behind her ear.

"It's so stupid." She scolds herself, averting my gaze by taking in her surroundings.

"Tell me anyway." She looks back up at me, eyes bouncing between mine as she takes in a deep breath.

"To make him think I was yours. That way he couldn't get to me because there was someone like you protecting me." The way she keeps her eyes locked on mine, when I know she wants to shy away after making such a bold statement is one of the many things I love about Ruby.

"I will always protect you. You should know that by now." Her vulnerability is quickly replaced by a flash of anger as if what I've just said sparked a dormant feeling to life.

"Then where the *hell* have you been the last six months? Huh?" My brows knit together in confusion. "You just quit the bar and disappeared then sent Tucker to play mailman."

She didn't read it.

"Ruby..."

"You know what? Let's not do this." She holds a hand up to stop me as I try stepping closer to her. "I'm sorry you got dragged into the bullshit from my past, but I can handle it. Excuse me, I have to go find my son." She starts walking away and I hate that it feels a lot like I'm losing her again.

But that won't stop me from trying to make amends. I know she needs space after everything that happened just now—so I'll give it to her. But I'm done staying away. I've waited long enough, I put in the work to heal, and though she may be refusing to acknowledge it right now, Ruby *is* mine. And God help the man who tries to touch her while she is.

"Consider our wedding officially *off.*" She stops and calls over her shoulder, making me grin instinctively.

For now, Honey.

MAX

Heading to the hospital. It's baby time boys.

TUCKER

Yes, Taylor is already yelling at me. We'll probably beat you guys there.

ME

On my way. ⚓, 🎈

"Oh shit, you really brought balloons?" Tucker laughs when he sees me walk into the waiting room.

"Don't be snarky just because you didn't bring something," I snap back.

"I brought the woman who will undoubtedly be buying clothes for this child every time we leave the house until it graduates."

"Alright, that's fair." I chance a look in Ruby's direction, but she, Leah, and Lauren are all huddling around each other, waiting for any incoming text updates from Taylor.

She seems different, but I'm not sure *how*. She hasn't looked my way, she hasn't spoken to me again, but there's an energy around her that just isn't *Ruby*. I may have been gone for six months, but I still know my girl and something is heavy on her mind. Maybe I really crossed a line at the soccer fields the other day, or maybe she's still mad at me for not being around as much. Regardless of what it is, or how much I want to work things out with her, this isn't the place and it's *definitely* not the time.

"IT'S A GIRL!" the three of them shout in unison, as tears begin to fall and they embrace each other. Not long after Max walks through the door, eager to introduce us to their new baby girl.

Chapter 22

RUBY

"How is any of this even possible? Can he really do this?" I feel like I'm having an out-of-body experience as I sit here in an attorney's office discussing the possibility of losing my son. My pride and joy, the reason I live, my *everything*.

The day after Hendrix's soccer game I was served papers that stated my ex was suing me for custody of Hendrix. After the initial shock and panic attack wore off, I spent the next day and a half googling every reputable law office in the area with an attorney I could afford.

"Unfortunately, he can."

"But he's not even on his birth certificate. He has no legal rights to him. Right?" I argue helplessly.

"In that case, he will probably request a paternity test first, and then see where things go from there. Unless you're wanting to skip that and just confirm the paternity without it." I let out a frustrated groan.

"Doesn't the state of Tennessee take into consideration that he's been with me for his *entire* life, that he's in school, he never misses a checkup at the doctor, and has a full support system outside of just me that ensures his well-being? He's safe. He's loved. He's healthy. What more do they need to see he's exactly where he belongs?"

I know the words coming out of my mouth make sense, so why the fuck is she shaking her head no at me.

"Since the father had no prior knowledge of the child's existence, he's claiming he was never given the choice to be involved in his life and help raise him." The tone of her voice, along with the words coming out of her mouth feel like needles in my skin. I can feel myself staring at her like she's from another dimension because she *has* to be if she believes any of the things she's saying.

"All of that is such bullshit." My eyes widen as I look back at her apologetically, though she just lifts a brow back at me. "He knew about him. He didn't *want* him, and he even went as far as to threaten me if I didn't *take care of it*. That's why I made sure he didn't know about him after that, he's *dangerous*. How does *none* of that matter? How is he still in a position to take *my child* away from me? A child he *did* know about and didn't want." My eyes are overflowing with tears, as she keeps herself mechanically professional.

"Do you have any proof of those things? A police or hospital report? Any witnesses? Threatening text messages? Handwritten notes or emails?" I hang my head, knowing my answer leaves us in the same position we started in.

"No."

"Did you ever file a restraining order against him?"

"No." Because to do that he would have to be notified about it, and I didn't want to give him any leverage to find me.

How did he find me?

She lets out a sigh, straightening her shoulders as she reaches across her desk.

"With you being a single mother, relying on his school and child-care to take care of him a majority of the time, the judge may see it as a good thing for him to finally get to know his father. Being in a more financially stable home, or a home with *two* parents—or both —could be good for him."

The fuck did she just say to me?

I've died and gone to hell, haven't I? Because this is my worst nightmare.

"Maybe if you were married and could offer the same support financially as you claim you can emotionally, things would look different for your case." I could rip this woman to shreds if I could do anything but sit here with my mouth hanging open right now.

She brushes it off as if there's nothing left to do. The finality in her voice makes me want to throw up in panic. That's it? He comes waltzing in out of thin air and starts making claims that are *bullshit* and actually stands a chance to take my kid because I'm not *married?* Fat. Fucking. Chance.

"But, I'm engaged," I blurt out, causing her to sit up straighter in her chair.

Shit. Shit. Shit. Why did I say that?

"Oh." Her brows knit together. "You hadn't mentioned that before." She flips through her paperwork, likely checking to make sure she hadn't overlooked that detail. "Well, I suppose that *could* help your side of things. Let's get that information added to your paperwork and go over some details."

That's why.

The smallest new hint of positivity in her tone almost makes me ill. As if I didn't stand a chance of keeping full custody of *my* son without being legally bound to another person. I smile and nod, giving simple one-word answers as she asks me things about my *fiancé*. Each vague answer I give makes me question my decision to bring him back into this even more.

For instance... *Name?*

"I would love to sit down with the two of you at some point and go over some things about the case, would that be okay with you?" Rounding her desk to see me out, I smile to keep the nausea at bay.

"Of course." I keep it together until I'm back in my car, then it hits me. I have to actually *tell* Tank about this now.

Shit. What have I done?

Knock knock knock.

Tank opens the door to his apartment, and all the air I'm holding in my lungs escapes when I see him. His dark brown hair is longer than usual, going all different directions like he just rolled out of bed, his beard is fuller making his green eyes stand out against the dark scruff and tanned skin, and he's wearing blue jeans with no shirt.

I can't stop staring at the tattoos that cover his chest and all the way up his neck, that is until I notice the defined "v" that travels well beyond the waistline of his jeans when he props his arm up against the door.

"Hey, Honey. Everything okay?" The deep rumble of his voice rattles me, reminding me of why I'm here.

"No." I shake my head, willing my voice to steady.

"How can I help?" He opens the door further, ushering me in. As soon as I'm through the threshold, and no longer distracted by his body, my mind starts going a million miles a minute.

"What's your name?" I blurt out frantically.

"What?" he asks with a laugh, closing the door behind us.

"Like your real name? Is Tank on your birth certificate? Is it short for something? When's your birthday? What are you even doing for work now? Oh yeah, and *where the hell have you been the last six months?*" I yell at him, feeling the warmth of a tear roll down my cheek. I know I'm only rambling because I'm completely panicked, but as I pace around his living room, he just stands there—watching as I yell at him.

It reminds me of the day he picked up Hendrix from school and spent the day with him. I got home to a clean house and hot dinner and I went on and on about how it and he just... let me.

"You've known me for two years, how do you not remember when my birthday is?" He shakes his head, looking genuinely confused. I shoot him an annoyed look, bothered by the fact that *that* is the detail he settled on questioning. Instead of answering him, I continue.

"How could you just leave me like that? After *everything* that happened, you just disappeared on me, on *Hendrix*. You crushed him, you know? You crushed him and you crushed me and I am *so SO* mad at you for it." I'm completely sobbing now, as I see the pain wash over his features. His brows knit together, jaw ticking rapidly as he visibly swallows. He looks like he might say something, but when he doesn't I ask the only thing I really need to know at this moment.

"Are you better now, Tank? Please tell me you're better now." I blink away the tears, holding my breath as I await his answer.

"I am. Much better than the last time we were here," he says, glancing around his apartment. I take a minute to look around, remembering every single thing I felt during the drive over here that day. Seeing him standing in the living room when I walked in opened my eyes to how much I truly cared for Tank.

"Ruby." He moves closer to me and I can instantly feel the heat radiating from him. "What happened?" I take a deep breath, breathing in his intoxicatingly sexy scent, as he runs his hands along my arms.

"He's trying to get custody of Hendrix."

"Not fucking happening." His jaw flexes with anger and instinctively I run my fingers along his jawline. His eyes soften at my touch, making the butterflies I had all but forgotten about flutter back to life.

"It might. Depending on what judge gets the case."

"How is that even possible?" he asks, shaking his head in disbelief.

"They're trying to make it seem like I've been keeping his child from him for six years, and since he's got money, and a wife apparently, they're painting it like he's *such* a suitable father. Which is the biggest fucking lie on the planet." Flashbacks of the last time I saw him begin fighting for my attention, so I squeeze my eyes shut to will them away.

"What did your attorney say? Do you have a good one?" he asks, studying me as I feel every nerve in my body telling me to run out the door. I nod in agreement that I have one, but I clam up at the thought of giving him a verbal answer about what she said about the situation.

This is crazy. Asking a guy I once considered my best friend— who I thought I would fall in love with—who then became a stranger for most of the year, to *marry me* so I can keep my kid. Why drag him into this mess? Sure he played along at the soccer field when I said we were, but he had no idea of the depth of the situation. How could he when I've never had the guts to tell anyone the entire story?

For all he knew he was helping me let someone down easy and that would be the end of it. But this is Hendrix we're talking about, and if there's one thing I know for sure, it's that I would do *anything* to keep him safe. Including fake a marriage.

And I have a feeling Tank will do the same. For Hendrix.

"That being in a serious relationship... that having a *fiancé*, could help my case tremendously. That it gives me less of an *edge* than that of a single mother who works in a bar and relies on friends and babysitters to take care of her child." I would laugh hysterically if I didn't feel like I was dying on the inside right now.

"Fucking legal system." He scoffs, rolling his eyes.

"Tank..." He looks back down at me. "I told my attorney I was engaged... To *you*," I admit sheepishly. His eyes widen slightly, though I can't quite get a read on what he's feeling.

"I think the only way I can win this is if I get married." As if the nausea from this situation wasn't bad enough, the vulnerability I am feeling right now is ten times worse. I'm not even sure I said it loud enough for him to hear me, and if I have to repeat it I might actually pass out.

My hands are shaking rapidly and my breath is stuck in my throat as he takes a deep breath in. Never breaking eye contact as he studies me closely.

"Okay," he says, walking over to his kitchen counter. He grabs a stack of Post-its and a pen, tossing them onto the table as he nods for me to come over.

"What's this?" I ask, looking up at him.

"Tell me what you need me to do and I'll do it." Emotion wells from deep in my chest, making my eyes water.

"Just like that?"

"Just like that."

"Are you sure?" A deep chuckle rumbles out of him as he smirks at me.

"Ruby, I've always known you'd burn the world down for Hendrix, I'm just gonna be there to hand you the matches." I smile in appreciation, wiping the tears that have spilled onto my cheeks as relief washes over me. For the first time since I got those papers, I feel like I may actually have a shot at keeping Hendrix with me— where he belongs.

"So what's this for?" I point to the stationary on the table.

"Terms to abide by. Write down what you want, what you expect from me when we go into this, and we'll sign our names to it."

"On a Post-it? What if I have a lot of terms?"

"I have another stack in the drawer." He shrugs, handing me the pen with a smirk on his face. I roll my eyes and take it from him, then I write down my terms and we sign it.

Terms of Marriage

For the duration of our marriage I agree to be Honest, loyal, and to keep my promises.

Above all else, I will Keep Hendrix safe. No matter what.

X Ruby   Tank

"One last thing," he says, tossing the pen on the table before grabbing my hand.

"What?"

"Ruby Ranes, will you marry me?"

Breathe, Ruby. Breathe. We don't need another see/smell/feel moment right now.

Six words I never imagined I would hear, especially from Tank, but my heart still stops for a moment when I hear them come from his lips.

"You don't have to do that, we both know this is strictly circumstantial. You don't have to make it seem... *real*." I drop my head, still embarrassed that I've dragged him into this at all, but all I hear is him snickering.

"Listen to me." He tilts my chin back up, something I've always loved that he does to bring my attention back to him. "If this is going to work, we're going to have to make it seem as real as possible. That means we play the part and we make it believable. I'm not letting you lose Hendrix, but if this is what it's gonna take, then we have to be all in for it. Are you sure you're ready for that?" I take a moment to appreciate the changes I see in the man standing in front of me today.

He's so steady in the midst of a storm that isn't even his to weather. He's confident in his ability to do this, when there was a time not so long ago that he would have run for the hills at the request. He would have tried to convince me he would only make things worse, but I see none of that self-doubt in him today. Is *he* ready to be all in for this charade? Because if I'm honest with myself, I don't know if I am. The feelings I've had for Tank are nothing short of complicated, and to marry him, *legally marry him,* and have to make it believable to anyone who may be watching—all while having no clue how he feels about me after being apart for six months— sounds like very dangerous territory to waltz into.

"For Hendrix?" I ask, unable to ask the question that's *really* burning in my mind. He nods once in agreement.

"Then yes. I will marry you." He gives me a questioning look, my last chance to back out. "I'm ready."

"Okay. Then we have a lot of details to discuss, *fiancée.*" He smirks, gesturing for me to follow him to the sofa. Still shirtless, dreamy as ever, and sending a rush of heat through my body at the sound of him calling me his *fiancée.*

Shit, I am so not *ready for this.*

"Hey, Tank?"

"Yes, Honey?"

"When did you get a puppy?" I point to the dog that just appeared in the hallway that could be Riley's miniature twin.

"Like I said, a lot to discuss." He winks, nodding over to the couch.

Chapter 23

TANK

IT'S true that I would do anything to help Ruby keep Hendrix with her and away from the asshole who shares his DNA, but I'd be lying if I said I'm not thrilled by the opportunity that's fallen into my lap. The time we spent apart was agonizing, yet necessary. For me to heal, to forgive myself, to accept things that had been keeping me in the dark, and to grow into someone worthy of her—her love, her time, her respect. I had every intention of proving that to her when she was ready to see me again, but now that I've realized she never read my letter, I wonder if she even cares about those changes at all. She thinks I abandoned her and Hendrix and without the explanation I *thought* I gave them, that's exactly what it looks like.

I'm not here because she still has feelings for me, or even because she missed me. I'm here because I inserted myself back into her life when I thought she needed me, and caused a problem only I can help fix now.

Ruby can think my participation in this is strictly to keep Hendrix safe—which will always be top priority—but she's sadly mistaken if she thinks I won't take this time to prove to her just how much we should be together. In a few days, Ruby will be my wife, and I fully intend to treat her as such.

"So, does Hendrix know about any of this yet?" I ask as Ruby's eyes roam around my exposed chest.

"Are we skipping the conversation about the dog?" she asks again, moving her gaze to have a nice little staring contest with the gorgeous brown and black Malinois.

"I got Maverick a few months ago. After spending a lot of time with Max and Riley, I thought he would be good for me." She nods in response as Maverick tilts his head to one side.

"Lay down Mav," I command, not missing the way Ruby begins rubbing at the goosebumps on her arms.

"I'm sorry, do you think you can put on a shirt?" she says, closing her eyes as she shakes her head in frustration.

"Weird request from my *fiancée*," I tease.

"Tank, be serious." She groans, giving me *the look*. The look that says *"please, for me"* that could get me to start wars for her without thinking twice about it. But the edge to her tone isn't one I'm used to, so I stare at her a moment longer in surprise.

"I'm sorry, I'm fucking starving and having a really shitty day. Plus, I can't focus when all of your muscles are staring at me so, can you... please?" She waves a hand up and down my body.

"Yes, ma'am." I grab a clean shirt out of the hamper on my coffee table, holding my arms out for her approval once it's on.

"Thank you." She sighs, looking at me bashfully before plopping down on the sofa as she lets her head fall back on the cushion. "No, Hendrix doesn't know anything yet."

"Do you think he'll be okay with it? Us getting married I mean. Do you think he'll understand?" I feel the nerves shaking in my chest as I sit down beside her on the couch.

"I don't know, honestly. I *hope* he will. I know he really looked up to you before–" she stops herself, quickly looking my way to gauge my reaction.

"Before I hurt you?" My jaw ticks as I try not to let the guilt and pain from that memory override all the healing I've accomplished since then. But fuck it's hard not to.

"Before you *left*," she corrects, causing a frown to appear on my face involuntarily.

"What?" A small smirk appears on her face as she turns her head to look at me.

"The night that everything happened, I was so worried that he would be just... absolutely traumatized. Ya know? But you want to know what he said to me?" Her eyes are glistening and I can tell she's fighting back tears.

"He told me that you once said you would never hurt me, that you would protect me because I was one of your *important people*," she says, using air quotes. "He immediately assumed that what happened between us was an accident and after making sure I knew we were safe—the way I always do for him—he was *so* bummed that he didn't give you the picture he colored." The countless emotions I'm feeling right now are making my head spin. I'm sad that I disappointed Hendrix, I'm angry at myself for not getting help sooner—to keep that night from happening in the first place—and astounded at the way he handled things at his age. Most of all, I'm curious about how *she* feels about all of this. But *wow* is the only word I can force past my lips.

"Was it true?" she asks, biting on the inside of her cheek. "Was I one of your most important people?"

"No. Not *was* true. It *is* true. You *are* one of my most important people, Honey. Always will be," I correct, taking her hand in mine as she studies my face. "Would it be okay with you if we told him together? Just in case he has questions about where I've been lately?"

"Of course." She smiles sweetly in agreement before confusion washes over her features. "So where *have* you been working? Since you left the bar?"

"I got a job as a personal trainer at Hall's Gym."

"I thought they were closing or something?"

"They had been talking about selling but I think one of their sons moved back to town to run it so they wouldn't have to," I explain, seeing the way her mind is somewhere else completely.

"Oh, good." The emptiness in her response almost makes me laugh. Like her brain is on autopilot for this conversation.

"Come on, let's go." I offer her my hand as I stand from the couch.

"What? Where?"

"Well, if it's alright with you, we're going to go tell Hendrix what's going on. I know it must be killing you every second that passes that you haven't told him." She smiles up at me gratefully. One thing I've always loved about Ruby's relationship with Hendrix is that she's always so honest with him. She doesn't brush things off as unimportant when he asks questions, so long as it's nothing *too* mature for him to know about, she tells him. "*Then* I'm taking you two out to dinner so we can put that hangry little beast back where he goes." I boop her nose and she rolls her eyes, but the sweet smile beneath tells me she's not really mad.

"Are you sure? I mean, I know we still have a lot to talk about," she asks hesitantly. I see the way her nerves are starting to take over, so I do what I've always done and lean in to kiss her forehead. Not missing the way her eyes fall closed as she releases a more steady breath.

"Look, we're about to have all the time in the world to catch up on current events. Let's go talk to Hendrix now." I see the relief on her face as she lets out a breath.

"Okay."

"And Ruby, never second guess my willingness to be by your side, you hear me?" She nods in agreement as curiosity sparks behind her eyes.

Good.

I want her to wonder if my words hold a deeper meaning. Because she'll find out soon enough what every last one means. No more staying away. No more uncertainty. When the storm finally settles, she'll know just how much marrying her isn't me doing her a favor, but *us* finishing what we never got the chance to start.

"It alright with you if Mav comes?" I ask, nodding to where he's sitting by the door waiting for us.

"Of course it is." She smiles over at him, making him tilt his head at her again.

Being back at Ruby's house isn't as hard as I thought it would be. I assumed I would be flooded with horrible flashbacks of that night, and that I wouldn't be able to shake the gut-wrenching feeling of failure, but I'm not. I remember the night vividly, of course, but that twisted part of my mind isn't in control anymore. I'm able to remember and regret the things that happened without it sending me into a complete spiral, which is giving me the reassurance I needed to really take on my role here.

The only thing making me nauseous now is waiting for Ruby to get back with Hendrix from next door. I have no idea what to expect when it comes to how he will feel seeing me again. Will he still be angry? Will it be like no time has passed? Will he have a thousand questions, or will we be back to where we started when he didn't speak to me at all?

My heart races faster as I hear them outside the front door. I love this kid, man. I can't stand the thought of him hating me. When the door finally opens, I rub my sweaty hands against my blue jeans as I stand up from the table. Hendrix freezes in the doorway and blinks a couple of times as if he's letting his eyes adjust. Then my heart completely stops at what he does next.

"Tank! You're back!" he yells, running over to me. His arms wrap around my legs and I feel tears immediately flood my eyes. I really thought he was going to hate me.

"Hey, buddy, it's good to see you." I do my best to keep my voice from wavering, but I fail. Ruby stands still in the entryway as tears fill her eyes, a look of shock painted on her face.

"Are you feeling better?" He pulls away staring straight up at me, I look at Ruby for further explanation but she shrugs in confusion.

"What do you mean?" I bend to his level, hoping he'll give us both a little clarification.

"Uncle Tucker told me that you had to go away for a while because you needed help to feel better. That's why I didn't see you for so long." He grabs my face in his hands, moving one hand from my cheek to my forehead. "So do you feel better now?" I've never wanted to thank my brother for sticking his nose where it didn't belong more than I do right now.

"I do, buddy. I feel a lot better. Thanks for asking." I smile at him, and he smiles back—showing off two lost teeth.

"I missed you a lot," he whispers, making it hard for me to catch my breath.

"I really missed you too, bud." He lets out a big gasp as he looks over at Maverick.

"Is that *your* dog?" He looks back over at me with wide eyes.

"Yep. That's Maverick, wanna go say hi?"

"Just a sec. I'll be right back!" he yells, taking off down the hallway. I can't help but laugh as I stand back up and start walking towards Ruby, who still hasn't moved from the entryway.

"You alright, Honey?" I place my hands on the back of her arms, rubbing gently up and down as she begins to relax.

"I just... I had no idea what to expect. I'm honestly shocked and so relieved by how well this is going." She laughs.

"Tank, Mom, come here!" Hendrix calls us over as he sits on the couch with Maverick at his feet. He leans down to let Mav sniff his hand before petting him gently on the head. Ruby and I take our seats, and with one of us on each side of him, he hands me a piece of paper barely containing his excitement as I unfold it. Warmth spreads through my chest when I look down to see a picture of the three of us playing soccer.

"Wow, little man. This is a really good picture." I smile at him but his features drop and he clams up a little bit.

"Thanks," he mutters under his breath.

"What's the matter, sweetie?" Ruby asks, pulling him closer, as his eyes trail up slowly to mine.

"I played soccer this year," he says sadly. "I wish you could have seen me."

"I saw," I tell him, nodding my head.

"You *did?*" He looks at me curiously, and I see Ruby mimic his reaction.

"Your very first game you were the only one on the team that even got close to scoring a goal. The next few games you were the *only* one to score. The night one of your teammates showed up in a cast you played goalie for the first time and stopped all but one ball from getting through. I was so proud of you because even when you got upset you took a deep breath and kept playing your best. And at your last game—*you* scored the winning goal." I poke his chest as his eyes grow wide. His expression is ecstatic as he hears me recapping his plays.

"You were *there?*" Ruby chokes out.

"For every game."

"But I never saw you." Hendrix frowns. I take a deep breath, trying to find the best way to explain myself. And with Hendrix, that's always with the truth.

"I know, buddy, and I'm sorry about that. I was trying to make sure I was all better before seeing you and your mom again. I had to make sure I was keeping you both safe."

"So you were watching, but you couldn't come to talk to us because you had to protect us?" he asks, picking up one of his toys off the couch. I avoid looking at Ruby at first, unsure how she may feel about me borderline stalking them, but when I finally do, she's staring back at me with misty eyes. And though I'm answering Hendrix's question, I'm making a promise to her as well.

"Yeah, bud. I'll *always* protect you." She blinks a few times as she looks away, readjusting her position on the couch. She uses my statement as a segway into why I'm here in the first place and taps Hendrix's to get his focus back on her.

"Hey, I actually have something to tell you. It's *really* important. Are you ready?" Hendrix nods again and Ruby glances at me before she starts.

"How would you feel if I told you Tank and I were getting married?" I can hear the encouragement in her voice, projecting that this is a good thing, but I can also see the nervousness in her eyes as she awaits his response.

"Like Uncle Max and Aunt Shane?"

"Yes, exactly." She smiles sweetly at him as he grows excited, then his face twists.

"Do I have to wear a suit again? That thing gave me wedgies." I can't help but laugh remembering how mad he was in that suit at the wedding. Then he lights up again.

"Does this mean I'll get a baby sister now? I like baby Cece, she looks like a baby doll but she's squishy." He makes little pinching motions with his fingers, making me chuckle.

"No. No suits, No babies." She cuts him off quickly.

Oh, I'd definitely put a baby in her.

"Oh. Okay. Then why are you getting married?" he asks. When I look at Ruby I can tell she's drawing a complete blank. I'm sure of all the questions she thought he might ask, *that* wasn't one of them. Because the *real* reason we're getting married isn't a reason she's ready to give him. So I take her hand in mine and fill in the blanks.

"Because, I can't imagine two people I would rather spend my life with than the two of you. I know I was gone a long time and that this might be a little confusing to you. But would it be okay with you if I married your mom, and stuck around for a while?" I smirk at him, and his smile lights up the entire room.

"Hell yeah!" I stifle a laugh as Ruby's mouth pops open.

"Hendrix Ranes!" Ruby scolds, making his hands fly up to his mouth.

"Sorry sorry sorry." His muffled apology comes out as she gives him a disapproving look. "I mean, *heck* yeah." I'm still trying to hold my laugh in when Ruby sends Hendrix to get ready for dinner.

"You're back for five minutes and he's already talking like you," she teases. I glance down and smile when I notice she hasn't let go of my hand yet.

"I'm sure you've said far worse than that," I argue playfully, squeezing her hand in mine. Though I wish I hadn't brought attention to it, because she immediately lets go.

"Absolutely not. I have the mouth of an angel." She tosses her hair behind her shoulder, and for a moment it feels like old times. When we would be cracking jokes together around the bar—usually at Marco's expense—with the mood light and a smile on her face.

I missed this. I missed *us*. But when she mentions her mouth, my attention immediately fails to focus on anything else, and her lips have me reminiscing. I run my thumb along her bottom lip, catching her off guard as her eyes snap up to mine.

"Maybe so, but I happen to recall how downright sinful you taste." She lets out a small gasp as my tongue swipes along my bottom lip and a grin spreads across my face. We both pull away when we hear footsteps approaching.

"Can Tank and Maverick go Trick-or-treating with us after dinner?" Hendrix asks, skipping into the living room. I look over at Ruby whose eyes are wide with regret.

"Oh, shoot. Buddy, I forgot to get you a costume," she admits, barely glancing at me out of the corner of her eye.

"Maybe I can wear my Spidey costume from last year?" He perks up, making Ruby laugh regretfully.

"Umm. No chance that's gonna fit you again unless you're going as Spidey turned Hulk." Hendrix's face drops slightly, and I can see the way Ruby is beating herself up over this. She's not the one to forget *anything* when it comes to Hendrix, especially not Halloween. This custody shit must be taking up more room in her brain than I realized.

"Maybe I can help." I give Hendrix an optimistic smile, making his face light up instantly. "May I?" Ruby gives me a curious stare but finally nods and I take Hendrix with me to grab a small duffle bag I keep in my truck before we head to his room to DIY a costume.

"Okay, Mom, you ready?" Hendrix calls, hiding us behind the wall that leads to his bedroom so she can't see us yet.

"I don't know, *am I?*" she sings out. Hendrix jumps out from behind the wall in the camouflage pants he's been wearing since I got here, a black long-sleeve shirt I found in his closet, and combat boots—complete with war paint and a Nerf gun. Then I follow behind wearing my uniform pants, boots, and a black T-shirt—and a little bit of war paint at his request.

"We're *battle boys!*" Hendrix yells, making me choke on a laugh.

"Sure, we'll go with that," I agree, squeezing Hendrix's shoulder. Ruby's hand comes up to her lips, hiding a smile as she looks at us.

"You boys look incredible." When she looks at me I can see the gratitude in her eyes, I give her a wink and call Maverick over to stand by us.

"Let's go get some candy then." I clap my hands together.

"We're still eating first, right?" Ruby asks, grabbing her keys from the counter.

"Of course, Honey. You ought to know I'm gonna take care of you first." I give her a wink, not missing the way she pulls her bottom lip in with her teeth as I walk past her.

After swinging through a drive-thru for some food, we stop at one of the most festive neighborhoods in the city to trick or treat. I thought Hendrix was being a little over-zealous when he took the pillowcase off his bed to use as a bag, but he filled the damn thing up more than halfway before we called it a night. Ruby has been talking about her feet hurting since we reached the end of the first road and though I take Maverick on runs regularly, I'm pretty sure he's been giving me the death glare since about the 20th house.

"Thank you for tonight, Tank. I really owe you for the way you came through for him. I can't believe I forgot his costume." She shakes her head, chastising herself as she leans against the frame of her front door. Hendrix is already in the house doing inventory of his candy, and Maverick took it upon himself to jump into my truck to lie down once we got back.

"Hush, woman. You owe me nothing." I smirk at her. "It was a lot of fun actually. I can't remember the last time I smiled that much." She looks up at me, the light from the front porch illuminating her brown eyes in a way that could have me lost in them for hours.

"Yeah, I've missed that smile," she says quietly, almost as if the thought wasn't supposed to be vocalized.

"I've missed yours too." I tuck a strand of hair behind her ear, fighting every cell in my body that's begging to kiss her. "Goodnight, Honey."

"Goodnight." She smiles, watching from her doorstep until I'm out of the driveway.

While Trick-or-treating the other night, Ruby and I were able to vaguely discuss when the wedding would need to happen—given the statement I made to her ex at the soccer fields—our backstory in case it comes up, and how we should tell the people closest to us. The conversation ended when we got back in the car to head home, but we did make a plan to tell our friends today when we all meet at the bar for weekly drinks—something I've missed tremendously over the last six months. I haven't missed drinking as much as I've missed being with everyone in one place.

"My brother. Welcome back to family drink night," Tucker says with open arms as I walk into the bar.

Curious glances are exchanged around the room, but all the girls end up looking straight at Ruby. I go in for a hug with Tucker and can't help but notice how Ruby's gaze is on *me*, while four others are on her. When I make my way behind the bar the looks of confusion don't stop, but finally Shane breaks the silence.

"So, what's going on? You haven't texted us back in *days*, should we be worried?" she asks, bouncing Cece in her arms as she sways back and forth. Tucker slides Taylor a water, catching an annoyed look from her as he takes her empty martini glass away, and everyone else looks at Ruby with anticipation.

"Sorry about that, there's just been a lot going on..." She glances at me with a look of nervousness on her face. When she begins chewing on her lip I know her anxiety is piquing, so I take it upon myself to relieve her of the stress.

"Ruby and I are getting married," I announce rather loudly to the group.

"Oh my god." Taylor chokes on her water, holding a hand to her chest as she coughs. With several mouths hanging open and looks of disbelief being directed at Ruby, I instinctively move closer, draping my arm over her shoulder and turning my face into her.

"Do you want to tell them or do you want me to?" I whisper in her ear, earning a look of appreciation from her when she pulls back slightly.

Those fucking eyes.

I could get lost in them for hours if ever given the chance.

"I got it," she whispers, taking a deep breath in.

"Hendrix's father recently showed back up." I notice how Ruby looks over at Max, and when I follow her gaze he looks more pissed than I think I've ever seen him before. "After finding us, I was served papers that he's suing me for custody."

"But why? After all this time, why now?" Lauren asks, genuinely confused. Ruby hangs her head as she fidgets with her fingernails.

Peeling off the plum purple nail polish before looking back up with misty eyes. I've never seen Ruby cry this much and I absolutely fucking hate it. Happy tears are the only exception, but the fact that she's sad and *scared* has me edging closer to the decision to take this guy out and eliminate the problem altogether.

"Because, *technically*, he didn't know he existed until recently," she says, not looking back up.

"Ruby, if you're not ready to explain this to us, you don't have to. You don't owe us an explanation. But, I *am* confused why you two getting married has anything to do with that," Shane interjects, squeezing Ruby's hand.

"I promise I'll fill you in on the details soon, I think I'm still in shock or something. But for now, I can tell you this—me being a single mother who works at a bar with no reliable spouse, no secondary income or care for Hendrix, doesn't look good for my case. Not when *he's* the perfect man on paper." Her tone is laced with bitterness as she trails off.

"That's fucking bullshit," Max growls from his barstool.

Ruby takes a deep breath in, shaking her head to compose herself like the badass we all know and love.

"Tank and I are getting married. He'll be my *reliable spouse*, and possibly my only shot at keeping my kid. And I need you guys to make it happen in two days," she says, holding her head high as she looks at the girls.

"You two are literally trying to kill me, aren't you?" Taylor says, glancing between Shane and Ruby. Shane just rolls her eyes, but before another word is said, Lauren is on her feet.

"Anything you need babe, that sweet boy isn't going *anywhere*."

"Yeah, there's no chance in hell this guy stands a chance against you," Leah assures her.

"Text me what you want and it's yours," Taylor agrees.

"Can I interest you in the world's tiniest flower girl?" Shane smiles, tipping Cece in her direction making Ruby cry, *again*.

"I don't know what I would do without you guys." Then she

turns to face me completely, not hiding behind a subtle glance or a whisper this time. *"Especially* you. I'll never be able to thank you enough for this, Tank." I admire her willingness to be so bold in front of all of our friends, but I am not quite ready to tell her what a pleasure it's going to be for me to do this. So I pull her into me and kiss her forehead. Saying all the things that words can't, once again.

ME

You sent $500 to Lauren Long via ApplePay

LAUREN

???

LAUREN

If that was an accident good luck getting it back.

ME

Can you take Ruby out today? Get manicures, or her hair done. Whatever she wants. I know she won't accept it from me, but I want today to be special for her & make sure she has a dress she loves.

LAUREN

Oh. my. Fucking. God. You're in love.

ME

Didn't ask for your opinion, Sour Patch. Can you do it?

LAUREN

You know you text me for a reason. Of course I can.

LAUREN

You're alright Landry, you know that?

ME

Just make my girl feel special until she'll let me do it myself. And don't mention any of this to her. Please.

LAUREN

#swoons

ME

I have no idea what that means.

Chapter 24

RUBY

LAUREN

Get dressed baby. I'm picking you up for some wedding day pampering.

ME

You don't have to do that Lu. You know it's not like that.

LAUREN

First of all, I'm already on the way so I'll hear NONE of that. Second of all, let's pretend that it is.

ME

Fine. See you soon.

I'M KIND OF glad Lauren insisted on getting me out of the house today, even if it's for something as silly as *wedding day pampering*. Hendrix demanded he hang out with the guys today and I've spent way too much time alone with my thoughts. My anxiety is at an all-time high now that I've had a moment to let the entirety of what's happening settle in and I feel like I've gone completely mad.

My ex is back.

No one knows *who* he is.

No one knows *why* I disappeared with Hendrix to get away from him.

And here I am. Getting my nails painted with my best friend, prepping for my *wedding* to my situationship turned future husband, as if everything is completely normal. All while being in a constant state of fear over losing Hendrix if this doesn't work out as planned.

I think I'm gonna throw up.

"So," Lauren says, abruptly interrupting my thoughts. "Are you a *white on your wedding day* kind of girl?"

"Lauren. Stop." I tilt my head giving her an annoyed look.

"*What?*" She feigns innocence.

"It's not *real*," I whisper, catching an eye roll from her.

"Can we just pretend for like five minutes that it is? I want to know what your dream dress looks like. What flowers are you carrying? *Where* are you getting married? Tell me the vision, because I know you have one," she insists, throwing my thoughts into high speed. And once the vision appears, it's hard to hold back from telling her what it is. So I cave.

"Yes. I'm a *white on my wedding day* kind of girl." I roll my eyes back at her. "There's this dress I saw online once and I've loved it ever since. It's completely silk, floor length, of course, with a slit up the thigh, and the sleeves kind of hang off your shoulders because the bodice is tight enough to hold it up. Oh, and a sweetheart neckline that makes the girls look good," I admit, feeling a bit embarrassed that I actually *have* thought about it, and never even realized how much. We both laugh when she realizes how into this I am.

"Keep going," she encourages. I roll my eyes again, sighing as I continue.

"Black roses with African lilies. I've never really thought of *where* I'd get married, though if it were a fall wedding–"

"How convenient," she interrupts dramatically, bringing attention to the fact that it *is in fact fall*. "I'd want it to be somewhere where we could see the sunset while we say our vows." I start to dissociate as I get lost in the idea of it all. The sun setting over the horizon, the sky looking like a painting straight from Shane's studio, while I stare into the eyes of the man I'm marrying, vowing to love him forever and him vowing to protect me and Hendrix no matter what. My heart thumps rapidly against my chest like it's trying to escape when the word *protect* floats through my mind.

"I'll always protect you."

"You see him, don't you?" Lauren's voice is much softer when she disrupts my vision this time.

"What?" I ask, noticing a dampness between my thighs that only ever shows up at thoughts of *him*.

"When you picture your wedding, you see Tank. Even in the fantasy—it's him isn't it?" My heart flutters and I feel as if the breath has been knocked out of me when I realize how true her words are. Because when I was looking into the eyes of the man promising me forever, they were the same bright green eyes I've gotten lost in countless times before. Though I have no desire to admit that to Lauren in the middle of the nail salon.

"Nope. It's you. I think you're my true love. Run away with me Lauren. Let's leave this cruel world behind, what do you say?" She can't contain her laughter as I go on and on like I'm trying to land a role in a Hollywood production.

"Well, you're *definitely* my type..." she says, playing along like she's contemplating it. "Ruby," she says in a more serious tone. "It's okay if it is him. If anything, isn't it better that way?"

"It's just so complicated. He was gone for *six months*, and it's not like we saw each other every now and then, it was complete silence. I know he had to take care of himself, and I get that, I really do. But I had to convince myself he didn't care about me at all anymore to keep from living in a constant state of heartache, and knowing he still saw *everyone else* but me, kind of made it feel true." I laugh sarcastically. "And *now* I'm literally *marrying* him. Within five minutes of being around him again, I dragged him into my bullshit in the most permanent way possible, without even a *Hey, how have you been?* I don't know why he would ever agree to this, I mean it's *crazy*."

"Ruby–" She tilts her head in disbelief, but I quickly shake my head to stop her from trying to make me see it differently.

"Look, I'll have plenty of time in the coming days to dish out necessary apologies. I'm just counting myself lucky that he even agreed to this in the first place. We both understand that this is strictly circumstantial—to give the appearance of stability to a judge in hopes they see how much Hendrix should stay with me. With *us*. We agreed to keep Hendrix safe, that's all this is. So why complicate it with old feelings that he probably left behind months ago?" I see her mouth pop open, but then it closes again and I turn to examine my nails.

"Okay. I'm sorry I brought it up. You handle this however you need to, and I will support you no matter what. Can you just do one thing for me?" she asks, making me look over at her once again.

"I'm scared to say yes."

"Just for today, keep pretending. Live in the fantasy for a little while. Then you can go back to your *circumstantial* way of thinking after you say I do." I give her a disapproving look, but she raises a brow at me in return. And if anyone knows Lauren, they know better than to argue with her. I swear if she ever got tired of being a real estate agent she would make a great lawyer.

"Fine." The devilish grin that appears on her face immediately after makes me wish I could take that one single word back.

"You're gonna be a wifey." She does a little happy dance in her chair, making her nail tech scold her.

"I regret everything that's transpired here today," I say quietly, shaking my head.

She smirks at me as she taps her phone screen, causing it to make a *bloop* sound from her sending a text.

Shit. What did I just agree to?

"Guys, what are we doing here? We have to go, or did we suddenly forget that I have to get married in like three hours?" They haven't told me *where* I'm getting married yet, which has my anxiety at an all-time high, but I trust these girls with my life, so I made the choice to trust them with my fake wedding too.

"Of course, we didn't forget. *That's* what we're doing here," Shane says sweetly as we stop outside of the courthouse—and for some reason, my heart sinks.

Where else should a fake wedding take place?

"Oh," I say, trying my best not to let my disappointment show. "Right. Of course." I try playing off my initial surprise, but as always, they see right through me.

"Come on, this way." Leah laughs, pulling me behind her. I glance at Lauren who has a smug look on her face and I can't quite tell what she's up to. When we stop again, I see it. Behind the courthouse is the most beautiful court*yard* I've ever seen. There's a large pond and the perfect view of the western horizon. The open field leading up to it has been transformed into the perfect outdoor wedding space with a flower-covered arch and exactly seven chairs.

"You didn't." I look at Lauren in disbelief.

"Just for today," she whispers, laying her head on my shoulder.

I take a moment to think about the day I've had with Lauren and the conversations that took place in the nail salon. The manicures, the hair appointment, the dress shopping where I found a simple white dress to wear tonight, and how I actually allowed myself to get excited over those things. Pretending it's real isn't going to make this *easier*, it's going to make it that much harder when I'm hit with a vivid reminder that it's *not*.

"Guys, I can't do this," I say, feeling dizzy from all the second-guessing. "I can't keep pretending this is all real. I mean, what the hell am I thinking? We should just grab a judge, and make it happen inside—quick and painless. Because it... it's gonna hurt too much to act like it's real when it isn't." I find myself on the verge of sobbing as they all take turns trying to calm me down. Pretending Tank and I are getting married because we're in love is only setting myself up for heartbreak—because we're not. I've been through that with him before, and I don't plan on doing it a second time.

"Ruby. Hey, *breathe,*" Lauren says, taking both of my hands in hers. "Okay. No more pretending then. But the dress, the place, and the fact that we're all here for you, none of that changes. We'll just refocus on *why* you're doing this, okay? For Hendrix, right?" I nod as she regains my focus. "So then, do *all of this* for him." She motions to the courtyard again, "Because he thinks it's real too." Tears begin forming in my eyes as her words sink in.

"You're right." I blow out a shaky breath.

"Now... We have one more thing to tell you," Leah says, looking around at the group nervously.

"What is it?"

"You and Tank have a room at *The Vista* tonight." No one moves, I don't even think they breathe as they await my reaction, and to my own surprise, I don't have one. Maybe my brain is shutting down due to how absolutely overwhelming this feels. Who knows? But maybe this will give us a chance to actually talk about the last six months, *and* what the next six may possibly look like without worrying if Hendrix is listening in. Maybe having a room somewhere away from the house will be a good thing.

"Okay," I say flatly. They all look at each other and shrug when they realize I won't be putting up a fight.

"Let's get you married then," Taylor says, breaking the silence as she links her arm with mine.

"I may have *one* other surprise for you," Lauren whispers as we walk across the street to the hotel. After seeing the last-minute venue they just took me to, I can only think of one thing it might be.

The dress.

How she found it, and how she *afforded it* is beyond me, but she made it happen. As I stand here looking in the floor-length mirror in what will be mine and Tank's room later this evening, I try my best to compartmentalize my emotions.

I feel absolutely beautiful. Exactly how a bride would hope to feel on her wedding day. Suddenly I'm worried I'll show up to Tank in jeans and a baseball cap thinking this is just another Saturday afternoon. I should know better though. At the very least Taylor will make sure he is wearing a dress shirt for this.

"One more thing," Lauren says, handing me a small box.

"What's this?" I turn to face her, taking the box and opening it to reveal a beautiful silver locket that has a sapphire in the middle of it.

"Something blue," she shrugs, looking into the box with me.

"You are the most incredible friend, you know that?"

"I do, thank you so much," she says, making me laugh as she grabs my bouquet of fake black roses and African lilies.

Lauren and I grew very close, very quickly, after being introduced. I can't quite put my finger on it, but something between us just *clicked*. I love every single one of these girls I call family, but if I were going to have a Maid of Honor by my side today, there's no doubt in my mind it would be her.

"But that's not from me," she says quietly, making my brows knit together skeptically.

Is it… from Tank?

I open my mouth to ask her where it came from but I'm stopped by the door to the room opening.

"Let's go, people. The boys are officially waiting," Taylor announces as she walks into the room, dropping a small black duffle bag on the coffee table. Lauren clasps the locket around my neck as I grab my phone, checking it once more before handing it over to Leah. Tank and I haven't talked much since setting this all in motion, so I'm a little shocked when I see his name on the screen.

TANK

See you at the altar, Honey.

Butterflies flutter to life in my stomach, though I'm unsure if it's from excitement or nerves. With no time to spare, that thought gets thrown onto the back burner as we make our way across the street. I'm so focused on not tripping, and remembering to breathe, that I don't even realize when we make it to the wall of hedges that hides me from the view at the altar.

"Max is on his way to walk you down the aisle." My eyes widen as Shane gives me a puzzled look. "What? Do you want to take a chance of tripping down this hill in that dress?" she remarks.

"*No.*" I mouth off. As soon as Max rounds the corner in a suit, I stand up a little straighter. He freezes in place as if he's been stunned while he takes in my appearance.

"You ready?" he asks, clearing his throat.

"As I can be." I offer a tight-lipped smile, as the girls scurry down the hill. When it's just the two of us, I feel this overwhelming sense of disappointment from Max.

"I'm sorry I didn't tell you what was going on." I drop my head as he walks over beside me.

"Ruby, you've been like family to me for seven years. You don't owe me or anyone else here an explanation. But I saw the pain in your eyes when you told us he was back. I just never want you to forget that you can come to me when you need help." A tear rolls down my cheek and I swipe it away before my makeup smudges.

"Well, I couldn't exactly ask for your help with *this,*" I tease, trying to lighten the mood. He chuckles and shakes his head.

"Yeah, I suppose not." His smile fades and he looks at me more seriously now. "You sure you know what you're doing?" he asks, sending me into an immediate panic.

"No." I laugh, "But we'll figure it out." We stand quiet for another moment before a thought comes crashing to my mind.

"Oh, shit." I look up at Max with wide eyes. "Um, I really appreciate you offering to walk me down the aisle, but uh, I think I need Tank." He raises a brow at me.

"Isn't it bad luck to see the bride before the wedding?" My face drops in annoyance.

"*Really?* You too?" He looks at me more curiously. "It's not real," I whisper, making him roll his eyes as he turns to walk back down the hill.

"Yeah, it is, Rubes. It's very real. The sooner you realize that, the better." His words make my stomach drop, he takes another step before turning on his heel. "By the way, you make a beautiful bride."

"Thanks," I mumble, then he's gone.

What the hell is that supposed to mean?

I mean, I'm not an idiot, I know this is *legal*, but if he meant what he said, in the same way *I* did, then I feel completely in the dark.

"Is everything o–" The deep voice that sends heat throughout my body causes my eyes to snap up instantly.

"Oh my god."

Oh my god.

He's wearing his Marine's dress blues, and he looks so fucking handsome.

Chapter 25

TANK

THE SLY WINK Lauren gives me as they take their seats lets me know she did what I asked. I'm grateful for her participation because I knew there was no way in hell Ruby would let any of this happen without the persuasion of her friends. My palms are sweating as I wait for her to appear over the hill. I can't wait for her to see the view—there's a light fog settling over the pond behind the courthouse and the sky is the most beautiful shade of purple tonight as the sun is setting and if that doesn't feel like fate, I don't know what does. A few minutes pass and Max appears, *without* Ruby.

Shit. What happened?

When he walks up to me he shrugs.

"She said she needed you." I'm not sure I've ever felt joy like this before. Hearing that Ruby said she needed *me*. I'm practically sprinting as I make my way up the hill, but when I reach the top, I still don't see her. I walk a few more steps and round the corner where a wall of hedges stands.

There she is.

When my gaze lands on her I have to blink a few times to ensure my eyes aren't playing tricks on me.

"Oh my god." The words slip past my lips before I realize I'm saying them out loud. Her eyes snap up to mine and a look of shock similar to the one I'm wearing spreads across her face.

"Honey, you look... *perfect*." Her eyes glisten as they make their way to mine after taking in my uniform.

"So do you." Her voice sounds so small today. Ruby is typically loud, confident, and unafraid to speak her mind, but today I can feel her holding back.

"Is everything okay? Max said you needed me?" I try to hide the pride in my voice, though I'm feeling it everywhere else. Her head drops as she picks at one of the black flowers in her bouquet. The most *Ruby Ranes* bouquet of flowers I've ever seen and I fucking love it.

"Yeah. I just..." She lifts her head, bravely looking me in the eye. "I am so sorry, Tank. For all of this. I know you had your reasons for putting distance between us, and I learned to be okay with that. But dragging you into this mess the *day* you showed back up in my life. I'm not sure I'll ever be able to apologize enough for that." Her lip quivers as she tries to keep her composure.

I want to shake her and tell her if she'd just read my letter, she would know why things were the way that they were. Then she might understand that the time we spent away from each other didn't make my feelings for her *change*, it only magnified them. Then she might know that being here with her today is the best possible outcome I could have hoped for. But I don't have time to tell her all of that now. Because there's a judge and a purple sky waiting for us at the bottom of this hill and I refuse to let her miss it.

"Ruby Ranes, you listen to me and you listen closely. Do not *ever* apologize for giving me the opportunity to stand here with you today. Because if I didn't want to be doing this, I wouldn't." Her eyes don't waver from mine as she takes in every word of what I've just said, nodding to let me know she understands.

I know she's probably still thinking I'm only doing this for Hendrix, but she'll soon learn that if it were anyone else but her, anyone else but *them*—I would offer to bury a man before committing myself to a marriage I wanted no part of. But it's not anyone else, it's Ruby and Hendrix—and when I pictured a future for myself worth living for, they were it.

"Are you ready?" I ask, tucking a stray hair behind her shoulder.

"I'm ready," she agrees. I offer her my arm and she links hers through it. Before we make it two steps, she pulls me back to stop me.

"Wait." She gasps. "I forgot the whole reason I needed you up here." My brows knit together in confusion.

"Which is?"

"What's your legal name?" She glances at my name badge that reads *T. LANDRY* and looks back up at me. "Or is it really Tank?" I can't help but laugh as I remember her barging into my apartment asking that very question a week ago.

"Uh, it's Tate. Tate Landry."

"Tate," she whispers, smiling to herself. "So where did Tank come from then?" She laughs, the sight and sound making time stand still as I take her in.

"Long story short, I ran Tucker over with our battery-operated Jeep...*several* times when we were kids." I chuckle, remembering how mad he would get when I would catch him and take him out at the heels.

"Oh my god, that doesn't surprise me at all," Ruby exclaims, laughing once again.

"Shall we?" She nods in agreement as we begin walking down the hill again. I glance down at her when she gets her first glimpse at the sunset, and the look in her eyes puts the most gorgeous sunset I've ever seen to shame. Nothing compares to the beauty that is my wife.

When we make it to the altar, I can tell the judge is saying something, but Ruby during golden hour is something to be savored. My attention only refocuses when the judge starts the Declaration of Intent.

We both make it to the part where we say *"I do"* but Ruby has barely looked up at me through the entire ceremony. I know this isn't ideal for her, but I need those honey-brown eyes on me. When I reach over and grab her pinky with mine she finally looks up, stealing my breath with one simple look. I can't believe we're actually here.

"Do we have the rings?" The judge asks, as panic immediately flashes across Ruby's face. I simply give her a wink and pull them out of my pocket. She looks up at me in surprise as I hand mine over to her.

"It is now time to say your vows. Ruby, repeat after me." And she does.

"With this ring, I thee wed. I do promise to love, honor, and cherish you, in good times and bad, for richer or poorer, in sickness and health, until death do us part."

But now it's my turn, and I won't do this without her full attention on me. When her hand is held out for me to slip her ring onto her finger, I lift her chin the way I've done so many times before, as I begin repeating our vows.

"With this ring, I thee wed. I do promise to love, honor, and cherish you, in good times and bad, for richer or poorer, in sickness and health. **Not even death shall part us.***"* I can see Taylor's mouth pop open from my peripheral vision, and Leah slapping Lauren's arm relentlessly. But my main focus right now is the way Ruby's breath picks up ever so slightly from my words. It's a small change to our vows, but one I will take very seriously.

See, I like to think death tried to keep us apart once– and failed. After months of healing, and learning what exactly I would live and die for—they're both *her*. I'd crawl out of the deepest of graves to be with her.

"By the power vested in me, by the State of Tennessee, I now pronounce you husband and wife. You may now kiss your bride."

Everyone remains still and silent, but Ruby's eyes stay locked on mine. Looking for an answer to what we do now. But before she can try to find a way out of it, I pull her in close and my lips come crashing down on hers. I don't know when I'll get the chance to make this happen again, so I take my time savoring every moment. When her hands find their way to the nape of my neck and she kisses me back, the small flicker of hope I've been holding onto begins to grow into a flame. Daring to burn down every wall she has up trying to keep this from being real.

Our friends applaud and cheer as Hendrix runs up to us, bringing our kiss to an end as he wraps his arms around our legs.

"This is the best day ever." He tilts his head back to exclaim.

"I agree." I smile down at Hendrix who looks between Ruby and me with the biggest grin on his face, but when I look up at Ruby, she still seems *off*.

"Alright little man, you ready to go?" Max asks Hendrix, picking him up like a football.

"Can we have ice cream tonight?" he yells through his giggles.

"I don't see why not. Cece is up and down all night, we might as well be too." Max shrugs, before planting Hendrix's feet back on the ground.

After we've said all our goodbyes and it's just Ruby and me next to the water, the tension filling the air is almost unbearable.

"So, Hendrix is staying at Max and Shane's?"

"Umm, yeah. They asked if he could stay over tonight to give us some time *alone* I guess." She laughs nervously.

"Okay. Well, do you wanna head back to the house then?" I ask, trying to break through her closed-off demeanor.

"Actually." Her head drops as she fidgets with her dress, allowing the slit to fall open just enough to show off her tattooed thigh. "We uh, have a room over at *The Vista*," she admits, as her cheeks turn pink.

"*Oh?*"

"Yeah, but we don't have to use it. The girls probably just got it for me to get ready closer to the courtyard or something." She waves a hand dismissively, making me smirk when I realize she's nervous.

"Let's use it." She slowly looks up at me, and I have to fight every instinct urging me to kiss her again.

"Are you sure? What about Maverick?" I love that she asked about him.

"Tuck can take him. He's always trying to steal him from me anyhow." I shrug.

"Okay," she agrees. I hold my hand out to lead her up the hill, but when we're only halfway up her heel gets caught in the back of her dress.

"*Shit,*" she mutters under her breath as she tries to unhook it.

"Come here," I say, scooping her up in my arms causing a gasp to escape her lips. "I got you." I walk all the way across the street and into the hotel lobby before planting her feet back on the ground.

"You did not have to carry me all this way." She smiles, adjusting the sleeve of her dress.

"What kind of husband would I be if I didn't?" I wink at her, grabbing her hand as we walk towards the elevators. Thanks to Lauren I already have a room key, and I *may* have called ahead to have the room "*tidied*" before we returned. When we walk in the door Ruby immediately kicks off her heels, shrinking about five inches then she rounds the corner and freezes.

"I can't believe them. This is way too far," she says in a quiet but angry tone.

"What do you mean?" I ask, setting my cap on the table.

"It's so stupid," she scoffs, though an embarrassed hue of red begins heating her cheeks.

"The girls tried to convince me to pretend that today was *real*. I agreed just to avoid arguing with Lauren, but they took it too far with this. I'm so sorry." She moves toward the bed, likely to begin removing the rose petals that have been placed on the mattress, but I quickly stop her before she has the chance.

"They didn't do it," I admit, seeing the confusion spread across her face. "I did." A deep blush appears on her cheeks as she nervously bites the inside of her cheek.

216

"Why?" she asks quietly, glancing at the bed then back at me. I hate living in this state of constant misunderstanding with Ruby. I never planned to come back and make things *more* complicated, but ever since that day at the soccer fields it's been nonstop planning—a backstory, a wedding, a plan to keep Hendrix *far* away from the asshole who's appeared out of nowhere to try and take him. But tonight it's finally just me and her, and I fully intend on clearing up any confusion that may still live in that pretty mind of hers.

"Because I wanted to." I shrug, smirking down at her.

"I don't understand." I sigh, leaning against the desk directly behind me.

"Well, that's probably because the only talking we've done in the last week since seeing each other again has been about today and everything leading up to it. But the six months prior are still a mystery, and you're confused. That sound about right?" She nods her head in response.

"Then allow me to make it less confusing for you." I pull a letter out of my pocket with her name scrawled on the envelope, and hand it over to her.

"What is this?" She takes the envelope and inspects it closely.

"That's the letter I wrote you six months ago." The confusion on her face almost makes me laugh. "A copy of it. I didn't trust that Tucker wouldn't end up losing the first one."

"Ah."

"But that's not what happened, is it? You got the letter, you just didn't read it."

"What are you, psychic now?" She tosses her hands in the air, getting worked up at my accusation.

"No, I just–"

"Tank Landry disappears for six months, comes back omniscient," she says as if she's reading the headline from a paper. "You know, texting still works too. Or hey, showing up in person. Telling me face to face why you're still going to see *everyone else* we hang out with, but not *me!*" she snaps, looking up at me as she gets all this pent-up frustration off her chest.

"You might want to stop yelling at me," I say, flexing my jaw as I notice her breasts straining against her white silk dress when she puts her hands on her hips.

"Oh really? And why is that?" As soon as the words leave her lips, I pull her body flush with mine, pressing her tight against my waist. Her eyes grow slightly as she looks down then quickly back up at me.

"Because it gets me hard when you're all worked up." She stands motionless as her eyes bounce between mine. "*Especially* when you're wearing *my* ring, in a wedding dress that I'm dying to see on the floor. Now, are you going to read the damn letter, or do I need to read it to you?" Her eyes are wild with emotion as she pulls away and rips open the envelope, and my heart begins to race.

I've been so sure that I handled things the right way, but at this moment I'm terrified I may have been wrong. That she'll read it and still not understand my reasoning. But it's a little too late for second-guessing. She unfolds the paper and walks over to the bed, sitting down as she begins to read it.

RUBY,

I HOPE YOU CAN FORGIVE ME FOR SENDING TUCKER TO DELIVER THIS LETTER,
BUT I KNEW IF I LOOKED INTO THOSE HONEY BROWN EYES OF YOURS,
I WOULD NEVER HAVE THE STRENGTH TO FOLLOW THROUGH WITH WHAT I HAVE
TO SAY. YOU KNOW THAT SPACE YOU TOLD ME YOU NEEDED? I'M GONNA DO
MY BEST TO GIVE IT TO YOU. BECAUSE I REALIZE HOW HORRIBLY I MESSED UP
THE OTHER NIGHT, AND I WILL DO WHATEVER IT TAKES TO MAKE UP FOR IT.
TO SHOW YOU HOW TRULY SORRY I AM FOR PUTTING YOU IN THAT SITUATION.
BUT I WANTED YOU TO KNOW THAT I'M GETTING HELP. WHICH IS ONE OF THE
REASONS WHY I'M WRITING YOU THIS LETTER. TUCKER HELPED ME FIND A
THERAPIST THAT HAS EXPERIENCE DEALING WITH VETERANS, AND I'M GOING TO
SEE IF SHE CAN HELP ME FIGURE MY SHIT OUT.

I WANT YOU TO KNOW HOW MUCH I WANT TO BE WITH YOU RIGHT NOW, BUT
I DON'T KNOW WHAT COMES NEXT, AND I DON'T WANT TO PUT ANY PRESSURE
ON YOU TO BE AROUND ME UNTIL YOU'RE READY TO BE. STAYING AWAY FROM
YOU IS GOING TO BE ONE OF THE HARDEST THINGS I'LL EVER DO, BUT IF
THAT'S WHAT YOU NEED AND IT MEANS I'LL COME BACK TO YOU A BETTER
VERSION OF MYSELF, A VERSION THAT PROTECTS YOU AND DOESN'T HURT YOU,
THEN I'M GOING TO DO WHATEVER IT TAKES, FOR HOWEVER LONG IT TAKES, TO
MAKE THAT HAPPEN.

I HOPE YOU'LL STILL CALL ME IF YOU EVER NEED ME, OR IF HENDRIX NEEDS
HELP WITH SOCCER. NO MATTER WHAT'S GOING ON, I'LL BE THERE. PLEASE TELL
HIM I'M SORRY TOO, THAT I MEANT WHAT I SAID WHEN I TOLD HIM I WOULD
PROTECT YOU, AND I PLAN TO KEEP MY PROMISE. YOU'RE MY GIRL, RUBY, AND
ONE OF THE BEST FRIENDS I'VE EVER HAD.

I HOPE ONE DAY I GET THE CHANCE TO SHOW YOU JUST HOW MUCH I MEAN
THAT. I'LL BE WAITING FOR YOU TO TELL ME YOU'RE READY TO SEE ME. THEN
MAYBE WE CAN START OVER?

ALWAYS YOURS, TANK

Chapter 26

TANK

"You stayed away for *me?*" she sobs as the letter falls onto the bed.

"I sure as hell didn't do it for myself." I laugh, bending down in front of her. "I was trying so hard to finally do the right thing when it came to you. I've never been a selfish man, but with you, that's all I ever wanted to be. So I spent those six months trying to find a way to redeem myself for the things I put you through, but I never felt successful. So I settled on just being better. After feeling like all I had ever done was screw things up between us, the least I could do was make sure when you saw me again, I was the best version of myself you'd ever seen. One of the reasons I quit the bar was to help me stay away from alcohol. I had gotten into a really ugly relationship with it, and I've been going to AA meetings ever since I left. I'm just... I'm really fucking trying to be better." She frowns at me as she takes my face in her hands, looking over every feature before she settles on my eyes.

"You don't have to keep waiting for redemption, Tank. What you did today for Hendrix and me, made every single redeeming quality you have outshine any mistake you thought you needed to make up for. I forgive you for what happened and for the way things ended."

My heart bursts wide open at the words I had no idea I even needed to hear.

"Can you forgive *me*?" Her words take me by surprise.

"For what?"

"For not opening your letter. For making you think I didn't want to see you for *so* much longer than I did. For today."

"There's nothing to forgive, Honey," I tell her, wiping away a tear from her cheek.

"Are you still interested in a fresh start?" she asks nervously.

"Not tonight." Her face scrunches in uncertainty. "Tonight, I want to treat you like my *wife*. If you'll let me." I see the way she swallows nervously, as her thoughts start running faster than she can think them.

"What do you mean?"

Oh, she knows exactly what I mean.

"I *mean*, I want to show you just how good I could be at being your husband." I run my hand along the thigh that's peeking out from the slit in her wedding dress.

God, there will never be anything better than seeing Ruby in a wedding dress.

"I want to show you every single thing I've wanted to do to you since the night you first kissed me." I notice as she squeezes her legs together and it gives me the most untamed feeling I've ever had. "I want to make you *mine* in a way that will consume your mind and leave no space for anyone else." She's biting her lip now and I'm not sure she even knows it. Her cheeks are more red than I've ever seen them and she looks fucking perfect. "What do you say, Honey? Can I make you mine tonight?" My voice is low—hopeful she will say yes. I'll make her mine one day, but doing it on our wedding night—no matter how fake *she* thinks it is—I can't think of anything more perfect.

"I don't know. Is that really a good idea?" she whispers, but when I look into her eyes, I see no conviction. Only pleading for me to tell her it is. That it won't change things and we can start fresh tomorrow.

"If your pussy is as wet for me as my dick is hard for you, I don't see how it could possibly be a bad idea." She pulls her bottom lip in with her teeth, and I can tell by the look in her eyes that she's ready to play. Her brow is raised and she tilts her chin up defiantly.

"It's not." A devilish smirk appears on my face as I slide my hand further up her thigh, disappearing under the white silk fabric.

"Should I see for myself if you're lying? I'll give you one last chance to confess." With her poker face firmly in place, she doesn't say a word. But when she spreads her legs slightly, I could absolutely devour her. A growl sounds deep within my chest as I run my finger along her silk underwear, and I can already feel how drenched it is.

"Naughty little wife." I shake my head at her. "What am I going to do with you?"

"I was told you were going to make me yours."

"So that's a yes?"

"I can't seem to say no when it's you," she admits, making my heart squeeze in my chest. I slide my hand up around her hip, still hiding away under her dress as I try to keep myself from ripping it off of her– for now.

"If you start to feel uncomfortable, or you change your mind at any time–"

"I won't," she interrupts eagerly, making me smile, but I continue anyway.

"*If* you do. Say yellow and we'll slow down, say red and we stop completely."

"That sounds so serious." Her eyes widen slightly.

"Honey, I don't know what all you've experienced at the hands of others, but I want you to know you're safe with me—*always*. Understand?" She nods in agreement. "Use your words, baby."

"I understand. Red stop. Yellow slow." She nods.

"That's my good little wife." I move my hand and immediately rip the thin string on either side of her thong, making her gasp.

"Now lay back and let me see that pretty pussy." Her body turns red from her chest up to her cheeks as she lays back on the hotel bed.

When I move the fabric from her dress I see her glistening from her wetness and it brings me straight to my knees. I run my hands along both of her thighs, kissing my way up past her tattoos until I plant one soft kiss to her clit. She sucks in a breath and I see her hands grip the edge of the mattress.

"If you're going to tangle those hands in anything baby, it better be my hair. I wanna feel how much you enjoy this." I start back, kissing and licking up every drop of her sweetness, and like the good little wife she is, her hands find their way to my hair.

Her moans and the way her back arches off the bed give me enough satisfaction I could stay here for hours making her feel good. I slide one finger in and her head falls back, short little breaths making her chest rise and fall. When she's ready, I slide a second finger in and she lets out a little whimper that has me rock hard.

"Eyes on me, Honey." Her big brown eyes lock on mine and it takes everything in me not to stand up and kiss her. My tongue flicks where I know she's most sensitive as my fingers curl inside her. I can see her swallow and the way she's getting closer to her release. Her eyes fall closed for a moment, but before I can correct her, they're back on me.

"Good girl." I stop long enough to praise her. Her walls tighten around me as another moan falls from her lips.

"Tank, I think I'm gonna–" I keep my rhythm steady, wanting her to feel every bit of her pleasure. Her fingers wrap around my hair tighter as she whimpers even louder. "Ah, Tank!" Her legs squeeze around my head as her walls clench around my fingers. I curl them again and again, lapping up every drop that she gives me until I feel her grip begin to soften. Her breaths are coming more quickly as I rub my hand gently along her thigh.

"Such a good little wife." She pushes to sit up on the bed, blushing and satisfied as she struggles to hold my gaze.

"That was… Wow." Her nervous little giggle makes me smile.

"But what about you?" she asks bashfully, as she finally meets my eyes.

"If you thought we were through here, you're sadly mistaken." I furrow my brow at her as I stand back up. She watches as I begin removing my dress blues, and when my jacket no longer covers my *very* obvious erection her eyes grow wide as she takes it in. When I remove my shirt I see the way her eyes drift over the tattoos covering my skin, but when I finally drop my pants, standing in only my boxers, her eyes become comically wide.

"You alright, Honey?" I chuckle as her eyes stay fixed on my cock.

"How is that... I mean it's not gonna–" She shakes her head as she struggles to finish her sentence.

"Words, baby." I encourage her, running my fingers through her hair. I'm not used to a speechless Ruby. I'm not quite sure what to think about her not smarting off to me.

"It's not going to fit. I mean, you saw what your fingers just did, *that* is definitely bigger than two of your fingers. No matter how big your hands are. Are you trying to kill me?" I laugh at how chatty she got from the sudden fear my dick might kill her.

"You're gonna be a mouthy little thing, aren't you?" She narrows her gaze, letting her eyes flick to mine from my cock that's already lined up perfectly with her mouth.

"For your sake, I hope so."

There she is.

She hooks her fingers into my boxers, pulling them down to free my cock before dropping them to the floor. I quickly kick them to the side and fist my length, pumping a few times as her eyes go from intimida*ting* to intimida*ted*.

"I can't use safe words if I'm choking to death, Tank." I can't help but laugh because, God, I love this woman.

"You take the lead, Honey. But, *if* I get carried away, just pinch me right here." I guide her hand to a spot right above my ass as she nods in agreement and I run my thumb across her red-stained bottom lip. "Open that pretty mouth wide for me." Her lips wrap around my cock and my jaw tightens instantly. The warmth of her mouth along with the fact that she's marking me with that lipstick has me struggling to let her be in control. She takes me halfway a few times as she finds her rhythm, before getting comfortable enough that I become familiar with how the back of her throat feels.

"*Fuck, baby.*" I grip her hair, still letting her take control, but when her tongue swirls around as she takes me down her throat I begin thrusting my hips as she bobs her head and I feel myself on the verge of release.

"Look at you, sucking my cock like such a *good* little wife." When her eyes meet mine I can't help myself, I feel like I'm about to cum all down her throat. I thrust harder twice more and she rests her hand on the spot on my back, but she doesn't pinch. I slow my pace, looking down to make sure she's okay, but when she looks up at me all I see is determination. She uses her hand to pull me in closer, and that's all I need to find my release.

"Where do you want it?" I ask, seconds before it escapes me. She closes her lips around my cock and bobs her head a few more times, giving me a very clear answer. When she swallows every bit of what I give her and I'm finally spent, she pulls away, rubbing her finger along her lip, making sure she's left nothing behind and I can't seem to focus on anything else.

No fucking chance I'm forgetting this come morning.

"How was that for a good little wife?" she asks playfully.

"You know, that sounds even better coming from your lips. Those perfect. Fucking. Lips." I wrap my hand around her neck, bringing her lips just a hair away from mine.

"Now lose the dress." I pucker my lips, letting them barely graze hers. When I take a step back I can see how nervous she's become.

"You okay, Honey?" I ask cautiously, cocking my head to the side. She nods her head but her expression doesn't change. She reaches her arms around her back, unzipping her dress as I watch her intently. Her eyes are locked fiercely on my own and she takes a deep breath before releasing the dress, letting it fall to her feet. I take another step back to fully appreciate the masterpiece in front of me as she unhooks her bra and lets it fall to the floor.

I was wrong, the only thing better than seeing Ruby in a wedding dress, is seeing Ruby naked.

My eyes begin roaming her body, and my dick throbs from how painfully beautiful she is. Her full, perky breasts, hard nipples, and tanned skin have me wanting to spend the next 24 hours kissing every inch of her. But my blood runs cold when I see a scar about four inches beneath her belly button. My eyes snap back up to hers quickly, and when I see her fighting back tears I start seeing red. I close the small distance between us, cupping her face in my hands and she tries to avert my gaze.

"Who did that?" I ask, not hiding the anger and hurt in my own voice. "Ruby, who hurt you?" She finally looks at me, *really* looks at me and I know. She doesn't even have to say his name.

"I'm gonna fucking kill him." I see as her eyes glaze over and she begins spacing out. I pull her into my chest, taking a deep breath as I try to calm myself down. I can't see red right now. I'm still going to kill him, but right now I need to take care of my wife.

"Come here." I pull away from her slightly with the intention of getting her into a warm bath, hopeful it will help her to relax and clear her head. There's no way we're doing this when she's hurting the way she is.

"Tank." She grabs my hand to stop me, squeezing it tight as her honey-brown eyes plead with me. "Can you just... will you make me yours now? *Please.*" Her voice breaks as she fights back her sobs.

"Baby, are you sure?" She nods her head quickly, resting her palms on my chest.

"I just want there to be you. Nothing but you. Please. Erase everything else, Tank."

"Of course. I'll never deny you what you need." I brush her hair back and kiss her forehead.

"Tell me your words." I press my forehead to hers, our eyes locking on each other.

"Red stop. Yellow slow."

"Good girl," I say sweetly as I pick her up, wrapping her legs around my waist. She locks them in place and while one of my hands keeps her supported against me, the other tangles in her hair, allowing my thumb to caress the apple of her cheek. I hesitate momentarily, but any doubt about what to do next disappears with her next words.

"Kiss me, Tank. I'm yours, remember? Make me yours." She's simultaneously breaking my heart and putting it back together as she makes her request. The pain in her eyes that she's asking me to replace is something I would walk through hellfire for. But instead, I do what she's asked. I kiss my wife.

Passionately.

Possessively.

In a way I pray will heal every part of her she feels like that asshole broke.

My fingers grip her ass tight, as she begins grinding her hips against me. Coating my abdomen with her wetness. My dick hardens instantly and I lay her gently on the bed never letting my lips leave hers. Her legs are still wrapped tightly around me, as I begin feathering kisses all along her neck, only releasing me as I move down to her breast. From there I kiss along her stomach until I make it to her scar. The same place one would be for a c-section, only it's much smaller and far less professionally done. I kiss it once, twice, three times before I hear Ruby crying. I bring my face back up to hers, watching as the tears roll out of her eyes.

"Baby," I whisper, my heart aching seeing her like this.

"Please don't stop." Her hand caresses my cheek as her finger-nails brush through my beard.

"I'll never stop. Not even death shall part us, Honey. I'll make sure you remember nothing but *us* from this day forward. I swear it." She shakes her head yes as I take her lips in mine once more. I guide myself to her entrance, breaking our kiss briefly.

"I'll go slow, I promise." I slide in just past the tip as her hands move above her head, gripping the sheets as I let her adjust to my size.

I keep my promise and go slow. Letting her wetness usher me in at just the right pace. I hear her moan *"yes"* at the exact moment I'm all the way in and there will never be a sound I love more than Ruby being satisfied. Her grip around my cock is downright intoxicating and takes every bit of self-restraint I have to keep my rhythm slow enough for her. I kiss along her neck until my lips reach the cusp of her ear.

"Only us, baby." I reach my hands up, interlocking our fingers as I make love to my beautiful wife.

"Only us." She agrees.

"Can you feel it, baby? How perfectly you were made for me?" My lips brush along the shell of her ear, as she lets out a little moan.

"*Yes,*" she breathes. "More, please."

Don't have to ask me twice, Honey.

I thrust into her harder, her eyes never wavering from my own. Something about staring into her eyes while she takes every inch of me is driving me absolutely wild. She squeezes my hand tighter as I lose control, increasing my speed while bodies collide and her beautiful moans are the only sounds that fill the room. I ram into her even harder, my cock hitting a spot it hadn't yet reached.

"Yellow!" she says, her voice full of urgency. I immediately pull back, kissing her nose gently as I look into her eyes.

"I'm sorry, baby. Are you okay?" I ask, pressing my forehead to hers again. Her breasts are pressing against my chest as she pants.

"I think so. You're just so... big. It almost feels *too* good. Like I can't breathe when you hit certain spots. Is that crazy?" I let out a chuckle as I reassure her that it's not.

"Not at all. Come here." I wrap an arm around her waist and pull her into me as I stand to walk to the head of the bed, sitting down so that she straddles my lap.

"Now you're in control, Honey. You set the pace and I won't take over unless you ask me to." She bites her lip as she raises up just enough to guide my cock into her pussy again.

"Is this okay?" She asks, grabbing the headboard behind me as her mermaid tattoo grabs my attention. I smirk and look back at her.

"Just dance baby." I see a light come on in her mind as she begins to expertly move her hips, taking me on the ride of my life. "Look at you, riding my cock like such a good little wife." I suck in a breath as she smiles at my praise, leaning in to kiss me. I wrap my hands in her long black hair, letting my tongue explore that perfect mouth of hers as she continues grinding her hips on me.

"Take over please," she whispers against my lips, making me smile.

I pull her up, positioning her to turn around on all fours. Once I'm back inside her, and our rhythm is set, she fists the sheets in her hands. When her moans become muffled by the fabric, I bring her back flush with my chest, allowing her sounds of approval to be heard more clearly. I take advantage of our new position and begin rubbing her clit with one hand while the other wraps around her throat to bring her lips to mine. I always knew my hand would look right at home around her throat, but I didn't realize just how right I was. My tattoos make the perfect necklace for my bride.

I squeeze gently, swallowing her whimper as her walls clench around me.

"Red!" She pulls away from me quickly as her breathing becomes panicked. I still my movements, pulling out before wrapping both of my arms around her in a gentle embrace.

"Okay. I'm listening. Which part?"

"My throat. I-" She shakes her head nervously.

"I hear you. I'm sorry that I scared you. I won't do it again." I promise her. She turns to face me completely, looking into my eyes hesitantly.

"I just... I got nervous because I... I liked it this time."

"This time?" I ask, trying to swallow past the hint of anger in my throat.

"Yeah, but the last time someone had their hand there...It wasn't for pleasure." She drops her gaze, clearly not wanting to relive whatever happened *last time*.

"Just tell me what you need, Honey, and I'll do it." I caress her arms, reminding her that I'm here for *her*.

"Show me it's okay to enjoy it. That you'll make me feel good and keep me safe."

"Are you sure?" She nods in agreement, but when I raise a brow at her, she verbalizes her answer.

"Yes. I'm sure." I kiss her lips soft and sweet before laying her back down on the bed.

"Keep your eyes on me, baby, and I'll remind you that you're safe." I lean down, bringing my lips to the cusp of her ear. "I promise I'll only ever make you feel good, Honey. So good you'll feel me for days after." I feel her nipples harden against my chest and my cock throbs, demanding to be inside her again.

Being with Ruby, making her *mine* in every sense of the word is an experience that I'll remember for the rest of my life. I know I promised her a fresh start tomorrow, but I don't know how I could ever go backward with her when we've reached *this* point in our relationship. I'm so fucking in love with her but I have no idea how or *when* to tell her.

I slide back into her, loving the whimpers she releases as I fill her completely, and wrap my hand around her throat again, keeping just enough pressure there to help her relax without taking her out of her safe space. When she begins rubbing her own clit the sight has me on the verge of release.

"Tank," she moans.

"That's my good girl. You know I'm gonna take care of you don't you?" She nods, as I replace her hand with my own.

"You know I'm gonna make you feel good and keep you safe?"

She nods again. "Come for me, baby. Come all over my cock and show me what a good little wife you are." As if we just needed one last bit of connection to finish, her eyes flick up to mine and we find our release together.

I lean down to kiss her before letting go of her neck.

"Nothing but you." Her smile is one of appreciation, as she rubs the pad of her thumb along my cheek.

"*Us,* baby. Nothing but *us.*" I correct her, before pulling out and gathering her in my arms.

"What are you doing?" She squeals.

"Taking care of my wife."

Chapter 27

RUBY

FROM THE MOMENT I saw Tank in his dress blues at the courtyard something told me he was taking this more seriously than I realized. He got a haircut, had his beard freshly trimmed, and looked so handsome it took my breath away. It was hard not to get caught up in the *what ifs* of it being real.

What if he really wanted to marry me?

What if we hadn't lost so much time?

What if this was the ending we were always supposed to have?

But my heart couldn't take me thinking that way if in the end none of it were true, so I had to turn it off. I was basically on auto-pilot during the whole ceremony, but when he changed his vows it sparked something in me that made me wonder if my *what ifs* weren't so far-fetched after all.

Not even death shall part us.

I wanted to stop the ceremony immediately and ask him what it meant, but I refrained.

Getting back to the hotel room was awkward at best, when I saw all the rose petals on the bed I thought for sure my best friends had lost their minds. But when Tank told me he had done it and gave me the letter I never read, I started questioning everything. I thought I wanted a fresh start with Tank, to pick up where we left off six months ago and take it from there, but after tonight I'm not so sure.

When he told me he wanted to make me *his*, there was only one part of me that had reservations. But I thought what could it hurt to take a chance? We could take things slow and just see where it would go. But from the moment he touched me, I knew I was screwed. Because everything about being *Tanks*—the way he looks at me, touches me, takes care of me—it all just feels *right*.

I knew when he told me to *lose the dress* what would happen. I knew he would see the scar, I knew he would be angry, and I knew the reaction that followed would tell me everything I needed to know.

He didn't go on a manhunt—which wouldn't have surprised me in the slightest—he didn't demand answers, or make me feel damaged.

He stayed.

He stayed and kept his promise to make me his, and made me feel pleasure and safety I've never experienced before. He stopped and listened when I used my safe words without ever making me feel like I was crazy or putting a damper on the mood. He loved me in a way I've only ever read about, and surely never thought *I* would have. I knew that it was okay to show that part of myself to him— the part no one else in my life has ever seen—because as much as I am his, he's mine too. Only I still don't know where he stands on starting fresh tomorrow after the way tonight went.

As we're standing in the shower together, I realize how desperately I want this to last. Him washing my hair and planting kisses on my shoulders and my neck, while I memorize his every touch. I remember the first time I met Tank and couldn't get over how insanely hot he was at first glance. Then the few times I saw him without a shirt on it took every bit of my self-control not to gawk at him. But tonight, seeing him completely naked for the first time, I haven't been able to look away. And I haven't *had* to.

His physique lives up to his name because he's *actually* built like a tank and being wrapped up in his arms is easily becoming my favorite place to be. The veins running through his arms and hands and the tattoos that cover his tanned skin are getting the attention I've wanted to give them for over two years now, and his dick will more than likely make me forget my own name before we check out of this hotel tomorrow. I'm not surprised that it's as massive as the rest of him, but oh my *god*.

"Like what you see, Honey?" he teases, as I run my hands along any part of him I can.

"Has anyone ever told you that you're a beautiful man?" He chuckles, spinning me around to switch places with me, shielding any water from hitting my face as he leans down and kisses me.

"You would be the first." He breaks our kiss only long enough to get those words out. Even though I still feel sore, my pussy can't help but clench when he wraps his arm around my waist to bring me closer to him. My arms wrap around his neck without hesitation and he pulls my legs up around his middle. His kisses move from my lips to my neck and my nipples harden as I arch into him from the sensation.

"You've ruined me, baby, how am I ever supposed to stop kissing you now?" he whispers in my ear, and I desperately want to tell him to never stop. That if he does I may actually die from the heartache.

"Maybe you don't." He rears back, letting those emerald green eyes study mine. I don't know why I feel the sudden need to hide after my comment. He's holding my naked body flush against his in the shower, after giving me the best orgasms of my life and a sense of safety I never thought I would have with a man. Even after every comment he's made tonight that leads me to believe he wants this, and possibly more, I'm scared to tell him what I want.

"What happened to a fresh start?" His brow furrows, making my heart race with anticipation. "Have you changed your mind?"

"What if I have?" It feels like time has frozen as he looks back at me contemplating—the only thing still in motion is the water running between us.

"I want you to be sure. I don't want you making a decision because you're caught up in the moment. Because once you tell me that you want this, Honey, there's no taking it back." I've never seen Tank look so... hopeful while waiting for a response from me.

"I'm sure." He smiles so genuinely when I nod my head in agreement, as I feel his length begin to harden against me. As he takes my lips captive in his, my hands tangle in his hair before I reach down and line him up to my entrance.

"Greedy little wife." He smirks against my lips, causing me to stop.

"Do you not want to?" I move my hand back up to his shoulder as his features harden.

"Let me make this *very* clear. I will never not want to be inside that sweet little pussy of yours." I gasp as he thrusts all the way in. "And I will always be just as greedy for you—if not more." He spends the remainder of our shower making me come not once, but twice more, before drying my hair and wrapping me up in a plush hotel robe to carry me to the bed. He gets under the covers beside me still completely naked before tucking me beneath his arm.

"Are you tired?" The deep rumble of his voice vibrates through his chest while he plays with my hair.

"Surprisingly, no," I admit, looking up at him. "You?" I mean sure, if I sat under the warmth of his embrace while he played with my hair like this for any length of time, I'd probably get the best sleep of my life, but I'm not ready to let this night be over.

"No." He shakes his head, kissing my forehead. "I think we should fill in some blanks from the last six months, don't you?"

"Yeah, of course." I sit up straight so that I'm able to face him. "What do you want to know?"

Everything.

I want to know everything I've wanted to ask him for the past six months about what drove him to almost leave us, to what he's been watching on TV in his spare time. He stares back at me patiently as I figure out how to ask him what I want to know, but the look in his eyes—the peace that hasn't always been there—makes me confident that we can have this conversation now, without fear or discomfort.

"Why did you do it? Why did you... try to kill yourself?" My voice is low, like a verbal tiptoe to help us ease into it. Regardless of how much it terrifies me to ask the question, I hold his gaze when I do. He lets out a deep sigh, taking my hand in his before he answers.

"Because, I really hated myself." His answer feels like a knife to the heart. "Or at least I thought it was as simple as that. I felt like all I ever did was fuck things up. No matter how hard I *thought* I was trying to do things right. I felt like all I ever did was fail. I let my team down when I broke my back, and again when I wasn't there during the mission that got Dom killed. I let you down–"

"I had no idea, Tank. I'm so sorry." He nods in appreciation but stays quiet. "And, you didn't let me down." I squeeze his hand in mine, doing my best to reassure him that I never felt that way. I was hurt when I didn't hear from him all those months, sure. But I know the reason behind that now and it was my own fault.

"I did though. I knew something was off and I just kept thinking I could handle it on my own. And we see how that ended up. It got you hurt and I almost took my own life because I was drowning in a darkness I couldn't even see. I let you down by trying to be in your life when I knew I shouldn't have been," he says, as I run my finger mindlessly along the palm of his hand. He looks down at it and smiles.

"I missed you like hell during the six months we didn't talk, but I'll always be grateful for the healing that happened during that time."

"Me too." I caress his cheek and when he kisses the palm of my hand, my heart begins to flutter. I clear my throat and return to drawing circles in his palm. "So I take it therapy has been going well then?"

"Yeah." He nods, starting to play with my fingers mindlessly. "It was really hard at first, Having to talk about everything and open myself up to bare my sins like that, God I hated it."

"You seem to do those things fine with me." His eyes soften when they land on mine.

"You're my girl, Ruby. You've always been the exception. Even more so now that you're my wife." My cheeks heat as he gives me a wink before he takes in a deep breath and continues. "To better answer your question though, I'm down to bi-weekly phone check-ins with my therapist unless otherwise needed, so yes. Therapy went very well." He has no idea how at peace my heart is from hearing him say that.

"Good." I smile up at him. "What else?" I ask, wanting to fill in every single moment I wasn't with him.

"Well, you've met Mav already," he says, making me nod in agreement.

"Right. Very briefly, but he seems great."

"He is." He laughs. "While I was in therapy I hung out a *lot* more with Max and Tuck. They helped keep me accountable and I really needed that, especially in the beginning. We'd hang at Max's a lot, or we would go to the gym, or the range and I found myself gravitating towards Riley more often than not, and she started doing the same with me. Which is weird because that dog and Max are like kindred spirits or something. Anyways, Max made the suggestion I look into getting a dog of my own, suggesting the same breed as Riley, and when we found Maverick we clicked instantly."

"Is he good with kids?" I know he's been around Hendrix once already, but their interaction was brief so I feel the need to ask.

"Do you honestly think I would get a dog that couldn't be around Hendrix?" He smiles at me, making my heart lurch in my chest. *Of course not.* "I think you and Hendrix will both fall in love with him. He goes with me almost everywhere, and he especially loves the days I volunteer at *The Veterans Center*. He gets all sorts of attention and just eats it up."

"Oh, you've been volunteering?"

"Yep. There's a living center that caters to the specific needs of veterans. I go as much as I can during the week. It really helps put things in perspective ya know? Plus I get to serve those who served our country a lot longer and a lot harder than I did. They're full of good stories and a really great outlook on life—most of the time. I've tried surrounding myself with people who understand me, and what I've gone through, and are supportive. It makes more of a difference than I realized."

"Do you think I'll be one of those people? That understands you and supports you?" I drop my gaze when I ask, afraid we've lost too much time and that maybe I won't know him as well as I did or *thought* I did.

"Honey, you understood me in ways I didn't even understand *myself* before all of this happened. I have no doubt in my mind you're still one of them because you're my missing puzzle piece—the only thing that's kept me from feeling complete until now." He threads his fingers through my hair, pulling me in to kiss me in a way that feels full of promise.

We stay up for hours talking about all the things we've missed over these last six months. He tells me about his therapist and the ways she's helped him to find closure, forgiveness, and healing. The coping mechanisms he uses when he gets angry and how the flash-backs and blackouts have subsided only to the occasional nightmare.

He fills me in on all the times he followed me around *Joe Goldberg* style just because he missed me, but was under the impression I wasn't ready to see him yet. The way my eyes begin to water when he tells me about the physical therapy he's been in to strengthen his back seems to bring out his emotions as well. He laughs as he swipes a tear away, looking up at me almost bashfully as he continues.

"What about you, Honey? What'd I miss while I was away?" He squeezes my thigh, his thumb caressing the inside of my thigh to the point I want to request we pick this conversation up later.

"Well, you really didn't miss much. A couple of lost teeth for

Hendrix, he started soccer—which you actually knew about—Marco finally learned how to make a Gimlet, and... yeah, that's about it."

"Whoa, hold on. If Marco learned how to make a gimlet, I fear that the end of the world is coming. It's only been like, what, eight years?" he teases, leaning against the headboard.

"Stranger things have happened." I yawn, as I feel exhaustion creeping over me.

"Name one," he argues, causing me to hold my left hand up, shaking my ring finger.

"Can't compare an anomaly to something that was meant to be, Honey." He winks at me, causing heat to rush to my cheeks.

I look down at my ring and study it closely for the first time since he slid it onto my finger. The band is black gold covered with small diamonds, with a pear-shaped center made of a double halo of diamonds and an amethyst in the center. My breath catches in my throat when I realize how much detail is in this ring. It isn't some bubble gum machine ring or something he picked up last minute. The purple stone in the center is a dead giveaway of that. When I look back up his eyes are already on me, watching as I process why he would put so much thought into this, *how* he could have when we had so little time to prepare for today.

"I *want* to be your husband, Ruby. I know that might be hard for you to understand right now given the circumstances of how we got here. But I'm choosing to see it as an opportunity to really give us a chance—is there *any* way I can convince you to do the same?" he pleads, having no idea just how much I want that too. How I want to dive in head first and hope for the best. But the tiniest hesitation living in the back of my mind still demands to be the loudest voice when it comes down to it.

Because while I wish we could stay in this moment forever, tomorrow is going to come, the ghosts of my past will still be there to haunt me—and I don't know how much he'll want to stay when he's met face to face with some of them.

"I want to say yes, but... there's still so much you don't know about my past. Things I wish I could take back, things that I'm not proud of..." My emotions get the better of me as I think of my perfect baby boy. "Things that brought me so much hurt, but ultimately gave me Hendrix and I just don't want you running scared if they get dragged out," I admit, toying with the sash on my robe to avoid meeting his gaze.

"Tell me every terrible thing you ever did, and let me love you anyway," he says the statement like a memorized quote, causing my gaze to narrow on him. "Tell me everything now, Honey. No more skeletons in the closet. We're going to bury them properly once and for all." I shake my head in disagreement as he tilts my chin up to look at him. "Let me prove to you that I'll still be here—by your side —even if everything else falls apart."

"I don't even know where to start." The words fall out breathlessly, so he takes the lead.

"The night you told me you had to leave Nevada, I wanted to ask why, but I could tell you weren't ready to talk about it. Maybe we can start there? Tell me what happened." I blow out a shaky breath, willing myself to open up to him.

"After I graduated college I had every intention of getting a job with my degree. I wanted to really make a difference by helping people, ya know? But after paying my tuition in full, and only working two days a week to keep my grades up, I didn't have enough money to get a place of my own and start completely from scratch. My parents weren't talking to me anymore after finding out about me stripping, so going home wasn't an option and I didn't have any friends I trusted enough to find a place with. Not after everything that had happened with the people I *thought* were my friends. So, instead of starting a new chapter and getting an apartment, and looking for a job in psychology, I checked into a sketchy motel and asked for more days at the club to help me save up. I was uh… a favorite back then. The other girls would always make comments about how the place was only packed on nights I was dancing, and that I always went home with the biggest tips." I scoff, remembering how isolating it felt when they would make those comments. All I wanted was friends who would be happy for me, but they never were. "I remember how I would always have to stay late to sober up or let Zay, the only *real* friend I ever made at that place, take me home after drinking with customers. Men would always want to buy me a shot before solos and since I was there for the cash I never said no.

"The night Mark showed up at the club, I don't know he just stood out from everyone else. And that was rare for customers at *Bad Bunnies*. He wasn't drinking heavily to the point of yelling slurs at the dancers, he sipped on one glass of whiskey the whole night and just *watched*. He was a big tipper, and at the end of the night, he stopped me and told me how great I was. I was waiting for some cheesy pickup line but he just offered to walk me to my car and that was it. He started showing up more regularly and it was always the same thing—a big tip and walking me to my car. Then one night he requested a solo and that's when everything changed. I had a buzz from doing pre-show shots with the girls, on top of drinking with the other customers, and I started running my mouth. I went on and on about how *nice* he was," I say in disgust, scoffing as I continue, "and then I said something I wish I could go back in time and take back. I asked him when he was going to take me home."

I see the way Tank's jaw flexes, but he keeps his features solid as he rubs my leg to comfort me.

"God, I was so stupid. I'll spare you the details, but he did. It wasn't until months of us hooking up and me ending up pregnant with Hendrix that I found out he was *married*." His jaw flexes again, but he doesn't interrupt.

"I was the *other woman* and I had absolutely *no* idea. I even waited to get an ultrasound before telling him because I thought he might be *excited*." I angrily wipe at the tears falling down my cheeks, feeling a wave of nausea wash over me as I wish I could go back and never even tell him.

"Everything about him changed after that night. He said it was my fault that it happened and to *get rid of it*—that he was done with me and had no intention of taking care of-" I stop for a moment trying to force the words out. "Of some slut who can't control herself. I felt so *dirty*, so worthless, and unwanted. Like by falling for someone I *thought* I knew and getting pregnant that I'd done something wrong."

"You did *nothing* wrong. You hear me. Not a damn thing," Tank interrupts, holding my face firmly in his hands, caressing my cheek gently with his thumb. I nod as he stares deeply into my eyes as if he's trying to be sure his words are getting through to me. Then he nods for me to continue.

"It took me a little while to get over the way things ended but I thought, worst case scenario, I would have the baby and raise it on my own. I never wanted anything from him, but I wanted even less after seeing who he *really* was.

"But one day he asked to see me, saying he missed me and wanted to talk about things and I stupidly agreed. I was so naïve to think things would end up being different between us, that maybe he had a change of heart about the things he had said. And even if he didn't want to *be* with me, maybe he wouldn't be so nasty about the baby. He walked in and the first thing he asked was if I was still pregnant. I wasn't sure by the tone of his voice what he wanted the answer to be, so I told him the truth. He slammed his fist on the dresser, knocking a flower vase over making it shatter while voicing his disapproval. He grabbed me by the throat and the last thing he said to me was *I'll give you one last chance to take care of this, or I'll do it myself.* He picked up a broken piece of glass from the table and when I tried to knock it out of his hand, he grabbed me by the wrist. He held it so hard it was bruised for days after. Then he used the glass to cut me on my stomach. A permanent reminder of the threat he made. That moment has haunted my dreams for over six years." I rub the spot on my stomach as Tank pulls me over to straddle his lap, rubbing my thighs in a soothing motion.

"The tattoo on your wrist. It's a tattoo of the bruise he left?" I shake my head, rubbing my thumb across the ink.

"I know it may seem morbid, or may not make sense at all to others, but I wanted a reminder of what I had been through, and what I was strong enough to walk away from. I wanted to be able to look back and see how far I'd come from the shit he put me through, *with* my baby alive and well." I can't help the sobs breaking free as I think about how badly I want to squeeze Hendrix right now.

"You're okay baby. I've got you now. You're safe with me." I take a steady breath, letting his words and gentle touch soothe me.

"I lied and told him I would take care of it the way he wanted so he would leave me alone. He didn't want anything to do with me anyway, so I figured if I just disappeared he would never know the difference. I would keep my baby, and be rid of him. When he walked out, I packed what few belongings I had and was leaving the motel within an hour. My phone had been going off for most of the time but when I finally picked it up, the messages sent me into a downward spiral. Every single one of them reiterated his seriousness about me getting an abortion. That if I did what he said, *no one would get hurt*. He doesn't deserve to be anyone's father. He never has." I get angry all over again as my heart yearns for my baby boy. The sweetest and happiest kids I've ever known. The one who's helped keep me whole, and reminded me how strong I can be.

"You're right, he doesn't deserve to be anyone's father. Especially not Hendrix. I promise you we're going to make sure that doesn't happen. Honey, look at me," he says, bringing my gaze up to him. "He had no right to *ever* blame you for anything that happened between the two of you. I will kill him for making you feel the way that he did and for trying to keep Hendrix from being born. Hendrix makes this world a better and brighter place, and I am *so* fucking proud of you for walking away and fighting, for the *both* of you. You deserve nothing less than someone who shows you just how wanted and worthy of love you are—because you *are*, baby. You're more worthy of love than anyone else I know."

Tank Landry, has healing powers through words of affirmation.

All I can do is shake my head to let him know I hear him because if I try to speak I'm not sure what will end up coming out.

"Wait...If he texted those things to you, couldn't that be used as evidence against him?" I shake my head, wishing it were that simple.

"I don't have that phone anymore. I lost it when I went back to *Bad Bunnies* to let them know I wouldn't be back. I didn't realize it until I reached Salt Lake City. At the time I saw it as a good thing since he didn't have a way to contact me, but I also didn't have any of *my* old contacts. I drifted from state to state, picking up any job I could to keep some money in my savings all while living out of motels. Once I got too pregnant to keep traveling, I stopped drifting. That's when I ended up in Nashville. I walked into Chattahoochies to see if they could use any temporary help, and the rest is history. Max took me under his big grumpy wing and not long after I was able to get a little two-bedroom house. Then along came Hendrix— my little miracle." We both smile as Tank continues to absentmindedly touch, stroke, or rub any part of me he can reach. Like he has an undeniable need to have some part of himself connected to me. If I'm being honest, I hope he never stops.

"That's why you've stayed at Chattahoochies for so long. You found your new family there." I smile, thinking about how much Max has been there for me throughout the years.

"Max really taught me to be strong, you know? I'm not sure he even knows it, but when I first started and was still so damaged from my past, I would cower at bar patrons getting too rowdy or making inappropriate comments at me. I was strong when I knew I needed to be, like when it came to leaving Mark, but with everyone else, I was a doormat. He would look at me and say, *Show 'em your backbone, Rubes. We don't take anyone's bullshit around here.* Then he would give them this look, letting them know that whatever I said next was to be taken seriously or they would be removed. I still hear his voice telling me that every time I have to tell someone to shove it where the sun doesn't shine." I laugh, noting the seriousness on Tank's face.

"You are by far the strongest woman I've ever met. You are the most incredible mother to Hendrix, and loyal to your friends. When I first met you, I remember thinking you were so unlike anyone else I'd ever met. You're quick-witted and beautiful, you radiate confidence and have no problem telling people when it's time to hit the pavement. You're strong and you would do anything to protect the ones you love. I learned *very* quickly that your personality matched the outward beauty you possess, which is what kept drawing me back to you when I knew I should stay away. But do you want to know what I've discovered I love most about you?" His green eyes are so serene as they study on my own, making my heart hammer faster inside my chest.

"What?"

"I love the way you let yourself be vulnerable with me. When you show me the parts of yourself you think will show weakness, it only proves to me that you're stronger than you think you are." I feel like I've cried more in the last week and a half than at any other time in my life, but nevertheless, more tears begin streaming down my face.

"Can I be strong *and* scared? Because I am still so scared I'll lose him." He cups my face in his hand, wiping away my tears as I lean into his touch.

"We won't lose him, but you can be whatever you need to be, as long as you're mine."

"I'm yours, Tank," I whisper, kissing the palm of his hand before resting my cheek against it again.

"Good girl." I smile at his praise, letting my eyes drift shut once again.

Chapter 28

TANK

My wife is the most beautiful human being in the world. She wields a strength unlike any other person I've ever known, and my love for her only grows with each passing moment. When she lifts her head from my hand, letting her sleepy eyes flutter back open, I unsash her robe and slide the fabric down over her shoulders to remove it completely. My dick begins to harden immediately at the sight of her and the blush that creeps over her face as I admire her beauty.

"Come here. You need to rest." I motion for her to lay beside me, tucking her under my arm as she hangs her leg over mine. Her breasts are pressed firmly against my side as she begins tracing the tattoos on my chest.

"Tell me something I don't know about you."

"What?" I laugh, her question catching me off guard.

"I want to know everything about you. The good, the bad, and the interesting."

"I thought it was the good, the bad, and the *ugly*." I tilt my head to look down at her, making her mimic my motion to meet my gaze.

"There's nothing *ugly* about my husband." Her cheeks turn rosy, as she fights back a smile. She moves to rest her head on my chest again, and I can't help the smile that forces its way onto my face. I quickly memorize the way it feels to hear her calling me her husband and how happy she looked while saying it. I think for a moment about what I could tell her that she doesn't already know and won't bore her before something comes to mind.

> *"In visions of the dark night*
> *I have dreamed of joy departed—*
> *But a waking dream of life and light*
> *Hath left me broken-hearted.*

> *Ah! What is not a dream by day*
> *To him whose eyes are cast*
> *On things around him with a ray*
> *Turned back upon the past?*

> *That holy dream–that holy dream,*
> *While all the world were chiding,*
> *Hath cheered me as a lovely beam*
> *A lonely spirit guiding.*

> *What through that light, thro' storm and night,*
> *So tremble from afar—*
> *What could there be more purely bright*
> *In Truth's day-star?"*

"So you read, nay, *memorize*, poetry?" I can feel her smiling and it brings a smile to my face as well.

"I do. Mostly Poe but a couple of others as well. I picked up a book in the airport on my first deployment and started reading it when I was overseas. It ended up being a nice distraction ya know?"

She turns to rest her chin on my chest as her honey-brown eyes look at me curiously.

"So what does it mean?" I begin brushing her long black waves that rest along her back as I do my best to explain it.

"Well, the way I see it is, he starts by writing about a dream he had where happiness left him, but it doesn't scare him because he's already living in a state of depression and darkness. What impacts him most is when he has dreams about joy and happiness because he can't relate to them. He doesn't interact that way with the world because he's living in the past, where that darkness keeps a hold of him. But then, he recalls a dream he once had that he considered to be holy. One that helped him escape the world of misery he had lived in for so long. But that's the beautiful thing about poetry, different people will interpret it in different ways."

"What you said earlier? About telling you all the terrible things and loving me anyway, was that a quote you'd memorized as well?" She lets her eyes lock with mine, and I intertwine my fingers in her hair, caressing her cheek with my thumb as I do.

"It was. But I still meant every word."

"You're full of surprises aren't you, husband?"

Fuck, she said it again.

"If you keep calling me your husband in that sweet-as-sin voice of yours, I'm going to have a hard time letting you sleep tonight," I warn her, but she only seems more encouraged as she drops her hand to brush against my hardening cock.

"But I'm not tired." Her mouth is saying one thing but her eyes are telling me another.

"Give me about five minutes of playing with your hair and I bet

I'll have you snoring." Her eyes fall closed as I begin massaging her scalp and she finally lays back down on my chest.

"Fine. Five minutes, but if I'm still awake after that. We do what I want," she says through a yawn, and suddenly I'm curious what it is that she wants.

"As you wish." Not even a minute later, I feel her body go limp. But of course, my beautiful bride doesn't snore, she sleeps as beautifully as she does everything else. Feeling her steady breaths against me and her body perfectly entangled with mine, my own sleep follows not long after.

Waking up this morning and realizing last night wasn't a dream was surreal. I slide out of bed to order us breakfast while Ruby sleeps because I'm sure she's exhausted after the night we had. I have no intention of waking her up until absolutely necessary, but she looks so fucking beautiful right now, it's hard to keep my hands off of her. The sheet is wrapped around her waist, her back fully exposed with her raven-toned waves splayed across the pillows. I quickly grab my phone and snap a photo, or three, of her before placing it back on the dresser. When I hear a soft moan from behind me, I turn around to see Ruby now lying on her back gripping the pillow above her but she's still very much asleep.

Naughty little wife. What are you dreaming about?

When my name falls from her lips in the softest whisper, my dick hardens instantly and I walk slowly over to the bed. When I move the sheet from around her waist, her legs are spread and she's dripping wet. I contemplate whether I should help her find her release or let her sleep, but what kind of husband would I be if I left my wife dripping and needy? I run my hands along her thighs, squeezing her hips as she moans again. Her body responds to me instantly as my tongue makes contact with her wet slit. A few moments later her eyes flutter open and she finds out that she isn't just dreaming anymore. I continue flicking my tongue along her clit as her eyes adjust.

"I thought I was dreaming," she whispers, biting her lip as she lets her hands find their way to my hair.

"You were. But I couldn't let you moan my name like that and ignore the fact that you needed me." I swipe my tongue along her pussy again. "You *did* need me, didn't you, Honey?" I ask, stopping to wait for her answer.

"Yes," she breathes. "Yes. I need you. Don't stop." I smirk, and do as she's asked. Her fingers snake through my hair as she grips tighter, breathing out little *yeses* as I bring her closer to her release. I slide one finger inside of her, gently working in a second as she arches her back. I curl my fingers inside of her, hitting the same spot I know drives her crazy as I lap up every drop she's giving me.

"*Tank,*" she moans my name as her orgasm takes over her, making her legs shake and squeeze around my head, but I don't stop until I know she's completely satisfied.

"Such a good little wife." She bites her lip, still looking as though she's dreaming but jumps when someone knocks on the door.

"*Room service.*"

"I got it." I stand back up and she lets out a little gasp. When I look down, her eyes are fixed on the erection that is not at *all* hidden behind my black sweatpants.

"You're going to answer the door like that?" Her eyes grow wide as she looks up at me.

"Well *you're* not answering like *that*, that's for damn sure," I tell her, nodding to her perfect naked body. "All this does is let everyone know I have a wife whose pussy makes me hard as fuck." Her whole body turns red as she grabs the sheet to cover herself back up. I adjust myself so I don't scare whoever is behind the door, then open it to retrieve our food.

Once I walk back in the room with the cart she gets out of bed, stretching her arms above her head before walking to the bathroom. It's so fucking wild to me how much things changed for us overnight. Yesterday she was so reserved and holding so much back out of fear, and today she's waltzing around our hotel room completely naked without a single care in the world. Exactly the way I want it to be. When she comes back in, she slides her underwear on and throws on a T-shirt before coming to sit on my lap.

"You ready to get back home?" I ask, assuming she's itching to get back home and see Hendrix.

"Yes and no." She takes a sip of her coffee, before looking over at me. "I'm beyond ready to see Hendrix, but I'm not sure I'm ready to get back to reality." She frowns.

"We're going to win this thing, baby. That asshole sperm donor doesn't have a chance taking Hendrix from us," I assure her, kissing her cheek before taking a bite of bacon.

"That's not all I'm talking about." She hangs her head, playing with her fingernails before looking up again. "Can I tell you something and you *not* think I'm crazy?"

"Of course you can. You should know better than to even ask." I raise a brow at her, making her smile.

"I'm gonna miss hearing you call me your wife all the time." I frown at her, making her roll her eyes. "I know it's so dumb, but–"

"What makes you think I'll stop calling you my wife? You *are* my wife."

"Yeah, but all of our friends think this is just some agreement we made to protect Hendrix. What will they think if you're suddenly calling me your wife and looking at me like…"

"Like what?"

"Like you've fucked me in a hotel shower and know how I taste." A devilish smirk creeps across my face as I remember *exactly* how she tastes.

"I don't give a single fuck about what everyone else thinks. I will call you my wife whenever I feel like it, and I will gladly tell them how fucking delicious you are."

"How will that look though? I don't see you for six months, drag you into this marriage, and then we're... *together*." Her question sends a wave of anger through me. Not at *her*, at the motherfucker who made her feel so used and worthless that she's questioning what it means to be with *me* now. I pull her legs over my waist, allowing her to straddle me as we sit on the edge of the bed.

"I hope it looks like I'm madly in love with my wife. That this whole situation is just the fate that brought us back together so I could prove to you just how much I want you, *need* you in my life. Don't you see it, baby? I don't want a fresh start, I don't want to pretend not to be entirely consumed by the way I feel about you. Because I have never loved anyone the way that I love you. Making you my wife was by far the best day of my life. It was never fake for me."

"You love me?" The disbelief in her voice almost breaks my heart.

"Not even death could keep me from loving you, Ruby Ranes." Her eyes immediately fill with tears as she brings her cool hands up to my face.

"Landry."

"Yes?"

"No, I mean. It's Landry now—my last name." My heart damn near bursts when I hear her claim my last name as her own.

"I fucking love you," I tell her again, capturing her lips with my own. I grip her ass and pull her in closer. Needing as little space between us as possible.

"I love you, more," she says against my lips.

"I need to be inside you. Right fucking now." She shakes her head eagerly in agreement.

Last night was such a turning point for the both of us. I was finally able to claim Ruby as mine, making her my wife in every possible way, while helping her to overcome the emotional scars left by another. Replacing every horrible memory of what she'd been through, with new memories of *us*. *This* is our fresh start—a life of love and honesty, protection and passion—one where we don't have to second guess where the other stands. I will spend every day for the rest of my life, showing her how deep my love runs for her. So that even long after I'm gone, she'll still remember how much she meant to me.

With our bodies covered in sweat, my forehead pressed against hers as I'm still buried deep inside her she stills my soul with her gaze.

"I love you, Tank." Her honey-brown eyes completely captivate me, the same way they always have.

"I love you too, Honey. Now let's go home."

TUCKER

Took Mav over to Max's so you could pick the boys up together. He did great but I gotta get to work.

ME

Thanks man, I appreciate you taking him so last minute.

TUCKER

Anytime.

TUCKER

How was it?

ME

Are you asking me for a play by play or??

TUCKER

What? Dude, no. Never mind. Go get your kids man.

ME

You can't be that fucking vague and not expect me to go there.

TUCKER

So you went there?

ME

Oh, man. Would you look at the time? Gotta go get the kids.

TUCKER

Chapter 29

RUBY

I'm married.

I'm married and I'm in love with my husband.

A husband whom I married five days after seeing him for the first time in six months.

And he's in love with me too.

It's fine. We're fine.

"You alright, Honey? You've got that *drowned your cat* look again." Tank squeezes my hand as we ride to Shane and Max's house to pick up Hendrix and Maverick.

"Technically, you have... A few times now." I glance over, waiting for the punchline to hit him.

"*Wow.* Okay. You went there." He looks at me in disbelief as we both start laughing.

"God, I love your laugh." Every word that rumbles out of his mouth seems to make me blush these days. "So, I don't want to start making assumptions but we never had the *move-in* discussion prior to all of this happening, but you *are* planning on letting me live with you, right?" I can't help but laugh at the hint of seriousness I can hear behind his playful tone.

"Oh, well... I mean, I guess it would look kind of suspicious if we *weren't* living together." I pretend to contemplate the decision as

I see his features begin to harden. "I guess we could make something work. The couch may not be quite big enough for you, but you could take my room and I could just sleep with Hendrix for a while." He looks over at me like I've completely lost my mind, seemingly unaware that he's still driving a vehicle as his eyes stay locked on me.

"Are you serious?" His blank expression and deep voice have me wanting to buckle over in laughter.

"*No!* Of course not." He lets out a sigh of relief, shaking his head at me as he faces the road again. "Do you really think after last night I'm gonna sleep anywhere but next to you?" I feel my cheeks begin to heat, as a smirk crosses his face. He brings the back of my hand up to his lips and kisses it.

"Good girl." He winks at me and then begins stroking my hand with his thumb. "We can pick up Hendrix and Mav first then head to my place to grab some of my things, if that works for you?"

"I'm just along for the ride. You lead, I'll follow." My words seem to shock not only Tank but myself as well. Never in my life have I put so much trust into one person. I've relied on myself for as long as I can remember, but there's something about *him*. I'd follow him blindly into battle because I undoubtedly know he would keep me and Hendrix safe.

When I look over at his dashboard, I see a coin of some sort tucked in front of his speedometer.

"What's that?" I point it out, causing him to pluck it from its home before handing it to me so I can look at it closer.

"I got that one yesterday." He nods, as I run my fingers over the words,

6 months sober. One day at a time

"I'm so unbelievably proud of you, do you know that?" He looks over at me with appreciation in his eyes, kissing my hand again with a nod.

"Thanks, Honey, that means a lot coming from you."

I hope he's proud of himself too.

We pull up to Shane and Max's house and before I have my seat belt unbuckled Tank is coming around to open my door for me. He offers me his hand to help me out and doesn't let go as we walk up to the door. My heart is racing as we get closer, wondering what everyone is going to think about this—about *us*. Then I remember what my husband said and I try my hand at *"not giving a fuck what everyone else thinks"* too. Max opens the door and gives Tank a nod as he greets him, then looks down at our intertwined fingers before looking up at me with a smirk.

"Told ya." I give him a confused look before our conversation at the courthouse comes sprinting back to mind.

"It's very real. The sooner you realize that, the better."

"Hello to you too." I roll my eyes at him as he opens the door wider for us to come in.

"Mommy!" Hendrix yells, running up to hug my waist as Riley and Maverick follow at his sides.

"Hey, buddy! I missed you so much." I squeeze him tight, looking down as his head falls back to look up at me. I'll never get over how quickly he's growing up. I take a minute to just *look* at him. His brown eyes and single dimple always act as a mirror to my own features, while his dark brown hair that hangs right above his eyes is in major disarray from sleeping.

"Tank!" he says with equal excitement as he throws himself into Tank's arms.

"Whoa, hey little man." Tank catches him just in time as Hendrix Koala holds onto him. "Did you have a good time?"

"Yes. I helped make Cece stop crying with my funny moves." He smiles proudly.

"Hey, sorry. I was just getting her down for a nap," Shane says, walking into the room holding a baby monitor. Motherhood really looks good on her. I'm sure she would argue that fact right now seeing as she's still in her pajamas, her blonde hair is thrown into a messy bun on top of her head and she has milk stains on her shirt that I won't be pointing out. But the happiness that radiates from her when she's talking about or holding Cece, tells me she was absolutely born to be a mother.

"Don't ever apologize to *me* about doing motherly things. You know I get it." I wink at her, leaning in to give her a hug. Max hands Tank Hendrix's backpack and Maverick's leash while Hendrix still hangs all over Tank like some deranged spider monkey, and I can't help but get this warm feeling in my gut that this is something that's going to become normal soon enough—Tank and I doing things together that I used to do alone.

"Thanks for everything. We better get going though. We gotta stop by the apartment before we head home."

Home. He called my house home.

"You're coming home with us?" Hendrix says excitedly, worrying me for only a second that I didn't think to mention that to him before. God, my mind has been shit lately.

"Sure am." Tank bobs Hendrix's head back and forth with his hand.

"Like forever?"

"Like for*ever*. That sound like a plan to you?" He stops moving him long enough to let him respond.

"Yeah!" He throws his arms around Tank's waist as Tank pats his back.

Forever.

"Let's roll then. Maverick, come," Tank commands, sending shivers down my spine at the authoritativeness in his tone.

"Bye Uncle Max, bye Shane." Hendrix hugs them both before barrelling out the door, racing the dog to the truck.

"See you guys later." I walk out behind Hendrix as Tank drapes his arm over my shoulder, kissing my temple as we walk over to the car. Hendrix wastes no time getting in and getting himself buckled, but before I get my door open Tank stops me and spins me around, putting himself between me and the truck.

"What's wrong?" He runs his fingers through the base of my hair, pulling me into him as his lips capture mine. I freeze for a moment before settling into him, wrapping my arms around his waist as the heat spreads through my body. Every touch, every glance, every kiss that comes from him makes me completely melt.

"It's been entirely too long since I kissed my wife." He winks at me, and I involuntarily bite my lip before I hear someone clear their throat behind me.

"Um. Hendrix left Spidey," Shane says, handing me a plush Spider-Man as I turn around to face her. She doesn't say anything else but the look on her face is practically screaming at me.

"Thank you, he uh, would definitely be missing this later." Nervous laughter fills the air as Shane stares back at me with a raised brow.

"Uh huh." She crosses her arms over her chest.

"Okay so, byeeee." I turn around and quickly climb into the truck, letting Tank shut the door behind me. As he makes his way around to his side I chance a look in Shane's direction and sure enough she's having a complete silent meltdown in her front yard.

OH MY GOD. She mouths. All I can do is shrug as she takes her phone out of her pajama pant pocket and starts typing while staring straight at me so hard I think it's digging into my soul.

Ding.

SHANE

Emergency girls night.

ME

Um, I think I'm helping Tank move into my house tonight.

SHANE

He's a man. He'll pack some underwear and ammo and he's all set. Don't try to get out of this.

TAYLOR

Jesus Shane. Has Cece not let you get any sleep? You seem catty today.

ME

She's fine. She's just freaking out because she saw my husband kiss me in her front yard.

TAYLOR

LEAH

TAYLOR

HUSBAND

LEAH

KISSING

LAUREN

😏 I'll host. Ruby will bring the tea.

ME

I'll have to ask Tank, he's the only one allowed to tell me what to do now. 😈

TAYLOR

SCREAMING!!!!

LEAH

ON THE FLOOR 💀 😵

LAUREN

Oh my god. I'm so happy right now.

LEAH

And here I thought the hotel room was a BAD idea. 😅 silly me.

SHANE

I will not be able to focus on shit else today, so thanks for this. 😂

"Jesus Christ. What's all that about?" Tank asks, nodding towards my phone as the text alerts continue going off.

"Oh, nothing. Just a little girl talk." His brow raises with suspicion.

"Mhm... Let's see it." He wags two fingers motioning for me to show him, but his fingers moving like that sends my mind somewhere *completely* different. He must see the desire in my eyes because he gives me a warning look before cutting his eyes to the back seat, leaning forward to whisper, *"Naughty little wife"* in my ear right before snatching my phone out of my hands.

"Ahh, too slow." He sticks his tongue out like he's a child, holding my phone up by his shoulder as goosebumps appear along my arms from what he said. "Here. I'm just messing around." He tries handing my phone back to me. I look down at it momentarily then back up at him.

"It's okay. You can look." He gives me a questioning look but when I give him a nod, he looks down and starts reading.

It takes him a minute to get to the part I'm anticipating a reaction from the most, but when he does I'm not the least bit disappointed. He leans back on the headrest and lets out a groan like it's paining him not to say all sorts of dirty things to me right now in front of Hendrix. I hold my hand out for my phone with a proud smirk as he plops it down while shaking his head at me.

"You're gonna regret that," he mumbles, just loud enough for me to hear and little ears *not* to.

"No chance." I pretend to put all of my focus back on my phone as he finally pulls out of the driveway, when in reality I spend the entire drive to his apartment thinking of all the ways he could try to make me regret giving him that kind of power over me—and why it *doesn't* scare me. On the contrary, it *excites me*. I know that because when I finally step out of the truck again, I'm uncomfortably wet from just the thought of it. We aren't even at Tank's place an hour before he's done and I can't help but laugh when I notice almost everything he has packed is clothes and ammo outside of Mavcrick's things—which honestly looks like *more* than what Tank is bringing for himself. There's a bed, blankets, toys, food, bowls, a harness. Basically, if it's in the dog section at Petco, Maverick has it.

"So, you're going to have guns in the house?" I ask as Tank shoves his handgun safe into a bag.

"Yes, is that going to be a problem?" He drops the camouflage tactical-looking bag next to his regular duffle before walking over to me.

"I mean. What about Hendrix? He's never been around guns. He doesn't know how dangerous they are. I just...I don't want them there if he could end up getting hurt."

"Baby, what's the most important thing in this world to me?" he asks, wrapping his arms around my waist, and pulling me into him. I take a deep breath, contemplating my answer.

"Making Marco's life miserable." His face twists.

"I don't give a fuck about Marco." I swat his arm, widening my eyes as I look around for Hendrix. "Try again," he instructs.

"Us?"

"Damn straight. You and that little boy in there are the only things that matter. So in case this wasn't clear to you before, I'll make it clear now. I will *never* put either of you in harm's way again. I have safes for all of my guns, and the only way to get into the one I keep my sidearm in is with my thumbprint. *No one* is getting in it but me, I promise you, Hendrix will be safe." He kisses my forehead, putting all my worries at ease.

"Thank you."

"For what, Honey?"

"Always reassuring me of things without making me feel crazy or dumb," I admit, laying my head on his chest.

"Ruby, you're one of the smartest people I know. Never forget that. Needing reassurance over the safety of your son shouldn't make you question that."

I can't believe he's mine.

"Hey Tank," Hendrix asks from right beside us.

"Are you my dad now?" I look down and see him looking up at

Tank with a sadness about him that's so rare it has me worried.

Shit, why is this coming up right now?

"Why do you ask that, Hendrix?" I turn to face him, brushing some of his long brown hair back out of his eyes.

"I don't know. You guys are married now, so that means Tank is my dad, right?" I look up at Tank, and when my eyes land on his I see something stirring in his mind, though I'm not sure *what*. I open my mouth to answer him, even though I have no idea what I'm going to say, but Tank grabs my hand and stops me.

"Would it be okay with you if we have this conversation at dinner tonight? We can get back home and order takeout and sit down and really talk about what this means for all of us. That sound like a plan to you?" He directs the question at Hendrix, glancing at me for approval as well. Then I watch my full-of-life child nod simply before returning to the couch with Maverick—who seems to be his new best friend—where he's been playing with bar coasters.

Did Tank take those from Chattahoochies?

"What's going on? I see that you're thinking something, can you let me in on it?"

"Do you trust me?"

"I do, but–"

"Honey, I assure you if this was something you needed to know right this second I would tell you."

"But I do need to know right now. That's my baby and if something is wrong I want to know." He takes a deep breath, reluctantly telling me what he thinks.

"I have a feeling someone has said something to Hendrix about not having a dad that's upset him." I feel my face heat instantly, from my head all the way down my neck as I think about someone saying something so awful to my baby.

"But if it is that, it needs to be handled with a little time and sensitivity. Can I ask that you follow my lead with this?"

"Why do you think that's what this is?"

"Because I went through the same thing when my dad died. And

I remember wishing so badly that he was still here when kids would be assholes about me not having a dad." My heart sinks as I think about Tank as a kid, remembering how he said he was bullied and wishing I could go back in time and hug him and tell him everything will be okay. Then I get angry again when I think that may be happening to Hendrix now too. I finally nod my head in agreement, wrapping my arms around Tank to comfort him and thank him before we grab their things and head home.

Chapter 30

TANK

AS MUCH AS I wanted to be thrilled when Hendrix asked if I was his dad now, I saw the look on his face, the quiet plea behind his eyes when he asked. It wasn't just curiosity, there was a specific reason he was asking. We got home, ordered takeout, and though she's trying to control it, my sweet wife is about to lose her damn mind not knowing for sure what's going on. I asked her to follow my lead, knowing there was a chance she'd tell me there was no fucking way, that he's *her* kid and she'll be the one asking the questions. But much to my surprise, she was willing to let me, so I truly hope I handle this right.

"Hendrix. Come here." I sit down on the couch, holding a photo album I grabbed earlier from the apartment.

"Are we reading a story?" He plops down right beside me, laying his head on my shoulder as Ruby joins us on my other side. When I open the book and Hendrix starts petting Maverick with his feet, I can't help but smile at how natural this all feels.

"Sort of. I wanted to show you this picture of me when I was little." I flip to an old family photo where Tucker and I are sticking our tongues out at each other, while my mother squeezes our shoulders in an attempt to get us to act right, and my dad is smiling ear-to-ear as if nothing in the world is wrong.

"That's *you?*" He giggles.

"Yep. That's me right there, and that's your Uncle Tucker." I point to each of us in the photo.

"Who are they?" He points to my parents.

"That's my mom and dad."

"Your dad was a police officer?" he asks in amusement.

"He was. He actually died while he was out trying to stop bad guys." A wave of sadness I haven't felt in *years* washes over me as I think about him. As if he can sense it, Hendrix leans into me, wrapping his arm around mine.

"I'm sorry Tank." My eyes sting as I rest my cheek on the top of his head.

"I missed him a lot growing up, it was really hard not having my dad around." His head drops as he mumbles into my chest.

"Yeah?"

"Yeah. Some kids weren't very nice about it."

"Did they say mean things to you?" I shake my head, worried I was right about why he asked.

"They did. They would tease me for not having a dad and that made me *really* angry." He looks up at me with hopeful eyes.

"What did you do?"

"For a long time, I didn't handle it well and I would get into fights with people when they would say hurtful things."

"Fighting is bad," Hendrix rears back, scolding me with his glare.

"Well... The way I did it, yeah it was bad. But eventually, I stopped fighting the bullies."

"What did you do instead?"

"I threw them into trash cans." He spurts out laughter, but I'm not saying it just to make him giggle.

"Tank Landry. No, you didn't!" Ruby exclaims, swatting my arm.

"I certainly did. I was bigger than most of the kids in my class so when they would say things that hurt my feelings, I would put them in the garbage where they belonged."

"Oh, Lord," she mumbles, running her fingers through her hair as Hendrix continues laughing.

"Hendrix." He looks over at me, and seeing that it's time to be serious again he takes a deep breath. "Has someone said something about you not having a dad that made you angry?"

"Yes," he admits, making Ruby sit up a little straighter.

"Who was it?" she demands, her mama bear coming out, ready to show her claws.

"Tommy," he mumbles.

"The Halloway kid? I thought you two were friends." Her tone drops from anger to disappointment while dots begin connecting in my mind.

"Wait, what did you say his name was?" I frown, looking over at Ruby.

"Tommy Halloway, why?" I can't help but let out a humorless laugh.

"Do you know his parent's names?"

"Um, Jim and..." I don't even let her get the other name out before I turn back to Hendrix.

"Hendrix, look at me." He looks up with anticipation in his eyes. "How many times has this happened?"

"I don't know. Like every day last week." I take a deep breath, trying to remain calm while the more untamed part of my mind is telling me to look this asshole up immediately and let him know just who he's dealing with.

"I am about to tell you two very important things and I need to know you're listening, okay?"

"Yes, sir." He shakes his head, never breaking eye contact with me.

"Just because you grew up without a dad around, doesn't mean you were any less loved. Your mama loved you enough to know your life would be better this way. You are the coolest, smartest, happiest kid I know and I don't ever want you to change. Especially not because some kid is being an asshole."

"*Tank*," Ruby scolds me as Hendrix snickers.

"It felt necessary to get the point across." I shrug.

"What's the second thing?" he asks, looking up like he's hanging onto every single word I say.

"Next time Tommy picks on you, you tell him I'm gonna put his dad in a trash can again."

"Again?" Ruby inquires. I smirk over at her but don't bother explaining.

"Can I watch?" He leans in with his voice low like we're trying to be sneaky.

"You two are going to be the death of me." Ruby shakes her head in disapproval.

"You bet." I lean in and wink at him.

"Hendrix, baby, come here," Ruby says, opening her arms for Hendrix to sit in her lap. "Do you want to know the reason you didn't grow up with a dad? I know we've never talked about it before and I think you're old enough now that I can tell you why it's always just been me and you." He nods before resting his head on her arm, looking up at her as she continues, "The man that helped me make you, was *not* a nice man. He was very mean, and he said really bad things to mommy. I didn't know that when we made you though. *So* while you were still growing in my tummy, I made sure we moved very far away from him. I wanted to make sure you grew up around nice people, who would help me take very good care of you." I can see her fighting back the tears, but one slips past anyway quickly rolling down her cheek. I go to swipe it away, but Hendrix beats me to it.

God, I love this kid.

"It's okay, Mommy, we're safe now."

"I know, baby." When she smiles at him a lump forms in my throat at their interaction.

"Because we have nice people in our life. Like Tank, he'll take care of us. Won't you Tank?" He looks over at me and dammit if I'm not crying now too.

"Always." I choke out.

"I love you, Hendrix. More than anything in the world. You keep being you, and don't you ever let mean people bring your spirit down. You hear me?"

"Yes ma'am. I won't." He smiles. "Because Tank will put their dad in a trash can." He *winks* at me, making me bark out a laugh.

"Okay, trash man, why don't you go get your pj's on?" She shakes her head as he hops off her lap.

"Yes ma'am." He bolts down the hallway making Maverick perk up from his spot on the floor. Ruby sinks into my side, wrapping her arms around my waist as she exhales.

"So, you know the Halloways," She states, looking up at me.

"Jimmy Halloway is the reason I got put into wrestling in middle school. I fought that asshole so many times I almost got expelled. Apparently, his rotten fruit didn't fall far from the tree," I scoff, running a hand through my hair.

"Thanks for making Hendrix laugh by saying you'd put him in a trash can again." She giggles.

"Well, I'm glad he found it funny but I don't lie to Hendrix. I will one hundred percent throw that grown man into the trash if his kid says some shit to mine." The words come out of my mouth before I can stop them and my heart immediately stops as I wait for her reaction. She remains still for a moment before slowly sitting up beside me, her black hair falling beautifully around her face. I can't quite get a read on the look she's giving me, so my first instinct is to apologize.

"I'm sorry. I don't... I didn't mean to say anything to overstep." She studies me a little longer, an agonizing wave of nerves settling over me before she finally speaks.

"You really think of him that way, don't you?" My mind quickly runs through memories of us playing soccer at the park for the first time, the day I picked him up from school and we went to Spurs, the protectiveness I feel over him that I've only ever felt for one other person—the woman who he gets his...*everything* from.

"Yeah, Honey. I really do." I struggle to get the words out without letting my voice shake. "I have for a while now, but I never wanted to seem like I was inserting myself somewhere I didn't belong. I love that kid, Ruby. I love him as much as I love you. I just want him to know I'll never stop showing up for him. That's part of why I couldn't stay away when I knew he started soccer. I needed to be able to cheer him on, even if he didn't know it, and tell him one day that I was there. That I never missed a thing." With tears streaming down her face she pulls me into her, capturing my lips with hers.

I wrap my hands around her waist as she climbs onto my lap, parting her lips to allow my tongue easy access to hers. Kissing Ruby for the first time six months ago was incredible, but making out with my *wife* is absolutely indescribable.

"Are you really mine?" she asks, rubbing the tip of her nose against mine.

"I don't think I've ever been anyone else's, Honey."

"Let's go to bed." She stands up from my lap with a smile, giving me those *come and get me* eyes.

I'll never stop chasing after you, little wife.

But before I chase after her I see her phone light up on the couch and take it upon myself to update the group chat.

> **ME**
>
> She won't be coming... for you.

TAYLOR

🙂

SHANE

😅

LEAH

😳

LAUREN

🥹 I'm done. 😘

270

Chapter 31

RUBY

"I THINK I LOVE YOUR HUSBAND." Lauren laughs, pouring our margaritas into glasses.

"Hey, watch it," I warn, giving her a playful glare. She gives me a surprised look with her mouth hanging open.

"Not like *that*, duh. But that text was *bold.*"

"Well, he wouldn't be Tank if he wasn't." I feel the butterflies fluttering around in my stomach just at the mention of his name.

"I think my mouth hung open for five minutes straight after that," Leah adds.

"I slapped Max so hard he thought something was wrong with the baby... that *he* was holding."

"You slapped him *while* he was holding Cece?" Taylor says in disbelief.

"Well, it's not like I slapped *her*. He has big arms, she was fine." Shane rolls her eyes, looking back over at me. "Seriously. You need to start spilling *now*. I have been completely unstable today waiting for information."

"We know," Taylor sasses.

"What exactly is it you want to know?" I could assume they mean just what happened at Shane's house, but there's also a whole lot of shit that happened to get us to that point.

"I... I have no idea." Shane's face drops as she realizes she actually has no clue what information it is she wants.

"Let's start with the fact that your husband is completely in love with you," Lauren announces, sipping her margarita. Everyone turns to face me again, making my cheeks heat instantly.

I ended up telling the girls about the few times Tank and I kissed shortly after the night they guessed something was going on between us. They freaked out, of course, but after he and I didn't talk for six months, it was like a silent understanding that we wouldn't discuss it again. Until now. Because *now* I'm married and head over heels for him.

"What makes you assume that?" I ask the question jokingly, but her response is not one I'm prepared to hear.

"Well, you don't send your soon-to-be wife's best friend on a mission to pamper her or buy her the most gorgeous locket I've ever seen without being madly in love with her," Lauren says, pulling the locket under her forefinger to bring attention to it.

"Wait, *Tank* was responsible for all the pampering that day?" I don't know why I sound surprised. Because it's not the least bit surprising that he was behind it. I absentmindedly grab my necklace, feeling completely awful for not having thanked him properly for it yet.

"Hold on, *best friend?* Who gave you that title?" Taylor interrupts loudly. Lauren gives her an annoyed look before turning to face me again.

"He didn't tell you?" she asks, looking genuinely confused.

"We uh, had other things to discuss. I honestly forgot I was wearing it." I run my fingers along the blue stone in the middle, wondering why he wouldn't have brought it up either.

"So you guys talked about things then? I mean, like why he was radio silent on you for so long and... everything else?" Leah asks as we all move to the couch in Lauren's living room.

"*Yeah...* He actually wrote me a letter that I never read. If I had, I probably wouldn't have lost so much time with him." I shake my head, putting thoughts of the locket in the back of my mind.

"Oh my god, he wrote you a *letter*? What a fucking romantic." Taylor fake cries into her margarita. Then she gasps dramatically, startling all of us. "*OH MY GOD!*" she screams, making Shane jolt in her seat and Leah almost spill her margarita.

"What?" we all ask in unison.

"We're going to be sisters-in-law!" she squeals. I get weirdly emotional at the thought of having a sister. One that I actually adore and get along with too. Taylor is the funniest person I've ever met, she's loyal to a fault, and much like myself, she doesn't take shit from *anyone*.

"Oh my god, you're right." I laugh, letting the tears blur my vision as she squeezes me in a hug. "Hey, if your husband fucks as good as his brother then double congratulations to you."

"*TAYLOR*. Decorum, please," Leah says, shaking her head at her.

"Well, I'm not sure a soul on earth could out-fuck my husband. But double thanks," I say, feeling my cheeks burn as the girls' faces all morph into pure shock and excitement.

"Tell us everything." Taylor squeezed my arm.

"Um, *no*." I remove her hand and place it back in her lap to reach for my drink.

"Buzzkill," Lauren mumbles into her drink again.

"Pause." Shane holds her hand up, trying to catch up to everything. "Ruby, do you love him? Like, actually *love* him? Is all of this legit now?" I shake my head, trying to fight back the emotion creeping up my throat.

"I love him so much that it scares me," I admit. "In one single night he healed parts of me I thought were damaged beyond repair. He never makes me question where we stand or how he feels about me. He makes me feel safe in ways I assumed were unattainable. I don't know how else to describe it, but I can't imagine having to live without him now." They all stare at me with adoration on their faces.

I can't help but laugh at what a sap I sound like. "I'm insane. I've been married for two days and already I'm acting like a melodramatic wife who would die without her husband." I roll my eyes at myself.

"And I think there's something absolutely beautiful about that, babe," Lauren says, bringing my attention to her. "Because when someone who's been fighting her whole life to feel safe can put all her trust into someone who makes her feel that way so effortlessly, they're meant to be. You guys may have had to fight like hell to get here, but you're *meant* to be together. No doubt."

I love my best friends so much.

"But okay. Will you at least tell us *some* details about the sex?" Taylor interrupts the moment with her brash request.

"Jesus Christ," Shane mumbles. I can't help but laugh when I realize she will not be giving up on this any time soon.

"I love you girls like sisters, but I'd *much* rather be at home with my husband right now." I give them a suggestive stare and they all start squealing and giving me *atta girl's*. Even though I meant that statement with my whole heart, I know he'll be there waiting when I get home, so I let myself enjoy the rest of the night with my girls. In the middle of our very deep discussion about what Lauren wants to do instead of real estate, my phone goes off with a text from Tank. He and Hendrix are both in sweatpants with no shirts and they're flexing in the bathroom mirror.

> **TANK**
>
> Hendrix wanted to show you how big his muscles are getting because he ate ALL of his broccoli with dinner tonight.
>
> I wanted to show you what's waiting for you when you get home. 😏
>
> **ME**
>
>
>
> **TANK**
>
> How much longer till you're home?

ME

Are you rushing me?

TANK

I'm picturing you on your knees with my cock
down your throat. Of course I am.

ME

I DO get a little handsy when I'm buzzed.

TANK

You're killing me, baby. Please come home to me.
😔

ME

I'll leave here in 10. 😊

TANK

That's my good little wife.

ME

😇

TANK

We're gonna have to hang that halo up tonight,
Honey.

"Come on, sis. I'll give you a ride," Taylor says, pulling me off the
couch.

"What?" I say, looking around as everyone cleans up the living
room.

"I know that look *and* that shade of red. You're ready to go
home," she teases, calling me out *very* accurately.

"Is it that obvious?" I ask quietly.

"Oh, babe. Yes. It is." We say our goodbyes and Taylor drives me
home, while I spend

the whole drive staring at the picture Tank sent me.

Not only because he's so hot I can't breathe when I look at him, but because he looks like a *dad*. Making sure Hendrix took a bath, getting him to eat his vegetables—which is a *miracle*—and more than likely doing all the boyish things with him that I could never do the same way he can. It makes me wish he *was* Hendrix's dad.

"Here we are." Taylor puts her car in park and I look up to see that we're already sitting in my driveway.

I have got to stop spacing out like this.

"Thanks for the ride, Tay." I lean over to hug her neck, noticing a strange look on her face when I pull away. "What's wrong?"

"I'm just so happy for you Rubes. I know you've got plenty of shit going on right now that could have you down. But the fact that you've found love and happiness in the midst of it all? You deserve this more than anyone else I know. Don't forget that, okay? That you deserve to be happy." I shake my head to thank her, unable to form a coherent sentence right now.

"Love you, girl. Now go see your boys." She winks at me, nodding up to the house.

"Love you too." I hug her once more before getting out of the car, and making my way up the sidewalk.

When I walk into the house and see Hendrix, Maverick, and Tank asleep together on the couch, my heart swells in my chest. I snap a photo of them, standing there a few more moments to just stare at them. They're still in their gray sweatpants and Hendrix is tucked safely under Tank's arm while Spidey plays on the TV. I'm not sure what's freaking out more, my mind, my heart, or my ovaries. I walk over and brush Hendrix's hair out of his eyes before running my fingers through Tank's in the same way—making his eyes fly open when I do. I see his chest rise and fall a little harder, as his grip on Hendrix tightens slightly. When his vision focuses on me, he relaxes again.

"Hey, it's just me. Sorry, I didn't mean to startle you," I whisper, careful not to wake Hendrix.

"Bout time you made it home to me, wife." He smiles sleepily at me. I lean down and kiss his lips gently, causing him to grip my hair and pull me in a little harder.

"I'm gonna take Hendrix to bed." I go to pick him up, realizing just how big he's gotten. He's more than half my size and it makes me sad to think about just how fast time flies.

"Here, let me do it," Tank offers, hooking his arms under Hendrix's knees and neck before lifting him effortlessly from the couch. "Come on, we can tuck him in together." He nods for me to follow him down the hallway to Hendrix's room, and of course, Maverick is right on our heels.

When Tank lays him down in bed Maverick jumps up, laying down right beside him. Hendrix takes a cleansing breath before wrapping his arm around Mav and falling right back to sleep. I kiss his forehead and whisper how much I love him before we finally leave the room. Once the door is shut, I waste no time throwing myself into the arms of my husband and he meets me movement for movement as he wraps my legs around his waist. He grips my hair in one hand, while holding me up with the other, letting his lips roam from my neck down to my chest.

"I missed you, little wife." He growls against my neck, sending a shiver down my spine.

"I missed you, too, my love." His grip on my ass tightens to the point I think I might have fingerprints left there tomorrow.

"Say that again," he demands, releasing his grip on my hair so I can look at him straight on.

"I missed you, my love."

"*Fuck*, I love the way that sounds." He smirks against my mouth before biting my bottom lip.

"More than this?" I ask before letting out a soft moan, letting my hips drop to feel his length harden against me.

Buzzed Ruby may be a little unhinged. But I know it's okay to be with him.

He hikes me up over his shoulder before storming off to our

bedroom. Once the door is shut and locked he tosses me onto the bed, leaning over me with his lips mere inches from mine.

"Nothing compares to hearing how much you love being *mine*, Honey." He stands up at the edge of the bed, dropping his sweatpants before wrapping his hand around his cock.

"Kneel for me, wife." Wetness pools between my thighs at his command. I stand up right in front of him, looking up as he narrows his gaze at me. Before I do as he's asked, I pull my Zeppelin T-shirt over my head and drop my jeans to the floor, showing off one of my favorite outfits I used to dance in. It's a red lace bodysuit with roses all over it. Once I toss my clothes to the side, I drop to my knees, gathering my hair to tie it up out of the way.

"You're fucking perfect, you know that?" he growls. I smirk at him and simply stick my tongue out to accept him. He may love the way I sound from him making me his, but the enjoyment I get from seeing and hearing how good I make *him* feel turns me on more than I knew was possible. I want this man to absolutely ruin my life. I continue taking him as far down as my throat will allow, knowing exactly when to suck down and when to stroke him with my tongue.

"*Fuck baby*," he grits out through his teeth before pulling away from me. I look up at him and pout. "You remember your safe words?" The look in his eyes is absolutely wild tonight and the excitement it sends through my body has my pussy aching for him.

"I don't need them." He tilts his head in confusion.

"*Baby*, I'm not sure how much control I'll have with you tonight," he warns, "I don't want to hurt you."

"You won't," I assure him. I reach around and pull my favorite part of this outfit off, handing him the silk ribbon from the decorative bow on the back.

"Eyes, mouth, or hands." I turn around and rest my hands on my ass, waiting for him to pick where he wants to tie it. He takes a step closer, bringing his body flush with mine and his lips to my ear.

"Are you *sure*?" I tilt my head to meet his gaze and nod.

"I'm sure, my love. I trust you." His jaw ticks as he captures my lips with his, wrapping his hand around my neck. My nipples harden when he squeezes a little tighter, pressing his cock against my back.

"Face down, ass up, and hands back," he commands, nodding towards the bed. Once I'm in position he ties my hands, rubbing my back down to my ass before ripping a hole in my outfit to give him a clear path to my entrance without removing my lingerie completely. I let out a little gasp as his finger glides through my wetness, then I see him drop to his knees before he pulls me to the edge of the bed, swiping his tongue along my pussy. My whole body tingles at the feeling of him absolutely devouring me. There's something exhilarating about being at the mercy of someone who will do things that would feel terrifying with anyone else, but you know you'll be safe with *them*. When he slips two fingers inside me, curling them in sync with the motion of his tongue against my clit, I can't help but moan his name.

"*Tank!* I'm gonna come." He continues feasting on me until I'm biting the sheets to keep from screaming.

I'm barely down from my orgasm when he slips his fingers out and thrusts into me, making me yelp. "That's right baby, and you're gonna give me a few more." His massive hands wrap around my waist, handling me like a toy made for his own pleasure.

A *few more?*

I feel lightheaded as he continues to ram into me deeper and deeper, hitting every single spot I need him to. I feel like I'm basking in the sun with the way the warmth is spreading through my body—pressure building as he fills me completely, unrelenting as I grip the sheets of our bed.

"*Ah, Tank!*" I scream into the mattress.

"That's it, Honey. Give it to me." And I do. Another orgasm rips through me, making me release the sheets to dig my nails into my palms. My screams are barely muffled as his absolutely punishing pace keeps me coming. One of his hands reaches around my waist, pulling me up with my back flush to his chest.

"You're okay, baby. You're gonna give me one more." I shake my head trying to tell him I can't, but no words come out. My chest heaves up and down as my chest rises and falls rapidly.

"Yes, you are. But I need you to be quiet for me so we don't have to stop. You don't want to stop, do you, Honey?" I whimper and shake my head no.

"Atta girl. Just one more." He kisses my temple as his hand wraps around my throat, his cock still buried inside me as he picks up his pace, causing my head to fall back on his shoulder. I can already feel the tension building again, making my head swim. I let out a loud moan and he brings his lips around to mine, doing his best to keep me quiet—though it doesn't work. I can tell I'm close and his kiss only spurs me on further. His name falls from my lips again, and he pulls away.

"Bite," he demands, moving his hand up from my throat to my mouth. "I'm gonna come with you this time, baby, so let me have it. Come for me, my perfect little wife." I bite down on his hand right by his thumb as my body trembles. I can feel him pulsing inside me as he groans and gently bites my shoulder. He kisses away the bite marks as his pace finally begins to slow down, and his fingers begin caressing my jaw in the most gentle way as he drags his lips up and down my neck.

"You okay, baby?"

"Yes," I say breathlessly.

"You felt safe?" The way he asks makes me love him even more.

"With you, always." I lean my head back to capture his gaze. He huffs out a laugh and smirks before kissing me again.

"You were such a good little wife for me."

One reason I loved dancing so much was because I felt like I was in control of my body. When that feeling was taken from me, I was sure I'd never get it back. I realize now that I was wrong. I just hadn't met Tank yet. He's given me the security I needed to feel in control again, even when I'm *not*.

He unties my hands and helps me out of my now-ruined body-suit, instructing me to lay down while he runs me a bath. The way he always takes care of me after we have sex is something I'm getting spoiled to *very* quickly. But I get the feeling that with Tank, it's not something that will stop any time soon.

After getting into our sweats, we unlock the door and climb into bed. Once I'm tucked under his arm with my head on his chest, Tank begins playing with my hair, something else I'm getting spoiled to.

My contentment is disrupted as I think about how I'm not quite ready to get back to reality yet. Max gave me some time off from the bar to get settled into my new normal, but that all ends tomorrow. It's back to work, back to the custody shit show, and even though I'm sure Tank will be glad to get back to his routine of going to the gym, volunteering, and whatever else it is he does during the day, I'm really going to miss being with him all day.

I think I may be dick-whipped.

That or this is what it feels like to be in love.

It's honestly a toss-up at this point.

Chapter 32

TANK

"*Get him restrained, Dom.*" *I hear Asher instructing.* "*You two, help him. Figure out what the fuck is going on with this guy, I'm going down to get Tank.*" *I try to roll to one side, then the other. Fuck—I can't move without feeling like my spine is about to snap in two. That or it already has and the shock hasn't let me feel it yet.*

"*Hey, man. Talk to me. You good?*" *Asher is down the stairs and by my side in a matter of seconds.*

"*I can't move, Ash. My back hurts like fucking hell.*"

"*Don't worry. We'll get you out of here. Quite the dramatic exit you took up there.*" *I laugh, sending needle-like pain all the way down my back.*

"*Fuck you,*" *I groan, making him force a smile as he calls for the MedeVac.*

In a blink, we're at the hospital and all I can hear is the annoying repetition of the machines I'm hooked up to.

BEEP. BEEP. BEEP.

Fuck, I don't remember it being this loud.

"*Turn it offfff,*" *someone groans, but there's no one in the room but me. I look around again, but still, I see no one.*

BEEP. BEEP. BEEP.

"Tank, I swear to god, turn it off," Ruby's voice finally breaks through the barrier of dream and reality, making my heart rate steady back out when I see I'm *not* back in the hospital. I can feel myself covered in sweat, the stress from that dream taking a subconscious toll on my body.

I let out a tired groan of disapproval when I realize it's my alarm going off, letting me know it's time to get back to the grind. I'd much rather stay in bed with my wife all day, but I suppose I am a little excited to get back to *The Veterans Center* this week. I reach over to silence the noise, but when I do I notice a tiny arm is draped over my face and Maverick is lying across my stomach.

No wonder my back was hurting in that dream. Maverick's big ass is making it hurt for real.

I lift the arm gently and let my eyes adjust to see Hendrix sprawled out next to me, with his head on my shoulder, arm on my face, and his feet on Ruby. I can't help but laugh at the fact that *I* got the good end of this bargain.

I slide out of bed, being careful not to wake them, but Hendrix jerks when Maverick jumps down—kicking Ruby in the leg. I hold my breath waiting for her to groan and wake up, but she simply picks up his legs and lays them over her stomach—as if she's done this a thousand times before.

Which she probably has.

I'm realizing in this moment, that I have no idea what *their* regular schedule looks like together. This is only my second day living here, so I'm sure I'll be filled in on everything I need to know soon enough.

After letting Maverick outside to do his thing, I flip on the light in the kitchen and start brewing a pot of coffee before getting a quick warm-up workout done in the living room. I don't like wasting time warming up at the gym, so I always do that at home. That way when I get there it's straight to the weights.

"If you do this every morning I might not be such a gremlin when I first wake up." I stop mid push-up and look over my shoulder to see Ruby leaning against the wall, holding a cup of coffee in her hands.

"Mornin', Honey." I smirk at her as she takes a sip of her drink, squinting her eyes as a sign she's smiling back at me. Her hair is clipped back, but pieces are sticking out every which way, and she's wearing a pair of boxer briefs that hug her curves just right with an oversized *Bad Bunnies* T-shirt.

Perfection.

I jump up and walk over to her, kissing her forehead before going to make my own cup.

"Do you always wake up this early?" I ask as she pulls herself up onto the countertop.

"When I smell coffee I do." She smiles.

"Noted." I put the coffee pot back and walk over to where she's sitting. "Tell me what a normal day looks like for the two of you."

"It's so early." She pouts, shrinking to lay her head on my shoulder. I cradle the back of her head and laugh.

My wife is not a morning person.

"Okay, we can talk about it later. Just tell me what I can do to help make your morning easier." She leans back and looks at me while she thinks.

"I don't know. I'm so used to the routine we have I wouldn't know how to pick something to *not* do."

"Alright, how about I watch you guys for today and see if I can fall into your groove tomorrow?" She nods sleepily. "My sleepy little wife."

"Very sleepy." She pouts again. I bend down and kiss her neck, loving the way she tilts her head to give me better access.

"I'll try not to keep you up so late from now on," I whisper against her neck.

"Just put energy drinks on the shopping list, I'll be fine." I smile even bigger as I stand up to look at her. She bites her lip, making a subtle ache for her shoot all the way through me. I place my hands on either side of her face, keeping her focus fixed on my eyes.

"I love you, Honey."

"I love you more." She smiles, grabbing the locket around her neck. "*Oh,* I meant to thank you for this." She pulls it out from beneath the collar of her T-shirt, running her fingers across the blue stone. "When Lauren gave it to me, I originally thought it was from her, but when she said it wasn't I could hardly believe it was from *you.*" Her cheeks turn the perfect shade of pink as she dips her head to look at it again.

"Did you not look inside?" I smirk, making her look up, narrowing her gaze on me.

"No, why?" I reach up and click the locket open, turning it around to show her the photo inside. It's the one of me and Hendrix at Spurs from the day she asked me to pick him up. When her eyes meet mine they're so full of love I wish I had a camera to capture it.

"Thank you, Tank. It's perfect. I can't believe I didn't open it," she whispers, shaking her head as she admires the photo again.

"I forgive you," I tease, kissing her forehead.

"I'm grateful." She reaches back up, quickly kissing my lips.

"I want pancakes," Hendrix grumbles from across the kitchen. When I look over at him his hair is complete chaos and he's rubbing his eyes with a grumpy look on his face.

So he gets his morning rituals from his mother.

"Then I am making pancakes," I announce, winking at Ruby before looking around the kitchen for ingredients.

"*Yes!*" he whispers, as he climbs up on the counter with Ruby. She slides back to sit cross-legged on the island while he lays his head down in her lap, telling me exactly how many chocolate chips to put in his breakfast.

I could get used to this.

WIFE

When would be a good time for us to meet with the attorney?

ME

I've got clients booked for all my afternoons the rest of the week, but I'm free tomorrow morning.

WIFE

Okay, how about after we drop Hendrix off at school?

ME

Sounds like a plan. Am I still picking him up this afternoon?

WIFE

Yes, please.

ME

Hell yeah.

WIFE

Don't you ever try to tell me he gets it from me. 😄

ME

😄 That's my boy.

And it feels damn good to finally say it.

We're a few weeks away from school being out for fall break and I've been thinking a lot about what that will look like for our new little family. Hendrix *used* to go to Betty's during holiday breaks, summer, and after school while Ruby worked full time, but I've had a few ideas on how that might possibly change. How I *want* that to change. I want both of us to be able to spend more time with Hendrix—for

Ruby to not have to work so much and me to be able to take him with me to volunteer instead of dropping him off at the sitter's house for the day. If he *can* be with us, I don't see any reason for him *not* to be. I want us *together*, as much as possible.

Like many other parents today, I decided to ditch the car rider line and walk up to get him myself. Boy, am I glad I did too because it seems a certain little rotten apple is picking on him right outside the school. Hendrix's back is to me, and little Tommy shithead looks so much like his father that it's unmistakably him. I stop briefly to listen to what's being said, still far enough away that they haven't noticed me yet.

"You probably just play with Barbie dolls and watch *girl* shows because you don't have a dad to do all the boy stuff with." My jaw ticks when I hear the words come out of his mouth, seeing the way Hendrix just stands there and takes it makes me proud and sad all at the same time.

"Well, say something you *weirdo*." Just about that time a man walks up beside Tommy and rests his hand on his shoulder.

"Leave him alone son, he can't help that he doesn't have a dad."

No wonder this kid is such an asshole, it seems his father never stopped being one.

I stalk over towards them just about the time I hear Hendrix speak up.

"I do too have a dad, and he's gonna put your dad in a trashcan, asshole!" Hendrix yells.

Oops.

"Hey, you watch your mouth you little–" I tap Jimmy on the shoulder, interrupting him before he can finish his sentence. He turns to face me with a confused expression—until he realizes who's standing behind him.

"I'd choose your next words to *my kid* very carefully," I warn.

"*Your kid?*" he scoffs.

"Yes, *mine*. You got a problem with that?"

"I have a problem with what he just said to Tommy." He looks over at Hendrix who has a proud smirk on his face as he watches us. Jimmy covers his son's ears before looking back at me. "He called my son an asshole." I can tell by his tone that he expects me to be shocked. Little does he know I'm taking Hendrix for ice cream after this for saying it and standing up for himself.

"Well, Jimmy, your kid *is* an asshole. Just like his father." I clap his shoulder, winking at Hendrix before continuing. "And what do we do to assholes who bully us, Hendrix?"

"We throw them in the trash," he says with a devilish tone.

"You're not serious. We're grown men now, you're not gonna–" I move so quickly he never sees it coming. In one swift movement, he's over my shoulder as I march around to the back of the school by the dumpsters, with Hendrix and the rotten apple on my heels. I toss him in and dust off my hands, making Hendrix beam with pride.

"Teach your kid some manners, Halloway. Maybe you'll finally learn some yourself while you're at it." I start walking back to the front of the school with Hendrix bopping along right beside me when Jimmy gets the nerve to speak up.

"Because you're *such* a great example for your kid?" he mouths off, making me backtrack over to him. I shove my index finger in his face, making him rear back a little to keep me from poking him in the damn forehead.

"I'm teaching my kid to stand up for himself. We don't back down to bullies who are just cowards taking their anger out on people. I'm showing him how to stand up for himself *and* others when necessary. I'm setting a *great* example for him, and you're sure as hell not going to be the one to change my mind about that." I back away with my chest heaving, getting out every word I wish I had said to him all those years ago.

"Let's go Hendrix." He grabs my hand as we make our way back to my truck, my mind reeling as I contemplate whether or not I handled that right. Maybe it was a little overkill. Am I really teaching him to stand up for himself, or am I just teaching him to out-bully the bully.

"Hey, Dad…" I freeze in the middle of the parking lot, hearing him call me that directly for the first time making my heart damn near explode. I look down as his big brown eyes that match his mama's look up at me in wonder.

"Yeah, buddy?"

"Do you think I can really protect people like you do?" I pull him over to the side of my truck, making sure we're out of the way of traffic, before bending down to his level.

"I do. Hendrix, you're the sweetest kid I know, and that isn't something that makes you weak. You're stronger for it. Because you care about other people. You have a quality not everyone else does. You are going to grow up to be strong and brave and I have full confidence that you'll protect the people you care about."

"Can I throw people into trash cans?" He leans in, raising his eyebrows at me. I can't help but laugh at the takeaways he always comes up with.

"For now, you just keep being kind and tell a grown-up when someone needs help. If you see or hear anyone in trouble, the best way you can protect them right now is to tell an adult. You understand me?"

"Yes sir." He shakes his head, making his hair fall down over his eyes.

"I think it's about time for a haircut, little man." I rustle his hair, as he nods his head.

"Yeah, I know. The shop is never open when mom is off work." He laughs, giving me an idea.

"You know what, I could use a haircut myself," I say, running my hand through my hair. "You mind going with me?"

"Okay!"

"Alright, let's go." I open the door for him to climb into his seat. "But we're stopping for ice cream first because I am so proud of you for sticking up for yourself today. Maybe just, don't call people assholes anymore, alright? I don't want to get in trouble with your mom." He giggles when I mention getting in trouble with Ruby.

"Yes, sir."

ME

> Got Hendrix. I needed a haircut so I brought him with me, mind if we get his done too?

WIFE

OMG yes! I've been needing to take him for weeks but they're never open when I'm off.

ME

> He said he wants to try something new, you cool with that?

WIFE

Please don't bring him home bald.

ME

> Woman, I love you but what the fuck?

WIFE

Sorry, I'm just not used to not being there.

ME

> You trust me with his life, but not his hair...

WIFE

Point taken. See you guys tonight. I love you.

ME

> I love you too, my little agoraphobic.

WIFE

As we're pulling out of the parking lot, Hendrix's gaze is fixed on something outside of his window, then he finally looks up at me through the mirror.

"My mom is great at doing boy stuff with me. She doesn't even like Barbies and she *loves* watching *The Avengers* with me."

"Yeah, buddy, your mom is the coolest."

"Yeah, she is," he agrees with a smile spreading across his face.

"Hey, who's your mom's favorite Avenger?" I nod towards him, my curiosity piqued.

"Captain America," he states simply, making me smirk to myself. *Hmm. Is that so?*

Chapter 33

RUBY

"OKAY, so it's one, two, duck. Back up, and do it again. Got it?" I hear Tank's voice as I walk through the front door, the deep swagger to his tone instantly putting me at ease.

"Got it," Hendrix agrees eagerly.

"Okay, tap gloves. Go." When I make it to the living room I see Tank sitting on his knees with punching mitts on and Hendrix with tiny boxing gloves and a practice helmet on. Hendrix punches the mitts like Tank told him to, then ducks when Tank tries to get a hit in. Then they do it again, this time Tank comes around the opposite side, and Hendrix still dodges his attempt.

"That's what I'm talking about man, good job." They do it one more time, but Tank gets a hit on Hendrix, making me gasp by default. Hendrix starts giggling uncontrollably as Tank scoops him up to check on him.

"Hey, Honey, I didn't hear you come in." Tank looks up at me with that perfect, bright smile that sends my nervous system into overdrive.

"Mommy!" Hendrix runs over, hugging my waist with his glove-covered hands. "I'm learning how to fight." He smiles, his cheeks squishing together from his helmet.

"Are you now?" I ask, looking at Tank for an explanation.

"I am. But he *knows...*" He prompts Hendrix to finish his sentence.

"It's only for self-defense." Hendrix recites proudly.

"And..."

"*You don't throw the first punch, but you make sure you throw the last,*" he says as if Tank's drilled it into his head within the three hours they've been together.

"That's my boy," Tank praises, unwrapping the mitts from his hands. He stands and walks over to me, spinning his ball cap backward on his head to kiss me before helping Hendrix take his gloves off.

"You know, it's hard to disapprove of you teaching him to fight when you're doing it in such an honorable way," I tease.

"I'm not sure if I should apologize, say thank you, or you're welcome," he remarks, throwing their gloves on the couch.

"Yeah, me either and I'm way too exhausted to decide right now. Where did these come from anyways?" I ask, grabbing one of the discarded gloves as I fall onto the couch.

"There's a little sports shop right next to where we got our haircut today, so we stopped in to kill some time. When I told Hendrix about how I used to fight, he asked me to teach him. So... here we are."

"Oh, that's right. I forgot about the haircuts. Should I be worried since you both have your heads covered?" I ask nervously since Hendrix still has his helmet on.

"No, I just have a habit of wearing this and you know... safety first." He gestures for Hendrix to walk over so he can help take his helmet off.

"Ready, Mom?" His face is so full of excitement, I better love whatever haircut he chose for himself today because I can already tell he's completely obsessed.

"I'm ready." I sit up a little straighter as he looks up at Tank, and when he winks down at him, they both take their hats off—revealing that they have the same haircut. It's just long enough on top to either style to one side or wear as a fohawk, with a perfectly blended fade, and they both look *so* handsome.

"Do you like it? I look *just* like Dad now." Hendrix smiles, looking up at Tank again, but this time Tank looks over at me nervously, though there's also a hint of pride in his eyes that makes me smile.

"You sure do. You two are basically twins." I smile at him, opening my arms as he runs over for a hug.

"I'm glad you like it." Tank leans down to kiss my forehead. "I'm going to start dinner." I'm stunned silent as he walks into the kitchen, leaving me and Hendrix on the couch while he cooks. I'm not used to this, *obviously*, but it feels good—being taken care of, having time to just sit with Hendrix and talk before we ever make it to the dinner table.

"So, tell me about your day. How was school?"

"Well... Tommy was being mean to me again today," he says, but he doesn't seem sad about it.

"I'm sorry, buddy. Did you tell Tank when he picked you up?"

"I didn't have to. He heard *everything* when he walked up to get me and when Tommy's dad said I couldn't help that I didn't have a dad, Tank threw him in the trash can. And I got to watch!" I have so many mixed emotions from this conversation I don't even know where to start.

"He did *what?*"

"He threw Tommy's dad over his shoulder and took him to the dumpsters behind the school. He told him that he was going to teach me to stand up for myself and be brave." He animatedly stomps through the living room, throwing an invisible person over his shoulder into an imaginary dumpster, smiling so big I temporarily let go of the arguments I have about the way that was handled. "It was awesome." He finally plops back down beside me.

"So, you started calling Tank Dad today then, huh?"

"Yeah. Because I *really* want Tank to be my dad. He is, isn't he, Mom?" My heart twists as his big brown eyes search mine.

"Let me ask you this. What do *you* think it means to be a dad?"

"I think dads play soccer and make you laugh. They get the same haircuts and keep you safe. They come to pick you up from school and take you for ice cream. Oh, and they protect you and love you *so* much." Tears fill my eyes as Hendrix explains every single thing that Tank has done for him that makes him think he'd make a good dad. "And Tank does *all* of that with me. And now that you're married, he gets to be my dad, right?"

"I think Tank makes the *best* dad," I agree.

"So, it's okay if I call him that now?" he asks hopefully.

"If that's how you feel and it's what you want, then of course you can, buddy."

"Thanks, Mommy." He wraps his arms around my neck as we fall back on the couch, giggling together as I tickle his sides.

"Hey, does everyone want cheese on their burgers?" Tank asks, appearing back in the living room.

"Yes, please," Hendrix and I both say in unison.

"Cool." He turns to go back to grilling but Hendrix scrambles to his feet and darts over to him, throwing himself into Tank's arms.

"Whoa, hey!" Hendrix wraps his arms around Tank's neck, squeezing him so hard I think he might choke him. "What's this for?" he asks with a smile, squeezing him back as his eyes cut to me.

"Thanks for marrying my mom," he whispers, though I can still hear him clear as day. "I'm *so* happy you get to be my dad now." Tank glances over at me again, this time with a look of elated surprise. I smile, nodding my head to let him know I'm okay with it.

"I'm so happy I get to be your dad too, buddy. You have no idea just how much." He closes his eyes as Hendrix nuzzles into his neck. "And thanks for letting me marry her."

"You're welcome," he says loudly, making us laugh as he pops back up and hops out of Tank's arms. When Tank heads back outside to grill, Hendrix appoints himself co-grill master and goes with him, so I take the opportunity to close my eyes and try to rest until dinner is ready. However, that plan only lasts long enough for me to get comfortable before my phone goes off.

Ding.

REMINDER: APPOINTMENT TOMORROW @ 8:30 AM
Morgenson Law Firm.

I lock my phone and toss it to the side, letting my head fall back on the couch as I let out a frustrated groan. There are so many moments where I almost forget *why* Tank and I got married in the first place. Finally admitting our feelings for each other and ending up in the situation we're in now feels like a fairytale that keeps getting disrupted by a harsher reality.

I wish this were all just some stupid nightmare that I could wake up from—only when I wake up Tank and I would still be together. Unfortunately, this nightmare I'm living is *very* real. At least through the storm, I still have Tank. His unwavering support and confidence that we'll get through this and come out the other side is the only thing keeping me afloat most days.

"Go wash up and then you can set the table, I'll get Mom." I hear the boys setting things down in the kitchen, and I can't help but fall even more in love with him and the way he's taking charge around here. Teaching Hendrix how to stand up for himself, taking him for a haircut without me asking, cooking dinner for us like it's just the most natural thing in the world. I'm not sure if he was worried about fitting into our lives and our routines, but in the same way, he's said I was the missing puzzle piece from his life—he was the one missing from ours as well. I only hope things can stay like this for us.

"Yes, sir." Hendrix's little feet take off down the hallway. My eyes are still shut when I feel Tank sit down right beside me.

"What's got my beautiful wife frowning?" he asks, pressing the frown lines between my eyebrows to smooth them out. I peek over at him with one eye, instantly melting when I see him staring back at me. He's got his gray baseball cap back on, and the black T-shirt he's wearing hugs his biceps so tight it looks like it could rip any second.

"Just being reminded about our appointment with the attorney tomorrow," I explain, making him nod his head. "Sometimes I just wish none of this was happening. That we could keep the family we're starting to build without all the bullshit from my ex." He studies me a minute before wrapping his arm around me, scooping me up and into his lap as my legs straddle either side of him. I let out a little squeal as he does, and he smiles when I begin to giggle.

"Baby, we're going to keep focusing on the little family we have here. That's what the judge needs to see anyway, right? That Hendrix has a home with two parents who love him and are doing everything they can to take care of him? So let's keep focusing on that, and I believe the rest will take care of itself." I shake my head, taking in every one of his gentle, yet masculine features.

"How do you do it? Stay so sure that everything is going to work out, even in the worst possible situation?" I ask curiously, running my hand along his cheek.

"Because, I don't believe I was given a second chance to plan for the worst-case scenario. I'm using every bit of faith and hope that I have to plan for our future together. Me, you, *and* Hendrix. We got this, baby." He gives me a reassuring wink before bringing my lips to his, sending an ache for him straight to my core.

"I'm hungryyyyy!" Hendrix yells from the kitchen.

"He acts like you when he's hangry," Tank says, standing from the couch with my legs still wrapped around him.

"Just accept the fact now that you have two of me, and it'll make your life a lot easier." He shakes his head, carrying me to the kitchen before putting me down to get our plates. When I take my seat next to Hendrix he's practicing his punches and ducking to avoid invincible blows.

"Give it time, you'll start to see a little bit of me rubbing off on him." Tank beams from the other side of the kitchen, making me smile.

I can't wait.

"Mr. Landry, Ms. Ranes. I'm so glad you were able to–" My attorney motions for us to have a seat in front of her.

"It's Mr. & Mrs. Landry," Tank corrects her, pulling my chair out for me to sit first.

"Of course, my apologies." She smirks, though it gives me an uneasy feeling the way she's looking at him. "I'm glad you were both able to work it into your schedule to sit down with me to discuss what happens next." She folds her hands on top of her desk, but I can't stop wringing mine. Tank notices and immediately grabs my hand closest to him, squeezing it firmly to reassure me everything will be okay.

"So, let's get right down to it. A paternity test has been requested, as well as a face-to-face after said paternity has been confirmed. He would like to meet his son."

"Absolutely not," Tank growls from beside me.

"Yeah, there's no way I'm taking Hendrix around this guy. Like I said before, he's dangerous."

"Though, not dangerous enough for you to have filed a police report or restraining order against him." I see the way Tank rears back at her words, confirming that I'm not crazy and this isn't a normal response from someone who's supposed to be defending our case.

"Is there a possibility that your judgment of the situation could have been obstructed by the emotions you were going through during the time you told him about the child? That you may have misread the situation altogether? Maybe you subconsciously knew that things weren't as bad as you were making them out to be, and that's why you never filed any claims." With every word that leaves her mouth, I feel like I'm on trial, and instead of her *defending* me, she's waiting, *hoping*, to see me lose.

Who the hell does she think she is?

"With the respect that you're due, ma'am—and believe me, it's not much—if my wife says this man is dangerous, then you are to take her word for it. You are in *no* position, whatsoever, to question what she's been through, nor her ability to recall it as it happened. Hendrix *will not* be going near him. End of discussion. Now, do you have anything *useful* to add to this meeting? Because you're about one idiotic statement away from being fired." Just when I think I can't love him anymore, he says things like that.

"Here's the paperwork for getting the paternity test done. I'll be in touch later this week about next steps." She smirks, shoving the paperwork at me. My eyes fall to it, then drift back up to hers. I'm still unable to speak, think, or come up with a reasonable explanation for how this is all happening. Tank takes the papers from her hand, crumples them up, and throws them in the trash before getting my attention when he squeezes my hand.

"Come on, Honey. Let's go." He guides me out, tucking me under his arm as we walk back out to his truck. Once we get inside I finally blink away the brain fog, looking over at him as he blows out a breath.

"Baby, I want you to know I am in no way trying to sound disrespectful right now, okay? But where the fuck did you find that woman?" He points to the law office we're still parked in front of.

"The internet. But she comes highly recommended by all her clients. I checked her out Tank, I swear."

"Okay. I believe you. Did you also happen to steal her lunch, or I don't know, slap her directly in the face the first time you met?" I can't help but snicker at his comment.

"*Tank,* be serious!" He laughs along with me, unable to fight the need to laugh to keep from screaming.

"I'm sorry, Honey. I'm just trying to find a reasonable explanation for why she's trying to victim-blame someone she's supposed to be defending." The word *victim* coming from his lips makes me feel a sense of weakness I've never felt while being with him—and I don't like it at all.

"I'm not a victim," I mumble, trying not to take my anger out on him.

"You're right. I chose my words poorly, but she *is* twisting all the information she's getting and putting the blame on you. We need to find a new attorney, immediately."

"Yeah, I think you're right. I'll start looking as soon as we get home." I lean my head against the back of my seat looking over at Tank, but something catches his attention, and his entire demeanor changes.

"Ruby. Tell me I'm not hallucinating, is that who I think it is?" I follow his gaze and immediately feel the color drain from my face.

"Oh, my god." I open the truck door and throw up in the parking lot, while the ex that's suing me, has his hands all over my attorney.

Chapter 34

RUBY

"SHIT, BABY. YOU OKAY?" Tank runs over to my side of the truck, side-stepping the mess to brush my hair out of my face. I can't fight the tears that immediately start coming, as my mind tries to comprehend what the fuck I just saw.

"*No*, I'm not okay. I don't understand what the *hell* is going on." I sob, wiping my mouth as I fight to keep myself from throwing up on Tank. He holds me against his chest, brushing my hair back and kissing the top of my head over and over.

"Shh, shh, shh. We're going to figure this out together, I promise. Starting by never speaking to that woman again." I take a deep breath, trying to reign in the wave of nausea still lingering. When I'm finally able to release him without losing my composure, he gets back in the truck and drives us home.

"I'm gonna tell Max you won't be in until later, if at all, and I will see if I can get someone to cover my clients at the gym," he says as I lay down on the couch.

"You don't have to do that. I'll be fine," I say unconvincingly as I stay zoned out on the TV that isn't on.

"You're cute when you're in denial." Tank takes a seat, lifting my feet into his lap as he waits for my response. I can't even find it in me to muster up a witty comeback or flirty response like I normally would because it feels like I have no idea what's real and what isn't anymore.

"Baby, I'm not leaving you when we have important shit to figure out. I'm gonna make some calls, you take a nap and I'll wake you when it's time to go get Hendrix. Okay?" He rubs my legs in a comforting motion, and I nod in agreement before he walks out with his phone already to his ear.

I close my eyes and try to get some rest, but every little detail about what's happened over the last couple of weeks floods my mind.

How did my ex even know about Hendrix?

How did he know where to find us?

Is the attorney I hired his wife or just another mess he's making?

Is he even still married or was I being played the whole time?

Did Tank and I even have to get married or could I have won this thing alone?

I sit up, grabbing a throw pillow to tuck under my arms as I let out a loud groan.

"Can't sleep?" Tank's voice catches my attention.

"Would you be able to right now?" I ask, playing with a loose string from the pillow.

"No chance." Taking a seat next to me, he wraps his arm around me.

"Are you already done with your calls? That was fast." I point to his phone as he slides it back into his pocket.

"Yeah, I called the gym and someone is covering for me, and I left messages at the other place." I nod robotically, still unable to get my mind to settle down.

"Tank?"

"Yes, Honey?"

"Can we go out and do something? Like a walk, or *anything*. I just really don't want to sit in the silence right now. It makes me too anxious." He leans back to look down at me, a devilish smile appearing on his face.

"I've got an idea." He stands up quickly, pulling me to my feet. "Get dressed." He slaps my ass, sending me down the hallway towards our bedroom.

"What about you?" I ask, looking him up and down as he stands in black jeans, boots, and a denim button-down.

"Once I take this off, I'm ready," he says as he begins unbuttoning the denim shirt.

"Then what's wrong with what I'm wearing?" I argue, folding my arms over my chest. I have on my nicest pair of jeans, a white silk button-up and a pair of black mules. He stops at the second button of his shirt to wag a finger up and down my body.

"You look like you just came back from your attorney's office. Go put on your *real* clothes," he says, making me roll my eyes.

"*Touché.*"

"Shake a leg baby, I'll be out front waiting." He winks at me, already helping to get my mind off of the horrible morning we had, and eager to see what he has planned.

I dig through my closet and drawers looking for something to wear, unsure *what* exactly I need to dress for. But instead of stressing over it, I play off Tank's outfit and keep it simple. I throw on my black denim shorts, white tee with skull hands doing *rock-on* signs on my boobs, and my combat boots. Tennessee is notorious for being unseasonably warm in the middle of November, and this just so happens to be one of the rare sunny and 65° days we get before it becomes so cold my nipples could cut glass as soon as the front door opens.

I make sure to brush my teeth prior to grabbing a claw clip and my leather jacket before rushing out the door. I drop my hair as soon as I see Tank standing next to his bike with a helmet sitting on the back for me.

"Are you serious?" I ask in excitement. "We're taking the–" When he turns around I notice he's wearing *my Bad Bunnies* T-shirt that I always sleep in, and I'm a little put off that it looks so much better on him. While it hangs off of my body comfortably, it hugs every single one of his muscles in a way that makes my mouth water. I freeze in the middle of the sidewalk, letting my mouth drop open.

"Are you wearing my shirt?" I roll my lips trying to hide my smile.

"Look, I got dressed in the dark, but once it was on I didn't want to take it off. This thing is so fucking soft," he explains, rubbing his hands over the fabric in an almost seductive way.

"I thought you learned your lesson a long time ago about getting dressed in the dark." I smirk, walking over as he grabs my helmet from the bike.

"Guess not." He winks at me, placing the smaller helmet on my head.

"What made you decide to take the bike?"

"Well, I figured what better way to get your mind off of things than with a little adrenaline?" He wags his eyebrows, making sure my helmet is on tight. "Hop on, Honey." He throws one leg over the bike, and I mirror his movements to climb on the back. His bike is way more sporty than Max and Tuckers. They both have the classic bikes while Tank drives one that I think they call a crotch rocket?

"Hold on tight." I wrap my arms around his waist, though I'm still a little far away from him. I think I'm too small for this seat—or it's just made *really* far back.

He starts the bike giving it a little throttle before immediately hitting the break, sending me sliding forward. My ass slides into place where my seat *actually* is and my arms wrap around him tighter.

So I was *not* sitting on an actual seat.

When he turns and winks at me it's like I can almost hear him call me his *good little wife*. He closes my visor then his own before we pull out of the driveway.

The rush from feeling the wind hit me at however many miles an hour we're currently going, is exactly the kind of distraction I was needing today. Once we're outside city limits, he turns down a back-road that winds uphill. I release his waist running my hands down his thighs, but when he reaches back and squeezes mine in return, it sends a different kind of rush through me. It's amazing to me how he always seems to know exactly what I need to help calm me down.

We keep down this path for about twenty minutes before we come to a lookout point on the side of the road. He pulls over, sending dust flying up around us before cutting the engine and helping me take off my helmet.

"Oh my gosh, this view is *gorgeous*." My mouth drops open as I see nothing but a sea of red, orange, and yellow leaves from treetops for miles.

"Mmm. I'll say." The desire dripping in his tone matches the look in his eyes when I turn around to see him staring at *me*. He's leaning back so casually against this bike, arms folded over his chest, looking like a freaking dream I'd love to have every night.

"Mr. Landry. Did you bring me up here just to get me alone?" I tease, walking over to throw my arms around his neck as he wraps his hands around my thighs just below the hem of my shorts. "Because you know... We were already alone at home."

"But, my girl said she needed to go out, so out we came." He smirks.

"How is it you always seem to know exactly what I need, even when *I* don't?" This makes him laugh, and I can't quite figure out why.

"Baby, do you realize that for the first two years I knew you, you did the same thing for me?" My brows draw together in confusion.

"Really?"

"Every single time I was about to lose my shit, *or* if I already had, you would show up at just the right moment to do or say something that would help me cool off immediately. It was weird, I could tell you had some enchanting effect on me by the end of my first week working at the bar. Maybe now I'm just getting to return the favor."

"Did you just call me enchanting? Because there's *no way* I'm not letting that go straight to my head." He pulls me into him, capturing my lips in his as he moves his hands from my thighs up to my hair.

"I can't think of a single better way to describe you, little wife, than pure magic." I subconsciously bite my lip, and he pulls it out with his own teeth before kissing me softly. "Especially the way you taste." He kisses me again.

"Are you saying you want a taste now?" I whisper in his ear, knowing exactly what it does to him. He pulls back with a hungry look in his eyes.

"Do *you* want me to taste you right now, little wife?" His deep voice rumbles, as he stands, grabbing my thighs again and turning to put my back against the bike. "Pressed up against my bike where anyone could drive up and see?" For some reason that sends a rush of excitement through me and I nod eagerly. He flicks the button of my shorts open effortlessly as he stares into my eyes. "I love it when my wife is a little naughty." He drops to his knees for me, kissing along my chest, down my stomach, and lifting my shirt to kiss my scar before he begins pulling my shorts and thong down. Just as they hit the ground I get a little anxious about someone *actually* driving by and seeing, but in true Tank fashion, he eases every bit of that worry. As soon as his hands are back on me, and he kisses me where I'm truly aching for him, my mind is cleared of anything but *us*.

"Nothing but *us*," I whisper the encouragement to myself as my fingers find their way to his hair.

"Damn straight." He smirks before letting his tongue swipe along my clit again. Just as he works two fingers inside of me, sending a tingling feeling all over my body, I hear a vehicle approaching and I freeze. My head snaps back up and I look over my shoulder to see a guy getting out of his small SUV.

"Hey, are you okay?" he calls out, slamming his door. With the way the bike is positioned, the only thing he can see is me sitting against the bike. Not my shorts around my ankles, and certainly not Tank on his knees completely devouring me.

"Tank, someone is coming," I whisper in a panic, though he never misses a beat.

"Yeah, it's gonna be you in a minute." When his tongue swipes along my clit again, I have to fight to keep in a moan.

"Yep. All good here," I yell, making him stop right in front of his vehicle.

"Alright. Just wanted to make sure you weren't broken down or anything." He has a confused look on his face as he places both of his hands on his hips.

"Nice bike. Is it yours?"

"Nope. It's my *husband's*," I tell him quickly, the last word coming out unsteady as Tank edges me closer to my release. I think Tank likes it when I call him *husband* because he starts going down on me at a pace that has me seconds away from having an orgasm in front of a total stranger.

"Oh, gotcha. He know you have it out here?" The guy chuckles at his own ridiculous joke.

"Yes, yes, *yes!*" I scream, pulling on Tank's hair, letting my head fall back as he sends me so far over the edge he has to hold my legs steady so they don't give out on me.

"Umm. Are you sure you're okay?" the guy asks, sounding *very* concerned and not the least bit enlightened as to what just happened. Tank lets me enjoy every second of my orgasm before he slides his fingers out of me, licking them clean and sliding my shorts back up my legs before standing up.

"I'd say she's better than okay. Right, Honey?" He wipes my wetness from his beard, and when I steal a glance over my shoulder at the guy he looks absolutely *mortified.*

"Oh. Oh shit. Oh my god. Sorry. I uh… I'm so sorry," the guy stammers, backing up to his car.

"Didn't bother us none, pal." Tank smirks and waves as the guy goes screeching off down the road.

"*Tate Landry!*" I swat his arm, making him laugh.

"Whoa, hey. Don't use my government name. That was hilarious." I shake my head in disapproval, dropping my head in my hands.

"Oh no, you got your jeans all dirty." I point out, making him shrug with another small laugh.

"Baby, no amount of dirt could keep me from getting on my knees for you," he says, wrapping me in his arms. "You down for a little adventure?" he asks, piquing my interest.

"Something *more* adventurous than a roadside orgasm in front of a stranger?" I say sarcastically, making him roll his eyes.

"Maybe not, but I was thinking we should hit up a tattoo parlor." My eyes narrow on him skeptically.

"For you or for me?"

"Can't do one without the other," he says in a knowing tone, leaving me completely in the dark. "What do you say, wife?"

"I say, let's go, husband." He smiles down at me before picking me up and kissing me in a way that leaves me dizzy before we jump back on the bike and speed down the road.

When we pull up to *After Dark Ink* I start to grow more excited because it's been *forever* since I got a tattoo.

"Tank, my man. Long time no see," the guy behind the counter says, greeting Tank with the well-known handshake-to-hug combo.

"Way too long, my man." Tank shakes his head in agreement.

"What can I do for you?"

"Well, Bruce, I need a couple of tattoos for me and my wife." My cheeks heat at him calling me his wife to someone else. Though with *that* voice he could probably call me a teapot and I'd melt.

"Right this way." He leads us to the back letting us sit right next to each other while Tank talks in hushed tones with Bruce and another artist whose name I learn is Izzy. All I can see is Tank flipping his hand around before Izzy comes to sit down by me.

"Do I get to know what I'm getting permanently inked onto my body?" I ask, glancing over at Tank.

"Do you trust me?" he asks, giving me that devilish grin that I love. I hesitate for a moment and when I don't answer right away he raises a brow at me.

"Of course I do." I roll my eyes as I lean back in the seat.

"Give me your ring." He waves two fingers at me, making me frown at him. I do as he says and he slips it onto my other hand. "Don't worry, this is only temporary."

The tattoo artists pay us no mind as they disinfect both of our hands and get to work. Bruce gets done with Tank's first and asks for his stamp of approval. I look up at Tank's face and notice that whatever he has, he *really* likes it.

"That all we getting done today? That was a quick one for you," Bruce says jokingly as I'm sure the rest of Tank's artwork took *hours* to accomplish.

"Actually, there is one more thing I want." He takes a few calculated steps closer to my chair, towering over me and making Izzy stop my tattoo.

"Bite." He holds his hand up to my mouth, and with my eyes locked on his, I bite down on his hand exactly where I know he wants me to, and I bite *hard*, making his jaw tighten when I do. He sits back down and Bruce wipes his hand with an alcohol wipe before tattooing my teeth marks into Tank's palm.

Holy shit, why is that so hot?

"Alright, you're done." Izzy smiles at me, as she begins putting her tools away. I look down at my ring finger and see *Not even death* on one side and *shall part us* on the other. My eyes begin to water as I look over at my husband, whose eyes are already fixed on me. The smile on his face isn't devilish or playful, it's that genuine, happy smile that he gets when something good happens for us. Like he's proud of the choice he made in bringing us here today.

I love it. I mouth to him, earning a wink in return.

I can't stop staring at my hand until we're back out in the parking lot. I think I *may* have mumbled a *thank you* to Izzy and Bruce, but honestly, I don't remember.

"What do you think?" Tank asks, holding his left hand up to mine to show the exact same tattoo on his ring finger.

"I think I love you more than you'll ever know. That every little thing like this that you do for me, for *us*, just proves that I fell in love with the right guy. I still can't believe I get to be your wife." My last words are almost a whisper as I continue staring at our hands.

"I promise to never stop doing these little things for you, baby. Because I never want you to forget how much I love, adore, and cherish you, my little wife." He leans in and presses his lips to mine, as different waves of emotions flood me. *Joy, disbelief, desire.*

"Where to now, Honey?" he asks, pressing his forehead to mine.

"*FOOD!*" I growl.

"Damn, I really thought you'd wanna go home and use my other tattoo." He clicks his tongue, pulling away from me dramatically.

"Food first, then that." I counter, making his face twist with interest.

"Okay. I can get behind that."

"You sure you're gonna make it that long?"

"*I'll make it.*" He pouts, but almost instantly his eyes darken and he leans in closer, stealing my breath. "But I can't promise I won't be thinking about fucking you the entire time we're there. How I can't wait to see you biting down on my hand while I bury my cock so deep inside you that your whole body is shaking from the orgasm I give you." My pussy tightens around nothing, and the sudden urge to have him deep inside me causes my heart to race. But when I bite my lip, ready to give up on the idea of food and beg him to take me behind this fucking tattoo parlor, he rolls his eyes dramatically and pulls me behind him.

"But no, let's go get some fucking french fries first." I can't help but laugh when he throws me over his shoulder to carry me the short distance to his bike. He drops me onto my seat and threads his fingers through my hair, kissing me until my lips tingle.

I still can't believe he's really mine.

Chapter 35

TANK

"Do you think it would be okay if I took Hendrix with me to volunteer today?" I run my fingers through Ruby's wavy hair as her head rests on my chest. Slow starts to the day have become one of my favorite things since marrying Ruby. Getting to lie next to her in bed, feeling her leg draped over mine, her scratching my side or tracing my tattoos while I comb through the tangles in her hair. It's the simplest things like this that make me realize just how madly in love with her I am.

"I think he would love that. You don't think they'll mind?" She lifts her head to face me, displaying marks from where her hand has been pressed into her cheek.

"Hell no. A kid as cool as Hendrix? They're going to adore him."

"Who's going to adore me?" Hendrix bursts into the room, running over to jump on the bed.

"Everyone in the whole wide world, probably," Ruby says, wrapping him up in her arms, and kissing him playfully until he's kicking his feet with laughter.

"I wanted to take you somewhere special today, you wanna go?"

"Heck yeah!" he yells as he starts jumping on the bed.

"Okay, then mister. You need to shower and brush your teeth," Ruby instructs, sending him out the door.

"Yes, ma'am!" He plops down off the bed and slams the door behind him.

"I would kill to have that kind of energy at eight o'clock in the morning." Ruby laughs as she falls back on her pillow.

"I don't know. I think his energy is kind of infectious. I feel wide awake now." I shrug, leaning over to kiss her neck. She smiles and lets out a pleased moan. "If you still need help waking up, I'd be happy to be of assistance." I slide my hand into her sleep shorts, feeling that she's already wet for me.

"But we have to get up and make breakfast," she argues, opening her legs a little wider for me. I let out a hungry groan as she bites her lip, letting a small giggle escape her.

"Um, it seems as though my breakfast is wet and ready."

"What is this place?" Hendrix asks, holding my hand as we walk with Maverick across the parking lot.

"This is where I like to come and hang out with some friends of mine every week. A lot of them served in the military just like me." I stop, kneeling down to his height. "These people you're about to meet are heroes. Some of them lost a lot trying to protect our country, so we're going to be very respectful of them, understand?"

"Yes, sir." Hendrix nods firmly, ironically saluting me.

"Let's go then." When we walk into the building I check in with the front desk and grab Hendrix a name tag. He takes his time looking around at everything before wandering into the dayroom. There are wheelchairs parked in front of the TV with *Wheel of Fortune* on, some guys are sitting in rocking chairs playing cards, and others are at tables studying their chess boards.

"Whoa, that guy has a robot arm!" Hendrix muses as Harold

looks up from the table. I'd be a little worried by his wording if it were anyone but Harold.

"Well, what do we have here?" he asks, making Hendrix stiffen beside me.

"Hey, Harold, you figure out how to play this game yet?" I tease, walking over to him.

"*Agh,* Don cheats." He waves a hand in front of him, reaching down to pet Mav. "Good boy," he praises as Maverick lays down by his feet.

"This your boy, Tank?" Don nods to Hendrix again.

"Sure is. Hendrix, come meet my good friends Mr. Harold and Mr. Don." I wave him over and he slowly makes his way across the room. Harold reaches out his prosthetic arm to shake Hendrix's hand, making him look up at me with eyes as wide as saucers. I can't help but smirk as I give him an encouraging nod. He reaches out to shake Harold's hand, but when Harold makes a fake zapping sound and jolts, Hendrix quickly pulls his hand back.

"Gotcha." Harold smiles, making Hendrix laugh.

"Don't scare the poor kid, Harry," Don scolds him.

"*Ah,* he seems tough to me. Are you tough, kid?" Hendrix nods.

"Yes, sir. One day I'm gonna be as tough as my dad." He looks up at me with a big grin, making my heart swell in my chest.

"Well, you already got the haircut for it, now you just need about 200 more pounds of muscle." Harold slaps my arm, as he and Don start cutting up. It's always the same with them.

You trying out for the next Avengers movie or something?

You get any bigger and you won't fit through the doors anymore.

"Alright, that's enough out of you two."

"You know how to play chess, Hendrix?" Don asks, pointing to the board with only three pieces moved.

"Yes, sir. My uncle Max taught me."

"Why don't you put Harold out of his misery and take over." Hendrix looks at Harold for approval before doing so.

"Be my guest." Hendrix walks up next to Harold's chair and begins playing.

"Look at that, Harry. The kid's doing better than you already." I shake my head as I stand back watching Hendrix fall so comfortably into place here.

"How did you get your robot arm?" he asks, propping his face on his hand as he studies the chessboard.

"Well, my regular arm was no good anymore so they took it off and gave me this one," Harold answers simply.

"Why was it no good?" Hendrix looks over at Harold with those big brown eyes of his and Harold tells him the story about how he lost his arm. Hendrix listens to every detail without ever losing interest, only taking his eyes off of Harold to make a move in his game with Don.

"I'm sorry you lost your old arm, Mr. Harry. But I think your new one is super cool." There's something about the innocent mind of a child that could bring a whole new perspective to the world.

"You think so, kid?" Harold and Don laugh, rustling Hendrix's hair as he makes his last move on the board.

"Yeah. You're like a cyborg or Iron Man—Checkmate." Hendrix beams as we all look at the board. Sure enough, he's captured the king.

"Don, I think you've finally met your match."

"Good game kid." Don extends his hand to Hendrix, who shakes it like a grown man.

"Alright, we're going to make some rounds, we'll holler at y'all before we leave."

"Bye, Mr. Don. Bye, Cyborg." Hendrix waves.

We spend the rest of the morning taking Maverick around to see people, helping serve breakfast, and talking with more of the guys about their time served. Hendrix seems to absorb every story like a sponge, intrigued by every little detail. While I help with maintenance on a few things, Hendrix busies himself by playing a few rounds of Go-Fish, and very animatedly telling people about how I threw a grown man in the trash can—which I'm sure I'll catch some grief over later. When it's finally time to go, I have to basically drag Hendrix out the door.

"You bring that boy back with you anytime, Tank. We could use a little ball of energy like him around here," Harold says as he makes his way back to his room.

"I think he would like that," I agree, glancing over at Hendrix and Maverick waiting for me by the door.

"You ready to go home?" Hendrix bounces to his feet, causing Maverick to do the same.

"Yes, sir. I can't wait to tell Mom all about Mr. Harold and his super cool arm." He begins pretending his arm can shoot lasers out of it.

"Hey, Dad."

"Yeah, buddy?"

"I'm really glad you made it back home," he says, catching me off guard a little.

"What do you mean?" I ask, stopping to really look at him while he talks.

"Well, some of those guys said their other friends didn't make it back home from fighting bad guys. And you said you used to do that too. So I'm glad you made it back home and got to be my dad." This kid has no idea the impact his little words have on my heart.

"I love you, Hendrix. I am honored that I get to be your dad." He smiles, throwing his arms around my neck before letting go again and starting back towards the truck.

"Can we go see Mom at work? I wanna tell her about our day right *now*," Hendrix excitedly requests. I glance down at the clock to see that it's just about lunchtime, and from the way my stomach growls right on cue, I take it as a sign to have lunch at the bar.

"Sure little man. Let's surprise Mom at work."

"*Yes!*"

"I gotta pee!" Hendrix yells as soon as we walk through the door of Chattahoochies.

"Okay, maybe don't announce it to the whole place though." I grab him by the shoulder and politely nod to the couple sitting at the booth closest to us. On our way to the bathroom, we spot Ruby and Hendrix suddenly forgets his previous urgency.

"Hey, Mommy! Dad and I had the *best* day today. I got to meet Mr. Harry, he has an arm like Iron Man. And I beat Mr. Don at chess, and then I played a *lot* of Go-Fish and told everyone how Dad put mean old Tommy's dad in the trash can, and then Maverick napped in Mr. Wilson's lap, and... it was the best. Day. Ever." He lets out a huge sigh of relief after his run-on storytelling, while Ruby's wide eyes bounce between us.

"Wow, that *does* sound like the best day. But you look exhausted buddy," she says, running her fingers along his cheek.

"I'm not tired." With his eyes only about half open right now, I beg to differ.

"Weren't you about five seconds away from peeing your pants, son?" I ask, reminding Hendrix of his mission.

"Oh, right! Gotta pee!" He starts running down the hallway again.

"We'll be right back."

"Okay." Ruby laughs as Maverick hops up in the booth with Riley and I follow behind Hendrix. I barely have enough time to check my emails before he comes busting out of the bathroom again.

"Feel better?" I ask as Hendrix walks out of the restroom.

"Yeah, that was a close one." The kid put away like three bottles of water while we were out this morning and never once stopped talking and playing long enough to go to the bathroom. I'm surprised he didn't burst in the truck on the way here.

When we make it back out front Hendrix runs over to the booth where both dogs are laying and snuggles up to them just as I catch a glimpse of Ruby at the end of the bar. I take a moment to admire the way she seems to float behind the bar. She never knew how much of my attention she held when we worked here together, but there were so many times customers would have to clear their throats or tap their glass on the bar to get my attention because it was always on her. The way she owns any room she walks into is downright captivating.

God, she's so fucking beautiful.

And apparently, I'm not the only one who thinks so…Before I can call out to get her attention a guy slides onto the barstool closest to her, grinning ear to ear while she's still facing the other direction. Every protective and jealous bone in my body starts itching as I walk a little faster in their direction.

"Excuse me, but what's a *gorgeous* woman like you doing working at a bar like this?" Ruby turns around quickly upon hearing the remark, but she doesn't look nearly as pissed off as I am. "Ooh, and the front looks even better than the back. What's a guy gotta do to get them digits?"

"First of all, you can fuck all the way off. Preferably back to wherever the hell you came from," I interrupt, watching as Ruby's eyes grow wide.

"Tank!" She swats at my arm, but I don't budge. I hold his stare until his eyes begin bouncing back and forth between me and Ruby.

"Look man I–"

"Was hitting on the wrong man's wife," I sneer, making his mouth drop open as he looks back at Ruby again.

"Oh, shit!" Ruby starts laughing as he covers his mouth with his hands. "You got wifed up?"

"I did. By the best, as you can see," she says, rubbing my arm as my anger begins morphing into confusion.

"Zay, this is my husband Tank."

"Well, he comes by *that* name honestly." He shakes his head in agreement, looking me up and down.

"Tank, this is my friend Zay. The one I told you about from *Bad Bunnies*," she explains, helping me to recall her telling me he was the only *real friend* she had while working there.

"Right, sorry. I'm just a bit protective over my girl," I admit, looking over at Ruby whose gaze is filled with delight.

"As you should be. I wouldn't have come in playin' had I known. I meant no disrespect." He holds his hands up defensively.

"So Zay, what are you even doing here?" Ruby asks as she rounds the bar to give him a hug. I know he's a friend, but I'm still fighting the urge to pull her back over to me.

"Well, I happened to see *this* and thought *no way is my girl working at a bar in Tennessee* so I had to come see for myself." He slides over a magazine displaying an article that reads "*10 off the grid places you should visit while in Nashville*" with a photo of Ruby behind the bar, looking like the fucking goddess that she is, but I can barely take the time to appreciate it since all I can feel is the heat in my ears from him referring to *my wife* as *his girl*.

Like fuck she is.

"Oh my god, I remember Max telling me someone was featuring Chattahoochies in an article, but I had no idea they took this picture," she says, holding the magazine up to read it. When her face drops from amusement to panic it's like I can almost read her mind.

Is this how Mark found her?

She looks over at me and when Zay sees the exchange he quickly changes the subject.

"So, has Melissa reached out to you about coming back for *One Last Dance*?"

"What?" Ruby shakes her head, trying to regain her focus.

"*Bad Bunnies* is hosting a theme night where they bring back all the old crowd favorites... Ya know, the ones that can still work the pole at least. I know for sure you were one of the names mentioned."

Absolutely the fuck not. Can he leave now?

"Oh, no I haven't heard from her. But I had to get a new number when I left so she probably didn't have a way to contact me," she explains.

"Well, if you wanna do it you should give her a call. She's still running the show up there and I know she'd love to hear from you. And the crowd would go nuts to see you dance again. You get it." He turns and nods at me, making me realize that I have in fact, *never* seen my wife pole dance.

"I think if I dance for anyone again it'll be my *husband*." She laughs, reaching over to squeeze my forearm, making my dick harden with pride.

"*Right*. Makes sense," Zay agrees with a humorless smirk. "Well look, I'm in town for a couple more days. I would love to have coffee and catch up if you have time. Here's my number, just in case." He slides a napkin with his phone number over to Ruby and waves on his way out.

"Good meeting you, Ruby's husband."

"Yep." I watch as he walks out the door before looking down at the napkin in her fingertips. "I don't like that guy." I lean across the bar as Ruby whips around, causing her black ponytail to brush against my face.

"Zay? Why? He's harmless." She laughs.

"He also strolled into the bar hitting on you in a *very* bold way. Unless you tell me he's strictly into men, I don't like him." This makes her roll her eyes as she makes her way back behind the bar.

"He's not into men, but Zay and I are just friends. We *were* just friends. It was never like that with us."

"Honey, I love you. But I saw the way he looked at you when your back was to him, and I saw the way he hugged you—which, by the way, I wasn't a fan of. You may not think there was anything there, but at some point or another, that guy had feelings for you."

"Tank, I love you too. But how can you know that just from a look?" She rests her elbow against the bar, mimicking my stance from a few inches in front of her.

"Because it's the way I've always looked at you. Like you're the only thing I see." Her face shifts from playful to serious as she stands up a little straighter. Crumpling the napkin in her hand, she walks over to the trash can and tosses it in.

"Okay then," she says simply. I stand up to my full height, not hiding the shock on my face from her action. I thought for sure she would argue with me more about why I am wrong, and try to convince me going for a cup of coffee would be innocent and then she could prove that they're *just friends.*

"You're all I see too, Tank. I don't *want* anyone else but you. And I never want to give you any reason to think that I would." I glance over to see Hendrix passed out in the booth with Riley and Maverick, just about the time Max comes walking back out front.

"I'm borrowing my wife," I tell him, ushering her through the door to the kitchen.

"Don't do anything the health inspector wouldn't do," he mumbles under his breath.

I'm going to do things that would make him weep.

When we stop in front of the walk-in freezer Ruby looks up at me in surprise. I open the door, pulling her inside after ensuring no one sees us.

"What are you *doing?*" she asks, folding her arms over her chest. "It's freezing in–" I take her face in my hands, kissing her with enough passion to melt every last thing in this freezer.

"I'm rewarding my wife," I say against her lips, wrapping her legs around my waist. I push her back against a shelf, kissing along her neck as I feel her nipples harden beneath her T-shirt.

"For what?" she whimpers.

"Plenty," I growl.

"For letting him know you're *mine.*" I bite her neck.

"For making it clear that I'm the *only* one who gets to see this sweet little body."

Another bite.

"And for only seeing me." I lick across the bite marks, soothing any pain I may have left behind.

"Of course, I'm yours, my love. I could never be anyone else's."

"God, you're such a good little wife," I whisper across her lips, biting her bottom lip until she whimpers again. My dick is pressed hard against my jeans as she tugs on my hair, grinding her hips in such a needy way.

"Max is gonna kill me," I say, planting her feet back down on the ground.

"What? Why?" she says breathlessly, gasping when I quickly pull her pants down below her ass.

"Because, I'm about to fuck you in his freezer." She bites her lip as I spin her around, bending her over until I see the wetness between her legs shining.

"You better be this wet for *me*, wife." I taunt her, letting my fingers glide across the wetness.

"I'm only ever wet for you, Tank." I feel her push back into my hold, making my dick throb against its restraints.

"Are you going to be quiet for me, little wife?" I ask, freeing myself from my boxers.

"Probably not," she admits, making me smirk. I line myself up to her entrance, wrapping my hand around her mouth.

"Bite." She does as she's told and the moment I press into her a muffled moan escapes her as her teeth sink into the marks inked on my hand. Feeling her warmth wrapped around me sends me into a state of euphoria as she whimpers with every thrust. She releases her teeth from my hand and I run my thumb along her bottom lip as I hear her whisper,

"Choke me, please." I pull her up, bringing her back flush with my chest.

Fucking dammit.

"Yes, ma'am," I whisper in her ear as my hand wraps around her throat. I feel myself getting closer to release as her head falls back on my shoulder. She starts to stutter out little *T's* like she's trying to scream my name, but the restraint on her neck won't let her.

"That's it. Give it to me, baby." I feel her body begin to tense as I slide almost all the way out before slamming back into her. I can feel myself hitting the spot that she likes when she tenses around me, so I continue to do so until I finally release her throat enough to let her moan out my name as she comes for me, sending me right over the edge with her. Our heavy breaths fill the silence as my chest heaves against her back. I wrap my hand around her throat again, tilting her head back so I can capture her lips with my own.

"Now you're going to work the rest of your shift with my cum dripping out of that sweet little pussy of yours. Reminding you exactly *who* you belong to, isn't that right little wife?" She nods her head with her eyes still glazed over. "You gonna remember how good I fucked you in this freezer every time you have to walk past it?" She bites her lip and nods again.

"You gonna come home and let me do it all over again?"

"Yes, my love."

"Fuck, I love when you call me that." I drag my nose along her jawline, breathing her in before dipping my tongue into her mouth, kissing her in a way that could have me standing in this freezer all day.

"I should probably get back," she whispers when I finally pull away. I growl my disapproval, making her smile up at me. Just as we finish getting ourselves dressed, the freezer door opens and Max looks over at us. Ruby quickly grabs a five-pound bag of cheese off the shelf, smiling so big I have to roll my lips to keep from laughing.

"We needed more cheese." She runs out of the freezer past Max, who is staring at me in disapproval. I plaster on a big-ass smile similar to Ruby's and stop right in front of him, giving him a wink while clicking my tongue.

"I swear to God I would fire you if you still worked here."

"Buuut, I don't." I clap his shoulder before walking off.

I can hear him mumbling to himself as I make my way back out front, but I don't even try to make out anything he's saying.

Hendrix is still passed out with the pups and I almost hate to wake him to take him home, but I have some calls to make and I'd much rather do that at home than here. So I walk over and scoop him up in my arms, as Maverick jumps down to follow me out.

"See you tonight, Honey." I wink at Ruby, making her cheeks heat instantly.

"See you tonight, my love."

Chapter 36

RUBY

"Earth to Ruby!" Leah waves her arms in front of my face, forcing me to refocus.

Well, if there's one thing my husband was right about today, it was the fact that I thought about nothing but him for the rest of my shift. It's been borderline torture to have to remember what happened in the freezer and not be able to run back home to him. You know, I used to have focus, drive, and determination to be the best at my job—now all I want to do is fuck my husband and watch movies on the couch with him and Hendrix.

He's ruined me.

He's turned me into a wannabe housewife.

"Oh my god, whatever sex memory you have on repeat up there better be a fucking good one," Taylor says, finishing off her martini.

"Why do you always think it has to do with sex?" Leah asks, leaning forward to look around Lauren who's sipping her margarita between the two of them.

"Leah, *look at her.* What else could it be?" I finally roll my eyes and rejoin the conversation.

"You're only partially right," I admit, taking the empty glasses from in front of them. Taylor sticks her tongue out at Leah like we're in middle school and I can't help but laugh.

"I've had a not-so-subtle reminder of my husband lingering for my entire shift so I'm counting down the minutes until I can go home."

"*Ow ow!*" Lauren hollers. Leah makes a little growl noise. Taylor drums on the bartop, and Shane's mouth falls open.

"*Here?*" Shane whispers. "*Where?*" Her eyes grow wide with scandalous curiosity.

"The walk-in freezer." They all begin to make dramatic screaming noises as I look around to ensure no one else can hear this conversation.

"Max would have a stroke if he knew." Shane laughs.

"Then maybe we should check on him…" Her mouth drops open even further this time, making the rest of the girls do the same.

"Oh my god, you got caught? That's so hot," Taylor exclaims.

"Only sort of. We were finished, thank *God*. But I sort of panicked and grabbed five pounds of cheese before basically running out so it looked suspicious. Not to mention Tank doesn't work here and getting cheese isn't a two-person job…" They all double over in laughter, and I can't help but do the same.

"I can't," Leah wheezes before almost falling out of her chair. Lauren tries catching her breath as she holds Leah up.

"Why *cheese?*" Lauren barely gets out, making me laugh even harder.

"It was the first thing I saw!" We're all laughing hysterically when Max walks behind the bar, looking at us all like we should be medicated.

"Oh, *honey!* I am so happy you're alive," Shane says dramatically before falling into another fit of laughter.

"I thought you weren't supposed to be drinking." He stares at his wife in confusion. Shane hasn't been drinking while Cece has been nursing because she's scared she'll get her secondhand drunk.

"Don't worry. She's sober." I assure him.

"That worries me more."

"We just thought you might be stroked out after finding Ruby…

and the *cheese*." You can barely make out what she's saying at this point, but Max hears enough to put two and two together. He looks over at me and gives me the *disapproving dad* head shake.

"I'm glad you're happy Rubes, but if you do it in my freezer again I'm making you work every shift with Marco for a month." My smile falls immediately, looking at him with a stone-cold face.

"You're mean." And I'll be damned if he doesn't plaster on the same big ass grin I gave him earlier before winking at me, clicking his tongue, and walking back to his office. When I turn back around all the girls have their lips rolled or hands covering their mouths to keep from laughing.

"Was it worth it?" Taylor whispers, leaning in closer to me.

"Oh, yeah." And the squealing starts again.

"Okay, okay, okay. We're gonna go so you can get ready to go home," Leah says, pushing her glass back.

"Bye. Love you guys." I smile, waving them off as they all pile out the door.

DING

HUSBAND

We need to talk when you get home.

ME

I'll start by saying those are my 7 least favorite words ever. Can you tell me now? You know I have anxiety.

HUSBAND

Sorry Honey, didn't mean to worry you. It'll be better to talk in person though. You off soon?

ME

20 minutes left.

HUSBAND

Drive safe. See you soon.

"You been having me followed, Ru?" That ice-cold chill shoots down my spine at hearing his voice. I quickly pull up my voice record app and start it before sliding my phone into my apron and turning to face him—just in case.

"What? No." Confusion covers my face as I realize I actually have no idea what he's talking about.

"Oh, really? Because I just *happened* to notice someone in a gray car showing up *everywhere I did* today." The slur to his words makes it no secret how drunk he is right now. But I still have no idea what he's talking about.

"I don't know anyone with a gray car, Mark. And you shouldn't be here. Go home."

"I wish I'd never seen you in that stupid mall." His voice trails off as he plops down on a barstool. I can almost feel my entire body lock up when I hear the words leave his lips.

"What?" I choke back the bile that's fighting its way up my throat.

"You know I'd spent *years* trying to get over you. Trying to forget you and the mark you left in my mind. Wondering every day if you actually went through with having our child." My features immediately harden at his words.

"Don't you *dare* call him your child," I grit out through my teeth. "Not after you told me to get rid of him. Not after you threatened my life if I *didn't* and not after you put his life at risk by assaulting me with a *fucking* piece of glass *IN MY STOMACH!*" I scream at him, not caring how everyone in the bar is now looking at us.

The sad look on his face pisses me off more than anything. I've never wanted to be violent with someone until now. I used to be scared of him, I would let thoughts of my past with him paralyze me, and was prepared for *years* to keep running if he ever found me. Now I'm ready to stand my ground, to fight to keep my kid, and to let him know he's messing with the wrong family.

"I wasn't right in the head, Ru. I didn't want to stay with my wife. I wanted to be with you. I wanted to start over and have the baby with you, really, I did. But there were circumstances that wouldn't allow me to do that, and when I couldn't have you—when we couldn't start a family together I just... I didn't want it to happen without me."

"Is that supposed to make me feel *better*? Am I supposed to *forgive you* for all the fucking trauma you put me through just because you were having a bitch fit over your own selfish mistakes?" He shakes his head, not meeting my gaze.

"When I saw you in the mall that day, I couldn't believe it was you. I was only supposed to be here for the weekend on business, but... When I saw the name of the bar on your shirt, I took a chance and looked it up. I came back the next day and sat right over there until I saw you, I had to make sure my mind wasn't playing tricks on me. I was going to get up and come talk to you, honest. Then I saw *him*. He was stepping in to protect you and giving you the shirt off his back. I saw the way you looked at him, and it made me so *angry*. Because that should have been me." The blood pumping so quickly through my body has me feeling like I'm about to pass out when I realize just how long he's known where to find me. "I decided that I should just go back home and try to forget about you again. That it didn't matter if you had the baby or not, but... a year later I still couldn't let you go. I couldn't stop thinking about you. Every day my mind was full of thoughts of nothing but *you*. So I came back, I just... I *had* to know if there was a chance for us. So I came back to the bar, waited until you got off and I followed you to see if you'd had the baby. When I saw you two together I knew I had to come up with a plan to get you both back. I just wanted a second chance to have the family we should have had." He reaches for my hand and I quickly pull it away. When my eyes finally refocus, the tears quickly start falling from them.

"You're sick, Mark. The fact that you think *any* of the things you did, *while still married*, were okay, just proves that. We will *never* be your family. My son has a dad now that *loves* him, and *protects* him, and has since *before* I ever even realized I was in love with him. *That's* the kind of man I want in our lives. Someone who will love him without expecting anything in return. Someone who does nothing but think about us, and puts us first. *He* is the father my child deserves, and the husband that *I* deserve. He's slowly started to erase every bit of damage you did to me, and he will continue to do so until you're *nothing*. You don't deserve a family. You never have and you never will. You will not win this case, Mark. You never stood a chance against us, now get the fuck out of this bar. And don't you *ever* come back." When I point to the door he grabs my wrist, wrapping his fingers tightly around it.

"Please, Ru. Just one more chance, please." I close my eyes and take a deep breath, fighting the panic I'm in, but when I open them again Max is pulling him away from me, shoving him back so that he staggers towards the door.

"If you're not out of my sight in five seconds I will call the police," he threatens, sending Mark running for the door.

Max rushes back over to me, wrapping me in his arms just as my legs give out on me. He keeps his grasp on me strong as every sob that I'd held back in Mark's presence comes rushing out of me. He pulls his phone out of his pocket and after one ring I hear Tank's voice and another sob breaks free.

"Your wife needs you."

"I'm on my way." No questions asked. No hesitation. Just like that.

Ten minutes. That's all it takes before my husband comes storming into the bar, eyes landing on me almost immediately. Like there's an invisible magnet that leads him straight to me.

"What happened? Are you hurt?" He bends down, cupping my face in his hands as he assesses every part of me.

"Where's Hendrix?" I ask, looking around for him.

"I dropped him at Betty's so I could drive faster. Baby, what happened?" I swallow past the cotton-like feeling in my mouth, as I try to get the words out.

"Mark came by..." Tank's nostrils flare angrily, but his touch is as gentle as ever. Holding me in a way that tells me I'm safe without him having to utter the words.

"What did he do?" I shake my head, unwilling to repeat everything that happened, and then I remember my phone. I set it on the table and press play on the recording I took while he was here.

Tank's chest begins rising and falling more rapidly when he hears me scream about Mark assaulting me, and I can see that he's trying so hard to hold it together. When it finally ends he begins pacing back and forth, running his hands through his hair and I can see him fighting to stay calm.

"Say something, please," I whisper. He finally stops moving and bends down in front of me again.

"You're the bravest fucking woman I have ever met. You know that?" Tears flood my eyes at his words, and I shake my head. "I'm so sorry I wasn't here with you," he apologizes, pressing his forehead to mine as his fingers travel through my hair.

"You couldn't have known he'd show up."

"I've been having him followed, Ruby," he admits with a sigh, leaning back as my stomach drops.

"What?"

"After we saw him with your attorney, I wanted to know *everyone* he had contact with. Every single person he knew was in a position to sway this case in his favor. The P.I. I hired told me today that he thought he may have been spotted, but that he'd found out something that he hoped could help us. That's what I was texting you about earlier but my first thought should have been to make sure he didn't come for you. I am so sorry that I didn't, baby." I cup his cheek in my hand, knowing all too well that he would never put me in danger intentionally.

"What did he find out?"

"The judge that approved the case is Mark's brother-in-law, and the attorney you hired, is his latest mistress." I have no words. He's sicker than I thought.

"But... he said he was trying to get back with *me*. Why would she help him do that?"

"My guess is he left that detail out of it and told her he just wanted a relationship with Hendrix, not you too." My ears begin ringing and I can barely focus on the words Tank is saying to me, but I still manage to hear the important ones.

"I reached out to a few people about our situation and they all told me the same thing. Mark would never stand a chance in this case without his dirty connections. Hendrix was never going anywhere, baby."

"Excuse me." I rush out of the booth, barely making it to a stall before I throw up everything I've managed to eat today. I fall with my back against the stall door, trying to wrap my head around even *one* part of all of this. Not only has the stress from this case made it hard enough to eat on a regular basis, but now it has me losing anything I do manage to get down.

Could it really be ending? With my luck, that seems unlikely.

"Honey, you okay?" Tanks' voice fills the bathroom, like a deep serenade for my weary soul, making it easier to breathe the second I hear it.

"I… have no idea," I admit honestly.

"Can I ask you something?" I roll my head along the door to look at him as he takes a seat next to me on the floor, taking the water bottle he offers me as he does.

"Yeah?" My brows knit together as I see the troubled look on his face.

"Are you upset that we got married? Knowing now that we didn't have to. Do you regret it?" I almost laugh at his question, but I don't even have the energy to do that.

Instead, I stare at my husband and let my mind go back in time, replaying every moment that led Tank and me to where we are now. I remember the day he walked into Chattahoochies—I was completely infatuated with him, even if I didn't want to be. That quiet, broody, and broken version of him that I still couldn't stay away from. I remember how even when he was fighting his own silent battles, he never let me fight mine on my own. Because of that, he became one of my very best friends—someone I could dance with in an empty bar, who knows my favorite color, and who makes me laugh constantly.

I think about the day in my kitchen when I thought we'd come to the end of something that barely got the chance to start, and the day after when I thought I was going to lose him forever. I realized then how desperately I wanted to be able to move past the hurt we'd both gone through and see what could become of us. I remember the way my heart hurt when he was gone from my life for six months while he healed—I'd never hurt like that before and I haven't hurt like that again since the day he showed back up at the soccer fields.

Tank Landry has always had a way of showing up for me exactly when I need him to and giving me a feeling of safety that I've longed for most of my life. He makes me feel brave, secure, and worthy of love without ever taking the credit for giving me those feelings. He's everything I never thought I would have in life.

"Marrying you, Tank Landry, was the greatest thing to ever happen to me. Don't you *ever* fucking forget that." Tears start to well in his eyes as he stares back at me in disbelief.

"It was never fake for me, baby," he reminds me, taking my face in his hand.

"Thank you... For finding the redemption you were searching for through marrying me—and loving me so fiercely, my love."

"I really want to kiss you right now." He leans in closer, pressing his forehead to mine.

"Please don't, my breath is really nasty right now," I say, making both of us laugh.

"Fine. I can wait," he agrees. "Let's go home, Honey." He stands up, pulling me to my feet. "I have a surprise for you when we get there, but we have one little stop to make on the way."

Chapter 37

TANK

IT WILL TAKE every ounce of my self-control not to take this guy out and bury him in the woods somewhere. The fucking audacity he had to show up at her work like that, saying all the bullshit he said to her. He doesn't deserve a next breath.

We pull up to the sleazebag motel he's been staying at, parking at the dimly lit end of the lot before I turn my ball cap around to shield my face.

"What are you going to do?" Ruby asks, unbuckling her seatbelt.

"I'm gonna stand up for my wife. Stay in the truck."

"What? No! You're not going up there alone," she argues as I lock the doors.

"*Honey.* Look at me." She locks those gorgeous brown eyes on mine as I lean down to her level. "Stay in this truck. I'll be right back." I grip her chin and pull her in for a kiss before she sinks back into her seat and looks at me pleadingly.

"Please be safe."

"Baby, he'd need a fucking army to take me down right now," I assure her before slamming the truck door and walking up to room number eight. I knock on the door twice before he finally swings it open.

"*You,*" he grumbles.

"Hey there, Mark. Make any horrible decisions today?" I ask rhetorically.

"None you should worry about." He smirks, trying to shut the door in my face.

"Oh, you thought we were done here. That's cute." I kick the door open, walking forward until we're almost nose to nose. "Because we're not through here until you understand just what lengths I'll go through to protect *my wife*."

"I'm calling the police." He threatens, reaching for his phone. A devilish grin appears on my face as I grab his wrist, in the same way, Ruby's told me he grabbed hers before—squeezing it until I can feel his pulse beating like a drum in my grip.

"You think you'll live long enough to get such an opportunity?" I ask, throwing his phone across the room before releasing his hand. Then he does the one thing I've been waiting for. He rears back and throws the first punch.

"Fucking dumbass." When I taste copper in my mouth I spit the blood out on his floor, before squaring my shoulders and taking my shot.

When my first punch lands, he nearly falls to the ground but I don't stop long enough to let him regain his bearings. I grab a handful of his hair, tossing him into the door before wrapping my hand around his throat.

"How's it feel, *Mark?* To be the one unable to fight back. To feel the air leaving your lungs with no plan of return. Not so good, huh?" He tries his best to pull my hand away, grunting like an idiot as his face begins to turn from red to purple. I toss him to the floor, walking across the room as he gasps for air.

"Ah, here we go." I smash a water glass on the dresser to shatter it before walking back over to pick him up off the ground. Once he's pinned to the wall again, I take the piece of glass in my hand and press it into his stomach, as he begins sobbing.

"You have no idea just how much you fucked up when you put your hands on my wife."

"She wasn't your wife back then," he argues as tears stream down his face.

"But, she was *always* meant to be my wife." I slam my arm against his chest harder, making his eyes squeeze shut. "Before you ever even laid eyes on her, before your *disgusting* fucking hands ever touched her, she was destined to be *mine*. You don't even deserve to breathe the same air as her, much less claim *her son* as your own. Give me *one* good reason I should let you live."

"So you don't go to jail?" His desperate response draws the most unhinged laugh from deep within my chest.

"You think I wouldn't gladly go to jail for her? I would endure *far* worse for her. She's *everything* to me. Do you understand that? That woman has saved my life in more ways than you can imagine. I would die a thousand deaths for her if it meant she was free of *you* and all the goddamn shit you've put her through," I yell, no longer able to keep my composure with him.

When I feel the glass cutting deeper into my hand I slice it across his stomach the rest of the way—making the incision deep enough only to scar, and not gut him like I've been imagining doing since I first walked through that door. I toss the glass to the side, squeezing my hands into fists as I continue my assault until he's unrecognizable.

I can feel how close to death I've brought him, and those tiny little demons I used to be so familiar with start crawling back out of the shadows urging me to finish him off—he deserves it after all. But as soon as I allow myself to smile at the thought, my vision is flooded with images of Ruby and Hendrix.

I start to see the life we've built together in just the last month alone, and what it could look like if we gave it a lifetime. The way Hendrix is starting to copy everything I do in an effort to be like me when he grows up. The way my wife looks at me now, the same way I've always looked at her—like I'm all she sees. It's true what I said before, that I would go to jail or even die a thousand deaths to protect them, but I think I'd much rather see what living life *with* them could be like instead.

So I pull back.

I don't let the demons win this time.

Instead, I let the angel on my shoulder—who looks a hell of a lot like my wife—have the last say.

"If you ever mess with my family again, I will finish what we've started here. Have I made myself clear? You either disappear on your own, or I'll do it for you." He nods his head vigorously, as he collapses on the ground.

"I expect the custody case to be closed by morning." I crack the door open, making sure no one is outside before slipping out and walking back to my truck.

"Oh my god…" Ruby says when she takes in the sight of me. "You killed him, didn't you?"

"You sound… I don't know, *proud?*" I ask, unable to pinpoint exactly what underlying tone my wife is using. She simply shrugs without another word, making me laugh.

"He was breathing when I left."

"Wow… okay." She picks up her phone and begins typing.

Not the response I was expecting.

"Honey? Whatcha doing?" I nod to her phone and she looks up at me.

"Telling Max and Tucker we don't need shovels." I keep waiting for her to giggle or raise her brows—the tell she has that lets me know she's joking—but she just stares straight back at me with that perfect little poker face of hers.

"You're serious?" I ask, making her turn her phone around.

ME

> We're at Mark's motel… Any chance you guys have easy access to some tarp and shovels? Just in case.

TUCKER

No tarp, but I have shovels and I'm familiar with the local Home Depot.

MAX

Will drop cloths work?

TUCKER

What the fuck is that?

MAX

The fuck you mean the fuck is that? Have you never painted before?

ME

Never mind. False alarm.

TUCKER

What a buzzkill. I was already in the truck.

"They're insane. Both of them." I shake my head.

"They're loyal is what they are," she corrects. "And you know damn good and well if the tables were turned you would have already been in the truck too." I take a moment to just look at her, so calm in the midst of something so brutal. I wonder if that has anything to do with the fact that she knows I'll always have her back. She made it clear today that she can stand up for herself and fight her own battles, but tonight when I chose to come out here, it was my way of showing her that she never has to do it alone. Never again.

My thoughts come to a halt when I see her eyes narrow on me.

"What?" I ask, a little frightened by what she may be thinking right now.

"I bet Clyde never made Bonnie wait in the car." I shake my head, stifling a laugh. Only she would crack a joke like that while I'm covered in her ex's blood sitting in a motel parking lot.

"You're right, baby. I promise from now on you can beat the shit out of your exes *with* me." She turns around to look out the windshield with the sassiest look on her face I've ever seen.

"That's all I'm asking for." I can't help but smirk as I let her have the moment before I hook my forefinger under her chin making her face me again. Her sass fades and she looks at me expectantly when she sees the serious look on my face.

"He's not gonna bother us anymore, baby. You're free."

"I was free the moment I became yours, Tank." I'd refrained from touching her up until now since I'm literally covered in blood, but I can't hold back after hearing her say that.

I pull her into me and she kisses me without hesitation as she crawls into my lap. My bloody hands tangle in her hair as she parts her lips to let my tongue meet hers, her hands travel down my body, teasing the button on my jeans before she pulls away from me.

"Take me home."

"As you wish, little wife."

"Did you want to go grab Hendrix while I hop in the shower?" I ask, unsure what exactly her motive was behind her *take me home* request.

"Betty said he's helping her bake pies for tomorrow and that she'll text me when they're done," she answers simply, sliding her phone into her pocket. "Plus, I'm a little dirty now too." She looks down at her body, pointing out how much blood got on her when she crawled into my lap.

"Let's get you cleaned up then." I smile before hopping out and rushing over to open her door for her. When we walk through the door I take our shoes and toss them in the basket before going to remove my blood-stained clothes to throw into the wash.

"Wait." Ruby stops me. "Didn't you say you had a surprise for me?"

Oh, shit. I forgot.

"I do," I assure her. "But don't you want us to get cleaned up first?"

"It can wait. I kinda like this look on you." She shrugs, looking up at me with those big, honey-brown eyes.

"Oh? What look is that, little wife?"

"Like you'd kill a man to protect me," she admits quietly, like she's almost ashamed to admit she enjoys that fact.

"I did far worse than that, Honey. He has to live with the fact that you'll *never* be his—all while knowing if he dares to come near you, I'll kill first and ask questions later."

"Are you really mine?" Her teeth pull her bottom lip in, as I fight the urge to pull it back out with my own.

"Only and forever." I lean in and kiss her gently. "Close your eyes." She lets out a little squeal and squeezes her eyes shut.

Instead of guiding her through the house, I throw her over my shoulder and carry her to our room. I plant her feet on the ground and spin her around.

"Keep them closed. *Shit.*" I hear her giggle as I struggle to find the remote. "Okay, open." I study her face closely as she takes in the corner of our room that has a red light glowing on the wall behind–

"You bought and installed a pole for our *bedroom?*" I squint my eyes, still unsure how she feels about it.

"Are you mad? I can't tell if you're mad or not." She lets out a laugh as she walks over to it, running her fingers along the cool metal.

"No, I'm not *mad*. Wait... Did you do this today?" She whips around to face me looking slightly panicked.

"Yes, and before you ask. Hendrix *did* help and he thinks it's to practice fire drills."

"Oh, dear god." Her head falls into her hands as she laughs.

"We'll get him a good therapist when he's old enough to realize what it was really for." I shrug, wrapping my arms around her waist as she continues laughing.

"You're unbelievable." She twists in my hold to face me. "But, I love it, thank you."

"You deserve to do the thing that makes you feel the most confident whenever you want to." I slide my hands into her jeans pockets, pulling her into me.

"So I can just call you anytime then, and you'll come running?" She wraps her arms around my neck, running her teeth over her bottom lip.

"Anytime, anyplace." I squeeze her ass so hard she whimpers, making my dick jump at the sound.

My lips land on hers with a desire unlike I've ever felt before. Knowing the custody case will likely be closing soon, knowing she *wants* this marriage as much as I do, and that having a future together as a real family is a possibility now, sends me into overdrive —like I need to make her mine all over again.

I step back, smirking when I notice a knick in the collar of her shirt. When I rip it straight down the middle she gasps, looking up at me with wide eyes—like she's trying to see straight into my mind. I toss the shirt to the side and unbutton her jeans, pulling them to the ground before backing up to the small chaise at the foot of our bed and taking a seat. I stretch my arms out on either side of me, readjusting to make myself comfortable.

"Dance for me, wife. *Please*." I demand—politely. She picks up her phone and taps the screen a few times before setting it down beside me. I look down to see a song called *Slayer by Bryce Savage* playing but as soon as my eyes are back on her, they don't dare to leave her body again.

She dances on the pole like she hasn't missed a single day in six years.

Climbing.

Spinning.

Dancing.

Hypnotizing me with every movement.

She walks over, dropping to her knees as she runs her hands up my legs, making my tongue swipe out to wet my bottom lip on instinct. When she stands back up she turns to face away from me, bending over to give me the most perfect view of her ass and... crotchless underwear.

Fuck. Me.

She continues dancing while facing away from me, and then she sits in my lap, spreading her legs to straddle me. Rolling her neck, she lets her black hair fall down her back perfectly. My lips begin feathering kisses along her shoulders and up her neck while goosebumps break out over her skin, but she never misses a beat—still grinding her ass against my rock-hard cock that's begging to be inside her right now. I put one hand around her neck, pressing her forward as I work to free myself from my jeans. When I pull her back up, she leans back and lets out a little gasp, surprised by the warmth pressed against her entrance. Before I can say another word she adjusts her position so that I'm already sliding inside her.

"I love when my wife is greedy with my cock." She begins bouncing up and down methodically, taking all of me while my fingertips dig into her waist. Without saying a word, she grabs my hand and begins guiding it up her body, passing her abdomen and breasts, stopping when I reach the base of her neck.

"You want a necklace, Honey?" I ask, inching closer to where she wants me.

"Yes, please," she whines, making a growl rumble out of me. With one hand around her throat and the other keeping rhythm with her bouncing on my dick I begin pumping into her harder, matching her rhythm. Her head falls back with a whimper as I begin hitting that little spot that will have her coming for me in no time.

"Tell me, Honey. Whose good little wife are you?"

"*Ah,* yours!" She answers breathlessly. I can feel her pussy begging to come, tightening around me as she's moments away from her climax.

"Say my name, baby. Let me hear it while you come all over my cock."

"TANK! I'm yours, I'm yours. Only yours," she cries out. While she's still riding out her orgasm, I stand to turn around, placing her on all fours while I continue fucking her from behind. She arches her back, dropping her head between her arms as she grips our bedsheets.

"Head up, Honey. Look at how well you're taking me." I instruct, making her look over at the full-length mirror propped against the wall. Her cheeks are flushed, that full bottom lip is trapped beneath her teeth and her eyes are full of desire.

"My perfect little wife."

"Fuck, Tank. I love you." I reach my climax as her words seep into my brain, emptying myself inside her, while her walls clench around me again.

"I love you, too, Honey. I could never not love you."

"Promise?" The quiver in her tone has me pulling out of her, unbothered by the mess it may make, to turn her around to face me. I hold my left hand up to hers, reminding her of my vows.

"Until I take my last breath and every day after that." Tears well in her eyes and I immediately start to worry. "Baby, what's wrong?" I take her face in my hands, searching her face intently.

"I'm just really happy with you, Tank. I don't want to lose you."

"You're never going to lose me, Honey. I promise. I'm yours, Ruby. Only and forever."

Chapter 38

RUBY

"Mommy. I got some bad news," Hendrix says, giving me a very serious eyebrow raise.

"Oh? What's the bad news?" I lean on my elbow, inching my nose closer to his as we sit next to each other at the kitchen table.

"Daddy makes better pancakes than you," he whisper-shouts in my face, giving me a good whiff of chocolate chips directly up my nose. I let out a dramatic gasp, leaning back with my hand over my heart, secretly loving that he calls him Dad now and loves his pancakes as much as I do.

"*What?*" He starts giggling immediately. "You mean all the special ingredients Daddy adds *that he won't tell me about*, taste better than the boring old pancake mix and milk Mommy uses?" I shoot an accusing glance in Tank's direction but he just smirks back at me.

"A *lot* better." Hendrix's brutal admission doesn't even bother me because he's right. Tank's pancakes are ten times better than mine. I get the feeling he could bake circles around me in this kitchen.

"Have I told you that you're my favorite kid in the whole world today?" Tank asks, smiling through a mouth full of pancakes and whipped cream. Hendrix winks and clicks his tongue along with two finger guns back at him.

"I'm gonna get you to tell me your secret recipe one day," I proclaim confidently.

"Good luck with that, Honey."

I can't get over how perfectly normal this feels. Spending Thanksgiving morning eating breakfast together while the parade plays on the living room TV. After my *husband* cooked breakfast while *our* son snuggled up with the dog on the couch leaving me to brew coffee and flip the bacon when instructed. Sometimes I want to pinch myself because it feels too good to be true. But I wouldn't dare do that now, I'd be too scared I'd actually wake up. I'd be fine living within this dream forever if that's what it was.

"Can we play Go-Fish now? I need to practice so I can beat Iron Man next week."

"I thought you called Mr. Harold Cyborg?" Tank asks, taking a sip of his coffee.

"Yeah, but Iron Man is cooler." Hendrix shrugs, hopping down from the table.

"Hold up. Dishes go where?" He comes to a halt as I point to his empty plate on the table.

"Oh, right. In the sink." He trots over and places his plate in the sink before running to the living room to grab the cards.

"He does know there's no strategy to win Go-Fish, right?" Tank leans to whisper, ensuring Hendrix doesn't hear him.

"You underestimate our poker faces and skilled questioning methods."

"Dear, God. I've married a crazy, competitive game-nighter, haven't I?" I smile wide as Tank takes our plates to the sink and Hendrix returns, tossing the playing cards on the table.

"Wait, these are just regular playing cards," Tank says in an almost questioning tone. "I thought he'd have like, I don't know actual Go-Fish cards." Hendrix and I both pin him with an unimpressed stare as I turn the box over that reads *Go-Fish* in black Sharpie.

"I'm just gonna sit here quietly now." He takes his seat across from me as I begin dealing the cards.

We play countless rounds of Go Fish—all of which Hendrix or I won —until Maverick lets us know he needs out, giving us a break from the table to get some fresh air. Instead of staying inside all day, I make sure the food I'm supposed to take for Thanksgiving dinner is ready to go, we grab the soccer ball and head to the park. As Hendrix and Tank are practicing dribbling the ball down the field and practicing passes, I get an email from our new lawyer that the custody case has been officially closed. When the boys take a break to grab some water, I see Tank check his phone and his eyes immediately find mine. He must have gotten the same email. He runs over from the other side of the park and lifts me into his arms, embracing me tightly as he kisses my neck repeatedly.

"This is our fresh start baby, me, you, and Hendrix." His deep voice is muffled in my hair as he speaks, "Our family against the world."

"Only and forever?"

"Only and forever," he assures me, capturing my lips in his before planting my feet back on the ground.

"Can you guys stop kissing? I need to practice my goal kicks," Hendrix groans from a few feet away causing us both to laugh. While still holding me in his arms Tank looks over at Hendrix. "Your dedication to the sport is unmatched, son." Then he looks back over at me.

"Let's go to the beach for Christmas this year," he says, making me rear back in surprise.

"The beach?" I laugh through the question.

"Well, I would say a cabin in the mountains but I've seen how you react to the cold, I thought you might like the beach better." He laughs, making an excellent and accurate point. I do *not* love the cold. "We deserve to do something special. It's our first Christmas together as a family. Why not?" He gives me a knowing look, hinting at the fact that we'll be celebrating the custody case being dropped without having to say it. I'm still so glad we found out it was all bogus before I brought Hendrix into it.

"Doesn't have to be the beach, we could still go to the mountains or New York and see the big ass tree, wherever you want."

"Can we do that though? I mean what about work and Maverick?"

"Well, I'm sure if you asked Max he would agree that you've earned at *least* a week off work, but I assume it's way more than that. I can get someone to cover my clients at the gym until we get back and of course, Maverick is coming with us." I can't help but bite back the huge smile trying to take over my face, but of course, Tank won't allow that. He pulls my lip out with his thumb.

"Baby, you know how much I love your reactions, don't you ever try to hide them from me." I let the smile completely take over, squealing as I throw my arms around his neck.

"So is that a yes?"

"Yes! Let's go to the beach."

"Hey, bud, what if I told you we were going to the beach for Christmas this year?"

"Does that mean we can't finish soccer practice?"

Oh, my sweet committed child.

"No, I mean we still have a month until Christmas. We can finish soccer practice." Tank assures him, making Hendrix's face light up a little more now.

"Oh, yeah! Will Santa still be able to find us? What about Christmas at Uncle Max's house? We always go to Uncle Max's for Christmas," he asks as we all walk over to the soccer ball together.

"That's true. You guys kind of have a tradition already. We don't have to go if you want to stay to have Christmas with our friends." Tank stops to look down at me.

"I think we can spend one Christmas away. Maybe we can celebrate with them early or something." He narrows his gaze, wrapping his hands around my waist to pull me into him.

"Okay. Counteroffer. What if we stay here for Christmas, and spend New Years at the beach instead?"

"I think that sounds like a great plan." I reach up on my tiptoes to kiss Tank just as Hendrix starts groaning again.

"Okay, okay, we're ready," I say, pushing away as Tank's hands linger on me for as long as possible.

"Change of plans, we stay here so Santa can find us, then we go on vacation after," Tank informs him as Hendrix kicks the soccer ball at me.

"*Sweet!* I've never been on vacation before." I see the realization hit Tank and the sadness on his face is almost instant. He glances over at me and I muster up a shrug and a half smile to try and play it off.

I hate that I haven't taken Hendrix anywhere cool for vacation before now, but with the fear of somehow crossing paths with Mark living in the back of my mind, I didn't want to leave the comfort of Nashville. Where I knew Max was always a phone call away if I needed him, and there were people here to protect us.

Hendrix is just now at an age where he'll actually be able to remember and enjoy a vacation though, and I can't think of a more perfect way to experience it than as a family of three. Well, four if you include Mav—and how could we not?

"Me either, but you know what? I think this is going to be the best first vacation *ever*." I give him a wink, making him smile.

DING

LEAH

Am I being a little clingy or does it feel like we haven't had girls night in a year?

LAUREN

Probably a little bit of both.

LEAH

☺

TAYLOR

Well, there's been like, a shit ton of stuff happening the last couple of months.

TAYLOR

Cece's teething and been attached to Shane's tit.

Rubes got MARRIED, fell in love with her husband, and is dealing with a shit bag ex that should go fall in a hole somewhere. Lauren is selling every house that's available in Nashville. And I'm still trying to figure out what color I want to paint our bedroom.

ME

When the hell did you become the stenographer of the group? 🦆

TAYLOR

God, I need a martini.

SHANE

Thanks for all of that, you psycho. Dinner is in 2 hours right? We'll pour it out Sweet Magnolias style after dinner.

ME

That actually sounds perfect. I kind of have a LOT to fill you guys in on.

LEAH

Thank God.

TAYLOR

I DO believe that's what this holiday is all about. 🙏

LEAH

It must be exhausting being you. 🙇

"Jesus Christ Le, did you make margaritas for the whole block?" I laugh, looking at the massive party-size pitcher of margaritas she's made for tonight.

"Listen, it's fall break. I can drink as much as I want tonight and not have to be up to listen to the screeching sound of my sweet little gremlins tomorrow."

"Leah, I think you might be ready for a career change if they're driving you to drink," Lauren teases while making sure all the dishes have serving utensils.

"Can you just let me live my life, please?" She rolls her eyes, making us all giggle.

"The party has arrived," Taylor announces as she, Shane, Tucker, Max, and Cece walk in the door together.

"Yeah, but I got here about fifteen minutes ago, thanks though," I fire back, making her mouth drop open.

"I think I'm in love with you." She runs over and wraps me in her arms.

"Sorry, that job is taken," Tank chimes in, wrapping his arm around my shoulders once Taylor backs away. When he caresses my jaw with his thumb Taylor's eyes could set me on fire with the questions burning behind them. We all fill our plates and sit around Lauren's massive dining table. We've started taking turns hosting holidays and this year Lauren had Thanksgiving.

Once the boys go outside to start talking about what their workout plan is for tomorrow, and the kids are both passed out in the guest room—Cece in her playpen and Hendrix on the bed with the dogs—all of us girls find a spot on the sectional to chat.

"How are you? Max and Tucker filled us in on what happened at the bar the other day." Taylor nods to Shane who has a concerned look on her face.

"Wait, we weren't informed," Lauren says accusingly, wagging a finger between herself and Leah.

"Yeah, just because we aren't fucking one of the brothers doesn't mean we should get left out." I close my eyes and shake my head trying to fight back a laugh.

"Yeah, I guess I can start there." I tuck my feet under myself as I sip my glass of wine. "Mark came to the bar the other day. He was completely drunk and acting like a fool, saying all this shit about wanting a second chance and... I actually recorded him, hang on." I pull my phone out of my pocket, holding it up to replay the events for all of them to hear. The anger, hurt, and comforting hand squeezes from every one of them make my heart full as I realize just how strong my tribe is. They all look like they're ready to go to war for me and I would undoubtedly do the same for them.

"What a fucking psycho. How did someone that unstable even get as far as he has with suing for custody?" Lauren asks.

"Ruby... What the hell happened between you two?" The pained look in Taylor's eyes tells me how much she's feeling the depth of this.

I tend to forget that Tank is the only one I've actually given all the details to about what happened between me and Mark. I felt like he was the only one that *needed* to know and by only telling him it wouldn't put me in a place to receive pity from others. But I should have known better than that. Like I've said countless times before, these girls are like sisters to me, I know they'll be supportive and not treat me like some fragile victim.

"So. Fucking. Much." My voice shakes against my will. They all give their quiet support, waiting for me to make my decision whether or not I'll share. I know they would accept it if I chose not to. That they would still be by my side and support me even if they never knew a single thing that happened. But I'm ready to put all of this behind me, once and for all. Tank and I are already starting to look to the future with our little family, so I need to fill them in now, so I can let it go. So I tell them everything. How we met, how we started "dating"—if you'd even call it that—how when I got pregnant I thought it would be a good thing but was quickly proven wrong. I told them about the last day I saw him, what he said and what he did, and how I never looked back.

"Such a fucking warrior." Taylor's statement makes me laugh because apparently everyone else could see it but me. I always tried to tell myself I was being strong, while secretly feeling like I ran away scared. Because at every stop I made I was looking over my shoulder—until I wasn't anymore.

"So, what happens now? Is your lawyer at least aware of this? Surely she will be able to present that to whoever she needs to and get this case thrown out, right?" Leah chimes in, breaking me from my thoughts. I take a deep breath, realizing just how incredibly out of the loop they've been during all of this.

"Right, well. My lawyer was actually sleeping with Mark—which explains why she was such an unhelpful bitch every time I spoke to her—and the judge who was supposed to take our case is actually his brother-in-law." They all sit silently and process as I finish off my wine in two big gulps. "Yeah."

"Ruby, how the hell could you not tell us *any* of this? We would have been there for you, we would have slashed some tires or put nair in her shampoo at the *very* least," Shane says sweetly.

"I swear I wasn't trying to keep you guys in the dark. You all know how much I love you, and that you're all like sisters to me, it's just…" I take a deep breath, trying to find the right words to describe where my mind has been.

"It's like ever since the day he showed back up, I've been stuck inside a tornado. Doing my best to focus on Hendrix so the impact wouldn't throw me out and break me. Then ending up with Tank happened *because* of everything with Mark and it all just felt so… unreal. Our wedding night was life-changing for me—and not just in a dirty way." I roll my teary eyes at Taylor.

"*Just.*" She snickers quietly, making Leah slap her arm.

"He helped me erase so much of the trauma Mark left behind. He was showing me how much he loved me before the words ever left his mouth, so when they actually did—I couldn't *not* believe him,

351

and I had already fallen for him too. Before I knew it, the tornado felt like a steady wind, and it was just the three of us left standing in it. The case got officially thrown out this morning. I am *so* sorry I haven't been able to include you guys more," I apologize, looking around to see tears falling from everyone's eyes.

"Don't you dare apologize. You're here now and you're happy," Leah says.

"And Rubes, you're *free*. Like, actually free of him now. Hendrix isn't going anywhere and you have a husband who loves you and God knows he loves that little boy of yours," Lauren adds.

"I love you guys so much." We all stand up and run into a massive group hug, complete with running mascara and sniffles.

"Now, who's ready to get a restraining order?" Leah exclaims, wiping under her eyes as we all laugh and do the same.

"Knowing Tank, he's already got it in the works," I admit.

"I don't think I've ever seen anything as beautiful as the way that man loves you and Hendrix," Lauren says as we all take our seats again.

"You know," I look around to ensure the guys are still outside, "I've been thinking about surprising him and asking him if he'd want to adopt Hendrix. Officially. I would have to ask Hendrix of course, but he already calls him Dad and thinks he hung the moon so I don't think he'd say no."

"I think that would make his entire life," Taylor says immediately.

"You think so?" I question.

"Sis, you have no idea how badly that man missed you while you two were apart. He would text Tucker at least once a day to check on you both."

"Same with me and Max. He always wanted to know how you and Hendrix both were. If you needed anything, how Hen was doing in school. He even made me drop packs of Sour Patch Kids in your backpack when you were having bad days." She laughs.

"That was because of him? I thought I was going crazy. They

would always show up the same day I finished a pack and then I would think I hallucinated finishing them in the first place."

"He'll do it. He'll adopt him on paper. Because it's very clear to anyone with eyes that he's already adopted him at heart," Leah says, making my stomach flip with excitement.

I'm gonna ask my husband to adopt my son.

"Okay." Taylor clears her throat. "Here's to making the guys cook for Christmas and ordering in the pies." She lifts her margarita glass in the air.

"Cheers to that." We all clink glasses and have a good laugh as the guys join us in the living room again.

Chapter 39

TANK

"WHERE'S MY BOY AT TANK?" Harold asks as soon as he catches sight of me.

"You know, I'm starting to think that's the only reason you look forward to my visits now," I accuse, causing him to shrug as he averts my gaze.

"I've never seen a kid win as many games of chess or Go-Fish in my life. He's some kind of secret genius or something. Smart as a whip and funny."

"Oh, it's no secret. He gets it from his mama, who he's spending the day with today," I explain, earning a look of disapproval as Harold grumbles back at me.

"*I'm sorry. We're currently at full capacity, but we do have a waiting list that you could join if you're interested,*" the voice of the receptionist, Tiffany, catches my ear as I hear her turn away yet another vet in need of care.

The Veterans Center is one of the few places in Nashville that offers top-of-the-line care for the men and women who need it. When I found out about it during one of my AA meetings, I came the next day to see how I could help. Doug opened the doors a few years ago, and the amount of people he's told me they've had to turn away makes my stomach churn. Tiffany, his daughter, works every clerical position you could imagine here from answering phones to sched-uling food deliveries, medical supplies, and linens. Doug's wife Lily is one of the reasons he opened this place to begin with. She was given horrible care at another facility and he was absolutely outraged. He spent the next year planning and getting funding to open the center, and now it's doing so well that they're having to turn people away every week.

"Tank, how you been my man?"

Speak of the devil.

Doug comes walking up to shake my hand, breaking me from my thoughts.

"Hey Doug, I've been well, how about yourself?"

"Ah, you know. One day at a time." He takes a deep breath, folding his arms over his chest.

"I do indeed." Doug has been sober for three years, and from AA meetings to the conversations we've had at the center, I know some days are harder than others for him to stick with it. We all have our moments.

"You know I'm here for you man. Just a phone call away," I remind him.

"Actually, I had something I wanted to run by you. You have a minute to talk?" His tone is serious, piquing my curiosity.

"Sure." I nod to Harold and Don as we walk back to Doug's office. He closes the door behind us and gestures for me to have a seat in one of the chairs in front of his desk.

"It's no secret that we're having to turn people away due to being at full capacity. It's been like this for some time now." I nod in agreement.

"I've been toying with the idea of opening another location, but between Tiff and I running things here, and Lily not doing so great—I just don't see how we could manage it."

"I hate to hear that she's in ill health, an expansion would be life-changing for some, but you can't overextend yourself, Doug, especially not when Lily needs you."

"You're right. And I have no intention of doing so. That's why I wanted to talk to *you*. How would you like to be a partner in *The Veterans Center*, and run the second location?" My eyebrows raise in surprise.

"I'd be honored but... why me?" His whole body shakes as he leans back in his chair, laughing at my question.

"Out of every person I've had come in here on a volunteer basis, no matter how long or short term they stayed—you've been the one with a fire behind your participation here. You want to help, you want this place to run smoothly, you want the tenants to feel comfortable and like they're right at home, not just in *a* home. You fix things without being asked, you see needs that others don't and you act on them without hesitation. If you ask me, you were born to do something like this." I'm stunned silent and completely humbled by his words. He's right though, I love coming here every week, helping out in more ways than just what's expected by volunteers. I enjoy bringing Maverick and Hendrix up here to help spread some smiles when things seem otherwise gloomy. But I'm not sure what that would look like for our family.

"I would love to. Can I talk with my wife about it and get back to you?"

"I wouldn't let you accept *without* talking to her first." He chuckles. "Alright, I'll let you get back to it. We'll talk again soon." He dismisses me from his office and all I can think about the rest of the day is that I can't wait to see what Ruby thinks about the idea. Because my mind is all but made up about it. Just as I am finishing up a game of poker with some of the guys my phone goes off.

TUCKER
Gym in 20.

ME
Yup. Leaving here soon.

TUCKER
Mav with you?

ME

Not today.

TUCKER

Dammit. Bring him over soon.

ME

Dude, just get a dog already.

TUCKER

Give me yours.

ME

You have problems. I'm on my way.

"Don't look now, but I think that girl is checking you out," Tucker says as I'm finishing my last few curls. "Like, she might actually be drooling."

"Are you sure it's not a bulldog? They do that too."

23. 24. 25.

I blow out a breath as I rerack the dumbbells. I don't bother looking around because I don't care who the fuck is looking this way, I'm not interested.

"Oh, shit. She's actually walking over." He glances over my shoulder and then quickly moves to grab his water from the ground.

"Dude, why?" I mumble, rolling my eyes in annoyance.

"Hi." Her voice comes out much too breathy. Why isn't it acceptable behavior to just pretend like you don't hear or see someone who's standing right beside you? I give her a curt nod before bending to grab my water.

"I heard Tony saying that you're one of the trainers here? I am actually looking for someone to train me, do you have any openings?" She lifts a shoulder in question, batting her eyes at me.

"Nope. I actually don't." I bring my water bottle to my lips, and she finds the courage to place a hand on my arm, squeezing the muscles I just finished working out.

"What a shame, you're probably like, the strongest person here." I cut my eyes to Tucker who throws his hands in the air as if to say *what the fuck?* Before I can tell her to remove her hand from my arm, it's yanked away.

"I suggest you keep your hand off my husband if you want to keep it." The girl's eyes grow wide and her face turns red as she takes a step back, readjusting her gym bag on her shoulder. Ruby turns to face me while the girl is still standing there in shock.

"Your...your husband? I'm so—" she stammers as she takes a nervous step back.

"Yeah. *Husband.* So the only one he'll be doing cardio or any other workout with, is *me.*" She turns to face me now. "Isn't that right, my love?" I hear the confidence in her voice, but I can also see the insecurity hidden in her eyes, and I won't stand for my wife feeling insecure over some random girl with far too much audacity. I smirk before I pull her into me, wrapping my hands in her hair as my lips come crashing down on hers. When her hands rub along my arms, I let out a hungry groan, making her smile against my lips. When I pull away I give her a wink and answer her question verbally.

"That's right, Honey." Ruby turns to face the girl who is surprisingly still standing there, watching us with her mouth hanging open like a Venus flytrap.

"So, find a different trainer. Or maybe even a different gym. But this trainer isn't available." The girl blinks a couple of times and turns to walk out of the gym.

"That was amazing," Tucker says with a big ass grin on his face. "I mean I was waiting for Ruby to drag her out the door by her hair." He laughs, letting out an exaggerated breath. "Man, I love your wife." He claps me on the shoulder, smiling at Ruby as she turns red.

"Alright, I'm hitting the showers before they close. Then I gotta get to the bar, catch you later." Tucker walks off, leaving Ruby and me by ourselves in the middle of the now empty gym.

"What are you doing here?" I ask, just realizing I didn't get a text from her.

"I'm sorry. That wasn't like me. I just... I was at the bar and Max said you were over here and I just wanted to say hi so he said Hendrix could hang out for a few minutes. I didn't mean to be all–" I shut her up by kissing her again, pulling her by the hips to bring her body flush with mine.

"You better not be sorry. I like it when you claim what's yours." I press my hardening length into her, making her gasp as she looks around us.

"And I am. *All yours.*" Her big brown eyes lock with mine as she bites her lip. "Just look at what you do to me. *No one* gets me as hard as you do, little wife." Her cheeks darken in color as she presses her body into me harder. I groan from the feeling of her against me. I look up to see Tony getting everything ready for closing, and since Tucker and I were the last ones to come in, I know the rest of the place is empty.

"Come with me." I grab Ruby's hand and my gym bag and run to the women's locker room. When I see it's empty I turn around and grab Ruby by the thighs, planting her ass on the counter as my lips find hers again.

"Tank," she whispers against my lips, making me move to kiss her jaw and along her neck. "What are you doing? What if someone comes in?" Her words are breathy as she rolls her neck to give me better access to plant kisses there.

"It would still just be me and you." I stand back, taking her face in my hands. "Not one single person could walk into this gym, or any other place on earth and get my attention the way you do. You're all I see, baby. Only and forever." She leans up and bites my bottom lip, completely rewiring my brain chemistry as my cock aches from how hard it is.

I pull her shirt over her head and let my lips find hers again, swiping my tongue along her lips before she opens for me. I palm her breasts in my hands, loving the whimper she gives me from the touch. I take one of her breasts in my mouth as she arches into me. When I bite down gently, she gasps as her nipples harden even more.

"Fuck," I groan, reaching into the shower to turn the water on. "Lose the shorts," I instruct, stripping off my sleeveless shirt and gym shorts as she slides her leggings down her legs, showing that she isn't wearing any underwear underneath.

Before she can ask again what I'm doing, I wrap one arm around her waist and carry her into the shower. She lets out a little squeal when the warm water hits our bodies, then she spins to face me while I hold her. When I first met Ruby, she would often wear this heavy-winged eyeliner that screamed *badass*. These days she goes more natural, letting her tanned skin and long dark lashes stand out without anything else surrounding them. Her honey-brown eyes pop as she looks up at me, and my heart squeezes at her beauty. She wraps her hand around my cock, pumping a few times while her eyes never waver from mine.

"Kneel for me, wife." She raises a brow at me. *"Please,"* I add, making her bite her lip as she drops to her knees for me. I fist my length, watching the muscle flex as she locks eyes with me with her mouth open wide. When she sticks her tongue out for me I can barely contain the growl that erupts from deep within my chest.

She begins pumping at my base with one hand as she bobs her head, taking me as deep as she can. When her throat tightens from her gag reflex I grip her hair and begin guiding her movements. Her tongue swirls around as her throat opens wider for me, driving me closer and closer to the edge. With my release drawing nearer all I can think of is how she must taste right now. I pull her up, guiding her to her feet as she looks at me in confusion. In one swift movement, I hoist her up by her thigh to wrap her legs around my neck, leaning her back against the shower wall. When my tongue parts her slit, she lets out a little gasp as her fingers find their way to my hair—exactly where they belong. She starts grinding her hips against my tongue, taking what she wants as my fingers dig deeper into her ass.

"That's it, baby. Ride my face. Give me every drop of sweetness you've got," I encourage her. Keeping in rhythm with her movements, it's not long before she's panting my name. Her legs squeeze tighter around my head and her back arches off the wall as she gives me every last drop.

"My good little wife, you taste so sweet." I plant one last kiss to her clit before I slide her back down to her feet.

"Turn around, Honey. Hands on the wall." I hover over her as she's still trying to catch her breath. I press my forehead to hers, closing my eyes to memorize the pattern of her breaths before turning her at her hips to face away from me. Her hands find the wall immediately and I line myself up to her entrance. She lets out a loud moan when I thrust into her, making me bring one of my hands down to wrap around her mouth.

"Bite for me, baby." She bites down on my hand where she always does when she needs to hold in those beautiful sounds of hers. Her little whimpers as I slam into her and the way her nails begin trying to dig into the tile on the wall get me closer to my release, but when she finds hers and basically screams into my palm, I'm done for. I empty myself inside her as her walls clench around me.

"I'll never get tired of fucking you. My beautiful, beautiful wife." I let my hands explore her body, planting kisses on any part of her that I can before I hear Tony's voice outside the locker room.

"Closing in five."

"Ok, thanks!" Ruby calls out since we're in the women's locker room.

Once we're dressed again, I grab my gym bag and drape my arm over her shoulder as we exit together.

"See ya tomorrow, Tony." I wave. He nods and opens his mouth to say something before a look of confusion washes over him. He looks from the locker room back at us, and I kiss the top of Ruby's head and give him a wink.

"Listen, I know you have to get to work but there's something I need to talk to you about later. It's a good thing, but if I'm asleep when you get home, will you wake me?"

"Of course."

"And, you know. You can get creative with it if you want." I smirk at her as we approach the door of Chattahoochies.

"Is there any other way to do it?" She winks at me, turning to walk inside.

I look around for Hendrix first, seeing him coloring in the corner booth where he and the pups always hang out, but before I can say anything to him Tucker grabs our attention.

"Um. Why is *your* hair wet Rubes? You didn't work out." He raises an accusing brow at us. Max looks up from where he's pouring two glasses of beer as Ruby's eyes bounce between the three of us.

"Oh, yes she did." She elbows me in the side making me wince.

"Jesus Christ, is no one's business safe from the sexual energy you two possess?" Max says, making Ruby's eyes widen

"Not when we've got lost time to make up for." I kiss Ruby's temple, giving her a reassuring wink.

"You know what, you two can give us shit all you want but don't act like *you* didn't fuck your wife on that pool table," Ruby says to Max, pointing to the pool table in the corner. "And I *know* better than to ride in your baby maker Bronco so both of ya, shut up." She looks between them, making Max's jaw tighten and Tucker smirk.

"As you were." Max clears his throat, running the drink order he just made.

"Honestly, I'm honored to call you my sister-in-law." Tucker nods, disappearing to the other end of the bar.

"I love it when you're feisty." Her smile spreads across her face as she giggles.

"I know, it's so fun."

"Hey, toots. Bout time you showed up," Lenny says, approaching us.

"You know, Lenny. You're the only one allowed to call my wife *toots and* keep his teeth." He lets out a raspy chuckle as he sits on a barstool a few feet away from us. I kiss Ruby one last time before grabbing Hendrix and taking him home to finally start planning our beach trip.

Chapter 40

RUBY

"WHY ISN'T Dad shopping with us today? We always go grocery shopping together," Hendrix asks as we push the red shopping cart through the store, filling it up with everything we're lacking for our trip to the beach.

"Well, Dad is at an important meeting today. You know how you go with him to see Mr. Harold and the other guys at *The Veterans Center*?"

"You mean Iron Man," he corrects.

"Yes, when you go with him to see Iron Man."

"Yeah?"

"Well, Mr. Doug, the guy who owns that place, asked Dad if he would want to run a second location, and he's going to do it."

"What does that mean?" he asks, hopping on the end of the baker to ride as I push it down the aisle.

"Well, it means that there will be a second building for people to go that need assisted living care, without Mr. Doug having to tell them their rooms are all full. There will be more space to help more people," I explain it to him the best I can.

"So Dad is gonna work there, like all the time?"

"Yeah, pretty much."

"That's so cool. Can I still go to work with him?" he asks as we stop in front of the tiny selection of beach towels. Shopping out of season for this trip is proving to be more challenging than I thought.

"I'm sure he would love that once they get everything up and running smoothly." I rake my eyes over the selection before propping my hands on my hips.

"Which one should we get for Dad?"

"That one!" He points to a Paw Patrol towel, making me laugh.

"Why that one?" I ask, seeing as how he hasn't watched Paw Patrol in like, two years, I'm surprised by his choice.

"Because, Chase kind of looks like Maverick." He pulls it from the rack, holding it over the basket. "Can we get it?" Even though it will look like a hand towel in comparison to my husband's masculine frame, there's no way it's *not* coming home with us.

"Absolutely." I smirk at him.

"*Yes!*" He pumps his fist excitedly before grabbing a Spider-Man towel for himself and a purple and white one for me.

After stocking up on towels, clearance swimwear, sunglasses, and slides for everyone, we check out and head to one of our favorite places for lunch. I guess there's a plus side to shopping for the beach in December—everything we *can* find is on major sale.

"Hey, Hendrix, I have something I wanted to ask you." We're sitting at a small table near the window, watching the cars go through the drive-thru while Hendrix makes funny faces at the cars that end up stopping next to us.

"Yes, ma'am?" He turns to face me, dipping his waffle fry in some ketchup before taking a big bite.

"How would you feel about asking Tank to adopt you?"

"What does 'adopt' mean?" A question I was sure he would ask.

"Well, you already think of Tank as your dad, right?"

"Yeah. The *best* dad." He raises a brow as he corrects me.

"Well, when someone adopts you it just means that–" Explaining adoption to a six-year-old is harder than I thought it would be. "It basically just means he's your dad on paper, not just in your heart. And you'd get to have the same last name as him."

"Oh, yeah, I want to do that!" His eyes light up as he grabs a nugget from his tray.

"Okay then. What if we surprise him and ask him while we're at the beach?"

"Yeah!" He jumps up and down, making my heart swell in my chest.

My baby boy is finally going to have the dad he's always deserved. Legally.

Our kitchen table currently looks like the summer section in Target threw up on it, and if we weren't supposed to be dragging the Christmas decorations out tonight I wouldn't care. Typically we get them out the day after Thanksgiving but things have been a little different this year and I'm okay with that. Hendrix and I gave up on trying to clean about a half hour ago and have been playing Go-Fish on the living room floor while waiting for Tank to get home. I told him I was planning to cook dinner tonight, but I physically cannot bring myself to cook in a messy kitchen, so I'm hoping we can order takeout instead.

"I win," Hendrix yells, just as the front door opens.

"I've created a card game monster." I smile as Hendrix winks at me.

"Hello," Tank calls as he kicks off his boots by the door.

"Dad!" Hendrix jumps to his feet and runs over to greet him, whereas I'm so tired I can barely move.

"My dude." Tank scoops him up in a hug before walking into the living room. "There she is." He smirks at me as he sets Hendrix back on the ground, laying on the floor with dramatic grunts before letting his head fall into my lap.

"Are we tired today, little wife?" he asks, biting my thigh before looking up to wink at me.

"*Exhausted*. When did shopping and getting lunch become so tiring?" I ask, running my fingers through his dark brown hair.

"You want to just get take out tonight, or order a pizza?" he asks, taking my free hand in his, and kissing the top of it.

"That sounds amazing." Both of our heads snap up when we hear Maverick growling, but we relax again once we see he and Hendrix are just playing with his rope toy.

"Not complaining, but are we taking the kitchen table with us to the beach? Cause it looks like it's got everything we're going to need on it," Tank remarks, earning an eye roll from me.

"*No*. I was planning on packing most of it after I got the house cleaned so it would be out of the way, and since we won't need it *here*. But then the house didn't get clean and my brain shut off so we started playing cards instead."

"Got it. *Well*," he stands, pulling me up with him, "I can either try and pack everything up—though I feel it would just get done twice. Once when I do it, and again when you *re*-do it. Or I can get the food and then take instructions when I get back."

"I'm sure you already know the answer to that *sooo*, I would like stir fry tonight please." A big grin spreads across my face as I throw my arms around his neck. He wraps his large hands around my waist and pecks my lips quickly three times.

"Yes ma'am. What about you, kiddo? Fried rice?" He nods to Hendrix, making him let go of Mav's rope, falling back on his bottom as his hands fly in the air.

"Fried rice!" he cheers. "Can I go with Dad?" He gives me the puppy dog eyes, and as much as I want to say yes to it, I know for a fact his room looks like the Goodwill donation center and I have no intention of cleaning that *and* the kitchen table.

"Not this time, bud. You have to clean your room." Tank moves to drape his arm over my shoulder.

"*UGH!* Fine," Hendrix grumbles. I open my mouth to correct his attitude, but Tank beats me to it.

"Hey. Watch your tone when you're talking to my wife, young

man." His tone is the perfect blend of authoritative and playful, making Hendrix look up apologetically.

"Yes, sir. Sorry, Mommy." He hugs my waist before marching off to his room to start cleaning.

"I'll be back soon." Tank kisses me once more before walking over to put his shoes back on. I run my hands down my face, willing away the procrastination I feel trying to tempt me to sit on the couch. "I'll tell you what. If you get half the kitchen table cleaned off by the time I get back, I'll reward you in a *very* memorable way." His comment immediately has my energy levels picking up.

"All of your *ways* are memorable so far." I walk over, running a finger teasingly from his chest to the top of his jeans.

"You better stop if you plan on eating tonight. You're one finger twitch away from getting thrown over my shoulder and hauled off to the room." I debate twitching my finger just to see how true his statement is, but I decide against it when my stomach twists with hunger pains.

"*Fine*. Be safe. I love you." I tuck my hands behind my back and lift my chin. He kisses me a little longer this time, and I take a moment to memorize the way his warm lips cover mine, melting me right down to my core. Even though his plans of *hauling me to the room* are tempting, I've been craving stir fry for weeks so I'm not risking missing my chance to get it.

"I love you too, my perfect wife." He cups my face in his hands, kissing my forehead before finally heading out the door.

I turn around and stare at the kitchen table—my Everest—and sigh.

You've got this Ruby. Just start.

I walk to the fridge and crack open an energy drink, taking a couple of sips as I hype myself up for the task. I carry all the things needing to be packed in mine and Tank's bag to our room, and everything that can go in the beach bag stays in the kitchen. When Hendrix finally emerges from his room I realize I've gotten half of the table cleaned off already.

"Mom, come look. My room is *so* clean." He waves me over. I grab his new swimming trunks, slides, and beach towel before following him down the hall.

"Show me," I tell him excitedly. Sure enough, his room looks immaculate. I'm kind of shocked because typically there will still be things on his dresser or they're all shoved in the closet floor, but not this time. "Hendrix, this looks amazing. I'm so proud of you. You didn't hide toys anywhere."

"Yeah, when Dad and I clean the house while you're at work he reminds me to appreciate my stuff. That if I love something I need to take care of it, and if I don't then maybe I didn't deserve it in the first place. And I really like my toys, Mom, so I gotta take care of them."

Why the fuck is this man so perfect?

"Well, that's a really excellent lesson your dad has taught you." I smile as I run my fingers through his spiked-up fohawk that he's been maintaining—as long as Tank has this haircut, so will Hendrix. "I am going to set your beach stuff on your bed so we can get it packed in a few minutes, okay?"

"Ok! Am I taking this?" He holds up his school backpack.

"No buddy, we're gonna use–" And then I realize something.

"Oh, shoot. We don't have suitcases." I quickly take my phone out of my pocket and text Tank.

> ME
>
> So, little hiccup. We don't have suitcases. 😬

> HUSBAND
>
> Do we need them tonight or can it wait?

> ME
>
> You saw the kitchen table, correct?

> HUSBAND
>
> Riiight. I can grab one while I'm out. What size?

ME

🍖 Big? And Hendrix will need one too.

HUSBAND

LOL. Okay. I'll send pics when I get there. Food
should be ready soon.

"Okay. Never fear. Dad is gonna bring suitcases home for us.
Why don't we finish cleaning up the house so it's all clean when he
gets here?"

"But I'm done." He looks around his room again, making me
laugh.

"Yes, your room looks great. But have you looked at your bathroom today?" I give him an accusing look and his head falls back.

"*Okay*," he drags. I clear my throat as he walks past me. "I mean
yes ma'am."

While Hendrix picks up his bathroom and wipes down the counters like I've shown him, I get the whole house vacuumed. I used to
vacuum once a week, *maybe*, but with Maverick around now I have to
tackle it at *least* once a day, though it could probably use more than
that. When I finally turn it off and check my phone I see the group
chat has started up.

SHANE

Virgin River time ladies! Cece and I are ready.

LEAH

Just poured my wine and made popcorn. 🍷 🍿

LAUREN

Same! 🙌

SHANE

God I love this show. I wanna move there.

LEAH

Yeah, I need a Jack in my life.

LAUREN
I'm more of a Brady girl. 😊

Just as I am about to text back my phone starts ringing and Taylor's name pops up on the screen.

"Hey, I was just about to text back, I swear. As soon as Tank gets home with dinner I'm gonna turn it on and try to watch it while I pack. We didn't have suitcases so he–"

"Rubes," the ominous tone to her typically bubbly voice makes my heart stop. "Tank's been in an accident." My blood runs cold as I look at the clock and see how much time has passed since I last talked to Tank.

"What?" my voice comes out in a whisper, as I feel my knees about to give out on me.

"You need to get to the hospital."

"Wh-what happened?" I choke out the words, leaning against the wall to try and hold myself up.

"I've called Max to come pick you up and asked if Hendrix could stay with them tonight. So just get some shoes on and get here soon okay? Tucker is on his way now and we'll be with him until you get here."

"Taylor, what *happened?*" I yell, my breaths start coming more quickly now as the panic begins to spread through my entire body. I hear her sigh before giving me the vague answer that makes me want to scream.

"The doctors will fill you in when you get here." The feelings of fainting and nausea war against each other as I try to find the strength to compose myself before having to tell Hendrix.

God, this is going to kill him.

"I'm done with my bathroom." Hendrix walks in the living room and faceplants on the couch dramatically. I take a few deep breaths, swallowing past the lump in my throat as I wipe the tears from my eyes.

"Hey, bud. Little change of plans for tonight." I try to make my voice sound as normal as possible, but it comes out high-pitched and uneven.

"No fried rice?" he asks, turning his head just enough to free his lips. I immediately feel the sting of tears reappearing in my eyes as a knock sounds at the door.

"Come in!" I yell urgently, making Max come barging in the door.

"Uncle Max!" Hendrix finds his second wind of energy, jumping up to run over to him.

"Hey, dude. Did your mom tell you that you're hanging with me and Shane tonight?"

"YAY!"

"Go grab your stuff. We gotta drop Mom off somewhere first."

"Do I just use my backpack Mom, or should I wait for Dad to get back with my suitcase?" Still turned away from him I throw my hand over my mouth to keep myself from letting out a sob.

"Your backpack will be fine tonight, buddy," Max answers for me, sending Hendrix to his room.

"Come here." Max pulls me into his arms and I sob into his chest. "It's gonna be okay. I'll get you to him as fast as I can."

"She didn't tell me anything. I don't know what happened, I don't know how bad it is. Do you know? Is he okay?" I look up at him, noticing a weary look in his eyes as he takes a deep breath in.

"An 18-wheeler flew through a red light and hit him, they're checking him out now. That's all I know." I push away from him and run over to the trash can before my lunch comes back up.

Flew. Flew through a red light.

"Ready!" Hendrix runs into the living room. My ears are ringing, my vision is blurry and I have no idea what happens between Max telling me what happened and us pulling up to the hospital. When Max parks his truck and squeezes my hand, I blink away the haze and slowly come back to reality. I take in my surroundings and see Mav and Hendrix in the back seat, I have shoes on and my purse is in the seat between me and Max.

"Keep us updated when you can. Hendrix and Mav will be fine with us for as long as they need to be." Tears burn my eyes again as I nod my appreciation to Max. I take a deep breath, wiping the tears from my face before forcing a smile as I turn to face Hendrix.

"Okay buddy, you have a great time with Uncle Max and Shane, and be super sweet to Cece. Okay?"

"Why are we at Taylor's work?" He looks out the window at the hospital and I fight with myself over what answer to give him. I always tell Hendrix the truth, but I don't want him to be crushed by this. So I settle with a simple truth.

"Daddy got hurt so I'm gonna go check on him. But don't worry, we'll get him all fixed up and see you soon okay?" A look of sadness and concern crosses his features as he pets Maverick.

"Will we still go to the beach? I really wanted to give him his surprise." I nod my head vigorously, trying to convince myself to think the best.

"Of course we will. As soon as Daddy is feeling better okay? But I really need to go check on him. I love you so so much." I reach back and squeeze him in an embrace before Max hands me my bag and I take off to find my husband.

Chapter 41

RUBY

I CAN'T REMEMBER the last time I prayed. Growing up my family went to church regularly and it was normal for us to pray over meals and at bedtime. I remember a pastor saying once that it doesn't matter *who* you are or *where* you are, that when you pray, God listens. I'm not sure I ever believed that, but right now a little faith couldn't hurt, and I find myself begging God to hear my simple request.

Please, let him be okay.

When I spot Taylor and Tucker, my knees almost buckle but I manage to make it to her arms and stay upright.

"Hey," her voice is muffled as our faces nuzzle into each other's shoulders. When I pull away, I look up at Tucker, seeing the subtle agony burning behind his green eyes, so similar to his brothers, only lighter. I wrap my arms around him and feel his chest sink as he wraps his arms around me tightly. I know that feeling, the silent cry you do when you're trying to be strong.

"He's gonna be okay. He's gotta be," I whisper, trying to convince myself as much as Tucker that I believe Tank is too strong to let this be the thing that takes him from us. He simply nods in response before standing up and wiping his eyes.

"Please tell me what happened now. Max told me he got hit, but what else?" I plead with Taylor, letting my eyes bounce between them. Tucker wraps his arm around Taylor, squeezing her shoulder as she begins.

"When he came in, the ER was a madhouse. There was another patient from the same accident that came in before him that I was assigned to, so I didn't see Tank when he was brought in. My patient didn't make it, so when I went to see how I could help the other person brought in from it, that's when I saw that it was him." Her voice wobbles as tears continue streaming down my face.

"But how bad was it? Why is he in surgery?"

"I don't know. I left to call you and Tucker and when I came back he was gone. I'm so sorry Rubes, I wish I knew more." The tightness in my chest worsens and I feel my already empty stomach begin to contract. The cold sweat that breaks out over my whole body comes so quickly I don't even realize what's happening until my eyes fall closed and I land in Tucker's arms.

The salty wind is blowing my hair as Tank and Hendrix run into the crashing waves. Hendrix is in his life jacket and Tank with an innertube and a smile on his face so big you'd think he was the child coming to the beach for the first time. I glance around at the almost empty beach before closing my eyes to let the sun soak into my skin. My husband really does know me better than anyone. New Years at the beach where it's still 65 degrees and nearly empty, this is exactly my speed. I hear Hendrix giggling and can't help but smile at the sound. A few quiet moments of nothing but the waves crashing to shore pass before I'm startled by the deep swagger of my husband's voice.

"Enjoying yourself, Honey?" My eyes fly open as a dripping-wet Tank stands above me, drying his hair with his Paw Patrol towel. He looks sculpted to perfection while wearing what I refer to as hoochie daddy swimming trunks. The ones that are long enough to not be gross, but short enough to make any woman that looks his way drool.

"I am, the view here is great." I lower my sunglasses on the bridge of my nose as I let my eyes glide seductively over his body, earning a growl of approval from him.

"Is that so?" He leans down, inches away from my lips. I drag my bottom lip through my teeth and shake my head.

"Mhmm." He pulls my lip from between my teeth with his thumb and captures my lips with his own.

"I love you, my perfect little wife," he whispers against my lips, rubbing the tip of his nose along the bridge of mine.

"I love you more." My eyes meet his and the peace I see behind them has a calming effect on me.

"Mom! Is it time for Dad's surprise?" Hendrix runs up to us, unbuckling his life jacket.

"Now?" I shouldn't be surprised by the fact that my child would pick the most random moment for this.

"Yes! I can't wait any longer!" He begins bouncing up and down in the sand, making Tank laugh as he looks between us.

"A surprise for me?" His brows knit together curiously. My heart begins to beat wildly behind my chest with anticipation. I don't know why I feel so nervous, I'm pretty positive he's going to say yes, but I guess old habits die hard, and mine just so happens to be to expect the worst. Suddenly I feel a wave of nausea creeping over me. My mouth begins to water and a cold rush shoots down my spine.

"Trash can," Taylor's voice demands just as my eyes fly open. I sit up and turn to throw up in the trash can that makes it to my side just in time. After trying to throw *nothing* up into the can, I wipe my mouth and take a bottle of water from Tucker.

"What happened?" I ask, looking around to see that I'm on a roll-away bed in the hallway.

"You passed out. Have you been feeling okay? You look really pale."

"It's probably just stress. This has been happening lately when I'm in high-anxiety situations," I explain, sipping on my water. Taylor's eyes narrow on me, though I can't read the expression behind them.

"What do you mean it's *been* happening?"

"When I get super stressed sometimes I throw up and get a little light-headed. I've just had a lot going on lately," I explain, frustrated that any attention is being given to me when my husband is going through God only knows what right now.

"Come on, I wanna get you checked out."

"No, Tay. I'm fine. I'm just worried about Tank. When is he supposed to be out of surgery?" I run my hand through my hair, looking up at the clock to see how much time has passed since we got here.

"I know you're worried about him." She takes my hands in hers. "We all are, but I want to make sure you're okay too. You could have an ulcer or something from all the stress you've been under the last few weeks. Okay? It won't take long and as soon as Tank is out of surgery we will go straight to him." I hesitate for a moment, not wanting to be anywhere else but here so the doctor can find us when they have information about Tank.

"I'll stay here in case the doctor comes out," Tucker says as if he'd read my mind.

"Fine. But as *soon* as that doctor comes out–"

"We go," Taylor cuts me off, agreeing to my terms.

"He fractured a few of his ribs, we did several scans and x-rays to ensure they didn't puncture any organs or cause any internal bleeding. We gave him some medication for the pain and we'll keep him here for observation overnight but he should be cleared to go home tomorrow." The relief that washes over me almost causes my knees to buckle, but I somehow manage to stay upright.

"Thanks, Doc," Taylor says as Tucker wraps an arm around each of us.

"He's in recovery now, the pain meds knocked him out so we're just waiting for him to wake up. You're welcome to go in and see him though."

"You go ahead, we'll be in later. I'll update Max." Tucker nods for me to go on.

"But you're his brother. I know you–"

"And you're his wife. You go. I'll see him in a bit." I nod and turn to follow the doctor to Tank's recovery room, clutching my bag like it will somehow help keep me on my feet.

When I see him, all my other senses go numb. I don't hear the doctor or the nurse talking, I don't feel anything besides my heart breaking, and all I see is him. Unconscious in a hospital bed with cuts and bruises all over his still strikingly handsome face. I drop my bag in the chair and sit on the edge of his bed, lifting his hand gently to hold onto it, needing to touch him in some way. To feel his pulse in my hands, to see that he's actually okay. Because for the entire time he was in surgery my brain could only think the worst.

That he may never come out of surgery, that like the other man from the accident, he wouldn't make it. That Hendrix would never get to share his last name and that our new little baby would never get to meet the incredible man who helped make him or her. Tears begin streaming down my face, landing on the ultrasound of the little life I've been carrying around for a few weeks now without a single clue. The little person who is half of me and half of the man I can't imagine living without.

"You better wake up soon so I can yell at you." I sniffle through a laugh, trying to keep myself from falling apart. "You scared the shit out of me." I wipe the tears from my eyes, running the back of my hand along his scratched-up face.

"You may not realize this, my love, but you've consumed every part of my life since the day we said *I do*. Losing you would completely destroy me. You gave me my life back, Tank Landry. You've reminded me that I am strong, brave, and–" I swallow past the lump in my throat. "Worthy of love from a man as honorable as you. You're everything to Hendrix and me. And you'll be everything to this little baby too, I just know it." I place my hand on my stomach, looking down at the ultrasound of our little peanut. Wondering if they'll have his beautiful green eyes and light hair, or brown eyes like Hendrix but have Tank's infectious smile.

"We're having a baby?" The rasp of his voice makes me gasp as I look up to see his green eyes watering.

"You're awake." My voice is a grateful whisper, held back by the wave of emotions I'm doing my best to conceal.

"We're having a *baby?*" he asks again, his chest shaking as a tear falls from his eyes.

"We're having a baby." I shake my head excitedly, holding up the ultrasound to show him. He takes it from my hands and studies it, squeezing his eyes shut as he pulls me into his chest. We stay like this for a while, my tears soaking his chest while his fall into my hair. He kisses the top of my head a few times before I finally sit up to look at him.

"How do you feel?" I ask, caressing his cheek as I let my eyes take in every inch of his face. He blows out a breath like he's contemplating how to answer.

"Like I got hit by a truck," he scoffs, taking my hand in his before letting his eyes meet mine. "But that pales in comparison to how I feel about having a baby with the woman I love. I know I'm already a dad to Hendrix, but with this one," he places his hand on my stomach, "I'll get to be there for it *all*. Every diaper change, every word, every step. I get to be a dad from the beginning this time, and I'm so fucking happy about it, baby." The emotion in his voice makes me smile in adoration.

"How are you feeling about it? Are you okay?" he asks, shifting in his bed to focus his concerns on me.

"I can't think of anything better than having a little human that's half of me and half of you. I was so scared today, Tank," I admit. He pulls my hand to his lips, gently kissing my ring finger before placing my palm to his chest.

"How many times do I have to tell you, little wife. Not even death could keep me from you, and if there's life after this, I will find you in every single one. My reason to live just grew by one heartbeat." I lean into him, gently kissing his lips as I silently thank God for the man I get to call mine.

"It is just *one* heartbeat, right?" Tank asks, his green eyes bouncing between mine.

"Yes. Just one." I smile, pulling the ultrasound back out.

"When did you find out?" he asks, rubbing the photo with his thumb.

"About half an hour ago. I passed out in the waiting room and Taylor insisted I get checked out–"

"You passed out? Did you hit your head? Are you okay?" He starts sitting up, putting all of his concern on me. I place my hand on his chest, letting him know he can relax.

"No, no. I'm fine. Tucker actually caught me." I smile. "Taylor and I didn't tell him, by the way. I wanted you to be the one to do it." He lets his head fall back on the bed as a smirk creeps onto his face.

"Oh, man. Tuck's gonna freak." He laughs. As if on cue, Tucker walks into the room, with Taylor not far behind him.

"If *you're* involved you're probably right." Tank's head lifts to look at his brother. "You seem to have a habit of giving me things to freak out about, little brother." Tucker walks to the far side of Tank's hospital bed, putting his hand on his shoulder.

"Seriously though, I'm glad you're okay." I see the way his jaw tightens, and my eyes bounce between the two of them. Tank squeezes my leg, glancing at me before looking up at Tucker again.

"I'm a little better than okay, actually." Tucker's head rears back, looking at us skeptically. "I'm gonna be a dad," Tank says, holding up the ultrasound of our little baby. Tucker's eyes widen as he looks around the room.

"You better not be fucking with me." He looks at Taylor first who quickly swipes a tear from her cheek. Then at me. Then back at Tank. "I'm gonna be an uncle?" he asks, his voice thick with emotion.

"Way to make this about you, but yes, you are," Tank answers.

Tucker grabs Tank's face in his hands, pressing their foreheads together as Tank wraps his arm around one of Tucker's. I can't fight back the tears as I see Tank celebrating the life of our baby with his brother. Tucker stands and rounds the bed quickly, pulling me off my feet into an embrace.

"Congratulations, Ruby." Two of the simplest words, yet they have me completely falling apart.

"Thanks, Tuck," I whisper as he places my feet back on the ground.

"Yeah, that's enough. Give me my wife back," Tank gripes, pulling me by the hand to sit back on his bed with him.

"Okay, well." Taylor clears her throat, walking further into the room and under Tucker's arm. "We're going to go. I'll check back in with you when I get here in the morning."

"Thanks, Tay." I smile at her, resting my head on Tank's shoulder as I settle into the bed next to him.

"See you tomorrow, brother."

Once Taylor and Tucker have left and it's just me, Tank, and little baby Landry, he kisses the top of my head, laying one hand on my stomach as we lay here staring at the ultrasound together until we both fall asleep.

"Dad!" Hendrix yells as we walk into Shane and Max's house.

"Freeze!" I yell, stopping Hendrix mid-run. "You remember how I told you Dad was hurt?" He shakes his head while still in a frozen running position. "Well, Dad fractured some bones right here, and he's still *very* sore—he will be for a while. So no jumping on him, no hanging on him like a jungle gym, just… treat him like you do baby Cece," I explain, making Tank side-eye me for the comparison. "Got it?" Hendrix nods again.

"Okay, unfreeze." He stands upright, walking over to Tank slowly as he rubs his hand along Tank's arm with a feather-like gentleness.

"Hey, Dad. I'm glad you're okay."

"Hey, buddy. Thank you. I am too." Tank smirks, ruffling Hendrix's hair.

DING.

TAYLOR

Did you tell them yet?

ME

Just got here. Doing it now.

TAYLOR

Call me, I'm on my break and I want to hear her scream when she finds out.

I dial Taylor's number, turning the volume down so no one hears it ringing before sliding the phone back into my pocket.

"So, listen. Tank and I have something to tell you." I look up at Tank, who can't hold back his smile, then back down at Hendrix before pulling the ultrasound from my pocket.

"You're going to be a big brother." Shane slaps Max's arm with such force *my* arm is stinging.

"We're gonna have a baby like Cece?" He gasps excitedly.

"We are. How do you feel about that?" I ask, my heart thumping wildly as I wait for his response.

"*ALRIGHT!*" he yells, squeezing me tight around my waist before looking up at Tank.

"I'm gonna squeeze you so hard when you're feeling better, Dad." He points at Tank, making him laugh.

"Sounds like a plan, buddy." I finally look up at Shane who looks like she's been holding her breath since the words *big brother* came out of my mouth.

"Breathe, Shane," I say, making a loud and *long* squeal come from her tiny body.

"OH MY GOD!" She runs over to wrap me in her arms. "Congratulations, mama," she whispers as my arms wrap around her as well.

"Congratulations, man," Max says to Tank, fist-bumping him since their usual handshake and hug combo would probably put Tank on his knees right now, which is a visual I wouldn't mind at *all*.

"Thanks, brother."

"Wait, who else knows?" Shane asks, unable to wipe the huge smile from her face.

"Just Taylor and Tucker... Oh, shi–oot," I say, pulling my phone from my pocket.

"Hello?"

"I thought for a minute there she had passed out. Thanks for letting me feel present for the moment. See you guys later," she says, making me laugh.

"Anytime. Talk to you later." I slide my phone back into my pocket to give Shane my full attention again.

"She wanted to hear the scream," I explain, making Shane roll her eyes.

"Why am I not surprised?"

"Let's go, Honey. I'm ready to take a shower and lay in my own bed."

We gather Hendrix's things, say our goodbyes, and load Mav into my car. Thank God for friends who drop your vehicle off so you don't have to Uber home from the hospital. The whole ride home Hendrix talks about all the things he'll do with his sibling if it's a brother, and all the ways he'll protect her if it's a sister, while Tank's free hand stays on my stomach.

"Would it be okay with you if we reschedule our beach trip for spring break or the beginning of summer? I just want to be fully healed so Hendrix and I can play in the water while you relax and take care of this little one," Tank suggests, making the dream I had while passed out in the hospital come rushing back to me.

"Sure, sounds like a plan." I smile in agreement.

"*So...* when are we getting fried rice? My bathroom is still clean."
Tank and I both stifle a laugh as we pull into our driveway.

"Okay, okay. But I'm having it delivered this time," I insist,
squeezing Tank's hand before pulling out my phone to place the
order.

No way am I letting him out of my sight for the next... ever probably.

CHRISTMAS DAY

"*But my heart it is brighter*
Than all of the many
Stars in the sky,
For it sparkles with Annie—
It glows with the light
Of the love of my Annie—
With the thought of the light
Of the eyes of my Annie."

The amount of poetry my husband has memorized impresses me
greatly. He's been reading to the baby every night since we found
out about him or her and I love every second of it. Hendrix is always
nearby with about a thousand questions about what it all means, to
which Tank is always eager to explain his takeaway from whatever is
read.

After telling Leah and Lauren at Christmas last night I thought I
would be mopping them off the floor there were so many tears. We
spent the rest of the night making a baby board on Pinterest while I

got to snuggle Cece. She looks so much like Shane it's ridiculous. But when I look up at the painting Shane gifted us for Christmas—a photo from our wedding day that Lauren snapped while Tank and I were looking down at Hendrix at the altar—and I secretly hope mine and Tank's baby looks like him. His deep green eyes, his dark brown hair, or his perfect smile. No matter who they look like though, I know for a fact they'll get plenty of his character traits because I already see them rubbing off on Hendrix.

We spend the rest of the day playing with Hendrix's new toys, watching Christmas movies, or snuggled on the couch by the fire while going through different baby names, while I pinch myself to see if this is really my life.

Loved.

Cherished.

Protected.

Pregnant.

Chapter 42

TANK

4 MONTHS LATER...

SPRING BREAK

THE MOMENT I saw that truck barreling down the road, I knew I had to act quickly. When I accelerated to miss getting hit directly, I thought I had escaped the crash altogether, but the 18-wheeler clipped the bed of my truck, sending me spinning into a light pole— right before another car followed, sandwiching me in between them.

All I could think of in that moment were Ruby and Hendrix and how there was no way I was leaving them behind, not like that. I fought to stay conscious until I was put under for surgery, and even then my mind was doing its best to keep my thoughts within reality. I dreamt of that night, how it would have gone had I made it back home with dinner and our suitcases. I could see us eating in the living room, packing for the beach, and watching my wife frantically scan every room to ensure we haven't forgotten anything, all while I assure her that we still had a couple of *weeks* before the trip.

When I could feel the pain meds wearing off, my dreams shifted to the present and I could feel *her*. Unable to find the energy to open my eyes yet, or even squeeze her hand to let her know I was with her, I could hear her voice and it's as if my soul sighed with relief. I could hear her telling me how much I've changed her life, wanting nothing more than to tell her that it's the least I could do since she changed mine first. My heart dared to stop when I heard her last statement. I forced my eyes open, seeing her looking down at her stomach, and the joy that filled every inch of my being was completely overwhelming.

We're having a baby?

I thought the words were confined to my mind only, but her head snapped up and the look in her eyes told me I must have said them aloud.

We're having a baby.

I'm going to be a dad.

That moment is one that will be locked into my mind for the rest of my life.

"Mom! Can we do the surprise now?" Hendrix's voice cuts through my thoughts, running up to where Ruby and I are lying in the sand. She sits up on her elbows, the cutest little baby bump I've ever seen poking through her black swimsuit even more when she does.

"Right now? You don't wanna wait until later?" she asks as he shakes his head vigorously.

"Okay. We can do it now." I sit up straighter, giving them a curious look.

"A surprise? What are you two up to?" Ruby and Hendrix give each other a sly grin and Ruby nods to Hendrix, moving to grab something from her beach bag. Hendrix jumps over nothing, throwing sand all over me as he plops down on my leg.

"I want you to be my dad," he says, making me rear back a little. I look over at Ruby who still has her back to me, then back at Hendrix.

"What are you talking about, bud? I am your dad." I tickle his side, making him fold like a table before he sits back up and looks straight into my eyes, the sun making the brown in his irises look almost golden.

"No, I mean *lethally*." My head snaps to Ruby who is now holding an envelope out to me.

"*Legally*," she corrects.

"Right. I want you to adopt me," Hendrix says, making my heart skip and my nose sting with emotion. I feel frozen in the moment, but when Ruby gives me a nod, gently extending the envelope further, I open it and pull out adoption papers, looking first at Hendrix who is grinning ear to ear, then back at Ruby.

"If you want to, all you have to do is sign," she says, looking at me with hopeful anticipation.

"Of course I do. You got a pen in that bag of yours?" She smiles, bringing her other hand around from behind her back with a pen in it. I sign them so quickly there's no chance you'll be able to make out my name, but I can't even care at this point. I pick Hendrix up, squeezing him in a hug as he grunts before wrapping his arms around my neck, squeezing me just as hard.

"I love you, Hendrix."

"I love you, too, Dad." When I put him back down, he grabs a bag of chips from the beach bag and starts snacking like everything is perfectly normal.

Meanwhile, I'm trying not to bawl like a baby in the middle of this fucking beach. I pull Ruby to her feet, grabbing her thighs before wrapping them around my waist. She shakes her head, letting her long black hair blow in the wind as my hands rest beneath her denim shorts.

"Three years ago, I walked into a bar to apply for a job I never even wanted to take, and was immediately intrigued by the gorgeous bartender with quick-wit and a soul-healing smile. I will *never* understand what I did to deserve the privilege of calling you my wife but I love you more than life, Ruby Landry. And even though I think we should have kept *your* last name 'cause it was *way* cooler." She lets her head fall back in laughter. "I am honored that you've taken mine, and allowed your son to take it as well."

"*Our* son. I'll never think of it any other way. We both love you more than you'll ever know and I can't wait to watch how much our new little one will fall in love with you too." I take her lips with mine, silently promising her a life full of love, laughter, honesty, and a safe place to run whenever she needs it.

"Party's here!" I hear Taylor's voice call from a few feet away.

"Aunt Taylor!" Hendrix yells, running to meet her.

"Hey, birthday boy! You ready for some s'mores?"

"Heck yeah! Are you making them?" he asks, making her shake her head.

"Absolutely not. S'mores have some sort of cruel vendetta against me, but Uncle Tucker's got you covered."

All of our friends managed to take the weekend to come down to the beach to celebrate Hendrix's birthday with us. Watching as everyone gathers around to start a fire, seeing the way they all love Hendrix and go the extra mile to show up for him, makes me grateful I found myself in the middle of this found family. I'm no longer waiting for redemption, I'm *living* it. Every day that I wake up married to Ruby, committed to the vows I made to love and protect her and Hendrix—as well as whoever this new baby will be— reminds me of why I was given a second chance. And I won't waste a single second of it being anything but grateful.

Epilogue

TANK

4 MONTHS LATER...

"We want to thank you all for coming out to show your support, for everyone who has donated to *The Veterans Center* to make this second location possible, and for the volunteers who will be here helping make sure our Veterans are getting the best possible care. You are making a bigger difference than you could possibly realize, so again, thank you," I announce from the middle of the common area.

The grand opening of the second location of *The Veterans Center* has gone over better than we could have imagined. Having the investors come and see what their money is going towards was my lovely wife's idea and it was genius, of course. I scan the room, my eyes landing on her within seconds, the same way they always have, admiring the way she looks in her fitted purple dress with our baby proudly on display beneath it. She's due any day now and I'd be lying if I said I wasn't growing impatient to meet the little nugget. Her eyes meet mine while we're both in mid-conversation, but I know the look without her having to utter a word.

It's baby time.

"If you'll excuse me for a moment, thank you so much for

coming out." I rush to Ruby's side, seeing a thin layer of sweat already coating her forehead as I wrap my arm around her back.

"I'm sure Taylor is so excited you're moving back. Congratulations on getting traded." She smiles at Sawyer, nonchalantly wrapping up their conversation as she turns to walk with me.

"Honey," I start as she lets out a long breath.

"I've been having contractions since we got here, but it's *time*. We gotta go." We start moving towards the door quickly as I look around for Asher.

"You've been in active labor for over an hour? And you didn't think you should tell me that?"

"Tank, not now. You can punish me for it in approximately 6-8 weeks." She smirks at me and I can't help but laugh.

"Only you would still be flirting with me when you're in the middle of having contractions."

"Have you seen you? It's hard not to." I finally spot Asher by the front desk and call him over.

"What's up boss?" Asher has come on as one of my first full-time employees and I couldn't be more thrilled to have him here. I missed my guys when I left the Marines, so having him around full-time is something I'm really looking forward to.

"I gotta get my wife to the hospital. You remember everything we went over in case this happened?"

"Yup. Don't worry, I got everything covered here. You guys go have that baby." He smiles, earning a sweet smile from Ruby.

Yup, still don't like when she gives those to anyone but me.

I do one more sweep of the room and make eye contact with Max and Tucker who are conversing with someone by the game room. I give them the nod and I know they know. We rush out to the truck and I drive as fast, and safely, as possible to get us there before she has this baby in the truck.

"I'm letting everyone else know we're going in. Lauren can bring Hendrix in a little bit," Ruby says, typing quickly on her phone.

We make it to the hospital in record time, and I grab the bags we've had packed in the truck for at *least* three weeks now, before running over to her side to help her out. As soon as her feet hit the ground, her water breaks. My eyes grow wide as her head snaps up to look at me.

"Up you go, Honey." I throw the duffle bag strap over my neck, scooping her off the ground, before booking it inside. We barely make it to the room before she's telling us it's time for her to push. I stand back, watching as my wife breaths through every contraction beautifully, planted firmly at her side as she squeezes my hand.

The doctor rushes in just in time, and as soon as he tells Ruby to push again—she does. Barely making as much as a grunt as he encourages her.

"Beautiful job. I see a head so big push with the next contraction." She shakes her head, breathing deeply as she waits for her next contraction. I look down and see the baby's head, as tears start to sting my eyes. I look back up at Ruby, her brown eyes fixed on me as she smiles sweetly, shaking her head before squeezing my hand again. She pushes hard, then rests, and with the last contraction, she pushes even harder– letting out one beautiful war cry before we hear our baby.

"It's a boy," the doctor announces.

We have a baby boy.

Our slimy, beautiful, mess of a baby boy. The doctor holds out the medical scissors,

"Wanna cut the cord, Dad?" I look at Ruby who, with tear-filled eyes, nods her head as encouragement. I cut the cord and let the nurses start cleaning him up, turning back to embrace my wife.

"You, are so fucking incredible," I whisper in her ear, pressing as many kisses as I can to her temple, cheek, and head as she wraps her arms around mine.

"Here you go, Mama." Ruby unties her robe, opening it to lay our baby boy directly on her chest, as she begins stroking his cheeks.

"He has your nose." She smiles down at him, while I allow myself to completely fall apart. I rest one of my hands on his back, and the other on Ruby, doing my best to not let my heart beat out of my chest.

"I thought of a name." Ruby looks up at me, and I take a moment to memorize every part of her in this moment. Her black hair, curly from her sweat and thrown into a messy bun on top of her head, her dark lashes that are still wet from her tears, and her tanned skin that's absolutely glowing right now.

"What did you come up with, Honey?"

"What do you think of Poe?" I can't fight the smile that takes over my face, looking down at our son again. I've read poetry to him every night since I found out about him, almost always something written by Edgar Allen Poe.

"I love it."

"Really?"

"Really."

"Are you ready to hold your son?" she asks, readjusting him in her arms to hand him to me. My heart bursts wide open as I prop his head up in the crook of my elbow. He lets out a little grunt and I look over at Ruby anxiously.

"He's okay," she reassures me. I can't stop the tears that start streaming down my face as he opens his little eyes and looks up at me.

"Honey, he's looking at me." I tilt him a little closer to her so she can see that his eyes have opened.

"He looks just like you," she whispers as tears well in her eyes.

We spend the whole two hours in recovery sitting next to each other on her bed, staring at our beautiful son. Whether he's nursing, or sleeping in his little blanket burrito, I can't seem to take my eyes off of him. When we finally move to a bigger room, Ruby texts Lauren to let her know she can bring Hendrix back. We want him to be the first to meet his little brother, so everyone else is just going to have to wait.

Knock. Knock. Knock.

"Come in," I instruct as Ruby sits up a little straighter in the bed.

She's changed from the hospital gown into some sweats and her favorite *Bad Bunnies* T-shirt. I swear she must have five of those things because I was *sure* I hid the one I wanted to keep.

"Mommy! Daddy!" Hendrix whisper-shouts as he runs over to me, hugging my waist before moving slowly to the bed.

"What is it?" he asks innocently, looking down at the blanket-wrapped baby.

"It's a little brother," Ruby answers, making his eyes grow wider.

"Hey, brother." Hendrix rubs his finger along Poe's forehead gently, making tears well in both mine and Ruby's eyes. And apparently, Lauren's since I can hear her sniffling from behind me.

"Do you want to know his name?" I ask, sitting down beside them.

"Yeah!" he says excitedly, though he never takes his eyes off of his baby brother.

"His name is Poe." He smiles, and then a look of realization comes across his face.

"Hey, like the poems you read every night." He smiles at me and I nod. "I love you, Poe. You're my best friend already."

Rip my damn heart out why don't you, son?

"Do you wanna hold him?" Ruby asks, making Hendrix nod his head excitedly.

"He washed his hands before we came in," Lauren informs us.

Ruby lets him crawl up next to her and places Poe in his hands, supporting his hold to make sure he doesn't let him roll away.

"So, I have some good news," Lauren says, walking over to the bed. "They accepted your offer. You guys got the house."

"Are you serious?" Ruby asks, looking over at me, grabbing my hand with her free one.

"Yep. We can go over details another time of course, but you got it. I'll leave you guys alone for a bit." She leans down to kiss Ruby's cheek before walking back out to the waiting room.

"We got the house," Ruby whispers, her big brown eyes set deeply on mine.

"We got the house," I repeat, leaning in to kiss my wife. We look down at the boys, *our boys*, who are already two peas in a pod and my heart is overwhelmed with gratitude.

"Thank you, Honey." I caress her cheek, making her look at me in confusion.

"For what?"

"For giving me the chance to build a life with you. I know our marriage happened somewhat urgently, and that you questioned things in the beginning, but I always knew you were meant to be mine. That *this*–" I look down at the boys again, "was the ending we were always supposed to have." I spin her wedding ring on her finger, bringing the purple stone back to the center. "That's why I bought *this* one month into the six that we spent apart." Her head snaps up, looking at me with wide eyes.

"Making you my wife was always my endgame. You're the only one I see. It's always been you for me, Honey." Tears fall from her beautiful eyes, making me swipe them away with the pad of my thumb like always.

"Only and forever, right?"

"Only and forever."

BONUS
Epilogue

RUBY

Whoever thought moving with a newborn was a good idea, had one single brain cell and used it improperly. It only took a couple of months to get our house sold and Tank has insisted on doing everything move-in related. Though I appreciate the effort he's putting into making this as stress-free as possible for me, the man can't organize a box to save his life—which is causing the stress he's trying to avoid. I'm pretty sure I saw my favorite coffee mug, Hendrix's soccer cleats, and some of Tank's underwear all in one box. I don't even want to know how those things ended up close enough to be thrown together, but I immediately made him stop packing and put him on *truck loading only* duty.

"Last one Honey. We are officially-" he leans down to kiss me while I bounce Poe in my arms, "moved in."

"I can't believe we're finally done." I look around our new home and take a moment to appreciate how much life has changed in the last few months. Our new home is much larger than the last with *plenty of growing room* as my husband put it. We have 2 acres of land for the kids and Maverick to run around on, and the view of the sunset every night is absolutely breathtaking.

"Mommy! Where's the box with all my toys?" Hendrix asks, digging through a cardboard box on the living room floor.

"I don't know, baby. We have a lot to unpack before we find them."

"I think *un*packing with these munchkins around is going to be harder than packing was," Tank whispers in my ear as he bends down to grab Poe from my arms.

"I think you're right." I widen my eyes playfully, just as my phone goes off.

TAY

Can Tuck and I have the boys tonight? Call me crazy but I sense you and daddy Tank need a kid free night to…"unpack" 😏 You know, really get to know the house. 😏

ME

Well, Poe isn't quite ready for sleepovers yet but a few hours alone would be life changing. When?

TAY

😈 Gimme gimme. Bring them whenever! The sooner the better.

"I also think Taylor might be psychic. She just texted and asked if they could have the boys tonight." I can tell by the way Tank's face lights up that he's got an idea of how he wants to spend that time—and it's *not* unpacking. My cheeks immediately heat from the thought. I love my sons more than life itself, but Poe has put a stop to our late-night *alone time* that we used to have after Hendrix would go to sleep and I desperately miss it.

"That's nice of them. Did she say what time?" he asks nonchalantly. I love it when he tries to act like he isn't excited when I know all too well that he is.

"Well, she said the sooner the better so I guess *now*." Tank nods as he pats Poe's bottom. Him holding Poe is the cutest and sexiest thing I've ever seen. He took on the role of Hendrix's dad so effortlessly and never treated him as a stepchild or any less of his own. But seeing him hold our *baby* who has *his* eyes, is a sight to behold.

"Now is soon. Now is *good.*" I can't help but giggle as he nods his rushed approval. "Grab Poe's bag and I'll make sure Hendrix is ready. Meet you in the car." He kisses my lips quickly as he rushes over to Hendrix.

We made it to Taylor and Tucker's in record time, barely making it through the door before Tank was throwing the diaper bag at Tucker. I had to swat his arm and remind him to tell our sons bye before he was grabbing me by the waist and whisking me out the door. As we're leaving Tank insists he run into the grocery store before we head back home. I was instructed to wait in the car, which is suspicious since we always go in together, but the grin on his face, when he hops back in the driver's seat, keeps my lips sealed from asking any questions that may ruin whatever plans he's come up with.

We pull up to the house and before the car is even fully in park he's unbuckling his seatbelt and leaning over to me. He wraps his hand around my neck, and pulls me into him, capturing my lips with his in the most passionate way it almost takes my breath away. It only takes me a few seconds to catch up before I place my hand on his jaw and turn into his touch.

"Get in the house. I need you naked in the next five minutes," he whispers against my mouth, making me drag my bottom lip through my teeth as I nod. I run into the house while he quickly grabs the grocery bag from the back and stalks towards the house. He looks absolutely primal when he steps through the threshold and the image sends a shiver down my spine. He drops the grocery bag on the kitchen table and raises a brow at me. I quickly pull my shirt over my head, and drop my shorts, not bothering to make a fuss over dropping my underwear and bra along with them. The hungry look in his eyes tells me he wouldn't allow it even if I tried. Once I'm completely stripped of my clothes, Tank's jaw flexes and he pulls his plain white T-shirt over his head in one swift movement.

"You are so fucking beautiful." He growls as he hurries to close the distance between us. Before I can say a word he's grabbing me by the thighs and placing me on our oversized kitchen island, making me squeal from the shock of the cool surface touching my skin. Our lips collide as his hands tangle in my hair, and I touch any and every part of him I can. I have missed this so much. The passion, desire, and the absolute *need* for each other that can only be expressed properly when we're alone.

"You smell delicious, little wife. Lay back and give me a taste." With butterflies in my stomach, I do as I'm asked and lay back on the cool marble. I let out a little gasp when his hands wrap around my thighs and he pulls me closer to him. I'm a little self-conscious about how I might look right now after moving and wrangling kids all day, but that feeling only lasts for a split second before he makes an *mmm* sound, putting my mind at ease. Then, without warning, his mouth is on me and my hands are in his hair.

"That's right baby, let me feel it." I look down to see the most devilish grin on his face and it makes me blush all over. The way he knows my body and can get me to relax enough to fully experience the pleasure he has to offer me is something I'll never get over. He kisses and sucks my clit in a way that sends me closer and closer to the edge of an orgasm until I'm crying out for release—and he gives it to me.

"Such a good little wife, you think you're ready for my cock now?" He kisses along my thighs before standing up and releasing himself from his jeans. His cock is hard and dripping with precum and I can't even stop myself from licking my lips when I see it.

"Yes, please," I answer, spreading my legs further and running my hands along my body to tease him.

"You're gonna be the death of me, Honey." He pulls me to the edge of the island until he's teasing my entrance. "And dammit, I'll die a happy man." When he plunges into me, the mix of pain and pleasure morphs into a euphoric feeling. I dig my nails into his arms as he kisses and sucks on my neck, making pressure build in my core faster than it ever has before. Being with Tank has always been an experience unlike any other. He makes me feel sexy, empowered, and craved in a way that always has me wanting more.

"Tank, I'm gonna come again," I cry out. I can feel the smile come across his face before he brings his lips to my ear.

"Give it to me, baby. I want every last drop to soak my cock." Goosebumps shoot down my arm as he wraps his hand around my neck and thrusts into me without restraint.

"*Ah, Tank!*" My head falls back, every wave of my orgasm making my head feel light as a feather as he empties himself inside me.

"*Fuck,*" he groans, bringing his forehead to mine as we both come down from our high. I open my eyes and they involuntarily land on the kitchen table where he threw the grocery bag earlier.

"Tank?"

"Yes, Honey?"

"I know this may not be the time to ask but, what's in the grocery bag?" He lets out a tired laugh and looks around before grabbing a decorative towel from the counter that got thrown out of a box earlier to clean us up with. After handing me my underwear and my *Bad Bunnies* shirt from the ground, he walks over to the table.

"Close your eyes," he instructs, earning a curious look from me before I squeeze my eyes shut.

"Okay, they're closed."

"No peeking." I hear him rustling through the bag and moving around the kitchen a bit before he finally tells me to open. It takes a minute for my eyes to adjust but when they do I see Tank standing in nothing but an apron that says *hot stuff* on it, with two oven mitts over his hands and I can't hold back my laughter.

"What on earth are you doing?"

"Well, the last time we tried making yours and Hendrix's favorite casserole together, it didn't end very well. So, I thought tonight we could try again. I want to make some good memories to replace the bad ones. And this time, ya know, I'm prepared." He waves at me with his mitt-covered hands making me laugh again. I hop down from the counter and run over to him and jump in his arms, wrapping my legs around his waist.

"I think that's a great idea." I lean down to kiss him as he tosses the oven mitts off to squeeze my ass. "Are you gonna cook in *just* that apron?" I ask excitedly.

"No." He chuckles. "I can't cook with my cock out, that's too weird. But I *can* do just the apron and my boxers if that's something you're into."

"That's fair." I giggle, earning a smile from him that melts me.

"Also, I have a new special ingredient of my own to try this time." He pulls out chili powder from the bag and shakes it. "Trust me, it's gonna be amazing."

As always, he's right.

We spend twenty minutes cooking in our underwear, laughing and kissing each other every chance we get, talking about all the holidays, birthday parties, and dinners we'll get to host here—replacing the bad memories with good ones.

After we finish our dinner, Tank runs us a bubble bath in our massive new jetted tub, which was a *major* selling point for me, and we enjoy the last bit of our uninterrupted time together.

"Thank you for doing life with me, Honey." He pulls my back flush with his chest, making the water swish around us as he kisses the top of my head.

"I would never want to do it with anyone else, my love." I tilt my head to look up at him as my hands trail along his muscular thighs and he leans in to kiss me again.

"Good. Because I'm never letting you go." He nips my bottom lip, grabbing my left hand with his to intertwine our fingers and line up our tattoos. "Not even death shall part us."

THE END.

ACKNOWLEDGMENTS

Lee Pirtle, my husband, my best friend, my hype man, my safe haven, the warmth of my soul. You "play the part" of a book boyfriend so well because it's simply your natural state of being. You love me better than any romance book could ever express, and for that I will forever be grateful. I simply could not have begun chasing this dream without you and your full support. My MMC's (Tank, specifically) are written the way they are because of your insight and commitment to bring light to men's mental health and I am so proud of you for not being afraid to speak out on the matter. Thank you for simply being you. I love you forever.

Kate, I don't know a better way to describe what you mean to me than that I have found a soul sister in you. Connecting with you a year ago was simply one of the best things to ever happen to me. Waiting for Healing and Waiting for Redemption wouldn't be what they are without you. Your input, ideas, and constructive guidance means the world to me. From the idea for Taylor and Tucker's engagement to every detail you put into the work you do to make my books look as outwardly beautiful as I hope they inwardly do, you are amazing and I simply adore you.

Erica, I am forever grateful that no matter how busy your schedule, you have kept a place for me in the midst of it all. I love you so much and working with you is such an honor. I always look forward to your voice memos and I hope we are provided many more opportunities to work together in the future. (aka, I'm never letting you go)

Keri, I don't know how I could have gotten through this book release without you. I am so grateful you accepted the position as my PA this year. Your comments while alpha reading and your spreadsheet expertise are only two of the *countless* reasons I love you. We make a great team and I can't wait to see what else we accomplish in 2024.

To my Content Creators and ARC readers, your love, support, and willingness to share my books with as many people as possible is something I will be forever grateful for. You all are so precious to me and I am absolutely thrilled to get to work with each and every one of you.

And as always, thank *you*, my readers. I can't imagine what my journey as an author would be like without your love and support.

ALSO BY SARAH PIRTLE

NASHVILLE NIGHTS SERIES

NASHVILLE NIGHTS

Milton Keynes UK
Ingram Content Group UK Ltd.
UKHW030250190324
439698UK00015B/1076